TEN REALMS: BOOK 1

The Two Week Curse

ALSO IN SERIES

The Two Week Curse
The Second Realm
The Third Realm
The Fourth Realm
The Fifth Realm
The Sixth Realm, Part 1
The Sixth Realm, Part 2
The Seventh Realm, Part 1
The Seventh Realm, Part 2
The Eighth Realm
The Ninth Realm
The Tenth Realm

TEN REALMS: BOOK 1

The Two Week Curse

MICHAEL CHATFIELD

THE TWO WEEK CURSE
Published by Vault
In association with Aethon Books

ISBN 978-1-63849-349-5 (hardcover)

First AETHON: Vault Edition: Summer 2026

Printed in the United States of America.
1st Printing.

Aethon Books
www.aethonbooks.com

Vault Storyworks
www.vaultstoryworks.com

Book design and art by Adam Cahoon.
Print formatting by Kevin G. Summers, Adam Cahoon, and Rikki Midnight.

TEN REALMS: BOOK 1

The Two Week Curse

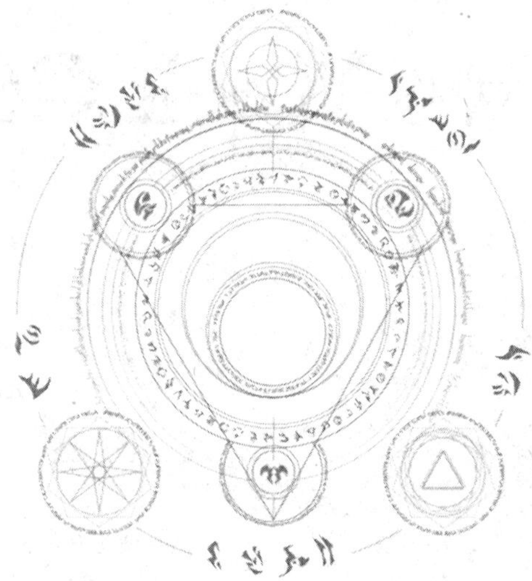

1

A REALLY SHITTY DAY

"They call it the two-week curse. What was originally being called an age of heroes, has now taken a drastic turn for the worse," the news reporter said.

Those in the room watched her, more out of boredom and the fact she wasn't another dude.

"She probably smells clean." Rugrat put together his rifle, working the action as a few in the room grinned and snorted.

"And that is not the downright creepiest thing I have heard all day," Honcho said, gliding by as he walked out of the room with his gear checked and his gun in hand.

"Better than being around you sweaty nutsacks!" Rugrat yelled.

"Like she'd let you within ten feet." Erik West checked his pouches and massive bag that held all manner of drugs, tourniquets, bandages, and other medical supplies.

"I'd only need ten feet." Rugrat waggled his hairy eyebrows. The man looked like a mix between a Russian bear and some Southern good ol' boy covered in more tattoos than a Russian gangster, who preferred to walk around in cowboy boots, his American flag short shorts, and a cowboy hat.

It might be wildly specific, but that was his usual outfit. He even had six pairs of shorts with the weight limit on the flight over.

"Dammit, Rugrat." Dillon shook his head.

"Two months ago, the first of the disappearances began, with people vanishing into thin air. Many are calling for answers, some people even saying that it's a government conspiracy. However, there have been no answers at this point. Without fail, people are disappearing roughly two weeks after they contract the curse. We now bring in our expert on the matter, Doctor Werstein," the lady said.

Rugrat snorted. "Wein-stein! Hah! Dick stain!" Rugrat laughed. "He one of your lot?"

Erik West had the unfortunate luck to have a German background—unfortunate because he had been stationed twice in Germany when he was with the United States Army. The running joke was that they sent him the second time because they thought he'd snuck his way into America but he didn't take the hint.

It didn't matter he didn't know any German, other than a few curse words he'd picked up along the way.

"See if I help you out if you get shot in the ass," Erik mumbled, just barely audible to the others in the room.

People snorted and laughed.

"Might finally mean he has to wear something other than those shorts!" Rossy laughed. The big Italian always sported a smile. It was hard to feel anything but goodwill for their leader. Even if he ate garlic as if it were running out of fashion and crop-dusted when dismounting, just so everyone would have to go through Rossy's "flavor of the day."

"Please tell me you haven't been having garlic today, sir," Dillon asked, straight-faced.

A devious smile appeared on Rossy's face. The sounds of gear being checked and weapons moved around came to a halt as Rossy ripped open a Velcroed pouch, enjoying every moment as he slowly pulled out a bottle from his vest as if it were his most prized possession.

"Aw, fuck! Hot sauce!" Keller said on the other side of the room. The look on his face made it seem as though he'd realized that there was truly no God or higher power to try to save him from Rossy's abilities.

Rossy simply smiled and displayed the triple heat specialty blend of fiery fury.

Erik unconsciously checked his shemagh, hoping it would be enough to save him.

"Ah, quit your whining." Rossy laughed and put it away. His demeanor changed and everyone's attention focused in on him.

"The curse has shown to have a symbiotic relationship with the host, in the first three days of incubation," Dr. Werstein said on the TV.

"Mute that shit. We've finally got the details. We're going to be moving from the compound to Camp D," Rossy said. The TV muted off in the corner as everyone listened in.

"Camp D? Shit, does that mean we're going through the shanty?" Rugrat asked.

"You got that right. Also, the body is going to be using their own vehicle and driver," Rossy said. Even though his tone was neutral, everyone could tell how pissed he was.

"What they driving?" Dillon asked.

"A flashy Benz," Rossy bit out.

"Oh, I hope they have a nice fucking ride in that mother fucker." Rugrat shook his head and cast a look to Erik.

Erik shook his head and shrugged. There wasn't anything that they could do to change their lot in life. If Rossy hadn't been able to change their mind, there wasn't any way they'd be able to.

Seems even when I'm working private instead of the big green dick of the army, I still get fucked. Erik grabbed his rifle as Rossy continued, loading a magazine.

"We'll be in the three Broncos—two up front, one behind the Benz. We're going to be taking the modifieds we've got. I want more firepower if we need it," Rossy said.

"The cops know our movements?" Erik asked.

"They do. I talked to our boy. He's not happy with having a Benz running about in the shanties, but there's nothing that we can do," Rossy said, holding Erik's eyes.

Erik nodded and the others in the room paid attention.

Rossy was their leader and shot caller. Erik was their combat medic but he'd been in the shit more than nearly anyone else and he'd earned his place as their second-in-command.

"We move out in twenty-five. Get your gear stowed." Rossy's eyes cast about the room. The noise once again picked up. The woman on the TV continued to talk silently. Someone turned off the mute as Erik checked his magazines and sidearm, loading it.

"Yes, after the incubation period, people report seeing a display in front of them, reporting on stats like Strength and Agility as well as Mana, which is a cultural reference to magic used in many different forms of media. Increasing these stats increases the person's natural abilities, well in excess of what a normal person can do." Dr. Werstein was pushed off to the side as a video appeared, showing someone picking up a heavy loaded barbell and laughing as they curled it with apparent ease.

"They are also able to cast spells." Another video showed someone in their backyard. The person mumbled a few words; fire shot out of their hand. The person behind the camera yelled, excited, as the caster laughed and joked around as the fire dimmed down.

Erik shook his head. *Could use some fucking magic on this run.*

His gear checked, Erik grabbed his bag and slung it over his shoulder as he grabbed his rifle with his other hand.

"Doc, what you think of that two-week thing?" Dillon, who was also ready, asked, a half step behind Erik.

"Think that it don't have much to do with me," Erik said. His nickname Doc was a moniker for nearly all medics in the armed forces.

He pulled on his ballistic eyewear that hid his eyes as he turned and slammed into the pushbar of the door. Light dazzled him and Dillon as the heat shot upward as they left their air-conditioned sanctuary.

"But magic, and stats? Sounds like some kind of messed-up video game," Dillon said.

"It'd be pretty kick-ass but who's to say that it'll happen to us?" Erik had dabbled in video games here and there, playing tabletops as well as Dungeons and Dragons on longer deployments.

"The whole disappearing after two weeks is kind of fucked up though," Erik said as they walked across the compound. There were tall buildings acting as overwatch, with the residences and command center in the middle.

They were on contract with one of the biggest copper mining companies in South Africa. It was their job to make sure that the higher-ups of the company got to where they wanted to go without being harassed, or to run security on the copper shipments.

They crossed the pavement as the heat beamed down on them.

"True that," Dillon agreed.

"Wait up!" Rugrat yelled from behind. He jogged to catch up. His helmet, attached to his vest, swung around as his bearded ass met up with them as they made it into a large metal shed. Inside, there was a large vehicle garage, from beat-up shit boxes that one might see on the roads, to premium sedans and up-armored trucks that looked beaten to shit but hosted heavy weaponry. These would be their rides. There was no hiding a Benz in the shanty town—might as well go with enough firepower to make the bastards think twice.

All the doors were open, with people dumping their gear into their seats. Rugrat got up into the turret, sweet-talking the fifty-cal machine gun as he checked over its working parts. With the dust and sand, keeping your gear clean was a necessity.

Everyone trickled in, storing their gear and making sure everything was how they liked it.

"Five minutes! Fire up the trucks!" Rossy yelled.

The three trucks came to life. Their beefy diesel engines chugged on air as the turrets turned from side to side, making sure that the motors weren't all gummed up with sand and shit.

"Load up!" Rossy called out. Everyone jumped into their vehicles. Doors slammed shut as the air con in each Bronco tried to cool them down.

"I thought they switched out this window," Dillon complained from the backseat.

Erik looked back to see that the window was spiderwebbed in a few places, showing where it had been hit by incoming rounds.

"Fucking Grade A." Erik shook his head. He unclipped his helmet from his vest and pulled the tactical helmet on. A red cross was on the side; scratches and dust covered the rest of its surface.

The Bronco lurched, following the lead Bronco out. They'd be in the second truck, with Rossy in the last Bronco so he could keep an eye on everything and be behind the Benz.

2
THE ROAD BACK

Erik half-listened to the radio chatter as their convoy ran across the compound. They passed through the snake-like entranceway of barriers, weaving in and out until they bounced onto what the locals called roads.

The trucks picked up speed and started to head out of the city.

They would be skirting the area that they referred to as shanty town before circling Camp D and coming back in another direction to try to keep the locals unsure of where they were.

Erik and the others looked outside of the Bronco as they raced through the streets, the lead Bronco using its horn to warn others away. They left the better areas of the city and moved through the shanty area.

Here, places were packed together, butting up against one another. Rusted metals, reclaimed wood, and plastics were used to create some kind of shelter for people to live in. Fires burned here and there as people looked out from the shadows, wearing all different kinds of clothing that they'd pieced together—much like their homes.

The turrets of the three trucks were all facing different directions, looking for threats as they rolled through.

Erik shifted his shoulders, adjusting his vest, and checked his rifle between his legs, pointed down at the ground.

They went over a large bump. Erik reached for the bar on the ceiling. "Fucking Christ there, Honcho!"

"Me no specken des Deutsch," Honcho, their Swiss driver, said with a grin on his face.

Dillon snickered as Erik shook his head.

"I know you can speak German, you Swiss fuck." Erik punched him in the shoulder.

"Well, be better to have a Bronco with some culture in it, not just you American fuckers," Honcho said.

"Hey, we're cultured," Rugrat yelled from above.

"Yogurt is more cultured than you!" Dillon said.

"Look at the brains on this one!" Rugrat sounded genuinely impressed by the retort.

"You wear a European bathing suit and a cowboy hat around the base!" Honcho yelled back as they hit another bump.

"Whoa, got me all tingly with that one," Erik said.

"I nearly fell out of my fucking swing!" Rugrat yelled from above, hammering on the ceiling.

"Explains a few things." Dillon laughed.

"Come here and let me kick you, you small fuck!"

"You're all gefickt," Honcho said as they swerved to follow the fucked-up road.

"You know what I hate? Those who can't understand other cultures and traditions, and the Swiss," Rugrat yelled from above.

"That doesn't make sense," Honcho yelled back.

"Shh! That's about the smartest thing his inbred mind can come up with—too much and he might just explode!" Dillon warned, being rewarded with a kick. "What was that for?"

"I dunno. Couldn't really hear it all but felt that you were saying something stupid," Rugrat said.

"Fuck, looks like he's a mind reader," Erik said to Honcho.

"Mind reader? I think he's just marginally less brain dead than the rest of you." Honcho flashed a brilliant white smile as they continued on their South African massage tour.

They left the shanty area; it took some time before they got to Camp D.

"Who the fuck named these places? Nothing cool like Alpha or Delta, just fucking D, like the dickhead who named them," Dillon said, getting a bit stir-crazy in the Bronco as they moved past the camp's security.

"Sounds like you'd be at home here," Erik said noncommittally, only paying half attention to Dillon's bitching.

"Wouldn't mind getting a vacation from you fuckers," Dillon said as they weaved through a security checkpoint with machine guns looking outward.

"Come on, admit it, you love having us around!" Rugrat yelled as they cleared the checkpoint, entering the main area of the camp.

"I can tell you with complete faith that the government lied in saying that you don't need a hockey helmet to go to work. Wait! Is that why you joined the army? They even gave you a free helmet!" Dillon asked, as if the stars had finally aligned and he'd gained a new truth.

"Marines, fuck boy!" Rugrat looked down the turret hole and yelled at Dillon.

"You were a Marine fuck boy?" Dillon asked slowly, a puzzled look on his face.

Rugrat started to swing his size-fourteen boot around.

"The children are fighting again, dear," Honcho said to Erik.

"Eh, one less kid," Erik said.

"Bronco Two, this is Three. Rugrat, will you stop kicking Dillon? Over," Rossy said.

"Bronco Three, this is Two. Currently having gladiator test for favorite child. Over," Erik replied without missing a beat.

"Bronco Two, this is Three. Understood. Five bucks on Dillon. Out."

Dillon and Rugrat's fighting died down. Dillon smiled while Rugrat's sand-stained face showed signs of a smile under his shemagh that covered the lower half of his face.

"Looks like I won't be able to tell the wife I've lost one now." Erik sighed.

"You married, Doc?"

"Three times. Fourth one's somewhere in Thailand," Erik said.

"But you're not married yet," Dillon said, confused.

"Never will be again," Erik said.

Dillon looked at him in confusion.

"He likes lady-boys!" Rugrat said.

Erik hit Rugrat in the leg.

"Ah shit, right on the nerve! My leg's numb!" Rugrat complained.

Dillon snorted, shaking his head.

The trucks had been to Camp D many times before and made it through the factory-turned-compound easily. They reached the larger reinforced building that was the headquarters of the camp. Bronco One and Two moved in front of the Benz that was resting there; the third Bronco boxed them in from the rear.

"Thailand, woo-hoo!" Dillon said.

"Thought you lived in Colorado?" Rugrat asked.

"Thought you were into women, not lady-boys," Honcho said.

"Well, you know, go for a little dip in Thailand, enough pay and they can all be my wives!" Erik said as the Bronco came to a stop. He heard the others snorting and laughing as he unlocked the door. He got out of the Bronco and scanned the area as he rested the barrel of his rifle in the crook of his elbow.

The trucks continued to run as everyone dismounted, looking around and stretching out the kinks.

"Fuck, Honcho—you wanna calm down that Swiss massage? There wasn't even a happy ending," Dillon said. Even as he stretched, he kept his rifle at the ready.

They milled around, talking to the others in the different trucks. Rossy had a talk with the driver of the Benz before he headed to Erik.

"So, diagnosis?" Erik asked.

"Brain fucking dead. This shmuck probably tongue punches his boss's fartbox every morning," Rossy said in a low voice. "The Benz is up-armored, but he seems to care more about getting to the compound in time for a dinner appointment than about being safe. Idiot looked up the fastest route from here to the compound, trying to argue with me that we need to take that way."

"I've got a cure for that." Erik tapped his rifle.

Rossy grinned, his eyebrows relaxing.

There was a commotion at the front of the headquarters to the camp, a bunch of suits and powerful-looking people smiling and laughing with one another.

Rossy flipped on his throat microphone. "Everyone get ready to mount up. Package is on the move."

The driver got out of his Benz that was running to open the door for his boss.

"See you in camp," Erik said to Rossy. The two of them separated and moved to their trucks.

"It's pizza night—wouldn't miss it!" Rossy shot back.

They got mounted up. Dillon took the turret this time, with Rugrat behind Erik.

The suit entered his Benz, and the driver rushed to his door.

"Bronco Two, this is Bronco One. You've got the lead. Take us home. Over," Rossy said.

"Bronco One, this is Bronco Two. Understood. Out."

The lead Bronco moved off. The second was starting to move when the Benz spun its tires, pushing to get in front of them.

"Silver Dragon, this is Bronco Three. Your position is third in formation! Over!" Rossy barked.

"We don't have time to wait around!" the driver said, not listening to radio procedure.

Rossy talked on a side channel. "Trucks, keep that fucker boxed in—can't trust him."

Honcho turned his truck, cutting off the Benz idiot.

"Why couldn't we put one of our people in there again?" Rugrat asked.

"Fucking union or some shit," Dillon said.

"Ain't no fucking unions around here," Honcho said.

"Still some dumb mother fuckers," Erik grumbled, shifting his shoulders and armor.

The Benz driver tried to get ahead a few more times but to no avail.

They exited the camp as Rossy kept berating the driver to stop pissing about like an idiot.

Erik looked at the Benz. The idiot was just making everyone's job harder.

The Benz calmed down after seeing that there was no way for them to get ahead. They rode through the rough landscape. It wasn't long before the road that was empty on both sides started to fill up with burnt-out cars, craters, and pitted roads with a shanty town on either side. They looked out for threats as they rushed past.

The roads started to get more complicated as they had to weave down streets, not slowing their speed any as they even forced some cars out of the way, charging forward. They'd rather do the insurance payout than get stuck.

People seemed to be watching them from every angle.

Erik gripped his rifle tighter as they continued on their path.

3
WHERE THE DEVIL ROAMS

They took a right, heading out of Gangster Alley, where a lot of the local gangs had claimed territory, turning it into a war zone.

The Benz surged ahead and rushed through the gangland, not following the trucks.

"Fuck!" Rossy yelled accidentally on the live channel. "Bronco Two and Three, this is Bronco One. Loop around and come get us. We'll follow Silver Dragon," Rossy hissed.

"Dillon, make sure that gun is live!" Erik's adrenaline spiked as Bronco Three picked up speed, not caring how rough it got.

"I said that it should be one of us driving," Rugrat said in the backseat as they bounced up and down, the suspension creaking and complaining.

They raced through the streets. People jumped out of the way of the modified trucks, leaving a trail of dust behind them.

There was a dull noise. Erik's head snapped to the side with the noise. He looked to Honcho and Rugrat in the truck.

"Sounds like a fucking IED!" Dillon yelled from above. The electric motor of the turret moved as Dillon looked out over the shanty town. "I see smoke!"

"Contact! Silver Dragon and Bronco One have been hit. Silver Dragon took most of the blast. We need immediate assistance!" The sound of gunfire could be heard in the distance and over the radio.

"We've got incoming small arms fire!"

"Rugrat, get onto higher, and get some of those QRF helo boys on standby ready to move," Erik yelled.

"On it, boss!" Rugrat confirmed.

"All call signs, this is Bronco Three. Bronco Two and Three will move to Bronco One's position. Our aim is not to secure the area but to pull out as fast as possible. Hellfire One will be moving in support. Understood?"

"Bronco Three, this is One. Understood!"

"Bronco Three, this is Two. Understood!"

"Paste anything that shoots at us," Erik reminded everyone.

The trucks turned onto a big road as people were running about.

"West, I got some fuckers running around with guns!" Dillon yelled.

"Don't shoot them until they give it a try!" Erik said, seeing them through his busted ass window.

"Hey fuckers! Over here! Come on, let me fucking shoot you!" Dillon yelled.

Honcho leaned on the horn as the group turned around. One with a machine gun tried firing from the hip.

Dillon's reply was much louder as he fired up his machine guns. A line of tracers left messy stains on the wall behind and no more bad guys running around.

They rushed past, the two gunners looking out for anything that might be a threat.

Rugrat was talking into his radio as they went over a small rise. Erik grunted as his head hit the roof of the truck. Rugrat's hand was on Dillon's belt, making sure that he wouldn't go flying out of the turret.

Bronco One turned and went down a side road.

"Contact!" Bronco Two called out. The heavy machine gun let out its deep bassy thuds as a rocket-propelled grenade hit a house, turning it into flying rubble as it exploded.

"Fuck me!" Dillon yelled. The turret moved as he tracked onto target. Tracers made short work of the thrown-together building, punching holes through it with ease.

The trucks continued at their best speed, not slowing down as they fought on.

Rugrat clapped Erik on the shoulder, leaning forward so he was right next to Erik's ear. "Call sign Hellfire is spinning up. Need fifteen!"

Erik tapped Rugrat's hand, confirming he'd heard him as they veered off their route. The shanty town was coming alive, people running away as the gangs rushed in.

Fuck. They finally turned onto the street that Bronco One and Silver Dragon were on.

Bronco One's front end was fucked while Silver Dragon was burning away, half torn apart by the explosive that had gone off.

Whatever had been used to make the IED was powerful to the point of reckless. The houses within fifty meters were shrapnel. Bodies lay here and there. People cried out in pain. Their pain was only quieter than the sounds of weapons fire.

The heavy weapons picked up their pace

"Bronco Two, cover us. Bronco Three will move to assist. We're going to hook up tow ropes and pull it the fuck out of here, now! Copy over!" Erik said.

"Bronco Three, this is Two. Will move to cover and support as you hook up to Bronco One! Out!"

Erik clapped Honcho on the shoulder. "Get me nice and close to them. Rugrat, get that tow hooked up!"

"Got it!" Honcho said.

Rugrat moved around in his seat, hand on the door as rounds sparked off the truck, Dillon firing back at where the muzzle flashes and whizzes came from.

"Coming up on it!" Honcho yelled. He slammed on his brakes.

Erik had to use the grab bar to stop going forward as he pushed the door open and jumped out of the truck. He slammed the door shut as he rushed for Bronco One.

Rugrat opened the back of Bronco Three and hauled out massive tow ropes, dragging them over to the truck.

Denners was up in the turret on Bronco One, firing and keeping the surrounding attackers' heads down. He was the one who had called in the contact report.

He had balls of fucking steel as Erik looked in on the rest of the crew. The driver, Keller, was slumped forward, blood covering him and the wheel.

Erik checked his pulse; finding nothing, he moved to the back of the truck.

Yoreck was banged up pretty bad.

"Yoreck, stop moving around, you fuck!" Erik yelled.

"Doc! Doc, that you? Fuck, man, it hurts!" Yoreck said, in clear pain.

Erik grabbed his collar and looked in his eyes. "Get your fucking shit together. You're fine, all right!" Erik used his command voice.

"Yah, got it!" Yoreck said, something switching in his brain as he did his best to stay out of Erik's way.

Erik checked him. He had cuts here and there; his left arm was fucked up and he had a scalp bleed. "Your chest hurt?" Erik pushed on it.

Yoreck let out a scream, making Erik wince.

"Sorry, dude," Erik said. He wasn't too bad, but he wasn't in a good way. He didn't know what was going on inside Yoreck but he didn't like it.

"Stay here, all right?" Erik said, looking at Yoreck.

"Got it, got it. Sorry, man," Yoreck said.

"You're all good. Don't worry about it." Erik rushed over to Rossy, who was riding shotgun.

Rossy was slumped in his seat, his face pale as his legs were covered in mangled metal.

"Fuck," Erik spat. He tore off his bag and started to pull out tourniquets. He wrapped them around Rossy's leg, knowing that they would need to be amputated anyway. He started treating Rossy as best as he could, setting up an IV and trying to get some more liquids into him.

"Hellfire. Hellfire, this is Bronco Three, you copy?"

"Bronco Three, this is Hellfire One. You are reading loud and clear. Over."

"Hellfire, I have one Pri-Alpha, one Pri-Charlie and one Pri-Foxtrot. Understood? Over," Erik said. Rounds pinged off the side of the truck as he pushed in closer to Rossy. He put the bag of saline up in the truck as he grabbed his rifle.

"Bronco Three, this is Hellfire One. One Pri-Alpha, one Pri-Charlie, one Pri-Foxtrot. Over."

Erik brought his rifle up and fired on where the rounds hitting near him were coming from.

Denners rotated his gun over and fired on the position, following Erik's tracers in.

"Hellfire, that is correct! What's your ETA? Over." Erik lowered his rifle and worked on Rossy again.

"Bronco Three, our ETA is ten minutes. Over."

"Understood. Bronco Three out."

"Rugrat, how them ropes going?" Erik yelled over the truck.

"First one's on, hooking up the second!" Rugrat yelled back.

"Rossy, dude, I need you, man. Come on, talk to me," Erik said as he did a more thorough check of Rossy, finding blood pumping out from his upper thigh.

Erik pulled out another tourniquet and strapped it around Rossy's upper thigh, tightening it as much as possible while squeezing on the bag of saline.

Rossy's body slumped as Erik's fingers moved for Rossy's neck, not finding a pulse.

He pulled out a field resuscitator, ripping off the different pads and putting it on Rossy.

"Please stand back!" the machine said. Erik hit the accept button as Rossy's body was shocked, making him jump.

"No pulse detected," the machine's voice yelled out as it tried to shock Rossy once again.

"No pulse detected," the machine mercilessly declared.

Erik grabbed his rifle and fired on the attackers around them, hoping to give Rugrat more cover.

"We're hooked up!" Rugrat yelled.

Erik was about to reply when he heard a buzzing noise.

He looked around before seeing a drone rushing toward him with an IED strapped onto it. Erik fired at the drone, trying to take it out. It swerved; one of its motors or something was hit as it skidded across the ground.

"No pulse detected."

The explosive on the drone went off and Erik was tossed backward. He screamed out as his legs and arm were shredded.

He tried to move his left arm and found that it wouldn't respond to him properly. It was becoming harder to move and he was quickly turning cold. "Fuck!" Erik yelled out.

"Honcho, we're all hooked up! Drive forward!" Rugrat yelled.

"Rugrat!" Erik yelled out, fear starting to take over as he forced himself to breathe and moved to grab tourniquets for his legs.

"West!" Rugrat yelled.

"Over here!" Erik tried to yell but his voice cracked and it was hard for him to do anything that didn't elicit pain.

He was putting on his first tourniquet, trying to get it tighter and tighter.

Rugrat came into view. He checked the area, firing on a few of the positions around the truck.

Honcho revved the engine on Bronco Three, pulling the tow lines tight.

"No pulse detected." The resuscitation machine zapped Rossy again.

"Pulse detected!"

Rugrat quickly grabbed Erik's vest.

Erik could swear that he saw a blue circle above him and Rugrat. A blue flame appeared in the sky above them, splitting into two and shooting into Erik and Rugrat.

Rugrat didn't seem to even notice as he pulled Erik back to Bronco Three. Erik screamed with the pain of his broken limbs dragging against the ground.

"No pulse detected, attempting to resuscitate." The machine attached to Rossy continued as Rugrat pulled Erik into Bronco Three.

"Get us the fuck out of here, Honcho!" Rugrat yelled as he pulled out gear from the back of the truck and started to patch Erik up.

Honcho fired up the truck, rocking Bronco One before hauling it forward. The tires rubbed on the ground as Bronco One was pulled out of the blast zone. Bronco Three strained against the extra weight but continued to pull Bronco One out of the crater it was in. The trucks moved as fast as possible, firing on the buildings to either side as they moved around the corners, getting out of Gangster Alley.

"Bronco Three, this is Hellfire One. We are three minutes from your location. Over."

Erik was feeling out of it from the pain as Rugrat stuck him with morphine and got on the radio to report the situation, moving Rossy from a Pri-Alpha to a Pri-Foxtrot.

Erik didn't remember much as they drove through the streets or the stop-off in a park as they loaded him up on one of the Hellfire helos and he shot off toward the hospital.

It was just a flash of memories as he didn't want to—or try to—take everything that was going on, in.

4

TWO-WEEK CURSE

All Erik remembered was pain, pain running through his entire body as if he was being torn apart from the inside. Then one day he woke up.

His legs were gone, his left arm too. They'd saved his life, but he had a two week curse.

He recovered faster than anyone else, and the doctors signed off on his papers, allowing him to be released, he didn't have anywhere to go, estranged from his family, his family were those that he had fought beside.

He would smile and joke when they came around but afterwards the mask would fall and defeat would consume him.

Erik didn't know how many times he had watched this interview.

"They call it the two-week curse. What was originally being called an age of heroes has now taken a drastic turn for the worse," the news reporter said.

Erik watched the report with dead eyes. It was the same report he had seen before he had gone out on his last patrol. He closed his eyes as tears appeared at the corners of his eyes. With a shaky breath, he was able to push down his emotions.

He once again focused on the television and the recorded broadcast that was now being shown to everyone who had the two-week curse to get used to their new circumstances.

"Two months ago, the first of the disappearances began, with people vanishing into thin air. Many are calling for answers, some people even saying that it's a government conspiracy. However, there have been no answers at this point. All we can be sure of is people are disappearing roughly two weeks after they contract the curse and they are never seen or heard from again. We now bring in our expert on the matter, Doctor Werstein," the lady said. "Thank you for coming on the show, Doctor Werstein. I'll jump right to the questions on everyone's mind. What is this two-week curse and why are people disappearing?"

"The two-week curse is hard to describe, but it looks like it removes the natural limitations of those who contract it, and allows them to gain access to Mana, magical power, like we see in video games and comic books," Doctor Werstein said in a serious voice.

"Surpassing limitations?" the reporter asked.

"Before, if you worked out, then you would tear the muscle fibers; they would repair, and you could lift more. There was an upper limit based on the strength of your bones, muscles, and body before it had negative effects. After reaching a certain threshold, your body can't improve anymore unless you focus on only training. People who exercise and who have contracted the curse have a numerical value of how strong they are. A normal adult male has a strength of about four, with women having a strength of three. Normal people can train all they want but they reach an upper limit of what their body can do. You can put in all the effort in the world but you can't defeat your genetics. With the cursed, it seems that the more you train, the more your body improves. It becomes increasingly harder to reach those higher stat levels, but there doesn't seem to be a limit for upward growth."

"So a human right now is limited in the stats they can reach, but a cursed has no such limitation?"

"Possibly. We have seen a slowdown in people reaching higher levels as they aren't able to get the nutrients or find environments to push themselves. With people disappearing after two weeks, few people are willing to do studies." Werstein shrugged.

"Tell us about that, the reason that it is called the two-week curse with the strange disappearances." The reporter leaned forward.

"Well, I'm a medical professional, but based on testing, this same Mana energy is used when they disappear. It seems that they are being teleported to somewhere. We don't know where." Werstein sighed.

"Is there any way to know why people are being targeted?"

"There are no common factors. People are picked at random," Werstein said.

Erik flipped channels from his bed, seeing other experts talking on the curse, then pictures and videos of people disappearing. The strange circle that appeared in the air and descended on the cursed. A flash of light and they were gone, a hole burned into the ground.

This was the new reality that he had woken up to.

With a thought, he called up his newest addition.

Character Sheet
Name: Erik West
Level: 0
Race: Human
Titles:
From the Grave
Strength: (Base 7) +0 (-3 due to injuries))
40
Agility: (Base 6) +0 (-4 due to injuries))
10
Stamina: (Base 9) +0 (-5 due to injuries))
60
Mana: (Base 2) +0
20
Mana Regeneration (Base 1) +0
0.95/s
Stamina Regeneration: (Base 7) +0 (-6 due to injuries))
0.95/s

He waved his hand. The vision disappeared but another screen appeared.

Title: From the Grave
You've died and come back to the land of the living not just once, but twice. You're a true survivor who has put one foot in the grave.
Rewards:
+0.50 modifier to Stamina and Mana Regeneration

He was a thirty-three-year-old combat medic without both his legs and his left arm missing.

He had less than two weeks, then he'd disappear.

He'd been doing private security work in South Africa, looking over VIPs and metal shipments.

All it took was a split second and he was no longer a soldier but a cripple. Silent tears appeared in Erik's eyes as he threw his body around. His *useless* nubs flailed around as if taunting him, telling him he wasn't a true man anymore, that he was worthless, some discarded piece of meat just surviving there.

A cruel smile appeared on Erik's face.

"Fuck. Even if it mattered, I'll be gone in two weeks." Erik snorted, looking back on his life, his three wives, loveless relationships. He didn't have children; he didn't want to bring them into this world of pain.

What did he have left? A cabin in the woods, a rack of medals, and an insurance company fighting with him about his benefits as he slowly drained his bank account.

Disappearing sounded kind of nice compared to this life.

All Erik could do was sit there, playing it back in his mind, remembering the last feeling of having limbs. Thinking of the others who had smiled and joked as they loaded into their trucks. The moments that they'd talked and laughed or got to know one another.

He couldn't help but think of the families. Honcho had a wife, with a kid on the way. Rossy was the father to two kids. Yoreck's family was close, with him having two sisters and three brothers.

Gone, and he was sitting here in a hospital bed with two weeks left.

He pressed the call button for the nurse.

"Is there anything that I can help you with?" she asked with a soft smile.

"I can't get to sleep; do you have something that could help me?" Erik gave her a smile, more for her than himself.

"Sure, I'll go get you something." She turned and left.

Erik pushed his head back into his pillows.

Here lies Erik West, used by many, loved by few and weakling.

He snorted at his own thoughts. He was a warrior, but when had he fought for himself? Now, when it was all coming to an end, he was filled with regrets and weakness. He wasn't a warrior charging forward into the breach; he was a sad man wasting away in some hospital till his time was up and they'd only need to change the sheets.

He didn't regret serving, nor did he regret his time with the military and private security contractors. He wished he had been able to pursue more things in life that the military had kept him from.

Thankfully the nurse returned quickly and added some new chemical to his IV.

"Thanks," Erik said.

"No problem." The nurse looked as if she wanted to say more. But what was there to say?

5
WOLF OR SHEEP

Erik woke up to the sound of snoring. He looked over to see a familiar sight. *Rugrat.*

They had served together since they left the military. They'd saved each other's lives too many times to count and they were brothers, even if they didn't have the same blood running through their veins.

Rugrat had been in the convoy. He'd been the one who had run through the bullets and carried Erik back to his truck and saved his life by putting tourniquets on his limbs.

Erik didn't say anything as he let Rugrat sleep in the chair. The man looked as though he had been through hell: his hair growing out, his cowboy hat off at an angle. The suit he wore looked as if it had been bought at a discount store and had been used too many times.

A nurse came in sometime later, opening the door. Rugrat's eyes cracked open as he looked to the nurse and the awake Erik.

"How are we feeling today?" the nurse asked.

Erik let out a long sigh and a shrug.

Looking between the two, the nurse gave a compulsory smile. "I'll bring some food around in a few minutes," she said before leaving.

Rugrat pulled himself up, his tan fading a bit as he leaned forward.

"How was it?" Erik didn't want to ask, but he needed to.

"They were nice ceremonies," Rugrat said, his voice forced as he looked at his hands. A heaviness fell over them as they sunk into their own memories.

"I heard that you're okay to leave?" Rugrat asked.

"Yeah, I would." Erik snorted, bitterness written all over his face. "Got the fucking two-week curse. Two weeks, I'm gone." Erik flicked his hand to the side with finality.

Erik instantly regretted his words as he saw the look of pain on Rugrat's face. It was as if he had punched him in the gut.

"You don't know that," Rugrat said, a defiant look in his eyes.

"Rugrat—" Erik started.

"Don't you start that defeatist shit with me. I just watched three of our friends get put in the ground in the last fucking week. I ain't having you give the hell up on me too. No one knows what happens when you disappear. What they do know is that the people who go can do anything before they leave! I heard that there was a person who had been stabbed but their body repaired itself!"

Erik gritted his teeth, getting frustrated.

Rugrat got up, pointing at Erik. "Are you a fucking wolf or are you a fucking sheep?" Rugrat's eyes burned into Erik's.

"I'm a fucking worm now!" Erik yelled.

"You're Erik fucking West—you're a fucking wolf." Rugrat poked Erik in the chest so hard it hurt.

Erik flopped onto the pillows, tears in his eyes as he let out a self-deprecating laugh. "A wolf, huh? Fat fucking good I can do."

Rugrat grabbed him by his hospital gown and yanked him up so Erik could smell the sweat and see the stubble on his face.

The veins on Rugrat's neck and hand popped out as he looked at Erik, as if searching for something, looking for that spark, that fighting spirit.

With a frustrated yell, he let Erik go and punched the wall.

Erik wanted to say or do something, but he felt like an empty shell, a being without purpose, without a use. Just a hollow shell no one wanted or needed.

Seeing Rugrat facing the wall, his shoulders slumped in defeat, hurt his heart. His anger and frustration rose. Instead of directing it toward himself, he directed it toward what had happened.

It was what Rugrat said. Anything was possible to the people with the two-week curse. He would beat this. He'd break this fricking thing.

There was always healing potions and healing spells in those games. Do I try and fight, even if for him, or do I just waste away here?

There was a noise outside of the room of people talking. Someone was raising some kind of argument.

Erik's jaw flexed. He knew that voice.

"Your parents arrived yesterday," Rugrat said, reading his thoughts.

Erik let out a deep breath. His brow pinched together and black lines appeared on his forehead as he rubbed his right temple. *All right, so I've got two weeks before I disappear. I need to know more about what this means.*

"Rugrat, you know anything about this curse?" Erik asked.

"I looked into it a bit. You see a screen in front of you when you woke up?" Rugrat asked.

Erik nodded.

"Well then, you've definitely got that. The screen showed your stats, I guess. You can upgrade them, get strong and use magic, like that Dungeons and Dragons stuff," Rugrat said.

"What about titles?"

"Titles?" Rugrat frowned.

"It gave me a title, something about nearly dying and coming back again." Erik shrugged.

"Oh, well." Rugrat looked awkward but then faced Erik right on. "You might have died on the operating table when they were getting you fixed up."

Erik pursed his lips, trying to assimilate that as his head moved back and forth slightly. "Okay, well, that's interesting to know." Erik didn't have time to think on all of that right now.

"How do you feel? Stronger?" Rugrat asked.

Erik moved around. He noticed that in his vision that there were two bars: one was blue, the other green. "You know what the bars mean?"

"They're your Stamina and Mana pool. It's the amount of actions that you can do before you need to drink or eat something, or Mana you can use on spells before you need to regenerate it," Rugrat said.

Erik took in his words and continued his investigation. His stumps were itchy. He checked on them, thinking that it might be a rash coming in. "The hell?" Erik looked at the skin that lay under the socks on his limbs.

The mangled skin should have taken a few months to smooth out, but now there wasn't a scar to be seen.

Hope rose in his chest, but he suppressed it. He didn't want to raise his spirits only to have them drop immediately afterward.

He put the socks back on.

"It's been nine days since you turned into a blue smoke machine, which means there are five more days," Rugrat said, holding nothing back.

The door opened. An older-looking gentleman with a refined bearing and a perfectly pressed navy-blue suit looked from the hulking cowboy-hat-toting man in the room to Erik.

Erik didn't miss the flash of disappointment in the man's eyes as he looked to Erik.

"Erik." A woman, wearing a skirt and matching blazer, pushed past him. She looked as if she were on the verge of holding back tears as she moved into the room toward Erik.

His features only hardened at these actions. His mother and father were upper-tier movers and shakers in medical and business circles. His father was a surgeon, while his mother was a business leader. The two of them had created a medical empire in various hospitals across America.

His father hid his thoughts through his patented Doctor West smile that made him seem carefree and laid-back, but underneath there lay the heart of a viper.

His mother was the one to play to people's emotions, using their guilt and emotions to get them to do what she wanted.

Out of the two, at least his father would lose the smile after he was home. His mother was manipulative and fake in everything that she did.

"Mother, Father." Erik looked to them both, his face pinched together.

"Erik dear, when we heard about you losing your limbs, we were distraught. We would've flown over." His mother held his head between her hands and looked into his eyes.

"Rugrat, get my discharge papers. Could you give me a ride home?" Erik asked.

"On it." Rugrat, sensing the odd atmosphere in the room, quickly left. The door closed behind him.

Erik's father frowned. "We told you again and again to come and work for the family hospitals. Your sister and brother both listened." His eyes thinned in anger as a snarl appeared on his face.

"Well, go see them. Seems that they're your perfect children." Erik had even less regard for the two snakes who were his siblings.

"Erik," his mother admonished. "We're family. Nothing can come between us!"

"We were never a family, just the surrogates for you. Doesn't matter much anymore," Erik said.

"You will be coming back with us to New Hampshire, where we will take care of you," his father said, brooking no argument.

Erik started to laugh, getting more and more crazed by the end of it.

Erik's mother moved away from the bed as she seemed to realize that her son was not the young and naive boy from before but a man who had been in battles around the globe, killing people for nearly half of his life.

"Good fucking luck. I can still beat you with just one fucking hand, you useless fuck. Even if I didn't, I've got the two-week curse. Try fucking 'helping me out' with that!" Erik laughed.

His father and mother looked to each other. They seemed to be communicating in gestures.

"Yes, to the two snakes in the room, I will be disappearing from this fine earth in, oh, another five days! So take a vacation in Colorado, say that you were consoling me, and fuck off."

His mother's face transformed in a second, a look of disgust and distaste there as she looked at her son. She didn't need to say anything. All the anger that she had hidden as she looked to draw him over to her side to do her bidding was removed. Finally, he saw her true face.

Rugrat opened the door. Her face turned into a saddened expression as she turned, hiding her face in her husband's shoulder.

Erik's father had a gloating smile on his face, hidden from Rugrat but visible to Erik.

"Let's go," Erik said. Rugrat helped him out of his bed and onto the chair. They left his mother and father in the hospital room.

They reached the truck. Again, Rugrat helped Erik up, throwing the wheelchair in the bed, and jumped into the driver's seat.

"You good?" Rugrat asked.

"I'm feeling better than I have in years." Erik smiled. It felt good to finally sever all ties between him and his parents.

Inside, he was still terrified. He wasn't ready to check out, but Rugrat made a good point. Who said that this was the end?

Rugrat patted Erik's shoulder. "Just the start of something new."

"Hmm?" Erik said, sensing something more in Rugrat's words.

Rugrat gave him a small smile. "You're not the only one with the two-week curse. Must be a damn virus. I've got it too."

Erik, shocked, didn't know what to say.

Rugrat shook his head and let out a short laugh.

Erik couldn't help but shake his head and snort. Rugrat started up the truck. Erik wanted to say something, but he knew Rugrat would dismiss it. Their brotherhood was stronger than blood. They didn't need to say anything.

Erik took a deep breath, calming his emotions.

Thank you, brother.

6

GUN NUT

With that, Erik and Rugrat had to make some hard decisions: which of their babies did they want to take?

"Dammit, how the hell am I taking any of my guns in a two-by-four meter space?"

"It's going to be hard," Erik agreed.

Rugrat had a sour look on his face as they drove along a bumpy road leading to Erik's cabin in the woods.

From what he found online, he drew two conclusions. Previous wounds before the curse would heal but at a slower rate. If someone was injured, they would heal faster than normal, but nothing death-defying.

Every time someone was hurt, the speed which they healed increased.

People's bodies don't only push past physical limits like how much they can lift, but also how many injuries they can take? Doesn't that mean that the more damage you take, the faster that you'll recover?

It was one hell of an idea, but it had far-reaching possibilities.

They made it to a hardware store. Erik drafted up a list and gave it to Rugrat.

He jumped out of the truck and went to get the items on the list.

Erik reached into the backseat, grabbing a knife that hung off Rugrat's bag. He rolled down the sock on his left leg.

He looked at the stump there right above the knee.

He started to think of how crazy this all was, that it was just him clutching at straws.

I might be, but like Rugrat said, isn't it better if I just tried? What's the worst that can happen? Erik paused for a moment. *Maybe I shouldn't think that while holding a knife.*

He shook his head and cut his leg with just enough pressure to break the skin and draw blood. He flinched slightly and put the blade away, setting a timer on the phone as he continued his research.

Erik looked over the different spells that had been created already and some of the hypotheses people had come up with for what worked, what didn't, and why.

It seemed like the spell and words weren't important, but rather the word association and one's thoughts.

For example, there was one person who yelled *meatloaf* and it turned the ground into a quagmire, then said *pizza* and created a sea of fire in front of them.

"I do not want to see that guy's cooking skills in person," Erik muttered.

He took a deep breath and put the phone down. He placed his hand on the leg he'd stabbed. "Heal." Erik watched the Mana bar in the corner of his vision. Nothing happened. He thought on what people had said in the video. He not only needed words but the intent and association.

He closed his eyes, thinking of his leg. He thought of how it must look like inside, based off the x-rays, the different scans, and what the doctors had told him.

He started to feel as if he were looking through his leg, seeing the skin, moving deeper through the fat, muscle layers, the nerves and tendons, blood vessels and to the bone and down to the marrow. It was as if he could see the burned-off nerves, the sealed blood vessels, and sculpted muscle to round out his nub.

He continued to look through the layers, as if he could look through it all as if it were a layered scan.

His head started to hurt and he felt tired. He opened his eyes. His Mana bar blinked at him. There wasn't much of the blue left in the bar.

His eyes went wide as he pulled his hand from his leg. His Mana bar stopped flashing so angrily. Every second, his bar increased in size; after two seconds, it stopped blinking and continued to grow, refilling itself.

Erik laughed to himself in victory. *If I can see through my leg, then there's nothing saying that I couldn't heal myself!*

Hope—true, tangible, and understandable hope—beat in Erik's chest as he sat back in his seat. He could cast a spell!

His lethargy only continued for a few moments before he jumped into action. He didn't have any time to waste!

Once his Mana bar was refilled, he placed his hand on his left arm. He once again remembered the same feeling from before.

He saw through it, seeing the interior of his arm in brilliant detail. He felt less strain as he looked at specific things. After nearly a minute, he had to stop as the Mana bar flashed at him once again.

"So the more in-depth my assessment, the more Mana that I consume," Erik said. It had been roughly forty seconds he had studied his leg for. "I didn't have to use a word, though." Erik turned thoughtful. "Maybe if you break it down, then you might not need the actual words but only the same visualization or cue to cast the spell?"

He once again started to go through the different spells people had shared. He went through the healing spells, paying attention to what people were thinking when they'd used these spells.

It doesn't seem like most of these people had a background in medicine. These are way too general. Seems that they were looking to just heal a wound, nothing overly complicated. Even some people said that it took them days to do something, but in time that their whole body felt better.

Erik closed his eyes. Instead of just looking to examine one thing, he tried to get a full scan of his body. He only got to see the muscle layer of his body when his head felt as though it were going to explode. He stopped. Sweat covered him. His heart raced and his adrenaline spiked.

A feeling of doom had filled him, as if knowing that doing anything more would have dire consequences.

"Okay," Erik said, pulling himself back together. "So, large-scale magic costs a lot, really fast. Small-scale is greatly reduced and specific casting costs even less, so working on a smaller scale and increasing looks like to be the best expenditure of Mana."

He waited the nearly thirty seconds it took for his 20 Mana to regenerate. It wasn't much, but to him, it seemed there were multiple ways to reduce the expenditure.

He reached with his right hand to his left arm nub. Unlike his legs, which had been cut off above the knee, he thought that this might be a bit easier and there was less to regrow.

He scanned his arm three times, getting a clear picture of what it looked like. Each time left him a little bit more tired, even as his Mana regenerated. He scanned his right arm, building up an image of it and checking over what the complete structure looked like.

After two scans, he grabbed Rugrat's bag again and found a marker inside. He circled his arm at the end of the nub.

"All right, well, all good ideas need to be proved or broken in the end."

He rested his hand on the nub again, focusing his mind on it. He felt the tug as he started to use Mana.

He thought of the marrow growing, the bone sheathed around it, the veins, muscle, tissue, tendons, nerves, fat, and skin. His entire body was drenched in sweat as he felt himself reaching his limits after only a few seconds.

With gasping breaths, he opened his eyes. His head spun and he felt dizzy. His green bar had dipped some as well. He looked to the mark on his arm. It seemed as if the nub had grown some, but if it had, it was so small as to be hard to measure.

He recovered his energy and once again sunk his mind into his arm and thought of his arm growing. It was slow, as if at a snail's pace. He didn't even take time to look at his arm. He stopped only when he was near exhaustion, pushing himself again and again.

His green bar continued to drop as he felt more and more drained. He didn't know how many times he had carried out what he had hoped to be a spell.

He looked to his arm to find that the line was now behind by a firm inch. Erik stared at it, dumbfounded. He laughed out loud and fist pumped into the air. "That's right, mother fuckers! I'm growing back my arm!"

He yawned, feeling tired and starving. He looked to his arm. His upper arm looked more defined, as if all of the fat from it had been drained out.

"So while I used magic to make the new limb, a part of the materials came from my upper arm," Erik surmised. "Going to need a ton more food and calories to keep this going."

He focused on his right leg and drew another line. As he thought of the different parts of his leg growing, he paused.

"I'll call this complex healing. It's really in-depth. What if I was to just pour Mana into my leg and stimulate it to grow? Like a tree." Erik recovered his Mana, thinking of what he wanted to do, the association between the word and the actions he wanted to happen. Once his Mana bar was filled, he put his hand on his leg.

"Minor Heal Wounds," Erik said. The Mana poured into his leg, slow at first, but then he found that he could speed up the rate at which he increased the Mana going into the spell as well as reduce it. He sped it up and could visually see a small section of his leg growing.

He recovered his Mana and tried it again and again. His upper leg became more defined as his leg grew. His leg was much larger than his arm but the rate of growth for his leg was matching it and he wasn't burning as much Mana.

Now he only had to think of the words *Minor Heal Wounds* and a blue glow would surround his fingers and his leg. It was barely visible in the dimming light of the day.

He moved to the other leg and used the concentrated growing spell that he'd used on his arm. He cast it on his left leg the same amount of times as he had on his right leg. It hadn't grown as long, but his left leg was thicker, its structure stronger.

He went to his right leg that he'd used the Minor Heal Wounds on and started to sink his mind into it. He tried to change the leg. It was much harder to do it to something that was already formed; there were a few slight issues but nothing that would have a great impact.

I'm going to need a lot more time to figure out more of these spells. Once I have a whole bunch of them, then I can use them for each situation.

He was thinking of using the spells much as a surgeon would use different surgical instruments to get the desired effect. It was medical instruments, drugs, and therapy all rolled up into one. The more he knew about each component or what he could substitute in, the faster his results would be.

Could I use something else to get the nutrients and stuff I need from? Maybe raw meat? Form it into what I need and fuse it together?

With just this one revelation of spells being able to heal, his mind started to open previously closed doors. He started to write down ideas that he had, losing the concept of time.

Rugrat chucked his new purchases into the rear of the truck sometime later, startling Erik.

He looked to see food supplies being tossed into the bed of the truck.

Rugrat tossed the cart into a bay and jumped into the truck.

"You get everything?" Erik asked.

"Yeah. What you been up to in here?" He looked to his bag that had been opened and the sheet of paper and pen in Erik's hand.

"Look!" Erik held up his left arm, a big smile on his face.

"What?" Rugrat asked after a few seconds, a perplexed look on his face.

"See that line?" Erik pointed to the line.

"What about it?" Rugrat shrugged.

"That was how long my arm was when you left the truck," Erik said.

"Wait, so, huh?" Rugrat looked at how Erik's arm was now a few centimeters longer.

"I can use magic! I can heal my arm and my legs!" Erik laughed out loud.

"Shit." Rugrat held his head and wiped off his cowboy hat, shocked by Erik's words.

7
RETURNING HOME

Erik continued to use his Minor Heal Wounds on his damaged limbs. It wasn't as comprehensive as the more advanced heal, but it allowed his body to heal faster.

He ate, researched, and continued to heal.

Rugrat was testing out his own abilities with a grip strength trainer. Whenever they stopped, he would be out of the car, doing push-ups or squats.

He didn't have any weights, but his strength was increasing bit by bit. Say he did two hundred push-ups on the first day; the second he could do two hundred and fifty, then three hundred, then four hundred, with no sign of slowing down. It became so easy he had to start doing handstand push-ups.

While he trained his body, Erik researched and healed.

He was eating all the time. His green bar that represented Stamina was already largely grayed out and he had to constantly eat to regain any sort of energy. Naps had become normal to him.

Erik chewed on jalapeno jerky as he sat back in his chair. "Huh." Erik let out a thoughtful sigh. It looked as though he was not the only person who had tried to take a few things with him. Several people had tried different things.

Some had worked, some failed. There were the more normal measures and the ones that just sounded a little bit crazy

"I think I was overestimating my abilities." Erik ran a quick scan of his arm where he had done what he had thought to be his in-depth spell.

The more he looked, the more he was assured. There had been issues in the area before; he had grown over them, but as he was making more of the new materials for his arm, he was finding that it was cleaner, there wasn't anything to be in his way.

"It would've been almost better if I started off from a stump than the formed nub that they gave me," Erik muttered.

"What are you talking about?" Rugrat asked.

"I only have a Minor Heal Wounds spell. I can use it in one area or I can use it on a larger area. Consumption varies, but it basically just speeds up the healing process. Well, more accurately, it stimulates the tissues to form. Well, I guess I'll find out when it comes to forming my hand," Erik said.

"Okay, got some of that—you've got two spells and it can heal you," Rugrat said.

Erik rubbed his head, a headache coming on.

"You okay?" Rugrat asked.

"Yeah, my brain just hurts."

"Happens to me all the time," Rugrat said.

Erik looked up at Rugrat with a raised eyebrow before snorting and shaking his head.

"Did you find out anything else?" Rugrat asked.

"I need to stab you," Erik said.

"Well, that wasn't what I was expecting," Rugrat drawled.

"I can cast spells, but they haven't been acknowledged by whatever system we have in our bodies. For the spells to be recognized, they need to be used on another person who is cursed. Now, most of the people who are cursed are at the same event or place at some time and they disappear at the same time. It looks like the curse targets an area, rather than a person, how we both got hit with it. Now we're from the system, but everyone else isn't. I can heal people all day long and get nothing, but once I heal someone else then the system that allows us to see stats will give me a pop-up," Erik said.

"All right, well, no need to stab me. I've got a cut on my knuckles." Rugrat held his hand out over to Erik.

"Heal," Erik muttered under his breath. Mana was drawn out of his body and a faint magical circle appeared on his finger above Rugrat's hand.

Erik frowned. It was as if he couldn't find Rugrat's hand.

He put the finger with the magical circle on Rugrat's cut. He saw the break in the skin, the tear through the muscle, the broken blood vessels and coagulating blood.

A glow appeared under the magical circle, feeling as the finger knitted itself together layer by layer.

Erik cancelled the spell. Rugrat looked at his hand before quickly looking up.

He yanked the wheel. They'd nearly come off the side of the road watching what Erik was doing.

"Well, the light show is new." Erik laughed as a screen appeared in his vision.

Skill: Minor Heal Wounds
Novice
Heal live matter
Consumption of Mana based on area and effect

Skill: Simple Organic Scan
Novice
See through organic materials (bodies)
Consumption of Mana based on area of effect

Erik wrote down the information before dismissing them.

It wasn't much information, but it confirmed some of his thoughts and created more questions.

"Did it work?" Rugrat asked.

"Yeah," Erik said distractedly as he pulled up his character sheet.

Name: Erik West
Level: 0
Race: Human
Titles:
From the Grave
Strength: (Base 7) +0 (-3 due to injuries))
40
Agility: (Base 6) +0 (-4 due to injuries))
10
Stamina: (Base 9) +0 (-5 due to injuries))
60
Mana: (Base 2) +0
20
Mana Regeneration (Base 1) +0
0.95/s
Stamina Regeneration: (Base 7) +0 (-6 due to injuries))
0.95/s

He studied the sheet in more detail. There was nothing like someone's Health points like there was in most Magic games that he had been part of.

One's health couldn't be easily broken down in numbers. They weren't pixels, each system related to one another.

There was no such thing as charisma, or intelligence; those were innate abilities that relied on the actions of a person.

Nothing was given; everything had to be earned.

"Yoo-hoo, earth to Erik." Rugrat waved his hand in front of Erik, trying to get his attention.

"Hey," Erik said, jolted out of his reverie.

"We're here." Rugrat turned off the engine and got out of the truck.

Erik looked out at the simple cabin. He liked his peace, so he'd bought twenty acres of land and built a cabin on it. He'd thought about just hanging out here, letting time pass him by, letting the world sort out its own troubles.

Now, he didn't have that sort of time left. He and Rugrat had less than five days until they were summoned.

Erik looked at his left arm. He felt like some kind of twisted comic book character as he looked at his adult upper arm and elbow that slimmed down into a toddler-sized arm and hand.

Erik couldn't help but make grasping motions with the hand.

I'm a T-rex!

Rugrat pulled out his chair, the noise making Erik clear his throat in embarrassment.

Rugrat and Erik worked together to get Erik into the chair. They'd gotten proficient as Rugrat helped him out at their motels, or when Erik needed to go to the washroom.

Rugrat didn't make any jokes and although he didn't say anything, Erik knew that Rugrat never would.

Rugrat rolled Erik toward the front door while muttering, "Home sweet haunted fricking house."

"Who has more supplies?" Erik asked.

"Who is crazier?" Rugrat didn't miss a beat, making Erik temporarily unable to reply.

"That's what I thought," Rugrat said.

Erik looked around the home. There was a workshop off to the side all locked up, then the main house. It was a two-story affair, simple and easy.

Erik took in a deep breath, a feeling of melancholy filling him. It was his home, but it would be ripped away from him.

All of his plans, his potential future, had been torn away by that improvised explosive device.

The two-week curse was the only thing that gave him hope. The more times he healed himself, the less Mana and Stamina he consumed and the more he was able to repair.

He knew that Rugrat was as confused and scared of what might come. Hell, they might die. Both of them didn't know. They would, however, face it as they always had: side-by-side with a gun in their hand, watching the other's back.

Erik looked around his home, using his wheelchair to tour around the first floor.

"All right, I'll go and get the materials moved to the workshop. You get some food and keep researching," Rugrat said.

"On it," Erik yelled back, hearing the door close a moment later. Erik was confused by his thoughts, the reality of Earth and the two-week curse clashing with one another, the fact that he could heal his wounds.

"If it hurts, then just keep on going. There's no path back anymore."

Rugrat stepped out of the house. His smile faded as his eyes turned dull. His excitement, his energy, it all seemed to drain out of him as the exterior door smacked against the doorframe.

In his eyes, he saw the friends they had lost, the funerals he had gone to. Seeing those widows, their children, the other military types who had served with them, talking to them over beers and telling them how it had happened. Seeing the coffin being lowered into the ground.

A chill seemed to pass through his soul as loss, knee-crumbling and future-ending loss made to cripple him.

Rugrat took a deep breath and focused his mind, raising his head as he gritted his teeth. He didn't look toward the house but headed for the truck and the supplies that had been stuffed into it.

I might not know what the hell this two-week curse is, what happens to us when we disappear, but I know that Erik needs me and that's enough.

Rugrat didn't know whether what they were doing would be wasted effort; it didn't really matter to him. As he threw the straps off and started to pull the steel out, he pictured the dead eyes, the lost look in Erik's eyes.

It was as if he was dead already on the inside. The anger that rose up in his throat as he yelled at Erik, Rugrat wouldn't admit it to himself, but those words were as much for himself as they were for Erik.

They might not want to keep going for themselves, but they'd push themselves for their brother, for the person who would stand beside them in thick and thin. This was one of those times.

Rugrat dragged the steel to the workshop, letting it drop to the ground. The noise made him wince, but the dull look in his eyes held a bit of hope.

"Maybe we need a new start? Something to take us away from this." Rugrat didn't really believe that Erik had healed his legs, but Erik thought so. "I just hope he doesn't lose too much hope if it doesn't work."

8

DIVISION OF TASKS

Erik heard Rugrat closing the fridge door in the basement and walking up the stairs moments later.

Erik cleared his head, forcefully pushing those thoughts and emotions to the side, becoming the Erik West he'd always been.

"Well, you might live in buttfuck nowhere, but, I'll say this, I'm impressed with your vault and beer!" Rugrat came up the stairs and shut the door behind him with a kick. He appeared around the corner with nearly a dozen beers and a grin on his face.

Erik couldn't help but chuckle at Rugrat's expression.

If there was one thing they could all agree on, it was their love for weapons and booze.

"Porch?" Erik asked.

"Sure thing." Rugrat took the beers out, then helped Erik outside and opened a beer for him. It was mid-afternoon. A cool breeze came through the surrounding forest.

Rugrat took a seat in a chair, crossing his cowboy boots and tilting his hat forward.

"Cheers." Erik held out his beer.

"Cheers," Rugrat said. The two of them tapped their beers on a nearby table before taking a long drink.

They just sat there for a bit.

"Nothing like a post-deployment beer," Erik said.

"Nothing quite like it, or the first country girl," Rugrat said.

The corner of Erik's mouth turned up at Rugrat's antics as they continued to drink.

"You have one hell of a hideout here," Rugrat said.

"Got everything you might need and a few things you might not, but it keeps me going," Erik said.

"Well, it's a good thing that you kept your right hand. Don't know what you'd do with all the time you have otherwise." Rugrat shook his fist up and down in the air.

"Fuck you too." Erik took a drink of his beer, his middle finger in the air.

Rugrat's solemn expression turned into a big smile as they sat and drank, shooting the shit and not even talking about Erik's wounds.

Erik woke up early, a headache brewing from the night before. He made to get up, finding he was on the couch. His left arm slipped as if it wasn't there. He looked over, and saw that it wasn't there.

Reality descended with a sigh as he felt the itchiness and the now dull pain of his missing limbs. He used his right hand to get up. He got on the floor and shimmied over to his bag. He popped some of the painkiller drugs and changed out of his clothes on the floor and struggled into his new set.

Rugrat woke up some time later. "Ready?" he asked.

"As I'm gonna be," Erik said. The painkillers started to numb the world again.

Rugrat made it clear to Erik he only had one job: to recover. Rugrat had carved out two circles outside of the cabin and was organizing his and Erik's supplies. He'd got deliveries planned; in his downtime, he worked out with the exercise equipment in Erik's workshop/garage.

His Strength had actually increased a point from his hard work. Seeing that extra Strength stat, he threw himself into exercising even more.

Erik opened his eyes with a gasp of breath as cold sweat flowed down his face. He slumped back into his chair. He was drained but recovering slowly but surely, a trickle of Mana flowing back into his body.

Erik was frowning at the ceiling as Rugrat walked in, covered in sweat.

"Dude, I know that they say size isn't everything." Rugrat couldn't hold in the laugh as he looked at Erik's "legs."

"They're perfectly functional," Erik said. The same thing that had happened with his arm happened with his legs. It was as if he were a child, growing once again.

He had full legs, knees, shins, calfs, ankles, feet, and toes—just they were about the size of a four-year-old's.

Growing them initially had taken time and an excessive amount of Mana and Stamina. The energy required to make them grow decreased abruptly.

"That's what they all say." Rugrat walked through the house, grabbing something out of the fridge, and headed back to the room. He tossed Erik a drink.

Erik grabbed it with his left hand; it had been fully regrown now. They had a day and a half before they were set to disappear.

Rugrat chugged a drink as Erik put the drink down.

"You know how I told you about those odd markings that are inside our bodies?" Erik asked.

"The two circles inside one another, thirteen of them throughout our bodies. I have three of them open—you've only got one?" Rugrat said.

"Yeah, I think that they're based on our Mana Regeneration. You have a Mana Regeneration stat of three while I've only got one. Also, when I cast a spell, then I feel the Mana coming in through the hole in the back of my head."

"Can we do anything for it, like open more of them up?" Rugrat asked.

Erik shrugged and grabbed the drink. "Hell if I know."

"Ready?" Rugrat put his drained bottle down and leaned forward so that his hands rested on one of Erik's legs.

"Go for it," Erik said.

Rugrat's healing spell wasn't as powerful as Erik's but every little bit helped speed up his recovery. A magic circle appeared around Rugrat's hands as power poured out of him and into Erik's leg.

Erik's fatigue only increased as his leg grew visibly before his eyes.

Instead of just pouring out all his Mana in one shot, Rugrat slowly introduced it into the spell, allowing him to keep just above his Mana Regeneration rate.

Erik braced himself and started to cast a healing spell on his other leg. Based on his senses, he worked to find the balance as well.

After ten minutes, Erik slumped back in his seat. Rugrat followed him a few seconds later.

Rugrat got to his feet and moved to the kitchen. He returned a few minutes later with a bag full of food. He threw Erik the majority of the bag, keeping some snacks.

Erik wolfed them down as Rugrat tore open a pack of jerky and started munching on it.

He didn't say anything as he kept eating and put one hand on Erik's left leg again. "Heal," Rugrat said, his voice tired, but his eyes focused on Erik's leg.

Erik continued to eat with him. While Rugrat got headaches from exhausting his Mana, Erik's Stamina decreased sharply. He had to keep on eating all the time.

They lost track of time as the sun started to set and the lights came on in the house. Erik and Rugrat only paused when Erik's Stamina was dangerously low or the Mana deficient headaches got too bad.

Erik's eyes were burning from the exhaustion. The darkness of night was already getting brighter as a new day was starting.

Rugrat slid in his chair, unable to stay upright as he passed out.

Erik looked at his legs. They were still skinny as hell, but at least they looked the right length now.

9
THE LAST DAY

Erik came to sometime later. Rugrat was stumbling through the house as though he were still drunk, holding his head as he drank directly from the kitchen sink.

Erik looked to his legs. His eyes hadn't lied—they were there now.

Erik gripped the armrests of the chair he was in. He gritted his teeth. Even with the headache mildly pounding away in his head, he was focused on his legs.

He pushed his body up. His legs felt awkward, but they responded to his thoughts. Erik stabilized himself before he pushed up, balancing his weight on his legs. They were incredibly weak. He could feel the strain of holding himself up on them.

Using the wall and the couch, he moved forward shakily.

His steps were sudden and jerky. It was as if he had sat on them for a long time. They were numb, but the feeling was coming back as blood flowed through them.

Rugrat looked over to see Erik moving forward shakily. His pained expression turned into a smile and then laughter. "You fucking beauty! Nothing can keep down the Doc!" Rugrat laughed.

Erik laughed. He tripped and fell over, but his joy wasn't diminished as he rolled onto his back and continued to laugh.

"I've got fucking legs!"

It was around midday by the time the two of them recovered enough for Rugrat to help Erik out of the house.

Erik leaned on Rugrat. His legs were already getting stronger. Erik's natural healing abilities had only increased with time. If he and Rugrat hadn't worked on putting him back together, then Erik's body might have recovered on its own in six months.

They went over to the garage/workshop. The truck, ATV, and car had all been moved out to clear space for the two circles that appeared in the workshop.

Discarded pallets lay around the room. Rugrat had broken items down into the components so that they were as small as could be. Boxes and anything that took up space had been removed.

Two semi-circle containers had been filled with necessary supplies and topped off with ammunition. Ropes in the center would allow them to climb into the middle and lower more gear over their heads.

"Good work," Erik said. Seeing all that Rugrat had done, he didn't know how he had enough hours in the day.

"I got your med kit supplies ready, but I haven't wrapped it all up. You want to check over it?" Rugrat pointed to gear off to the side where needles, bags of saline, bandages, tourniquets, drugs, and myriad medical equipment were laid out.

"Help me over there," Erik said. They didn't have time to mess about. There was just one day to go before they were summoned.

Erik went through the medical supplies. By nighttime, everything was packed up in the summoning circles. More gear was packed in around it. If they had more room, then they'd try to take as much as possible.

Erik's legs were good enough to help Rugrat with everything.

Then they turned to personal gear.

Erik checked on his plate carrier, rucksack, weapons, and other extras. He modified it as he could before there was nothing more to do.

They sat out in front of the house, looking at the garage and workshop, the two of them drinking beers.

Everything had been a whirlwind since Rugrat showed up in Erik's hospital room.

Unbidden thoughts appeared in his mind as his eyes moved to the stars.

Keller, Honcho, Yoreck—they'd been his friends, his buddies. Here he was, his arm and legs returned to him, but they hadn't made it.

A heavy silence descended as Erik raised up his bottle. "To the fallen."

"To the fallen," Rugrat said. The two of them hit bottles, tapping them against their chairs, and took a deep drink.

They nursed their drinks, thinking on the past. There was no grand ceremony or fanfare. Simply two men saying good-bye to their brothers.

"Well, even if it's the end tomorrow, we've got good company waiting for us," Rugrat said.

"That we do," Erik agreed.

A part of him wanted to just rest, to put it behind, but another part of him, the part that had driven him for most of his life, hungered for what was to come. He wanted to see what was on the other side of this summoning. He wanted to guide his own life.

10
TEN REALMS?

Erik woke up the next day with a mix of emotions.

He went downstairs and went outside to look over it all—trying to take it in, to settle himself down. It was the same kind of nerves he got when he was just about to go on deployment. But now there was no talking to anyone else to see what would happen next. This was the big leap for him.

He walked for about an hour or so before returning to the house.

"Erik, Erik!" Rugrat yelled, running around the house in a panic.

"I'm here, dude. What's up?"

"Shit, ah, nothing, sorry—didn't know where you were." Rugrat calmed down. "Thought I'd missed you already."

Erik could only pat Rugrat on the shoulder awkwardly.

They ate some food, stuffing themselves as much as they could as they didn't know when or where they might get their next meal.

"Time to get suited up?" Rugrat asked.

"Yeah," Erik said.

They grabbed their vests, pulling them on, checking their loaded magazines, their weapons, then gathered their guns together. Erik was hauling two gun bags with a pistol on his chest and his personal rifle hanging from his vest.

They helped each other get their rucks on, checking the other out.

They checked the time and got situated inside their tubes, affixing the extra overhead storage.

"Fuck, I hate the waiting part!" Rugrat yelled from his tube.

"And it hates you!" Erik yelled back, bracing his weapon.

Erik heard a wrapper being opened.

Erik laughed. "Twinkie?"

"You know it!" Rugrat yelled back. "Twinkies will never die!"

Erik shook his head. He was about to say something else when he suddenly closed his mouth. The air felt different, as if it were suffused with power. "Looks like this is it!" Erik yelled.

Erik felt an almost tugging sensation on himself, Mana, its now familiar cool but also comfortable feeling, surged through the workshop, creating a dust cloud around the two metal cylinders Rugrat had made.

A light appeared underneath Erik's feet and above his head. The magical circles were being created.

"See you on the other side, brother!" Erik yelled.

"Come on then!" Rugrat yelled into the skies.

Abnormalities found

Light surrounded Erik. Everything seemed to disappear. He knew he was somewhere else but he couldn't move, his every movement locked down.

The Mana surged and Erik's world changed.

He dropped slightly. Erik ripped on a pull tab, cutting the straps around the cylinder. They dropped outward and gear pouring out everywhere.

Erik raised his rifle, scanning the area. "Rugrat!" he yelled out.

"Good!" Rugrat yelled back.

They were in a forest but it didn't look like any that Erik had seen back on Earth. There were massive mountains in the distance that shot through the clouds.

The forest looked to be untouched, with colors that one wouldn't see in a normal forest. A fog moved over the ground; random glowing lights appeared in the forest.

The two of them looked around, checking that there was nothing around them.

They lowered their guns and looked to each other just as a screen jumped up in their visions.

Welcome to the Ten Realms!
You have been randomly selected to join the Ten Realms. One may choose to ascend the Ten Realms, thereupon making a request to the Gods of the Realms.
Only those who are Level 10, 20, 30, 40, 50, 60, 70, 80, and 90 may ascend to the next realm.

Fortune favors the strong!

Quest: Welcome to the Ten Realms
Requirements:
Reach Ten Realms Totem (Marked on map)
Rewards:
Guide to the Ten Realms
Minor ring of holding
Minor Mana recovery potion
Minor Stamina recovery potion
1000 EXP

Quest: Opening the Fourteen Gates
Congratulations! You have opened your first Mana gate, unlocking this quest.
Requirements:
Clear all of your fourteen gates (1/14).
Rewards:
+1 to Mana Regeneration base stat.
Undergo Mana Body Rebirth.
+14,000,000 EXP

You have reached Level 1
When you sleep next, you will be able to increase your attributes by: *5 points.*

0/300 EXP till you reach Level 2

You have learned the spell: **Minor Heal Wounds**. Your spell book has been updated.

You have learned the spell: **Blood Force**. Your spell book has been updated.

You have learned the spell: **Simple Organic Scan**. Your spell book has been updated.

You have gained a Map! Do you wish to accept this gift?
YES/NO

Erik dismissed the screens with a thought.

Rugrat and Erik walked closer together, their eyes still scanning the area.

"Looks like a bunch of this didn't come through when we were on Earth, must only work here. You see one of the screens talking about Experience?"

"Yeah, get three hundred and we can be level two's. Those circle things must be Mana gates. Mine said three," Rugrat said.

"Mine said one," Erik said, confirming it to them both.

Rugrat pulled the earpiece out from his ear. "Other than all the cool new gadgets, it looks like electronics don't work."

"We've only got four guns each and all of these supplies in the middle of nowhere," Erik said. His body was tense but he still felt some relief.

"Well, we aren't dead. I'd say that right there is a good start." Rugrat chuckled, the adrenaline still simmering in his veins.

Erik started chuckling and then laughing. "Fuck." He sighed, letting out all of his worries and fears.

"Ten Realms—doesn't sound so bad. Sounds kind of interesting," Rugrat said.

"Fortune favors the strong—little overbearing, ain't it?"

"Guess we'll have to find out. I'm going to use that map thing," Rugrat said.

"All right." Erik kept an eye out as Rugrat accessed his character sheet. It actually appeared in the air, he noticed. Before, the information on their character sheets had only appeared to them. There was no way to share it other than telling or recording it.

Erik still couldn't read it, but it showed that things were clearly different here.

Erik's body felt *right* here. It was as if he had been at high altitude and was now coming back down to the sea, getting his first clean breath of air.

"So, we're in a forest of some kind. Got a mountain range going from north to the east. Got some signs of a dirt road, it looks like. There's a marker leading to a city called Chonglu. Weird. This map is like GPS located—got a path to the main road and everything, or I can move the path if I want to. Says that it's about sixty kilometers away," Rugrat said.

"Three-day hike?" Erik said.

"Yeah," Rugrat agreed.

Erik looked at his watch. "No idea what time is like here, though my watch seems to be working." He realized how checking his watch on some other planet was not going to work.

"Let's get situated, sort the gear, then head out in a day or two," Rugrat said.

"Agreed," Erik said.

"Welcome to the Ten Realms," Rugrat said.

"If you're the welcoming committee, I need to get a damn ticket the hell out of here," Erik said, relaxing a bit.

11
REACHING LEVEL ONE

Erik and Rugrat started to clear the gear away. The guns that they hadn't picked had been turned into rough ingots. Erik was happy that none of them were loaded.

They pulled apart their own guns, put them back together, and used string to pull their triggers. All of them worked. Rugrat took first watch as Erik went to sleep.

You have 5 attribute points to use.

Erik saw his character sheet floating in front of him.

Character Sheet
Name: Erik West
Level: 0
Race: Human
Titles:
From the Grave
Strength: (Base 7) +0 (-1)
60
Agility: (Base 6) +0 (-2)
20
Stamina: (Base 9) +0 (-3)
90
Mana: (Base 2) +0
20
Mana Regeneration (Base 1) +0
0.95/s
Stamina Regeneration: (Base 7) +0 (-2)
1.75/s

If I up my Mana Regeneration, that will mean I cast spells with greater frequency and for longer periods of time. What do I need Strength for? I'm pretty strong on my stats now that I have all my limbs back. My muscles still aren't fully developed. A little slow right now but improving that fast enough so don't really need Agility right now. Stamina, now that means I can do more stuff for a longer period of time—kind of useful—but Stamina Regeneration means I'll need fewer breaks. Mana—well, I don't have spells that need that much Mana. Plus, with a high regeneration, it will be hard for me to really make a dent in the overall Mana usage. Erik pondered what to do.

Okay, so I need to do physical labor. There are only rudimentary roads from what I was seeing, so going to be on foot most of the time. If I could run faster, then that would be useful. All right so, one point into Agility, two into Stamina Regeneration and Mana Regeneration.

With Erik's thoughts, his character sheet updated and he accepted the changes.

Erik woke up some time later with Rugrat shaking him awake.

"West?" Rugrat asked.

"Yeah, I'm up," Erik said, his head blurry as he started to get up and out of his sleeping bag. He felt stronger, his body more powerful.

"Took some time to wake you there," Rugrat said.

"Just made it to level one, —put attribute points into my character sheet." Erik recalled what had happened right before he had gone to sleep.

He quickly pulled up his character sheet to look for changes.

Character Sheet
Name: Erik West
Level: 1
Race: Human
Titles:
From the Grave
Strength: (Base 7) +0 (-1)
70
Agility: (Base 6) +1 (-2)
25
Stamina: (Base 9) +0 (-3)
90
Mana: (Base 2) +0
20
Mana Regeneration (Base 1) +2
1.35/s
Stamina Regeneration: (Base 7) +2 (-2)
2.15/s

Clearly his dream wasn't just a figment of his imagination. He quickly told Rugrat what had happened.

Rugrat spent some more time awake, looking over his stat sheet before he got into his sleeping bag.

Erik was only able to wake him three hours later.

Rugrat, once coming to, quickly checked his stats. "Well, looks like we can only apply the attribute points when we go to sleep. Though when I trained my body and increased a stat level, it was like I broke through a barrier, allowing me to directly use my extra strength right away. Also it went straight to the base stat, not what I'm guessing is that modifying stat."

"Hopefully we can start to get some more answers at this Chonglu City," Erik said.

They gathered the supplies together that they had brought with them. They broke down the cylinder and moved around the forest, creating a few different caches with materials and items that they might need. It took them two days, with Erik and Rugrat working out as much as possible.

Erik was finally rewarded on his second day.

Your base stats have increased!
Stamina +1

Character Sheet
Name: Erik West
Level: 1
Race: Human
Titles:
From the Grave
Strength: (Base 7) +0
70
Agility: (Base 6) +1
35
Stamina: (Base 10) +0
150
Mana: (Base 2) +0
20
Mana Regeneration (Base 1) +2
1.35/s
Stamina Regeneration: (Base 7) +2
2.55/s

The other thing that they found was that their weapons had stats.

GM6 Lynx (Big Momma)
Damage: Unknown
Weight: 11.5 kg
Health: 100/100
Base Value: Unknown
Range: Long range
Requires: .50 BMG Ammunition

Erik and Rugrat toured the area, getting it burned into their minds so that they would be able to find it no matter what. As they did, they came across different plants and items.

Erik was passing a kind of fern when he took a knee.

It gave off a calming smell. Just breathing it in, he felt as if his body was lighter and healthier.

Erik looked at the plant for a few more seconds. "Well, got to take some risks." He grabbed his blade and dug around the fern's roots. He quickly pulled it and a clump of dirt free.

You have successfully retrieved Forest Fennel!

You have learned the skill: **Alchemy**
Alchemists are said to open the world with a pill, potion, or powder. Masters of poisons and body-altering consumables, their craft can bring out a person's ability and open new paths to their future.

Skill: Alchemy
Level: 1 (Novice)
No bonuses at this time. You must prove your skills first.

Erik's lips curled upward at his small victory.

Quickly he stuffed the plant away and moved back to camp.

"Rugrat," Erik said as he found the large man burying another cache of supplies.

"What's up?"

"I just got the Alchemy skill from doing something in this world. I think that if I was to heal something then, like how spells were recognized back on Earth, I might unlock the healing skill as well," Erik said.

Rugrat let out a long sigh as he got out of the hole. "All right, but you're going to have to stab me."

"This'll just hurt a bit."

"You're stabbing me, not giving me my latest run up of shots," Rugrat complained.

Erik quickly cut Rugrat's bare arm.

Rugrat let out a grunt and shook his arm at the pain as he pressed his teeth together.

"Big baby." Erik put his hand on Rugrat.

The magical circle appeared as he cast his healing spell with no problem. With his practice, for the two of them casting a healing spell took but a thought now.

The wound in Rugrat's arm healed up quickly.

"Fucking stabby mcstabface over here," Rugrat complained, wiping away the old blood on his arm.

Erik's face turned to joy as screens appeared in his vision.

You have learned the skill: **Healer**
You have delved into the arts of a healer, a noble and lofty skill. Your abilities are still simple but with more patients and practice, your skills will evolve.

Skill: Healer
Level: 1 (Novice)
No bonuses at this time. You must prove your skills first.

He let out a pained yell as he looked down at his arm and the grinning Rugrat.

"Sorry, I slipped. Let me help you out there," Rugrat said.

"You little shit," Erik complained as Rugrat healed him.

"Booyah—healer extraordinaire. Watch out, West." Rugrat laughed.

Erik's hand moved to his side where he had stuffed the fennel into his pocket.

"Oh, I found this in the forest. When I pulled it out of the ground, I unlocked the alchemist skill," Erik said.

"You want to make potions now?" Rugrat asked.

Erik opened his mouth and then shrugged. "I don't really know enough about it. If it's like the games, then I'd be able to make potions to restore Mana, Stamina, and heal, be bandages on steroids."

"Could also maybe make gunpowder, or find something like it," Rugrat said.

"Still far off. I won't make any decisions until we know more."

"Well, it should only be a day or two before everything is hidden away and we can set off," Rugrat said.

Erik nodded. He was cautious, but he was also excited. He was in lands unknown, a land that had magic and fantasy. There was no knowing what they might run into.

Erik was one of those combat veterans who embraced the fight. It was only when everything that was on the line he felt alive; it felt as if he served a higher purpose. He got things done and he charged forward. *That* was called being alive. Here he was in enemy territory and he didn't know anything. It was a blank landscape—it excited the hunter, the combat medic that rested within him.

12
EXPERIENCE

Erik and Rugrat woke up early, packing their gear away quickly. They cleared out the area around their camp.

It was hard to see any signs of where they had been as they checked their maps. Erik had used his as well by this time. They pulled their rucksacks on and checked their weapons before they moved off on their plotted route.

As they were walking, Erik started to feel tired. He took a leaf from a forest fennel and chewed on it.

Even if it had a bad reaction, he could heal himself.

Stamina Regeneration increased by 0.50/s for 2s

A faint power entered Erik's body, revitalizing his body.

125/300 EXP till you reach Level 2

"Rugrat, eat this." Erik passed the other man a leaf.

"All of that from a leaf? Is that much of a stamina regeneration increase?" Rugrat asked.

"Like I know anything more than you?" Erik sighed and walked ahead of Rugrat.

They continued on their path as they heard different monsters in the forest roaring and making noise at one another.

"High right!" Rugrat yelled. His silenced personal rifle fired as a snake with wings dropped from a tree onto the ground. A faint gray tombstone appeared above the snake. Erik and Rugrat didn't have time to look at it closer before a coughing war cry rose up from the surrounding area.

"Contact!" Erik yelled, pulling on his quick detach straps. He and Rugrat put their rucksacks in front of them as they were back to back.

A hissing noise came from the trees above as a flying snake shot out from a tree. Its mottled greens and browns made it hard to see before it launched its attack.

Erik fired in its general direction and one of his rounds hit the snake. As a tombstone appeared above it, a faint golden energy came from the snake and entered Erik's body. The same powerful feeling that had come from eating the forest fennel appeared in his body. It seemed to pause for a second, as if reaching a bottleneck before exploding forth. Screens tried to pop up, but Erik dismissed them before they formed as he grabbed the Mossberg on the side of his rucksack, pulling it out of its holster.

Mossberg 500
Damage: Unknown
Weight: 3.4 kg
Health: 100/100
Base Value: Unknown
Range: Short range
Requires: 12-gauge Ammunition

Although Erik had taken nearly twenty rounds to put down the one snake, Rugrat had needed five. After all, Jimmy "Rugrat" Rodriguez was a proud graduate of Marine Corps Scout Sniper School and more ranges, backyards, forests sand dunes, jungles and about everyother place he could get a gun and shoot it.

More of the flying snakes came out of the trees. Erik fired and turned, sending clouds of buckshot at the snakes, turning them to mangled corpses.

"Reloading!" Rugrat yelled, changing out magazines as Erik continued to fire.

Rugrat started firing again. "Back in!"

"Reloading," Erik said a few moments later. The flying snakes were coming from everywhere. He quickly started stuffing shells into the shotgun; he didn't even get to fully load before he fired on a nearby snake.

They weren't strong but there were many of them.

Erik felt a pain in his left leg. He looked down to see a flying snake buried in his leg.

You have been affected by the Winged Forest Snake's poison. -1.0/s Stamina for 5s. With chance of paralysis

Erik called up a healing spell, looking at the snake that was glaring at him. He grabbed the snake and his combat knife, stabbing the snake until a faint tombstone appeared above it. The snake was buried deep in Erik's leg. He didn't have time to get rid of it; he dropped his knife at his feet and pumped his shotgun, taking down three of the winged forest snakes in one blast.

There were tombstones all around Erik and Rugrat as a faint bloody smell started to rise from the ground.

A deep roar came from within the forest.

The snakes let out angered cries as they started to turn around and run.

Erik and Rugrat were quickly reloading.

Once he was done with his weapon, Erik pulled the snake out of his leg and sheathed his blade again.

"Contact!" Rugrat yelled, shooting at whatever he had seen. Erik checked his arcs before looking over where Rugrat's tracers were going.

A massive ape ran across the forest ground, dust being picked up in its wake as it jumped up into the trees, moving through the forest with ease.

Rugrat's rounds cracked around it, before three hit the ape's chest.

It was rocked back by the rounds and dropped to the ground. The forest went quiet.

Erik looked around. Other than the tombstones above the dead winged forest snakes and the ape, there was nothing to be found in the area.

"Let's get moving quick," Erik said.

"Check the tombstone on that snake next to you."

Erik reached out with his hand. When he touched the tombstone, a menu descended.

Winged Forest Snake Loot
Winged Forest Snake Scales *Damaged*
Winged Forest Snake venom pouch (Empty)
Winged Forest Snake meat
Take all?

Erik hit the *take all* part of the screen.

No storage device detected. Will drop in real world.

The snake's corpse turned white, being replaced by the three piles of items.

Erik was interested by the materials but he didn't have the space or time to collect them.

He quickly got his rucksack on and holstered his shotgun on its side again as he grabbed his personal rifle.

"Cover me." Rugrat moved to the ape. The tombstone flashed for a few seconds before the ape's chest seemed to open. A brown orb appeared, moving to Rugrat's hand. He stuffed the one-inch brown marble into his pocket.

Erik didn't ask as they set off at a jog, checking their surroundings for any other sneak attacks.

It was sometime later that they slowed down. They dropped their packs and scanned the area. The regular noises had come back to the forest. The great fight before seemed as if it was nothing to the beasts here.

Erik and Rugrat listened for anything that might be following them for a few minutes before they relaxed.

"Fuck me." Erik sighed.

"No thanks." Rugrat pulled out the marble from his pocket and tossed it to Erik as he leaned against his rucksack on the ground.

Monster Core
Rank: Common Mortal grade
Weight: 0.2 kg
Base Value: 5 Silver
Characteristics: Unknown

Do you wish to absorb this Monster Core?
YES/NO

Erik tossed it back to Rugrat. There was an undeniable power held within it. "Well, I hope that one silver and fifty coppers is worth something," Erik said.

"I wonder what would happen if we absorbed it." Rugrat looked at the marble before tucking it back into his pocket.

Ever since the battle had started, an exclamation mark in the top right of his vision had appeared. After the first couple of notifications came in and he dismissed them before the screens could totally form, none had appeared.

He thought of the exclamation mark in his vision and was bombarded with screens.

You have learned the skill: **Marksman**
Ranged Weaponry is familiar to you. You have far to go before gaining the title of a Master but with practice, you will get there.

Skill: Marksman
Level: 6 (Novice)
No bonuses at this time. You must prove your skills first.
You have learned the skill **Blade**
You're handy with sharpened steel but the path of Master is not one can get to by just repeatedly stabbing their target.

Skill: Blade
Level: 1 (Novice)
No bonuses at this time. You must prove your skills first.

You have reached Level 3
When you sleep next, you will be able to increase your attributes by: 10 points.

2,075/2,700 EXP till you reach Level 4

That golden energy that had entered his body from the snakes he killed must have been a visual aid for Experience. Erik didn't fully understand just what that meant right now.

"Let's find somewhere to set up camp. We've still got a long way to go," Erik said.

They gathered their gear and moved on. It wasn't long until they found a place to camp. Erik took first watch.

He used Simple Organic Scan to look inside his body. He wanted to check on the snake poison. It had been tearing up his body internally, trying to knock him out and send him into a state of paralysis. Erik had fought back with magic, but he hadn't had time to see whether there were hidden injuries.

When he looked through his leg, he was surprised. Instead of showing weakness, it appeared to be stronger.

Erik checked over his body. Not only was his leg in better condition, it seemed as if these changes were spreading slowly throughout his body.

Seeing as it wasn't anything bad, Erik could only shake his head, not knowing what to do. Four hours later, he woke Rugrat. He knew with the increase in stats it wasn't easy to wake someone.

Rugrat took his place and he got into his sleeping bag. When he closed his eyes, he was greeted with a familiar sight.

You have 10 attribute points to use.

Erik thought on his character sheet and what he wanted to do moving forward. With Strength, he could hit harder; Agility, his reactions were faster, his control greater. Stamina and Mana didn't need to be explained.

Erik placed two points into Strength and Agility; the remaining six he split between Mana and Stamina Regeneration. They would allow him to cast spells or fight for longer. With their guns, it only mattered how long and far they could run, or their reaction speeds.

He looked at the final character sheet.

Character Sheet
Name: Erik West
Level: 3
Race: Human
Titles:
From the Grave
Strength: (Base 7) +2
90
Agility: (Base 6) +3
45
Stamina: (Base 10) +0
150
Mana: (Base 2) +0
20
Mana Regeneration (Base 1) +5
1.95/s
Stamina Regeneration: (Base 7) +5
3.15/s

13
HELPING FROM AFAR

When Erik and Rugrat woke up the next day, they found that as they moved through the forest, many of the creatures quieted as they got close.

They increased their pace, half jogging through the forest, trying to make sure that they didn't bust up their ankles. Rugrat had put his stats toward his Strength and Agility so he was able to quickly outdistance Erik. He slowed down so that they were always close to each other.

There was no hiding the shock in each other's eyes at the speeds they were traveling at or the way that they had gained superhuman abilities.

If this is just level three, what would level ten or level twenty be like?

It wasn't until the afternoon of the second day since fighting the snakes that they paused their movements. They reached a cave. Several wolves moved around the cave in groups.

Erik and Rugrat looked at each other. They had experienced the advantages of gaining Experience through killing but they weren't reckless. These wolves weren't small by any means and they gave off a faint pressure that made Erik not want to underestimate them.

They skirted around the cave and headed downwind. As they did, it took them closer to the rough dirt road that led to Chonglu. They followed close to the road for a bit, looking for a way to cut back into the forest as they'd entered a hilly region.

Rugrat held up his hand, halting Erik.

Erik took a knee and scanned the area behind them as Rugrat scanned the area off to their front left. He moved back to Erik and tapped on his armored shoulder. "I think I hear sounds of fighting, like metal on metal," Rugrat whispered.

Erik couldn't hear it, but he nodded, trusting Rugrat. "You take lead and we'll check it out?" Erik said.

Rugrat nodded. They dropped their packs. Rugrat took out his modified M40A6. It was identical to his service weapon as a Marine scout sniper. He slung it on his back. The two of them moved forward, Erik just slightly behind Rugrat as they stayed low.

Rugrat stopped and pointed to the road. Next to it, a person was looking in the direction they had come. They were wearing rough pelts, with dirt on their face and a crude rusted sword in their hand.

To Erik, it looked like a lookout if he'd ever seen one.

They kept moving. A notification appeared in Erik's vision, but he dismissed it.

They moved onward toward where the noises were coming from.

Erik and Rugrat got to a small rise where there was a break in the tree line, giving them a view over the fight.

There were three carriages under attack. The first two carriages had been abandoned. The simple large creatures that looked like oxen pawed the ground, anxious with the spilt blood. There were some fifteen fighters on the side of the traders and thirty on the side of the raiders who were attacking them from either side.

Archers were in elevated positions raining arrows down; melee types fought one another on both sides. Six people were on the ground. Two of the traders had already been killed by these archers; another two had been killed by the raider melee types and then the final two had fallen to the blades of the traders' melee fighters.

If nothing changed, then the traders wouldn't survive.

"Give me the women and goods—I might even let you live!" A large man yelled as he swung his sword at one of the defenders, forcing them back.

The other raiders renewed their attacks against the relatively weak traders.

The traders all had ugly looks on their faces. They usually traveled with their families and their women. Although they were fighting alongside their fellow traders and husbands, all knew the grim reality if they were to fall into these raiders' hands.

Rugrat and Erik glanced at each other. Rugrat nodded and cleared a place on the ground quickly, pulling his rifle from his shoulder and pulling out its bipod.

Erik turned and braced himself against the small hill they were on. He sighted on the scout who was looking from the battle to down the road.

Erik found that his aim was drifting less, that his breathing was easier than normal.

He controlled his breathing before slowly pulling back on the trigger. He fired a quick double tap. His first and second round hit the lookout, dropping him to the ground.

Erik's exclamation marker blinked but he ignored it, looking back on the fight around the carriages. None of them heard anything from the silenced rifle.

Erik moved next to Rugrat, using a fallen log to steady himself.

"Good to go?" Rugrat asked.

Erik got himself ready and checked his aim. "Good."

"Archers, then the leader."

"Understood," Erik said. They were some two hundred meters away and elevated compared to their targets.

Rugrat fired first. The suppressor cut the noise of the rifle as Rugrat changed his point of aim and worked the bolt action as Erik fired, his round taking down another archer.

The remaining two archers on their side were starting to realize something was wrong as Rugrat's second round found its target. Erik hit the second archer but didn't kill them right away.

They let out a scared and painful howl before being cut off suddenly with Erik's second round.

The leader and the raiders started to look around to see that their four archers supporting them from behind on one side were dead already.

Rugrat fired again. Erik could only praise his abilities. With his rifle, Rugrat was a terrifying individual.

Erik picked out raiders who were outside of the fight and started firing, not caring about hitting them in the head and killing them silently.

They went down in pained cries, their armor unable to stop Erik's rounds.

Erik checked his aim as his targets were sprawled on the ground, screaming out in shock and sudden pain.

The leader was still on his feet, even with three rounds in him.

Rugrat put a fourth in the man's skull, dropping him.

The raiders had gone from twenty-eight fighters to seventeen in just a few seconds and they had no idea where their attackers were.

Also, their leader who had organized them all and was their strongest fighter had his head explode and was lying on the ground, dead.

They started to run in all directions.

The traders held where they were, getting in attacks on the raiders' backs, killing two more and wounding three before they were able to escape.

Erik and Rugrat took down targets of opportunity, adding another three to their count before there were no more raiders they could hit easily.

Erik checked the position that he had been firing from, quickly policing his brass and stuffing it into his cargo pockets.

Rugrat did the same with his expended cartridges.

They only had a limited amount of them and they didn't want to put any to waste.

Seeing that all their gear was tucked away, they headed away from the road, not wanting to meet the traders or the raiders they had been fighting.

They were heading off as a man's voice sounded out. "Thank you for your aid!" the man yelled into the forest.

Erik and Rugrat didn't slow their steps as they grabbed their rucksacks and then headed off deeper into the forest.

It was some time before they stopped and took stock of their gear.

You have learned the skill: **Stealth**
You know when to pick your fights and when to sneak about to get an advantage over your enemy.

Skill: Stealth
Level: 5 (Novice)
No bonuses at this time. You must prove your skills first.

Skill: Marksman
Level: 18 (Novice)
No bonuses at this time. You must prove your skills first.

Stealth Attack, hitting a target while undetected in stealth your attack is X2 stronger.

You have reached Level 6
When you sleep next, you will be able to increase your attributes by: 15 points.

7,700/23,000 EXP till you reach Level 7

"Made it to a level twenty-three Novice Marksman." Rugrat pulled out his M40 and checked it.

Erik checked his magazines and moved them around. "Well, we also know a few things. One, that the people here are human, that they use creatures other than horses. They carry out trade; they wear simple fabrics that we might find in history on Earth.

"These guys were all fighting with their strength, not magic, so maybe they haven't put in any points to their Mana, or they just have a few of their Mana gates open, like us. Also, health is definitely not based on hit points," Erik said as he worked.

"Hit points?"

"In some games, the people you're fighting have a certain number of hit points. You have to wear these down before you beat the creature. I didn't see anything like hit points. Everyone died as they would back on Earth."

"Though that boss raider," Rugrat argued. "When the first round struck, it punched a hole in him but it didn't exit. It was like his skin was as strong as body armor. I put the second shot into him and it was the same. His first wound was starting to recover when I took his head off." Rugrat stared into nothing as he recalled what he had seen.

Erik turned thoughtful. "Hopefully we'll find out more when we head to that town outside of Chonglu."

Rugrat nodded, putting his M-40 away in its gun bag. "You forgot the biggest thing."

"What's that?" Erik asked.

"We could understand them," Rugrat said.

Erik sat there, stunned. Between Rugrat and him, they knew five different languages. He hadn't even thought of it. They were on another planet, but the boss raider and the man who had thanked them had both been speaking English.

Erik and Rugrat went to sleep and did their watches. Rugrat was the first to go to sleep, with Erik going after him.

He quickly organized his attribute points, increasing his stats.

Character Sheet
Name: Erik West
Level: 6
Race: Human
Titles:
From the Grave
Strength: (Base 7) +4
110
Agility: (Base 6) +6
60
Stamina: (Base 10) +0
150
Mana: (Base 2) +0
20
Mana Regeneration (Base 1) +10
2.95/s
Stamina Regeneration: (Base 7) +10
4.15/s

Erik had continued down his previous path, putting Stamina and Mana Regeneration ahead of all else. Five went into Mana and Stamina Regeneration each, then with three going to Agility and two to Strength.

As Erik slept, the Mana in the surrounding area was stirred up.

Rugrat went on alert as he readied his rifle.

A faint blue gas gathered into a lazy tornado before being drawn in to Erik's body.

Rugrat looked at Erik. He could see a faint blue outline in his body. It was like his circulatory system but more rigid. It started at Erik's wrists, extending up his arm to his back; from there they connected, stretching up to the top of Erik's skull and then down through his back, tracing down his legs to his ankles.

After just a few minutes, the wind settled down, the night returning to its normal quiet as Erik continued to sleep, ignorant to what had happened.

When he woke up for watch, Rugrat told him what had happened.

Erik also found that there was another screen waiting for him.

You have reached the Vapor stage
+1 to Mana Pool

Quest: Mana Gathering Cultivation
The path of a Mana Gathering cultivator is not easy. To stand at the top, one must forge their own path forward.
Requirements:
Reach Mana Mist Level
Rewards:
+2 to Mana pool
+10,000 EXP

Erik used Simple Organic Scan and looked over his body to see what changes had gone on.

A series of channels ran through his body, linking his Mana gates together. The small channels were filled with a faint blue vapor that contained a powerful presence. He knew that this was Mana; he didn't know what the significance of it was or why it had changed.

They ate a boring breakfast of rations, but they were excited. Today they'd be checking out the town on the way to Chonglu City to gain information; the next day, they would be in range of the actual Chonglu City.

They trekked through the forest. They'd slowly plodded along before but Erik and Rugrat were now jogging through, confident in their new abilities and reaction times.

They would have been scared to twist their ankles in the past; now they weren't worried in the slightest.

Even if they did, they could both heal the injuries.

They reached a hilly area that allowed them to look over the town.

It was simply built, with only two or three stone buildings; the majority were wood, or mud-made inside their mud walls.

Around the small town were rough farmlands. It might look simple but based on the dangerous animals in the area, the little town had needed to fight for its current position.

Rugrat used his M40 rifle scope while Erik used spotting binoculars.

There were guards on the walls. They wore rough metal chest plates. The rest of their clothes were heavily padded to blunt any blows that landed on them.

People came in from the surrounding areas; traders had set up a few stalls inside the town, selling select goods and foodstuffs.

Erik and Rugrat had been hoping that the town would be a bit bigger. The bigger it was, the easier it was to get lost in. They didn't want to stick out, just gather information and understand what the Ten Realms was about and complete their quest.

"Let's move on," Erik said. They cleared up their gear and moved on toward Chonglu. It was nearing mid-afternoon when they got into sight of Chonglu. Once again, they set up camp and started observing the city.

Its walls were made from rock, standing ten feet tall. Their guards didn't have the lazy air that the town's guards had. They were alert and focused as they patrolled the walls, or they collected tolls at the gates.

There was a lot more traffic at the city as well.

The town served as the lifeblood to the surrounding farmers, but the city was the true gate to higher positions and places.

In the middle of the city, an obsidian pillar stood one hundred meters tall, much taller than anything around it.

There were different colored bands ringing it, with the top band being white, the next one gold, two silvers, three copper, and Erik saw two bands that were black.

Checking their maps against what they were seeing, that obsidian pillar was the location of their quest, the Ten Realms totem.

There were clear districts in the city and the noise of people going about their business could be heard far and wide.

The city hosted a population of some ten thousand people. Wood and stone buildings dominated most of the city. There was a trading and warehouse district, a residential district, a crafters sector, and houses for the nobles and ruling family of the city.

Erik scanned over it all with his binoculars. "Looks like there is a fee at the gate."

"We're going to need something to cover ourselves up. Our clothing and gear looks totally different from theirs," Rugrat said.

"You got your woobie?" Erik asked

"Never leave home without it."

"We drop our rucks here, take our personal weapons with us, wear woobies, then we go to a store, get a cloak to hide what we're wearing," Erik said.

"Okay, and I think I have a way for us to get into the city," Rugrat said, focusing through his scope.

"Huh?"

"Looks like some people who don't have actual coins use a barter system. We'll trade that monster core in for some change, so we at least have some local currency," Rugrat said.

"What do you think that they'll trade with us?"

"You got some jerky and nuts? A bag of that should be good."

"I'll get it together. You keep an eye out." Erik shifted to back where their packs were.

"On it," Rugrat said, not looking away as he continued to scan the city. His eyes could pick up a lot more than Erik's and he had training that made him much better than Erik was at scoping out a city.

Erik got together a few small bags of meat and nuts. He looked over at Rugrat lying on the hill and the city beyond. Just a few weeks ago, he had been moping around in a hospital when Rugrat came around to kick his ass and pull him out of his funk.

Since then, Erik had turned his situation around. It had gone past in a whirlwind. He pressed his lips together as he took in a big breath. If not for Rugrat, he didn't want to think on what kind of situation he might be in.

He held up his hand, letting Mana seep out from his channels and appear as a mist in his hand. "Magic, huh? Let's see what other secrets you're hiding, Ten Realms." A smile crept onto his face, a dense look in his eyes as they focused on that totem.

The next day, they were wearing their poncho liners, hiding their gear underneath. They had hidden the rest of their gear and had left their helmets with it all, so they wouldn't stick out, or at least stick out less.

They headed down toward the main road leading to the city. They walked up it toward the city, their hands on their weapons under the poncho liners.

People looked at them, assessing whether they were a threat or not. Not many people moved close to them.

Erik and Rugrat listened to their conversations. It looked as if everyone spoke English. They didn't question it as they reached the line moving through the gates.

There were people of all kinds of backgrounds: mercenaries for trading groups, traders, farmers with goods to sell, or young people looking for a better life in the city.

14

CHONGLU CITY

"Get out of the way for Young Master Silaz!" a voice yelled.

People hurriedly moved out of the way. Erik and Rugrat moved as well. They looked as a group of ten armored knights giving off a dangerous pressure charged forward. They rode what looked to be horses, but they were much stronger, their hooves like thunder as small dents were seen in the road.

Behind the guards, there was a carriage pulled by two horses. It was covered with ornate metalwork and had an emblem on it.

Four more knights on horses followed the carriage as it thundered toward the gates. The city guards moved out of the way with a dark expression on their faces as the carriage rushed through. They didn't do or say anything as they moved back into place after the last horse had passed.

"That must be the young master of the Silaz house. I heard that they are a great trading family dealing in monster cores and metals!" one of the people in the line said.

"Monster cores? Aren't those things only too rare? One must kill a beast that is level three or higher to get even a chance of finding one," another replied.

"The Beast Mountains are only four days' travel," the first person said.

The second person scoffed. "Beast Mountains? That place is better to be called a burial mound of experts. Many people go there looking for fortune, only to be turned to bones!"

A third person interjected. "The Beast Mountains might be a place of great danger, but it's also a place where one can find many natural treasures. Not only monster cores—there are the different ingredients that they might be watching over. The stronger beasts can have their skin turned into armor, their bones refined into Alchemy concoctions and weapons. Even eating high-level beast meat can increase one's Experience!"

"Do you think that it would be as easy as just walking into the Beast Mountains? There is a reason that the Silaz family and not the people who go to Beast Mountains are one of the strongest families in Chonglu City." The second person spoke up again, halting his words, clearly not willing to waste them on these two fools.

Erik cleared his throat, turning to one of the people beside him. "Are the Silaz family that powerful?" he asked, his stomach tight as he readied himself to run.

The woman frowned and let out a snort. "They are one of the three dragons, other than Lord Chonglu himself. Only the other two families Xun and Chung can keep them in check."

Erik nodded as if in agreement. Inside, that tension was dissipating. It looked as if everyone everyone spoke English; he might have a different accent, but people didn't find it too strange.

They moved with the line to the front of the gates, where a guard waited for them.

"Three coppers," the man said lazily.

"We don't have the coppers unfortunately, but we were hoping that these meats and nuts would be enough?" Erik said as Rugrat held out a few bags.

The guard frowned and then grabbed one of the nuts, chewing on it. His eyes went wide.

He looked around to see whether anyone was listening in as he asked in a low voice,

"Is this covered in salt?"

"Some of them are," Erik said slowly. *Crap, wasn't salt worth a lot in the past?*.

The guard quickly waved his hand; the bag of jerky and nuts disappeared as six coppers appeared in his hand and went into the collection box next to him.

Erik and Rugrat's eyes were focused on the man's hand where a simple ring was. They could swear that the bag had disappeared into that ring.

"Please have a good visit to Chonglu City," the guard said respectfully, cupping his hands and bowing slightly.

Erik and Rugrat repeated the same gesture back awkwardly.

"Thank you for your hospitality." Erik led Rugrat past the guards and through the city gates into Chonglu City. They had finally arrived.

People were moving all over the place. Past the entrance square, there were stalls running through the two main gates of the city.

The smells of food being cooked, sounds of metal being hammered out, and the chatter and liveliness of the city greeted them both as people bartered for better prices or looked to sell what they had, or simply just talked to those they knew.

"Should we go and see if we can find where that Silaz family does business? We'll be able to trade our Mana core in there," Rugrat said.

"Sure," Erik said.

They moved through the city. They got some weird stares as they were in odd-looking clothes. In the city, there was everyone from nobles to farmers and others from countries close and far. They might laugh and joke about their clothes, but they didn't stand out too much.

After some inquiries, they learned where the Silaz did their business and the storefront they ran.

They used their markers to put a marker on the location they had been given.

They walked through the streets, reaching the store without much trouble. They were just moving to a counter when there was a commotion at the front of the store. Rugrat glanced over it as Erik moved to the man at the counter.

"Hello, I was wondering if I could sell this." Erik held out the monster core that they had gained from the ape.

The man took the core from them, looking at them both before he pulled out a monocle and looked at the monster core closer. There was lettering around the monocle and a faint blue crystal that glowed slightly.

"Earth Rank low grade, Earth attribute, from a silver rendall ape. I can give you two silver," the man said.

"Young Master Silaz is so dominating. I heard that you went to the Beast Mountains yourself to collect monster cores!" a woman said in a flattering voice.

A young man laughed down her comment, clearly enjoying it but wishing to appear more mature. The other ladies around him thinned their eyes at the one who had spoken.

"It was a tough trip, but I have found I am interested in settling down more," Silaz said, hinting to the ladies, whose eyes turned red.

"You must be tired, Young Master Silaz. I know a few massage techniques to help you relax," another one of the women flirted.

"Massages? I know the perfect place to have a private meal, without so many voices," another shot back.

"I'll take it," Erik said to the man behind the counter, seeing it all and not caring about it.

The man quickly pulled out two silver coins and passed it to Erik. The monster core disappeared behind the counter.

"Thank you for doing business with Silaz's trading house," the man said with a warm smile.

"Have a good day," Erik said with a quick smile as he and Rugrat moved toward the door.

A guard moved toward them, looking at them with fierce eyes, as if warning not to get close to the young master, who was only slowly walking into the store, blocking the entrance.

Erik and Rugrat paid little attention to him.

"Does he need fifty feet to walk in the door?" Rugrat sighed as they were just about out of the store.

"You two there." Young Master Silaz's voice cut through the store as Erik and Rugrat were about to step out of the store.

The guards at the entrance closed their halberds, stopping Erik and Rugrat from exiting.

Erik and Rugrat looked at each other.

Rugrat had a big smile on his face as he moved toward the two with halberds.

"Hello, boys. How's it going? I hope you don't mind if I stand here. Some lovely weather we're having here—you know, blue skies, clouds, sense of bloodshed in the air." Rugrat laughed a little bit.

Erik looked back into the store, his hand on his personal weapon hidden underneath his woobie.

"I have never seen people like you before. You must not be from around here," Silaz said, lazily looking at the rings on his hand indifferently.

Erik didn't say anything. Instead, his eyes were bored. He had been yelled at by some of the hardest men he knew; he'd lived in life-and-death scenarios. Having some rich kid posing and trying to seem powerful in front of him wasn't a big deal.

I've heard that red with a side of brains is really in this season for interior decorating. Erik even started to imagine how he would paint the area behind the little upstart.

The little idiot didn't have any idea of what was going on in Erik's mind.

"Those clothes—I've taken an interest in them." The boy waved at Erik and Rugrat's woobies.

"That's nice. Don't swing that way, though. Thought you liked women?" Erik asked with a confused face, his eyes looking at the women around him as if he were confused.

Rugrat laughed as the guards' faces darkened and Young Master Silaz's expression stilled before a dense smile appeared on his lips.

"I've never met someone as *daring* as you two. Here I was, merely wanting to gain some souvenirs from foreign trash, but looks like trash doesn't know its position!"

With his words, the guards moved forward slightly, ready to attack.

Erik looked to Rugrat with a questioning look.

"Don't look at me. Looks like his head's so far up his ass, he came full circle." Rugrat shrugged.

"Didn't think of that." Erik nodded as if the world's secrets had been revealed to him.

"You!" Young Master Silaz's face twisted in fury.

Just as he opened his mouth again, there was a deep laugh from the street as the two guards who were blocking the gate opened their halberds.

A man wearing well-maintained armor entered the store with a smile on his face. But his eyes held none of the warmth on his face.

"Young Master Silaz, it is a surprise seeing you back so soon from your expedition. I hear that it was a rather…*wet* trip," the man said with a friendly smile.

"Lieutenant Hoste." Young Master Silaz squeezed out a forced smile, the murderous intent clear.

"Ah, hello there, travelers. You must be tired after coming to our great Chonglu City. There is plenty of food and drink to be had!" Lieutenant Hoste smiled.

"We will thank Lieutenant Hoste for his hospitality." Erik didn't really want to get into a fight. With it being inside a city, if there was bloodshed then it was likely that they would have to run from the city guard. Erik wasn't looking forward to that if things turned bad.

Erik bowed slightly and headed out of the store, Rugrat beside him.

Young Master Silaz's eyes moved to some of the guards around him who pulled out devices, talking into them as he opened his arms wide. "What can my humble store do to help you today, Lieutenant Hoste? I did not know that you had the budget for our wares."

Erik and Rugrat didn't continue to care for the rest as they headed away from the store and moved through the streets. They could both feel the eyes on them as they moved.

"I've got one on the roofs to our right, on top of the tailor shop. There's another tailing us on the street, by that wooden post with the rat skewers," Rugrat said.

"Mm, lovely," Erik said sarcastically.

They continued to move away from the store.

"Break up and meet at the tailor shop at the south end of the totem square?" Rugrat said.

"Got it." Erik diverted down an alleyway as Rugrat walked into a busy diner.

Erik broke out into a run. He moved through the alleyways quickly, then slowed down once he got back out to the main road, quickly and quietly blending in and sitting down in a group of people.

He watched as the tail on the rooftops rushed over, scanning the crowd quickly before heading off in another direction.

Erik got up and moved toward the tailor shop, changing his directions a few times to make sure no one else followed him.

He entered the shop, finding a few people talking to the tailors in the shop.

A woman looked at his attire and moved toward him, a smile on her face and a series of pins in her shirt with a tape measure around her neck. "Hello, might I be able to help you?"

"Please. I am looking to get a big cloak against the elements," Erik said.

"Certainly."

It wasn't two minutes later that Rugrat entered the store. He was larger and drew more eyes.

Erik waved him over as he looked over a rack of different cloaks. They were made to drape over armor already, so they were suitable for what Erik and Rugrat needed.

Twelve coppers later, they were outfitted in local cloaks. One couldn't see their vests, pants, or weaponry. Their boots were the only things that were visible at the bottom of the cloaks.

After settling up, they headed out of the store.

Around the large totem that reached up into the heavens, a defensive wall was manned by guards. They seemed ready to receive people if they came through the totem.

Erik and Rugrat moved closer to the totem. The rough gravel road gave way to smooth and level stone that enclosed the Ten Realms totem.

As they stepped on it, a screen appeared.

Quest Completed: Welcome to the Ten Realms
Requirements:
Reach Ten Realms Totem (Marked on map)
Rewards:
Guide to the Ten Realms
Minor ring of holding
Minor Mana recovery potion
Minor Stamina recovery potion
+1000 EXP

8,700/23,000 EXP till you reach Level 7

15

WELCOME TO THE TEN REALMS

A blue light appeared in front of them. They hastily grabbed at the object held within that blue light.

Glancing around, they saw a few sets of eyes thrown over in interest.

Not wanting to attract more questions, they both headed out of the square as quickly as possible, making use of streets and clusters of people to disappear into the city once again.

They found themselves at a restaurant sometime later. They ordered some food and got a secluded booth.

Erik opened the screen that had come with the object he'd opened. It was a simple-looking ring with a line of lettering on the inside of it.

Tutorial: Storage items
The minor storage ring, like many storage items, contains a special set of formations that allow one to store items within a space that is larger inside than outside. The size of storage space varies on the quality of the ring of holding.
To bind the ring of holding, one must erase the mark of the previous user and apply their own mark by dropping blood onto it. Once bonded, the ring of holding will be accessible only to the user if their mark remains.

Erik quickly pricked his finger and put some of his blood on the ring. He felt a connection establish between him and the ring. He sent out a thought and he was able to see everything inside the ring.

There were the minor potions for Stamina and Mana recovery, though the thing that drew Erik's attention was the *Guide to the Ten Realms* book.

Erik looked around in the city. It was easy to see that several people had these storage rings or other items that allowed them to store more items on their person.

Erik tested it out, holding his woobie that he'd wrapped up. It disappeared into his storage ring. He summoned it out again and it reappeared in his hand.

"With this, we can sort out all of our supplies," Rugrat said to Erik in a low whisper.

Erik looked at how much room was in the storage ring. "We'd need to get larger versions."

"That's just a problem of money, and two silvers seems to go pretty far," Rugrat said.

Erik and Rugrat's food arrived a short time later.

The smell of the food was heavenly after being on rations for half a week. Rugrat and Erik had a deep aversion to anything that even looked like a ration now.

They spent the rest of the day wandering around the city, getting to know it and seeing where different stores and places were.

Rugrat took them to the smithing area of the city, looking over different places there.

"Are you interested in becoming a smith?" Erik asked.

"Well, with our gear right now, if any of it breaks down, we've got some replacement parts, but nothing else. Also, if we lose our brass, then we're going to be screwed if we need some more. If one of us was able to smith out those parts, then we wouldn't have to worry about it."

Erik nodded. Rugrat's thinking made sense. They had a limited number of resources right now. When they used a round, they might have the parts to reload it, but they only had a limited supply. Eventually they would run out.

After touring the city for a long time, Erik checked on a few places, including the different apothecaries, which were the closest that people in the First Realm, unless they had a strong background, came to touching Alchemy.

The healers were swamped. There were always people needing healing. Though healers weren't ones to waste their time and Mana.

There were two healing houses and then several different apothecaries.

Erik looked over the different things that they were selling, including services. What he saw on the healing side made him want to shake them.

These people knew how to use a few healing spells, but they clearly didn't care to learn anything about a person's biology. Why would you need to when the healing spell worked just fine? Rugrat's knowledge of the human body was greater than their revered ancestors through a rigorous first aid training he'd undergone.

Erik, who had been a combat medic, had greater knowledge, could only see their abilities and shake his head. If medics back on Earth had these abilities, fatalities would plummet.

As it was getting close to night, the two of them headed out of the city and moved for where their gear was hidden in the forest.

They stored their gear in their storage rings and set up camp.

While Rugrat was on first watch, Erik pulled out his sleeping bag and a glow stone he had bought. He used the sleeping bag to block the light and pulled out the thick book in his storage ring.

It was a simple-looking book, with the cover showing the Ten Realms totem with its ten rings. Above it, written in gold, were five simple words: *Guide to the Ten Realms*.

With a deep breath and a sense of anticipation he had since getting the storage ring, he opened the book and started reading the first page.

There was basically two ways of increasing one's strength in the Ten Realms: Body Cultivation and the Mana Gathering system.

Body Cultivation walked down the path of enhancing their body through rare resources, Alchemy concoctions, or being tempered again and again to increase the basic strength of their body.

As one increased the strength of their body, their Agility, Strength, and Stamina would increase in leaps and bounds. Walking this path, they would have to endure great pain, destroying and reforming their body repeatedly to advance their strength.

This required healers or healing concoctions to keep the Body Cultivation practitioner from dying. They could also use concoctions created by alchemists to increase their body's abilities. Using too many pills could weaken one's foundation, though.

The cost was not simple, and alchemists were incredibly rare in the Second Realm. In the First Realm, they were nearly nonexistent.

The second system, the Mana Gathering system, could be improved in a couple of ways. The simplest was increasing Mana Regeneration. If one had more than ten Mana gates open, or their Mana Regeneration stat was at ten points or higher, they would step onto the path of a Mana Gathering practitioner. Erik had already taken this step as he had acquired the first level, Mana Vapor. Once his stats increased to twenty, then he would automatically gain the Mana-like mist; at thirty, this mist would condense into a Mana drop. Increasing past this level would require the practitioner to intervene as the next stage was forming one's Mana core; five drops had to be compressed until they formed a core within their body.

With each increase, their bodies would gain a greater Affinity toward Mana. Their Mana pool would also undergo an increase.

This was the simplest method. Other ways people could advance down the path of Mana Gathering practitioner was to, as Body Cultivation practitioners did, alter their body so that they could increase their body's Affinity to Mana or control over it.

Alchemy concoctions could alter one's body to increase the Mana that they could hold, artificially increasing the density of one's Mana, or its purity.

Also, one could take pills or undergo training to advance their own path to power at a faster rate.

As the body was the foundation of the Body Cultivator's path, the Mana gates were the foundation for Mana Gathering practitioners.

At birth, people would find that they had different number of Mana gates open. The more Mana gates they had open, the higher their comprehension and control over Mana. They gained a natural advantage in the amount of Mana they could pull into their bodies and were tempered from birth with Mana running through their bodies.

As one progressed through the realms, becoming higher, the natural density of Mana was greater; with this, the children were blessed with having more Mana gates open naturally. Some healers and alchemists were able to open the Mana gates of others artificially.

The higher the realm, the greater the treatment, it seemed.

Now, although these two paths were taken to strengthen most people, they were meant to augment and complement the main system that ran the Ten Realms: the Experience system.

Experience was the essence of everything in the Ten Realms. As every action created entropy, the Ten Realms created Experience.

Creatures could increase in level by just existing, absorbing the Experience of the Ten Realms, or through killing one another and consuming their flesh and monster cores.

As a human's skills increased, they were rewarded with Experience. For building or destroying, they gained more Experience and more power. Killing another creature, they gained a portion of its lifetime Experience. Creating a sword, they gained Experience for improving.

Humans could also increase their Experience over time without killing or creating. They would need to undergo meditation, drawing in the energy of the Ten Realms. It was much harder and took longer, but it was possible.

One might have hidden injuries that kept their body back from absorbing more Experience from the world. Healing these hidden wounds could directly increase their fighting strength and their overall level. Taking pills that were made from items with concentrated Experience could directly raise one's level. Though the Ten Realms weren't simple: Alchemy concoctions would only be effective one or two times and they would accumulate toxins in the body. One needed to remove these toxins so that they would be able to get the full benefit of later Experience-enhancing concoctions or resources.

Erik closed the book as Rugrat tapped on his shoulder. Erik put the light stone and the book away carefully. He took his watch, filled with more questions than when he had started reading.

Rugrat got under a cover and started reading the guide book as well.

16

TESTING INFORMATION

Erik used his Simple Organic Scan spell, looking at his Mana system in greater detail, from the Mana gates and channels to the area between the bottom of his rib cage and his bellybutton. This was where his Mana gathered and his Mana pool was.

He focused on trying to control the faint blue mist in his veins.

At first, nothing was going on. Remembering how spells worked and the different ways that people created spells back on Earth, Erik imagined the Mana moving through his body toward his Mana pool. He thought of a few different things before he sensed a change in his Mana's movement.

Mana Manipulation
Move your Mana in a more precise manner.
Substitutive effect; does not cost Mana but allows spells greater focus.

Erik felt his ability to move the Mana increase. He drew more in toward his Mana pool, but after a certain time he felt a full feeling that turned uncomfortable the more Mana he drew into his Mana pool.

He stopped after a few minutes, letting out a gasp of air. His eyes opened as cold sweat covered his forehead.

The Mana dispersed through his body once again, that pressured feeling falling away.

Erik moved to Rugrat's pack and pulled out the wrist strength device there. Along its side, it showed different numbers to show how much pressure was being exerted.

Erik squeezed three times, remembering the three numbers.

Erik pulled out his blade and rolled up his sleeve. He shook his head and jammed the blade into his forearm before he could think about his actions fully.

He let out a groan through gritted teeth, his healing spell activating according to the pain. It was now an immediate response.

Erik didn't pull the blade out as he continued to heal. His Mana bar decreased as Erik stared up into a tree, tapping his leg and breathing through his nose and forcing it out through his teeth.

His Mana reached about twenty percent when he pulled out the blade. He was at just five percent Mana when the wound sealed up completely.

Erik took a few moments to gather himself, feeling light-headed from it all.

He took the grip strength tester and squeezed it three more times. His strength had increased by at least five percent.

Erik waited for his Mana to fully recover, completing two of the three tests he'd thought about. It didn't take long until his Mana bar was full.

He focused his attention on the Mana gate in his left wrist. He studied it and compared it against the Mana gate at the back of his head that was open.

Erik used his newly found Mana Manipulation spell. The more he used it, the easier it became. It was even faster to get used to compared to the healing spell as it was moving Mana through his body, not working on multiple different systems in his body to repair his injuries.

He gathered Mana vapor together and drove it toward the Mana gate. The Mana hit the gate with a bang that ran through his body and made his hand shake.

Erik's eyebrows rose as he gathered more Mana together and forced it at the Mana gate. It shook and rang hard, the tremor reaching his upper arm now.

Erik let out a sigh, thankful that the first method had worked. If it hadn't—well, let's just say he didn't want to be stabbing himself all day long.

His eyes focused on his wrist as he gathered up his Mana, shaping it into spears, directing them through his channels and striking his Mana gate. They struck again and again, the ringing increasing in frequency. A slight cracking sound could be heard by Erik as he sped up his hits, compressing his Mana to the limit and sending it hurtling at his Mana gate. Part of the Mana was being absorbed by the Mana gate each time. Another cracking noise rang through Erik's body. His Mana system hummed as he drew in Mana through his head Mana gate and directed it straight into his wrist Mana gate.

Unknowingly, his control over his Mana increased as he could compress it tighter and guide it easily through his channels, increasing the speed of his attacks.

Erik lost sense of time. His eyes scanned the area but his mind was focused on his Mana gate. Cracks visible to Erik had spread across the Mana gate and there was a faint wisp of blue in the two circles.

Under Erik's relentless attacks, the gate weakened to the point of no return.

Erik barely registered as the first part of the gate disappeared, dissolving.

His eyes sharpened, coming out of the dull, repetitive process. As Mana was stirred up in the surrounding area, it centered on Erik's wrist. The blockage in his Mana gate dissolved as his Mana channels went in reverse. Instead of sending Mana at the gate, it was coming through. The dim lines around the gate turned brighter until Erik could see two rings underneath where the Mana whirlpool was located.

Erik felt his entire body being suffused with power. It was as if he could run a kilometer without tiring, or go days without sleep. He was drunk on power as Erik felt that power start to settle down, his Mana pool refilling quickly.

Erik, who had closed his eyes as that power rushed in, now opened his eyes, a faint blue light fading in their depths.

You have opened another Mana gate!
+1 to Mana Regeneration

Quest Updated: Opening the Fourteen Gates
Congratulations! You have opened your second Mana gate.
Requirements:
Clear all of your fourteen gates (2/14)
Rewards:
+1 to Mana Regeneration base stat
Undergo Mana Body Rebirth
1,400,000 EXP

Erik bit the inside of his lip in thought, his brow furrowing. The Ten Realms guide hadn't been explicit but it seemed from the information and the way it was talked about, most people would find it hard to open more Mana gates.

"I can probably open another Mana gate tomorrow," Erik said, looking at his right wrist.

If others were to learn of how easily Erik had opened a Mana gate or his thoughts, many wouldn't know whether to laugh or cry. Unless someone had a great backing or a lucky break, then they might never open another Mana gate than the ones they had at birth.

Erik had more questions but he only had the introductory book on the Ten Realms, after all. If he wanted more information, then he would have to seek it out himself.

Erik wanted to test out the mediation and gathering the Ten Realms Experience, but to do so, one had to close off the outside world.

With stabbing himself and opening his Mana gate, he had been aware of what was going on around him at least.

Erik looked up at the two moons in the sky; the third one had gone down a little bit ago. He pulled out a pad of paper and started to jot down plans and ideas. He still had plenty of testing to go through.

Wren Silaz carried the fragrance of women and drink as he walked back into his home, his smile containing a sourness. The guards around him seemed to be farther away than normal as they made sure not to draw the young master's attention.

"I heard that there was an altercation at the store." A calm voice that contained a hidden power rolled across the courtyard.

The guards dropped to their knees in salute as a man reading a scroll looked up. He wore simple but elegant robes, the Silaz family crest on his chest. His eyes were clear as he looked at Wren. Looking between the two, one might see the similarities there.

"Father." Wren cupped his hands and bowed to this man, not daring to show any hint of rebellion.

"Speak." Elan Silaz had established the Silaz trading house, bringing the family great prosperity and opening up their path to the top. He had three sons and one daughter. Wren wished to take over the business while Elan's other sons and daughter looked to join a powerful sect, advancing to the Second Realm and increasing the strength and backing of the Silaz family. The strong ruled; the weak obeyed: this was the Ten Realms' unwritten rule.

Wren couldn't hide his anger fully as he relayed what had happened with the two foreigners once he had returned to the store. His voice filled with displeasure and exaggerated the actions the two had made against him.

Elan's scroll disappeared into his storage ring. Wren's words halted as he looked at his father, whose eyebrows were slightly pinched together.

"These two that you looked down on were able to turn in an Earth rank low grade monster core. Based on Appraiser Gu's comments, they didn't seem too interested by the core and showed interest in the silver they were given. They are not from around here, so they were likely trading the core to see what the local currency was. They gave off the feeling of being level six or a low level seven. When leaving the store, even though you had them tailed, they were able to escape your tail's eyes. Then you punished your people for their failure." Elan's voice held a note of reprimand at the last sentence.

"I have already sent apothecaries to see to them, the money of which will be coming from you, and a repayment for the injustices they have suffered. These two men are not simple, Wren," Elan said.

Wren ducked his head, not willing to look into his father's eyes.

Elan sighed gently, seeing the clenched fists of his son. He was still a young man and liable to make mistakes. Wren had been given his warning; now he would watch to see what Wren would do.

Elan hoped to groom him, but one needed to have a few failures and to have their rebellious nature tamed if they were to lead the Silaz trading house.

17
JOBS?

Rugrat talked over breakfast about the different things that they had learned.

Erik helped Rugrat learn the Mana Manipulation spell and he set to opening his Mana gate in his wrist as well.

Rugrat had been researching different skills. There were reams of them, from heavy and light armor, to cooks, farmers, sneak, mercantile, woodsmen, and so on.

Many people unlocked multiple skills, but trying to level them all was a waste of energy.

The main path that most used was building up different skills that complemented one another and the way that they fought and their needs.

Rugrat wanted to pick skills that would augment his abilities learned as a Marine sniper and then other skills that would support that, such as being a smith to improve and maintain his weapons with the materials available in the Ten Realms.

Erik's mind went a bit differently. If he was able to focus his effort in increasing the strength of his body, that, with his healing abilities, would make him damn hard to kill. He would be able to keep people off Rugrat as the other supported him with long-range support.

Erik didn't want to have to learn how to fight with a blade or a two-handed sword; he was a decent shot and he had been in a number of different fighting clubs. He could use his rifle at range, his fists in close range.

He was also drawn to Alchemy. The thought of making powerful concoctions, the fact he could rely on himself to make Body Cultivation and Mana Gathering aids excited him. It gave him a challenge, something that he wanted to overcome.

They had some eighty coppers, which was pretty good; most farmers might earn two silver every month on average.

When they had been checking stores, looking for more or larger storage rings, they'd been left in shock.

They had Mortal grade minor storage rings that could hold one meter square of goods and were sold for three silvers. A Mortal grade simple storage ring had two times the space, but they cost thirty silvers. This was seen as a great expense that only the nobility or well-to-do idols could buy. The traders in the area didn't get these rings due to their high cost, instead choosing to move with their carriages stuffed with goods.

Unless Erik and Rugrat wanted to reveal their odd background, they needed to gain an income in Chonglu before they returned to where they'd buried their gear.

"We've got to get jobs," Erik said.

"I was already checking out some of the smithies. There are some places looking to hire and if I was able to get a few smithing technique books, then I could increase my ability quickly," Rugrat said, revealing why he was so interested in the smithies in Chonglu the last day.

"Technique book?" Erik asked, missing something.

"Basically, you open them and they upload their information into your mind. Magical memorization," Rugrat said.

Just this by itself would be earth-shattering back home; here it was a well-known fact.

"Though they're expensive. The rarer and more powerful, the more money needed to acquire them," Rugrat warned, seeing the light in Erik's eyes.

Erik let out a grunt, his hopes dashed as he continued to eat his breakfast slop.

"If I'm working at the smiths, what are you going to do?" Rugrat asked.

"Heal people. I can rent a stall for twenty coppers a day. People want to have a check-up, I can do that for two coppers; they want me to heal something, I'll barter with them." Erik shrugged. He didn't want to make money off people's misery, but seeing the condition of people in Chonglu and those waiting outside the healing houses, there was a demand among the poorer citizens.

Under his care, he'd make sure that they had the best treatment with no problems that might appear later, like a bone that was only partly healed as the healer wasn't willing to spend their Mana on some poor person offering all of their savings because it wasn't the high bounty one might get from working on a noble who had a training accident.

"Well, it looks like we have a plan," Rugrat said.

It wasn't long until they were back in the city. They entered right in the morning, the two of them separating and making a plan to meet up at one of the inns later.

They'd looked into communication devices and the sound talismans; they'd found it cost five silvers each.

Erik went and found one of the city civil servants off to the side of the marketplace. Though there were stalls that ran through the city, there was a dedicated market square where most sold their goods or services.

"What do you need?" the civil servant asked in a bored voice as he looked up from what he was writing.

Erik glanced down and saw that he could read what he was writing and he smiled at the civil servant. "I would like to rent a stall for the day."

The man frowned and looked over Erik. "Twenty-three coppers." He held out his hand.

Erik's smile turned a bit forced but he couldn't really argue. He took out the coins and passed them to the civil servant.

He pulled out a piece of wood with a number on it. "Here's your pass. Return it by seven tonight. Look for the stall location on the map." The man waved at the map on the side of the stall. The money was split, twenty going into the collections as three disappeared skillfully into the servant's ring as he continued to write on the scroll.

"Thank you." Erik looked at the map. He was off at one of the corners of the market.

He headed off for the stall. He found that it was surrounded by people selling animal feed and different large farm implements.

The stall wasn't anything much, a few chairs and a simple table with an overhead covering.

He took out a piece of wood and a brush with ink. He remembered what he had seen on the healer house's doors. He changed the wording a bit and looked to his neighbor.

"Excuse me, can you read this?" Erik asked.

The person frowned, starting to look angry.

"Sorry, I'm not from around here," Erik said, trying to patch over whatever he had done wrong.

The man let out a huff, still looking angry. "Not many people can read around here. Best to get a crier to tell people your goods."

Erik looked around. People were yelling out their goods, adding to the market's atmosphere. Now it made sense.

"Thank you. Do you know where I might be able to hire a crier?" Erik asked.

The man looked Erik up and down. "I have a cousin who could do it, eight coppers."

"Two," Erik said.

The man's eyes thinned as he pressed his lips together. "Best I can do is five."

"Three and I won't tell him," Erik said.

The man's face split into a grin as he held out his hand. Erik smiled and dropped three coppers into the other merchant's hand. "Pleasure doing business with ya. Name's Olik."

"Erik."

Seeing people coming toward his stall, Olik quickly made the coin disappear and he called over a teenager, quickly talking to him and pointing at Erik and then going back to his stall to greet customers.

"Mister Erik, my cousin Olik said you had some work for me." The boy smiled, a number of his teeth crooked as he showed signs of a rough life.

"What's your name?" Erik asked.

"Vand."

"Well, Vand, I'm looking to sell healing. Simple ailments, two coppers. Larger ailments depends on the case and resources." Erik paused for a moment. "Tell people that I won't charge them unless I have cured them."

Vand gave Erik a quizzical look. "Are you one of them healer types?"

"Yes." Erik nodded.

"The healing houses kick you out or summin'?"

"No. I'm not from around here, so I'm not part of the healing houses." Erik smiled.

"Oh." Vand nodded. "All right, so two coppers for minor ailments, more for major, you'll only pay if you get healed."

"That's it," Erik said.

Vand nodded seriously, his lips moving as he said the sentence over and over again, memorizing it.

Seeing the determined look in the boy's eyes, Erik nodded to himself.

"I think I've got it. I'll do my best, Mister Erik," Vand said with a goofy smile.

"Very well, I'll be here." Erik nodded.

Vand hurried off as Erik checked out his stall in greater detail. He moved his chair in front of his stall, putting the sign up on the stall's countertop. He leaned back in his chair, taking in the market as he looked at ease. People threw a few glances over to him, their brows pinching together.

Those in stalls around him were working hard to sell their goods and draw more paying customers. Erik was simply sitting there as if enjoying the sunny day, wasting his twenty coppers rental fee with no worries.

After some time, Rugrat found himself in front of a poster board. The wall was covered in positions for hire.

Finally his eyes caught one that looked interesting.

"Smithy's assistance required. Raise your smithing skill level and earn four coppers a day assisting a high-leveled Novice Smith. Must have at least seven Strength and five Stamina. Report to Wen Kun's smithy." Rugrat read out the posting. The rate of pay was less, but with the allure of learning from an actual smith, it only made sense.

There were barely any who had reached the Apprentice level in a crafting skill; most learned it in farming or cooking. Smiths mostly maintained items; few of them would actually make weapons and armor. After all, most people were farmers, not warriors.

Rugrat knew that it was a long shot; he had some general knowledge on metal, but it was off television shows, documentaries, or random articles he had seen before. He didn't have a formal education that focused on smithing.

If I have a basic understanding of smithing, then I can possibly use what I do know from Earth to increase my ability.

He checked the directions and took down the posting. He headed off toward the crafting sector of the city.

The smithies were all packed together, covered in black smoke and ash from the furnaces that worked constantly.

It took him some time to find Wen Kun's smithy. The place was in even worse condition than the other smithies, tucked away with three furnaces going. Still, people were lined up with different farming implements needing to be repaired, or buying new items.

Rugrat waited in the line as it moved up. A fat man sat at the counter. His face made him look as if he were constantly annoyed.

"I came here for the posting." Rugrat put down the ad on the counter.

The man looked from the ad to Rugrat, sizing him up. "You'll do," the man said. "Gu Shi, I've got a new coal stoker for you!" the man barked.

A man who was hammering out a hoe looked up. He had a beard, was covered in soot and looked brawny. Burn marks could be seen on his hands and arms. He sized up Rugrat before letting out a grunt of acknowledgement and returning to his work.

"Go over there and do whatever Gu Shi tells you," the man at the counter said, Rugrat no longer his problem as he looked to the line. "Next!"

Rugrat moved through the smithy. The floor was covered in discarded metal and scraps. There were smiths hammering away on metal, beating it into submission, then throwing it back into the furnace, heating it up again, keeping it constantly heated before they kept beating on the metal.

"Stoke the fires, keep it hot all day," Gu Shi said, his hammer falling between words. He checked his work as Rugrat moved over to the side of the furnace where there was a simple bellows and a hole where coal could be thrown in.

"It's not hot enough!" Gu Shi yelled out in anger.

Rugrat moved quicker, grabbing the shovel and tossing coal into the furnace.

Rugrat felt as though he were in basic training again as he dealt with Gu Shi's grumblings while he did his best to keep the furnace constantly hot for Gu Shi.

Rugrat watched the other people fueling the furnaces, as they used the bellows and tossed in coal, to keep the furnace at peak heat.

Through his observations and trials, he was able to get a hang of the bellows and know when to toss coal in or wait. As it got easier, Rugrat started to watch the smiths.

He tried to burn their very actions into his mind, looking to connect it with what he had learned and knew from Earth.

As he worked and watched, he listened.

Gu Shi was a person of few words but the smiths and the other furnace feeders talked freely. They were all doing simple work; they'd get bored easily if they couldn't do anything else.

"I heard that there's some good work in the Beast Mountains," one of the furnace stokers said.

"Yeah, if you want to get killed." An older smith laughed, the others smirking.

"My cousin went off. Now he's a true sword warrior. All of the girls flock to him when he comes back into town. Even got two Lesser Mortal beast cores by himself!" the stoker defended.

"He's the lucky one. Most people who head to the Beast Mountains turn into beast food. Unless one gets into one of those good mercenary outfits," the other smith replied.

"Though with all of the rare materials, beast meat, hide, and even monster cores, you'd be a made man!" The stoker continued to talk about his dreams.

"If you can somehow kill a lot of monsters, yeah, you might make a lot of coin to retire and live out the rest of your life. Hell, might be possible to ascend to the Second Realm. Staying alive is the issue. There are thousands of monsters in the Beast Mountains. All of them fight one another, but they hate humans even more," the older smith said, seemingly taking pity on the young lad. "Just don't forget your friends here when you write up your will!"

The others laughed as the young stoker closed his mouth, flushing in embarrassment.

Beast Mountains? I wonder if they'll be like that gorilla? Rugrat thought.

After seeing Gu Shi work for some time, Rugrat spoke up as he was resting.

"Mister Gu Shi, how much does an iron ingot cost?" Rugrat asked. Being a stoker wasn't that glamorous. He'd watched the smiths for some time and got some basic understandings of how to work with metal.

Gu Shi smirked. "Thirty-three coppers each, though for a go-getter like you, why not get a smithing manual for five silvers. Or better yet, one of the three forging blueprints in Chonglu City!" Gu Shi raised his voice so the other smiths and stokers could hear him.

They all laughed and jeered at Rugrat. To them, he was just a simple beginner who wanted to jump from Earth to the heavens in a single leap. *How could it be that easy! Didn't he see the suffering that they went through?*

Rugrat frowned. *Shit. Well, looks like I'm going to need to make some damn coppers!*

18

HEALING STALL OF THE CHONGLU MARKET

"Tsk, what a waste of coppers, coming out here to sit around and not sell anything," one person said as they were waiting for the goods to be loaded into their cart.

"He just showed up today," the person loading the cart said.

"Some people don't want to put the work into earning money," another agreed.

Erik heard this but he didn't care. Instead, he was looking around his stall with distaste. If this was back on Earth, he would have fired himself for offering health services out of this stall. There was food, animal feed, animals themselves—all kinds of possible infections just waiting around. Though with magic, the risk of infection? Gone with a simple spell. Antibiotics? What was that? A health potion? Some healers even used the same bloodied tools on different patients, not needing to wash them as their healing spells cleared out any infections automatically. Some of the patients might even be stronger against different infections as their body, following the Body Cultivation path, had defeated it and become stronger.

Erik sighed to himself as he sat there. He pulled out his guidebook and started reading as the day continued. It started to look as though his idea hadn't worked.

Knowing that few people could read, Erik didn't think it would be a problem if he read the guidebook.

Erik heard a yell as someone started screaming. His lazy demeanor vanished and his book disappeared; he was ready to pull out his rifle as he looked over in the direction of the noise.

People around Erik felt the pressure, looking at him in a slight shock.

Most of them weren't that high of a level. The pressure Erik was giving off didn't match with his laid-back appearance. The dangerous and cold atmosphere made some of those from a higher level look at one another in shock.

A man had been loading barrels of drink onto a cart and one of the planks had moved, the barrel coming back on him and crushing his leg.

Erik saw that people were looking over but few were looking to help him.

The people at the store came out with sour expressions.

The injured man was barely twenty years old with a crushed leg.

Erik quickly moved over, scowling as people were looking at one another.

The owner was frowning but it was clear he didn't know what to do. In this kind of society, there was no such thing as worker's comp.

"Give me some room." Erik didn't move the barrel that was on the man's leg. His hand rested on the leg and he used his Simple Organic Scan.

His face turned serious. Not only had the barrel shattered the man's leg, it had sent bone shards into the main artery that ran through his leg. He was bleeding internally.

Erik stood and grabbed the barrel. With a yell and a grunt, he picked it up and tossed it away. "This is gonna fucking hurt." Erik looked into the man's eyes as he held his shoulder and his other hand grabbed his leg.

There was a grinding sensation in his hand as the boy cried out. The others around all winced and moved away.

"Hold him down!" Erik said, looking to one of the strong men nearby.

"What are you doing to him?" the man demanded.

"Healing him! Now hold him down or else watch him die!" Erik barked.

The man gritted his teeth and held the screaming man to the ground by his shoulders.

"You—get his other leg," Erik barked.

The clear command in his voice made the other man move to help.

Erik held down the top of the injured man's leg. He used a healing spell to stabilize the man. A magical circle appeared around his left hand; his right hand moved down the injured man's leg, pushing and twisting the four different sections of bone back into place.

The man passed out from the pain as Erik worked quickly and efficiently.

The bone was all lined up as he cast a healing spell with both of his hands. The man's leg started to straighten out as the artery was sealed up. The blood was pulled back into the man's body; the bruising and swelling started to fade as the man's pasty and clammy appearance started to reverse. Veins were reconnected and the bones fused back together.

Erik looked over the man's leg once more and checked the man's body. He used his healing spell to clear up some bruising on the man's brain before he released his hands.

The people who had been watching had seen the boy's leg coming back together in shock.

"He must be from the healing house," someone said as Erik leaned back, clearly drained. The two strong men released the man on the ground, their faces pale from shock. They had seen the changes from up close.

"Healing house? Have you seen them ever work on someone before they asked for money?" another person chided.

The man woke up screaming, making many jump away in alarm. The man seemed to discover himself and where he was as his screams died down, replaced with heavy breathing and a look of confusion.

He looked down at his leg that had stopped hurting. His whole body shook as he looked at the tired man who was slowly getting up.

"You probably feel hungry as hell. Go have a big meal and you'll be fine. Check the plank next time before you try to roll a barrel up it," Erik advised.

"Y-yes." The man looked at Erik with wide eyes.

Erik patted the boy on the shoulder and stood. He returned to his seat and pulled out some jerky he had, feeling hungry after everything.

As he was eating, he checked his notifications that had popped up.

9,180/23,000 EXP till you reach Level 7

Skill: Healer
Level: 18 (Novice)
No bonuses at this time. You must prove your skills first.

Erik nodded to himself. One's skill level was not only based on the amount of times they performed an action related to a skill. If one showed advanced knowledge, then the skill would increase rapidly. If not, then no one would care to learn anything, simply repeating the same process over and over again to become masters.

People continued talking to one another as the boy was pulled to his feet and walked away by his friends, shock still on his face.

They grilled him as more than a few curious gazes were shot over to Erik and his stall.

Sometime later, a middle-aged man walked over, holding his hat in his hands. "Mister, are you able to heal others?"

"Depends what it is. Minor problems, two coppers; major problems, it depends on the resources needed. I won't charge you unless the person leaves my stall healed." Erik raised his voice a bit so that others could hear before quieting his words. "What is the issue?"

"My father, he had a bad case of coughing, but now all the strength has left him. He made me take him out to the market, but he can't walk more than five minutes without wheezing," the man said.

"Is he nearby?" Erik asked.

"I can bring him to you!"

"I'm young and my legs work fine. Is he in the market still?" Erik asked.

"Yes, yes!" The man's hands shook in excitement.

"Lead on," Erik said. This was the first real business he had; no one had shown up at his stall yet. If he was correct, the old man had some kind of cold or infection.

They walked through the different stalls before reaching an old man who sat at a tea shop. He was coughing heavily till his face turned red. When he stopped, he leaned back in the chair, all of the energy gone from him.

"Dad, this man here is a healer. I brought him here to take a look at you," the man said.

"There's no need to waste a healer's time on this," the older man said, hurriedly standing before another coughing fit shook him again.

He dropped into the seat as Erik put his hand on the man's back and used his Simple Organic Scan.

"Your father has liquid in his lungs and a nasty infection. It's only a minor affliction," Erik said.

"Two coppers was it, sir?" the man asked, trembling.

"That's right. I'll heal him first," Erik said.

The old man was wheezing, trying to get his breath back.

Erik cast his healing spell on the man and watched what happened inside his body.

He wasn't directly healing the problem. Instead, it was as though he were rapidly increasing the rate that the old man's body healed and his immune system worked.

He watched as the infected tissues weren't magically replaced but the healing spell increased the rate that the immune system functioned. In just a few moments, the old man's immune system had created an immunity to the infection and overpowered it, the man's body clearing it out of his system.

Hidden injuries within the man's body that hadn't healed were revitalized. Small breaks in the man's hands were healed. Unlike how when someone usually broke their bone, the bones didn't simply fuse and leave a weakness there; instead, the bone was regrown completely and the break became stronger.

Erik had seen this in the man with the broken leg, but after seeing two patients, he could confirm his original thoughts.

The old man's wheezing was cleared up. He looked tired but there was a glow to his eyes as his normal complexion returned.

Erik pulled his hands away from the old man, a small smile on his face as he was thinking on what he had seen.

I need to get more healing spell books!

19
FOCUSED HEAL

The old man took a deep breath in and out. A look of joy filled his face as he didn't find any difficulty in doing so.

He laughed out loud and made to stand up as Erik held him down gently but firmly.

"You had a nasty infection. Your body is going to need food. Also, that annoying pain in your left hand should be fixed." Erik smiled.

The man wiggled his fingers and his shock only deepened.

The young man held out two coppers to Erik.

Erik held out his hand; the middle-aged man looked stunned as he dropped them into Erik's hand, as if expecting something else to happen.

"Good to do business with you. Please let any of your friends know that if they need some healing to come over to my stall. I'll be there today and tomorrow," Erik said with a smile that was slightly forced. He didn't have the funds to keep on paying for the stall as well as a room in the inn.

Erik turned and left.

"Thank you, master healer!" the old man said gravely, cupping his hands and bowing deeply from his seat.

"No problem." Erik returned the gesture and left easily.

He checked on his blinking exclamation mark symbol, finding two screens.

10,520/23,000 EXP till you reach Level 7

Skill: Healer
Level: 20 (Novice)
No bonuses at this time. You must prove your skills first.

He moved through the market again. He wandered through the market a bit to waste some time before he needed to sit at his stall again.

He got near his stall to find that a few dozen people were there with bandages, or other ailments.

Erik moved past them and sat in the chair out front of his stall.

The different people there looked at him. He looked back at them before shrugging and started to open his book. He wouldn't go to each of them if they weren't willing to come forward.

Finally a woman with a bad complexion walked forward.

Erik put his book away and smiled at her.

"Are you able to heal people?" she asked in a faint voice.

"One of my specialties." Erik smiled.

"I had a nasty cut, but now my entire body is in pain."

"Did you cut yourself on metal?" Erik asked.

"Yes." The woman sounded shocked.

Erik pulled out another chair from behind the stall and put it down in front of his chair. "Please." He waved to the seat.

The woman sat down hesitantly.

"I'm just going to check on your condition." Erik held her wrist in his hand and used Simple Organic Scan. Based on her symptoms, it looked like she had tetanus.

Erik quickly used his healing spell. He pushed until he was at fifty percent Mana and continued to let it flow as fast as his Mana regenerated. That additional Mana gate being opened really helped him.

The woman's appearance got better rapidly before she looked completely healthy.

"Two coppers if you're happy with the healing," Erik said.

"Yes, thank you so much." The woman passed him two coppers, tears filling her eyes.

"Don't worry. I think that you should now be immune to rusty tools," Erik said. Everything he had seen showed that once someone had overcome a problem, then they would never encounter it again, at least as far as infections went.

Two screens popped up.

11,300/23,000 EXP till you reach Level 7

Skill: Healer
Level: 24 (Novice)
No bonuses at this time. You must prove your skills first.

Based on what Erik had learned, one would go from a Novice to an Apprentice once they reached level twenty-five, which would gain them a bonus and Experience.

The next person walked forward with a hobble, their leg in a splint. "Could you help me, mister?" the man asked.

"Please take a seat," Erik said. The man did so and Erik put his hands on the man's leg. The bone hadn't set right and it would lead to the man not walking normally again in his life.

"Tell me if you feel anything." Erik wasn't sure what would happen as he put his hands on the man's leg and used a healing spell.

The man's face went pale as he screamed out.

Erik released his hands as the man was holding his leg, hissing through his teeth.

Erik only quickly glanced at the screen that appeared before dismissing it.

11,320/23,000 EXP till you reach Level 7

"The bone hasn't healed right. There are two treatment methods. One, I heal it as is. It will take longer and be painful, as you've experienced. Or the second, we re-break the bone and I set it. Again, going to hurt, but it will take just a few minutes. If you have anything that you can get to numb the pain, I would suggest getting it if you wanted to continue," Erik said.

The man looked at Erik. Seeing his clear expression and the steady way that he talked, the man nodded.

"If we re-break it, I'll do it at four coppers; if the slow heal, ten coppers." Erik really wanted to just break and set the bone. It would be simpler.

"Thank you." The man nodded. He got up and walked away.

Erik thought on what had happened in the man's leg. The bonds on the bone had weakened as the muscles around it moved the bones into their true position. The process was slow. Erik increased the power going in for a split second and it sped up, but it was clearly incredibly painful.

Also, when he didn't completely heal the man, he had only gained a small Experience increase.

Erik looked up and another person moved to the chair. It was a mother and her son. Erik looked at them both. The little toddler was lethargic as his mother told Erik about the toddler's declining health.

A little healing spell and the little boy's viral infection was cleaned up.

Erik was even shocked himself. Viral infections were not something that could be cleaned up with antibiotics, but healing spells, with enough time, had been able to defeat the virus.

The boy's body even became stronger as the virus had a tempering effect on his body. Unknowingly to others, the little boy had stepped on the path of Body Cultivation, his eyes brighter as his muscles contained greater power and his circulatory system hummed with vitality.

The mother thanked Erik profusely, trying to give Erik more than his two coppers. He didn't accept more than two, gaining the respect of others watching.

"Did you see that? Refusing her money? What can the healing houses do but take our money?" someone said.

"Right! He's indeed a master healer that we have the luck of meeting!"

"Master healer? Really, you think this foreigner is a master healer? I've seen master healers heal people back from death's door with only a magical incantation that had a magical circle half a meter in diameter! He only uses healing spells that are a few centimeters wide!"

Erik's eyes hid a little joy, not at the words that were being spoken but at the screen that had appeared in front of his eyes.

Skill: Healer
Level: 26 (Apprentice)
You have become familiar with the body and the arts of repairing it. Healing spells now cost 5% less Mana.
Upon advancing into the Apprentice level of healer, you will be rewarded with one randomly selected item related to this skill.

You have received the spell book: **Focused Heal**
+10,000 EXP

You have reached Level 7
When you sleep next, you will be able to increase your attributes by: 5 points.

2,600/34,000 EXP till you reach Level 8

The rush of Experience was one of the largest Erik had gone through. He let out a cool breath as he felt himself breaking through that next bottleneck.

He quickly checked his storage ring, finding the Focused Heal spell book located inside. It was an unexpected reward; the guidebook hadn't said that he would earn an extra reward.

He cleared his throat and looked to the next person. "Please take a seat." He smiled. This was just power leveling!

Erik's stall was no longer quiet as people watched him heal people in the street, having them take a seat, tell them his problem, telling them items they would need to bring back to be healed, or healing them directly with his magic.

Quickly, word spread of the healer at a simple stall in Chonglu's trading district. Vand returned to the stall after some time. Instead of sending him out to call in more people, he had him move through the line that had formed, keeping it orderly and out of people's ways. Having so many people visiting, the surrounding businesses were doing a quick business, with some of the smarter ones bringing over food vendors who helped to feed the hungry people leaving Erik's stall.

20
HEALING HARVEST

As it reached the end of the day, Erik could only heal those who were the worst affected in line and give the others pieces of wood with numbers on them, telling them that if they came back with the piece of wood, he would serve them in order the next day.

This allayed some of the grumbling as Erik made his exit from the market.

With just a half days' worth of healing, Erik had earned two and a half silvers. His inner greed demon was rubbing his hands together at so much silver. He checked on the notifications in the corner of his vision.

Skill: Healer
Level: 38 (Apprentice)
You have become familiar with the body and the arts of repairing it. Healing spells now cost 5% less Mana.

33,320/34,000 EXP till you reach Level 8

Money in the bank, Exp in mah body and a skill on the rise—damn, I love it when a plan works out!

Although the money was nice, every time he used his healing skills, he was able to test out new ideas and gain a different understanding of the human body in the Ten Realms. As a combat medic, he had to deal with a lot of knowledge of what was happening inside the body without being able to actually see it. It was more of a guesswork. Now he could directly see what was happening inside a person's body with the Simple Organic Scan, and then affect and change it with healing spells and techniques and methods that he had learned in his training.

He had made a list of notes while he worked on people, jotting down thoughts and ideas that he had come up with.

His skill level was skyrocketing upward and he would have healed people for free if it wasn't for his need for resources. Just the Experience and knowledge was worth more than money. After all, most people needed to use technique books or have a teacher to teach them. At this point, Erik only needed to rely on his past training and experiences and adapt to the new use of spells.

Erik pressed his lips into a line. He was so close to becoming level eight. He'd found that healing the same kinds of wounds led to less Experience each time. Like killing creatures, it was slightly level dependent, but the big modifier was based on the severity of the affliction. The closer someone was to death, the greater the Experience he would get from healing them.

The higher the level, the harder it was to heal them.

He also found that as people leveled up, their bodies had a distinctive change. By dealing with tens of people from all kinds of level ranges, Erik had gained a sense for this. He could guesstimate someone's level based on the fluctuations in their aura. As someone increased in level, they would absorb a tremendous amount of the Ten Realms' energy, the golden-looking energy of Experience. It gathered in a person's body; then, when someone went to sleep and changed their stats, that energy would refine and increase the ability of that system: Strength was muscle density; Agility, twitch muscle formation, increased neuron firing in one's brain and reinforced tendons and ligaments.

Increase in Mana pool? One's dantian and their Mana channels would be tempered, increasing the purity of one's Mana, removing impurities contained within.

Leveling up surpasses human boundaries. According to the guidebook, one doesn't always need to level up to gain these benefits. Through special techniques or resources, one can increase the level of their Mana purity; they can temper their bodies and more.

This, like magical spells, surpassed the boundaries of fact on Earth; here it was common knowledge.

Erik walked up to an apothecary stall where an older-looking woman worked with mortar and pestle to create her remedies.

"Hello, I was wondering if you have any more Wraith's Touch salve?" Erik asked. This salve was what the man with the mangled leg had brought back. With the salve, he didn't feel a thing even as Erik re-broke his leg.

Seeing its effectiveness, Erik wanted to make sure he had some on hand if he needed it personally.

"Certainly. Five coppers," the lady said.

"I'll take ten of them," Erik said.

The woman looked surprised but quickly got the ten pots gathered together.

Erik passed her the coppers and the pots disappeared into his storage ring. He grabbed some food from stalls he passed and continued on his way.

It wasn't long until he was at the Wandering Stallion Inn. Rugrat wasn't there yet so Erik settled in a corner, getting a beer and opening the guidebook.

He went through it, checking a few of his questions against the book's information before putting it down.

One of the barmaids came over, seeing that Erik's drink was low. "Another?" she asked.

"Please. Also, do you know where one might find out more information about Alchemy?" Erik asked.

The women's eyebrow raised, looking over Erik before resting her hand on her hip. "The apothecaries are all Novice alchemists in some fashion, but most of them don't have any kind of books to learn from and have to find the path of Alchemy themselves. If you've got the coin for it, then the Blue Lotus can find you anything. Though down here there's not much left after the other realms have picked through their wares."

"Thanks." Erik gave her a copper coin.

Her tired look turned into a smile as she put the copper away. "No problem. One beer coming right up!"

Erik smiled at her as she walked away.

She was just coming back when Rugrat entered the room. He was covered in soot; his shirt was stuck to him and he was wearing the local clothes that they had both bought. Rugrat was a large man and fighting for most of his life meant that he was always heavily muscled. Combined with his workout regime and the changes that they had gone through since entering the Ten Realms, he drew more than a few eyes.

He scanned the room as he walked up to the bar.

People looked away. He was just another worker, nothing more.

Erik waved him over and he put in an order before moving to join Erik.

"How'd the smithy go, and you did heal yourself up, right?" Erik said. That soot didn't look good for one's health.

"No worse than gas mask training." Rugrat smiled. Even though he seemed tired, there was a determination in his eyes.

Erik rolled his eyes as Rugrat stole his beer and finished off the remainder.

"Good thing I didn't take any longer." The barmaid laughed as she put down two new glasses.

"Angels are real." Rugrat laughed, winking at the barmaid, and started gulping from the beer.

Erik passed her a copper for the two drinks. She moved away as Rugrat surfaced for air.

"We need more money," he said in a rush.

"Nice to see you too." Erik drank from his beer. With his silver coins, he was feeling pretty secure about their financial future as long as he could keep on healing.

"I got taken on as an Apprentice smith, but these guys are making mostly simple tools and the like. Most of the weapons and armor-related tasks are done by the big shops and most of it is maintenance as weapons are so costly. If I was to rent out a work area, it would cost ten coppers for the day, though I would need to supply all of the materials and tools. Another thirty for the tools. Then each iron ore is some fifteen coppers. Refined iron ingots are thirty-three coppers. Say I make five weapons a day, that's five to ten ingots," Rugrat explained.

Erik's previous confidence dimmed. It didn't seem to be cheap at all to raise a crafter in the Ten Realms. Just the resources needed were incredibly expensive.

"To accelerate growth and learn the basics, I'd need to get a smithy training manual. Those books can cost two or three silvers by themselves and then the good technique manuals are even more expensive."

"So we'd need what, ten silvers to have you set up comfortably and able to focus on just smithing?" Erik asked, turning his beer glass.

"Yeah." Rugrat slugged back more beer.

"If you had ten silver, what would you do?"

Rugrat leaned back in his chair, looking up at the ceiling to collect his thoughts. "First, get a general smithing manual. I have a lot of theories and ideas from back on Earth, though I don't know how to translate that over to the Ten Realms. Then I'd get a forging blueprint, or a few of them. Then a bunch of iron ore and time at the smithy."

"Wouldn't getting the iron ore slow you down?" Erik asked.

"Yes, but the more I know about the basics, the stronger I can be moving forward. If I don't know how to even make iron ingots then I'm going to be going forward half blind."

Erik nodded in agreement. It made sense to him.

"Then, with the iron ingots, I would make and destroy items as much as possible to keep down needing to get more iron ore, unless I could make something for coin."

"All right, how much is a blueprint?" Erik tapped his beer glass in thought.

"There are only five different blueprints that are up for sale in Chonglu: one for a dagger, another for horse shoes, another for a breastplate, and two other tool types," Rugrat said. "I'd go for the dagger. There's a lot more work needed, but with the one blueprint I would be able to learn a lot of different forging techniques. It would cost forty silvers, based on iron. It would sell for fifteen coppers. If I was able to get a usable grade, they would sell for twenty coppers. Maybe thirty if I got it up to excellent grade."

"Forty silvers?" Erik asked, alarmed as he leaned forward, his eyes almost coming out of his skull.

"The dagger blueprint isn't limited in materials, so if one has Mortal grade steel or even Divine grade iron, they could use the blueprint to make a dagger. Divine iron isn't even sold in the first four realms," Rugrat said.

Erik calmed down. It made sense—this blueprint could be used across realms with all kinds of materials, making it very versatile and usable anywhere in the Ten Realms.

Just raising that kind of money would take Erik twenty days healing people if he was to continue at his current rate.

"Who is selling the blueprint? Can we barter with them?" Erik asked.

"The Blue Lotus Auction House is the one selling it." Rugrat sighed.

"Are there any forging technique books in Chonglu?" Erik asked. Clearly Rugrat wasn't looking to make these daggers for the money, but to increase his skill level. If they could get him technique books for cheaper, then it would help them greatly.

"Yeah, Blue Lotus again," Rugrat said sourly. "Sixty-five silver for a basic forging technique book, five gold for the refining technique book that will allow someone to raise Mortal grade steel to Earth grade."

Erik sighed as well. A heavy atmosphere surrounded them as they played with their glasses.

"How did the medical stuff go in the market?" Rugrat asked, changing the subject.

Erik told Rugrat everything that had happened.

"You reached Apprentice grade?" Rugrat asked with a laugh. A few people glanced over before talking to their fellows in a low whisper.

"I don't think that it's so normal here," Erik said in a low voice.

Rugrat nodded, grimacing at his slip-up.

"I got a spell as well. Maybe when you upgrade to Apprentice then you'll get something to help you," Erik said.

"Going to take a long time hammering things out," Rugrat complained.

Erik, who'd been picking up his drinking glass, paused, setting it down. "What if we don't need technique books?"

"Hmm?" Rugrat asked, his attention fully on Erik.

"Look, we know quite a bit just in random knowledge from Earth. Technique books download information into our brain and they're a great help. What's to stop us from just reading normal books?" Reading was something that only the upper class did as they knew how to read and write. Although normal books were cheaper than technique books, their information might not be any less powerful if one was to come and understand what was contained within.

"To learn Smithing, I'll need to read?" Rugrat looked dejected before drinking from his beer. "Shit. All right. I've done worse."

"I know your love for comic books," Erik said.

"They're pictures, though!" Rugrat complained. "Only had room for fifteen of them." Rugrat sounded as though someone had kicked his dog.

"Though the money problem is a real one. Clearly the First Realm doesn't have the resources that we need to increase in overall level. We need to level up and get more money so that we can go to the Second Realm and increase our skills and strength." Erik's words were met with a nod.

"Amen to that, brother." Rugrat held up his glass.

They cheered each other.

Rugrat had already taken a big drink when a puzzled expression appeared on his face. "So, how are we going to increase our level? And get money?"

"Healing," Erik said.

21

SILVER AND EXPERIENCE GAIN

Rugrat went to gather more information, though Erik knew that he would be looking for books on Smithing as well.

Erik didn't worry. He gave Rugrat all of his coinage and headed up to his room. Rugrat had been shocked at the amount he had earned, but he seemed hopeful. With this earning potential, he was no longer hesitant about healing people instead of spending his time trying to glean something from the smithy. He only earned three coppers there because he was not only working, he was learning from the lead smith.

Seeing the straw bed, Erik pulled out his sleeping bag and air mattress instead.

With a wave of his hand, the Focused Heal technique book appeared.

> **Technique Book: Focused Heal**
> Do you wish to activate this Technique book? Doing so will destroy this Technique book.
> *YES/NO*

"Yes," Erik said.

The book's pages opened. The first page flipped over, complicated runes showing on the page. The pages started to turn faster and faster. A light shone in Erik's eyes as scenes, thoughts, and information appeared in his mind. A growing pressure could be felt in his head as the information came faster and faster.

The book snapped shut with a dull sound.

Erik was left reeling as the book dissolved in front of him.

Erik rubbed his head at the headache between his brows as he kept his eyes closed, fighting the headache that had come with using the technique book.

Finally, after a few minutes, he was fine to open his eyes.

Focused Heal
Journeyman
Focused general healing spell. Instead of healing a large area, you can focus your healing power into a controlled area.
Consumption of Mana based on area and effect.

He didn't have a target for the healing magic but he felt that he would be able to cast the spell without issue.

It added a greater depth to Erik's knowledge around spells.

Before, he had needed to use the placement of his hand to use his healing spell to greater effect. Now he could use it in a localized area. Still, it didn't merely fix the wounds; it would look to enhance the speed that the patient's body recovered. With his normal heal, this meant he was wasting energy on small things like the cuts one had on their hand, or an ingrown hair instead of right on the injury. At least now he could focus on the injury site. Still, it was too general for Erik's wants and needs. He wanted to get a spell that would allow him to heal a person system by system, from the bones, making musculature, to nerves and so on. Based on what he had learned, it would cost less Mana and it would be much faster.

Without a patient, Erik didn't have anyone or anything to practice his new spell on. He wasn't disheartened as he turned his focus inward, looking over his Mana system.

He could use the mist-like Mana in his veins with greater control as he looked at his new target: the Mana gate in his right wrist.

Before he started to attack it, he studied the Mana gate in his left elbow.

When looking over his left elbow, the corners of his mouth lifted upward. As Mana flowed past this "dead" gate, a little bit of Mana was being absorbed. If Erik's actions the other night were like breaking down the door with a battering ram, then what was happening to his left elbow's Mana gates was like a rock being eroded over time by water.

Weakening the gate, even a bit, would make Erik's attempts to open it much easier.

He took a deep breath and rolled his shoulders, getting comfortable as he looked at that right wrist Mana gate.

He compressed and formed his first faint Mana spear and directed it through his Mana channels, striking the gate with a dull thud that rang through his body.

Erik continued on, increasing the speed and power of the Mana vapor-created spears.

From the outside, one would only see his shaking body while inside Erik could only hear the ringing of his Mana gate being struck again and again.

Once again, things like time started to disappear as Erik heard the first cracking noise.

He forged onward, increasing the speed that the attacks landed on the Mana gate. He wasn't a man to give up with just a small victory. He forced more Mana through his body. His Mana channels felt painful and raw as he embraced the pain, welcomed it.

Pain tells you that you're alive! Erik let out a yell as his Mana channels from his center up through his spine and down through his shoulder and arm were lit up with blue lights. If one was to look closely, they'd find that those blue lights looked like spears.

Rugrat came back some time later. Seeing that Erik was working on opening more of his Mana gates, he left him to it.

Erik continued to fight the Mana gate as the sun started to rise again.

Finally there was a breaking sound as the Mana gate gave way and the surrounding Mana once again rushed toward his body. The last resistance gave way and a new thread of Mana entered Erik's body, drifting through his Mana channels and increasing the density of his Mana.

Erik fell backward, his eyes barely open as he looked at the two new screens.

You have opened another Mana gate!
+1 to Mana Regeneration

Quest Updated: Opening the Fourteen Gates
Congratulations! You have opened your third Mana gate.
Requirements:
Clear all of your fourteen gates (3/14)
Rewards:
+1 to Mana Regeneration base stat
Undergo Mana Body Rebirth
1,400,000 EXP

A victorious smile spread across his face as he finally let sleep and exhaustion take him.

Erik was greeted by a familiar sight.

You have 5 attribute points to use.

He placed one into Strength, one into Agility and Stamina Regeneration, with the last two going to Mana Regeneration.

Character Sheet
Name: Erik West
Level: 8
Race: Human
Titles:
From the Grave
Strength: (Base 7) +5
120
Agility: (Base 6) +7
65
Stamina: (Base 10) +0
150
Mana: (Base 3) +0
30
Mana Regeneration (Base 3) +12
3.75/s
Stamina Regeneration: (Base 7) +11
4.35/s

Erik woke up feeling invigorated. He took a few moments, enjoying the feeling of newfound Strength and the Mana flowing through his body.

With a smile, he headed downstairs and got some food.

It wasn't much later that Rugrat came down from his room as well.

"So what did you find last night?" Erik asked.

"First, I went to go and check on the Blue Lotus. They're an auction house, one of the strongest, that is found throughout the realms. No one, not even Lord Chonglu himself, is willing to go against them.

"They hold a high position but they don't flaunt it. They act as an opening to the rest of the realm and the higher realms. They've got all kinds of goods that would be incredibly rare in this realm. They sell only quality goods or goods that people will fight over," Rugrat said.

"What about materials?"

Rugrat shook his head. "The fact is that there are only a few people in the First Realm who are able to reach the Apprentice level, at this stage in the upper realms. This is just the starting stage. Once one reaches the Journeyman stage, they're seen to have a use and a future. From low Journeyman to a high-level Journeyman the difference is heaven and earth. A low Journeyman can be employed anywhere. A high Journeyman could own their own workshop in the Mortal grade realms."

Mortal grade realms referred to the first three realms, while Earth referred to the Fourth, Fifth and Sixth realms. There was still Sky, Celestial, and Divine above them, but these realms were places where even a local farmer would be more powerful than all the experts in the First Realm.

"There's also differences in skills, such as a formation carver is much harder to find than a smith. The resources for a formation master are harder to find than the materials for a smith at the same level. Though if a formation master and smith are to work together, they'll be able to create an item much more powerful than if they were to make it alone. Trying to sell these rare materials in the First Realm would be a waste," Rugrat said.

Erik nodded. If the value of these items weren't realized, then the Blue Lotus would take a great loss. The basic foundational books would be core inheritances in the First Realm, allowing the later generations the ability to advance quickly into the Second Realm and establish a firm foundation to advance further.

With there being few to no other places that had these books, Erik and Rugrat would need to fight for these manuals and books with all that they had.

Which meant they had to gather as much money as possible.

"I don't want to be the one, but might you be spending your time better healing with me?"

Rugrat grimaced. He really wanted to advance his smithing.

"Look, we can probably get you up to Apprentice, which is a smooth ten thousand Experience and some kind of random item or spell. Maybe it's an item that we can sell? Also, if we're both working, we can be faster. We could be earning ten silver a day if we just worked from morning to night," Erik said.

Rugrat wasn't a combat medic but he had extensive medical training just based on being in the military and different programs and qualifications he'd gained. Compared to the knowledge of the common people, he was a genius doctor.

"All right, we'll do that then." Rugrat held out the coins that Erik had given him the night before.

Erik waved him off. What was his was Rugrat's.

"Let's get to healing," Erik said.

They headed for the market, getting food along the way.

Erik headed into the office of the civil servant, paying the fee and bribe without being asked, getting him a pleased smile from the man there.

"I've heard good things about your stall. Keep up the good work and the other stalls around you might become prime real estate," the civil servant said.

Erik's ear picked up on a money-making scheme. "As long as mister is willing to cut me a fee, I'll be willing to send my patients there, as long as the prices aren't too high," Erik said carefully.

The civil servant sat back, appraising Erik. "Very well. Same prices. With the greater number of people, it should still capture many's interests."

"Two apothecaries and some food places would be the best suited," Erik thought aloud.

"Very well. I will make sure that there is a patrol nearby to deal with any issues," the civil servant said.

Erik nodded. So far nothing had gone wrong but if people got rowdy, things could get out of hand. Having the guards nearby to keep the peace would be a great help.

"Thank you for this opportunity." Erik cupped his hands and bowed his head.

"No need for that." The civil servant laughed, getting up from his seat and pulling Erik up. "I hope for a long and prosperous relationship." The civil servant smiled, holding out a stone token. Instead of being a daily pass, this was a weekly one.

Erik made to give the man more money.

"Don't worry about the fee. This is the least I can do." The civil servant clapped Erik on the back.

"Thank you," Erik said honestly. It was clear the benefits he could earn from this partnership.

"No worries. I might have some patients in need of your care in the future," the civil servant said.

"If they are people known to mister, then I will do my best at a reduced rate."

"Thank you greatly, master healer," the civil servant said. "I will see you out."

After Erik left, the civil servant returned to his office. Sitting there was a young-looking man with a powerful aura.

"Guard Captain, it is all sorted out. We will be able to observe from close to see his skills." The civil servant bowed to the man deeply.

He might take a bit off the top here and there, but his loyalty was to Lord Chonglu and the city. He had brought the information of the healer to the guard captain. Not many might know but Lord Chonglu and the guard captain had been looking for healers in the shadows for a month now.

"Well done, Pirez." The guard captain stood. "Make sure you make a full accounting."

"Yes, sir," Pirez said in a grave tone. Everything he took for himself was marked down. As long as he did so, the lord and others left him to it. If he could create more business, then they were happy to let him take his little kickbacks.

"I hope that he is able to help." The guard captain's gaze contained some softness and fear before quickly disappearing as he left Pirez's office.

Erik met with Rugrat and headed for their stall. It was the same as yesterday: already there were people lined up.

Vand was also there.

Erik paid him eight coppers directly.

"Today, I want you to organize the lines. This here is my friend Rugrat." Erik waved to Rugrat at the side. "He's able to heal as well. If there are any issues, let us know," Erik said.

"Yes, Mister West." Vand nodded seriously.

"Good lad." Erik clapped the boy on the shoulder. He might be simple, but he did everything to the best of his abilities.

"If you were here yesterday, please have your tokens ready!" Erik yelled out to the forty or so people who had gathered.

Tokens appeared in their hands as those without them looked over in jealousy.

"We'll do triage. You deal with the simple wounds to get started; I'll deal with the severe ones. Once your progress slows toward the healing skill, take on more of the advanced healing cases," Erik said to Rugrat.

"Got it," Rugrat said. Erik had told him all of the healing secrets that he had learned in the last day. This, combined with his knowledge, should allow him to quickly advance into the healer Apprentice level.

They quickly started, checking tokens and working through people in order, then triaging the patients afterward. Those with the worst afflictions were sorted out quickly, moving through.

The guard patrol kept coming around, maintaining order as the stores around had people moving out as food stalls and apothecaries replaced the animal feed and tool stalls.

Their Experience, coin purses, and skill levels continued to grow as people came to watch or be healed. Word quickly spread.

22

SHIFTING POWERS

"I heard that Little Brother suffered a loss upon your *glorious* return." A burly-looking man laughed as Wren entered a bar with his gaggle of followers.

"Older Brother Yui," Wren grit his teeth and greeted his older brother.

A number of his followers looked at the large burly man with interest, the women trying to entice him.

He took in the sights, but seeing the awkwardness of his younger brother made him snort.

"Don't tease little Wren like that." A faint voice carried through the place from a curtained-off VIP area.

The curtains were parted by servants as Domonos, their eldest brother, who was being served wine and grapes, looked up from his activities.

"Elder Brother," Yui said, his face solemn, not daring to slight his older brother. He might look kind but he was a vicious person and fighter. Going against him, one had to guard for hidden wounds that would affect them later on in life.

He truly didn't show mercy to his enemies or those who stood in his way.

Wren perked up. A joyful smile appeared on his face. After all, his tendencies were the most similar to his oldest brother. Wren might be the youngest and his fighting abilities might be the weakest, but with his eldest brother's backing, no one would dare to slight him. Wren was called the young master as he would inherit the Silaz business; Domonos was called the young lord as he would be the one to bring the Silaz family to new heights. He had already been selected by a sect in the Second Realm and he was waiting for them to descend for a nearby challenge before they would ascend, taking him with them and bringing him into the sect.

"Aren't we all of the Silaz family here? Should we not pick one another up?" Domonos asked lightly. His smile seemed carefree and gentle, making those who didn't know his nature smile, while others shivered.

Yui cupped his fists to Domonos and bowed deeply. "Eldest brother's words truly bring new light to my eyes. I was blind before."

"Wren, it has been some time since we drank together. Won't you share a drink with your eldest brother?"

"Certainly, Elder Brother. It would be my honor." Wren still looked up to his brother, as all young brothers would, seeing them as the ruler of all.

A calculating flash passed through Wren's eyes as he moved to his brother's private curtained-off area.

It wasn't long until they got on the subject of the two men and their audacity to verbally spar with Wren and how they had been able to escape Wren's hands.

Wren was filled with joy as he saw Domonos frown slightly.

"Father might be scared with you confronting them, but if I was to do it, then it would cut out the problem at the root," Domonos said.

"Thank you, brother. I will surely look for some way to pay brother back. I hope that you were able to enjoy the gifts that I sent you up on hearing that you made it into the Willful Institute," Wren said. The two brothers shared a smile.

Domonos let out a short laugh. "Indeed, you might be the youngest but your mind is sharp," Domonos praised.

His friends had dark smiles on their faces. It looked like the young lord would be moving again.

Grandmaster Eri was the leader of the Healing Moon House. As such, he was not expecting someone to barge into his own study as he was taking his afternoon tea.

"I am sorry, Master, but I couldn't stop myself anymore," Xui Deng, one of Grandmaster Eri's direct disciples declared as he dropped to his knees in front of his master, prostrating himself before him.

Eri had no time to try to stop or question him as Xui Deng's words came out like a river.

"A number of the peasants have been talking about a man who is healing their wounds without asking much in the way of compensation. They say that he is a healing grandmaster like yourself. Even going so far to say that your grand healing spells look powerful, but they are not as good as the healing that this man provides," Xui Deng said, his anger and frustration suppressed. His master was the most powerful healer in all of Chonglu and the surrounding region. The other healing houses might try to compete but he knew that his grandmaster was the greatest of them all.

Grandmaster Eri's expression darkened slightly. "I have heard that there was a slight commotion. I did not think it would reach to the stage that they were questioning our healing house!" His face turned red as his beard quivered in anger. He took a few moments to compose himself.

The truth was that Grandmaster Eri knew his own faults. He was a high-leveled Apprentice healer. In the First Realm, that might count for something; in the higher realms, that was barely passable. Instead of relying on his abilities, he took on a greater managerial role. Only by relying on a few Mana potions was he able to cast powerful healing spells for longer to shock the younger generation. Establishing him as a grandmaster who sought to improve their skills instead of flaunting his own.

He and the other healing house elders would get into confrontations but the simple fact was that they wouldn't dare to try to overthrow the other. It would bring the people's retribution and the strength they would lose would be even greater. Instead, they looked to put on displays of their healing power to awe the masses and draw greater patronage from the nobles for their exclusive services.

Now this man had come along and he was throwing them all in the dirt. Not only was he charging just a few coppers, he was doing it in the market without needing any grand scheme.

From what Eri had learned, this man wasn't just some kind of hoax—he was the real deal.

That was much harder to deal with.

"Use the Black Blood poison. If he wishes to say he's a healer, let's see what happens when he comes up against a truly life-threatening issue," Eri said.

"Yes, Grandmaster," Xui Deng said, the fervor in his eyes only increasing.

Grandmaster Eri nodded. The boy might not be the brightest but his loyalty was one of the best, making him the most appropriate student who would ignore his shortcomings and look to extolling his virtues to all he met.

Xui Deng acted quickly. He found out where Erik and Rugrat had been staying and then sent out some of the guards from the Moon Healing House to watch the location.

He himself moved into the crowd around the healing stall.

Not only was there the previous man proclaiming himself as a healer, there was a second, larger man with him.

Healers? They look more like brutes. Xui Deng sneered to himself as people lined up to get healed. The two moved through them too quickly to be real healers, taking only the smallest donations and making sure that they weren't bankrupting those who came to see them.

They even grabbed subpar "medicines" from the apothecaries. This further affirmed Xui Deng's beliefs. No healer in their right mind would rely on apothecaries or alchemists. Alchemists and healers were at odds with one another through the realms. One using the aid of the other was practically unheard of.

Xui Deng looked over their primitive ways and couldn't contain himself anymore. He quietly called up one of his people. "Go and use this on that shorter one." Xui Deng held out a needle covered in Black Blood poison.

"How will I get close to them?" the guard asked.

"You'll need an injury. Don't worry, I'll be sure to heal you," Xui Deng promised.

The man had a grim look on his face, hesitating.

Xui Deng glanced at the other guard.

He stepped forward and grabbed the other man's arm.

"Grit your teeth." A sickening cracking sounded as the man let out a scream between his clamped lips. His arm bent the other way now.

He grabbed his now broken arm. Xui Deng waved his hand toward the two healers.

23
BLACK BLOOD POISON

Erik was tired. He'd made sure to keep at least ten percent of his Mana at all times. He found keeping this buffer meant he had less headaches and didn't feel as tired.

The glow around his hands disappeared as the person in the litter looked at Erik with shock. Her family members held tears in their eyes as one stepped forward with twelve coppers.

Erik smiled awkwardly and could only accept them, knowing that the family wouldn't take no for an answer.

"You'll need some rest, plenty of food and water. You'll be up and about in two, maybe three days." Erik smiled.

"Thank you, healer," the woman in the litter said, trying to get up and bow to him.

"Rest. I don't want to have to heal any other issues," Erik chided as she let him push her back onto the litter.

The family gave their thanks and moved out of the way. There were plenty of others waiting to be healed.

Erik looked at the next person. The pale man's arm was facing the wrong direction, making Erik grimace at its unnatural angle.

"Ugh, that looks painful. Four coppers, and I'd suggest getting some numbing agent," Erik said.

"I'm fine. I'll pay five if you heal it right now," the man said.

Erik wanted to argue, but seeing the look in the man's eyes, he wasn't to be refused. Erik shrugged and leaned forward, holding the man's arm gingerly.

The man let out a hiss of cold air as the broken bones rubbed against one another.

Erik started to use Simple Organic Scan, examining the wound and lining up the bones.

He didn't see the vicious look that appeared in the man's eyes as a needle appeared in his good hand and he jabbed it into Erik's unprotected neck.

Erik grabbed his neck and jumped backward. Alarm appeared on his face. He used a healing spell as he looked at the man with the broken arm.

"West?" Rugrat yelled, sensing something wrong and seeing him hold his neck.

"Fuck!" Erik yelled. He felt something was wrong. His veins turned black as weakness spreading from his neck to the rest of his body.

The patient laughed and started to run away.

Rugrat's face turned calm, his eyes cold.

A murderous aura spread over the crowd. It was as if two dragons had been awakened.

Cold fear covered the area as Erik shot forward, his increased Agility and Stamina being put to use as he felt Rugrat rushing toward him, covering his actions.

The patient looked back, a look of fear in his eyes as he looked at Erik's expressionless face.

Erik's arm sneaked around the man's neck as he drove the combat knife up and under the man's rib cage, turning and ripping it out.

The man let out a sigh as his lung started to deflate and fill with blood.

Erik let the man drop as he was already fighting for air.

His vision started to swim as people looked at the dying man and Erik, who was covered in blood. He staggered back a bit, using his healing spell. It was having some effect but he was fighting a losing battle.

"We need to move," Rugrat said. Killing people inside the city was a sure-fire way to be killed yourself.

The guards might have not come over to find them yet, but they were patrolling the area. It wouldn't be long until they arrived.

Erik nodded, putting away the blade in his storage ring.

People were looking at them in horror. Their auras didn't show any of the calm mercy of before. Erik and Rugrat had been fighting as soldiers since they were old enough to join the military; they'd killed many people in their time and helped others.

Normally they didn't even exude any pressure. Now their anger had been revealed; the pressure of a combat veteran weighed down on everyone.

Rugrat led the way, barging a path through people.

Erik followed him as they heard yelling from behind.

"Talk to me," Rugrat said as Erik's face continued to pale and his reactions became sluggish.

"He gave me some kind of poison. It's in my blood." Erik didn't hide anything.

Rugrat didn't say anything.

Erik pulled out his minor Mana recovery potion and downed it in one go. His Mana recovery increased by one point for thirty seconds.

He constantly cast his Focused Heal spell, but the poison had spread to his heart and was being pumped through his entire body. Black veins stuck up across his body.

Erik stumbled, almost falling down. Rugrat grabbed him, holding him up as they saw guards behind them.

Erik wrapped his arm around Rugrat, who took off. Erik had been putting his attribute points into Mana Regeneration; Rugrat had been training his Strength and Agility to the max.

Rugrat's steps took them down an alleyway. He used the sides of the alley to get higher until they landed on a rooftop. A lady screamed as she was putting up the house owner's clothes to dry.

Rugrat went through the clothesline as Erik tried to focus on the poison. He coughed, tasting the tang of blood in his mouth. His blood was turning darker and darker, black in some places as it started to melt him from the inside.

Clearly Erik's attempts to directly heal his blood weren't working.

Circulatory system, toxins in the blood, liver and kidneys.

Erik's aims changed as he used Simple Organic Scan, looking at his failing liver and kidneys.

He used Focused Heal on both organs. They started to change. Erik wasn't trying to heal his entire circulatory system, so he could pour in more power to the two organs, increasing the rate at which they recovered.

As the black blood entered, it seemed to weaken, only a small bit, but Erik hoped his Simple Organic Scan wasn't wrong.

He continued to heal and looked around. They were nearing the eastern gate that led toward the Beast Mountains.

He was getting weaker, his body being destroyed from the inside. He was burning all over. It was as if he was liquefying internally.

Rugrat jumped across rooftops as guards continued to follow them.

The guards could defeat level eights easily and working together, they could stop a level ten from doing as they pleased. Erik was out of the fight for now and Rugrat had to look after him. Being only level seven, he had to run, or else they'd get trapped. Also within the city there was a formation that increased the power of the guards; if they got close enough, they could use the formation to restrain someone and increase their own power, allowing them to fight more powerful opponents.

"Shit, there's no buildings near the wall," Rugrat said, his pace not slowing in the slightest as he rubbed his storage ring, ready to pull out his service rifle and deal with these people.

"Don't kill them if you don't have to. That guy was sent by someone. If we kill a guard, then the Chonglu guards will come after us."

"Don't worry, I'm not that stupid," Rugrat yelled as he launched himself off a roof. He landed in a cloud of dust. People moved away from him as they inflicted fear into those around them and ran off.

Erik coughed weakly. The blood was dark and had a foul smell to it.

"Sir! That healer killed a man with a broken arm. It looks like he was affected by something. His partner picked him up and is running with him toward the eastern gate!" Liam, the lieutenant in charge of the patrol "assisting" Erik and Rugrat, while secretly keeping an eye on them both, reported.

"What?" Captain Quinn yelled as he stopped in the middle of the street. The guards around him all paused as those around looked over at the usually calm Captain Quinn. His aura of a level ten made those nearby lower-leveled people shake.

Quinn decisively turned toward the eastern gate and took off running. The guards around him followed as he pushed his speed to the maximum.

"Clear a path!" His voice boomed as he rushed through the street. People moved out of his way, paling at the power rolling off him.

"Sir, they're only level sevens, but their aura, it feels like they're gods of death," Lieutenant Liam Hoste said seriously.

"Who did the man belong to?" Quinn asked.

"I don't know. The main healer killed him immediately before succumbing to whatever is affecting him. It must be some kind of poison."

"We can't let them away. We need their help! Don't harm them!" Quinn launched himself down an alleyway, jumping over people, his guards following right behind him.

"Yes, sir!" Liam said, but from his tone Quinn could sense how difficult Liam thought it would be.

Quinn made good time as he reached the eastern gate. He could see the guards chasing from the marketplace over.

He had only stopped as a large man carrying his friend appeared.

It was the two healers, but they didn't seem like healers anymore. Quinn's sharp eyesight allowed him to see the other man's veins that had turned black and the healing magical circles on his body.

The wave of murderous intent made his knees shake. He had been in many life-and-death situations, but in front of this man carrying his brother out of danger, he felt as if he'd met a death god.

How many life-and-death situations has this person been in to create such a powerful aura? Quinn felt that he wasn't able to pull on the full power of his body under this kind of pressure.

"Move or die." The large man's voice was cold, emotionless.

Something appeared in his hands. Quinn had never seen anything like it before in his life, but the man wasn't slowing his pace at all.

"We want to help!" Quinn yelled.

"Move or die." The man raised the long object in his hands.

Quinn's heart missed a beat. "Clear a path!" he yelled, making sure his hands were away from his weapons. This man might be a level seven but Quinn didn't have any confidence dealing with him or that weapon.

The large man continued through the gate. No one looked to stop him.

"I'll remember this, Chonglu City!" the man yelled as he cleared the gate. The object in his hands disappeared.

Quinn felt the pressure on his body decrease as it got farther away. Silence fell as he felt cold sweat running down his back.

Clearly the two men were close. Quinn couldn't help but shiver as he thought of what might happen if the healer died.

He needed to report this to Lord Chonglu. He was the most powerful man in the city; he might know what that thing the man was holding, or have a plan of how to move forward.

Quinn didn't want to bother Lord Chonglu as he had his own concerns, but if this man returned, Chonglu City might not exist anymore if that man felt they had led to the death of his brother.

24

CITY LORD AND HIS WORRIES

Lord Chonglu looked to the two beds with a soft smile on his face, pain hidden deep in his eyes. His frame was thin and the air around him stale as he looked at the two small children resting within the beds. Their pale faces and weak bodies attested to the dire situation they were in.

Chonglu saw the time. He rose and pulled out a healing potion as he moved to the two children.

The door opened. Lord Chonglu's kind smile vanished as power seemed to roll off his body, declaring him as a level fourteen being.

Captain Quinn stepped inside. He dropped to his knee immediately, his face pale under the pressure of Chonglu's circulating power.

"My lord, I have found a healer who was able to heal people who the healing houses denied in minutes." The captain didn't hold anything back, knowing that his lord's anger was easy to ignite these days.

The lines on Lord Chonglu's face slackened. "Shut the door and speak, Captain Quinn," Chonglu said, his voice softer. Captain Quinn had become close to his children, looking after them as if they were his own.

Chonglu had been trying to track down his wife—his children's mother—and administering his city. He barely saw his children. It was only when the poison buried within their bodies ignited he pushed it all away, standing guard over their beds night and day to care for them personally.

Chonglu moved to the two children, one a boy and one a girl, twins.

Their weak bodies trembled as if cold but sweated constantly.

Quinn closed the doors as Lord Chonglu administered a Health potion to his two children.

Quinn quickly sank to his knee again once the doors were sealed. "The unknown man set up a stall in the market. He was attacked by a man and given a poison. His brother carried him out of the city. If he dies, I fear that his brother will slaughter Chonglu City."

"Who dared to attack a healer in my city?" Chonglu asked with a deep voice.

"I believe it was the Moon Healing House. We are looking into the matter," Quinn said.

Normally Chonglu would have Quinn look into the matter, punishing those who dared to kill in his territory. Now with his son and daughter badly wounded, this mysterious healer had a higher position in his mind.

"If they come seeking revenge, we will give them the people who were behind this plot. If they go too far, then I will deal with them," Lord Chonglu assured Quinn.

"They don't even have a backing of a Second Realm sect or person. All they have is the place they've carved out of being pious saints." Chonglu scoffed, shaking his head. They were nothing more than a group that acted as noble hangers-on. If they stopped him from finding a healer for his children, he'd happily destroy their position in his city.

"Investigate well. Hopefully that healer recovers," Chonglu said, with a tired sigh that seemed to come deep within his soul.

He smiled faintly at the small girl beside him as he moved some hair away from his daughter's face, before he moved to his son. His mind worked it over. They had called upon healers from all over the First Realm. It was a vast place, but the rewards he had put up were incredible.

Healers were a rare brand of people. To raise one's healing ability meant that they would have to focus on the mysteries of the body to fix and repair instead of working on their strength or their magical abilities.

Clearly, if this information was right and the Moon Healing House went after this healer, then his skills weren't a fabrication and at a level where it threatened them.

What other options do I have? Lord Chonglu rubbed his finger against his son's cheek.

"Go." Lord Chonglu's voice was quiet but it didn't diminish the might in it. He moved back to his chair between the two beds and sat down, as if a dragon once again returning to his slumber.

"Yes, my lord." Captain Quinn quickly left the room and closed the door behind him.

Xui Deng's face was pale as he walked through the Moon Healing House, his actions wooden and his eyes haunted.

He had been born and raised by the Moon Healing House from a young age. He'd rarely left the city other than to follow his master. Even then they'd been greatly protected.

Few if any people were willing to anger a healing house and their disciples. Doing so would bring down the wrath of many warriors and people looking to gain their favor, or use their services.

Now, Xui Deng didn't feel secure in his position.

A shiver ran down his back at those auras. They weren't healers; they were bringers of death and destruction. The shock of their auras, revealing their anger, made Xui Deng's heart race.

He made it to his master's quarters, numb as his master's servant went to make sure that he was ready to receive guests.

Not long afterward, his master walked into the room, looking out over the city.

"Master, I have erred." Xui Deng dropped to his knees. If there was someone who could make this right, it was his master. He relayed everything that had happened.

His master's face turned grim as he heard it all. "He killed the one who poisoned him right away?" Grandmaster Eri asked.

"Yes, Master."

"Good, then there will be no one to question. Make sure that you clean up any loose ends. With them killing someone inside the city, Lord Chonglu shouldn't let this go," Eri said confidently. "Even if he was going to let them go, to gain favor with us in order to heal his children, he will do all in his power to appease us."

Xui Deng was stunned by his master's ability. Not only had he resolved Xui's fear in a few short words, he had shown the power he had over the city lord himself.

"Will we get someone to heal his children?" Xui asked.

"Their affliction is a deep one and something that only the higher-ups would be able to deal with. It will take a lot to take them from their own positions. We must make sure that Lord Chonglu knows the grace that we give to him and will pay the fee due," Eri said in a righteous voice.

New strength came into Xui Deng's body. The bracelet on his arm vibrated, telling him that a message had arrived.

Seeing it, Eri waved his hand. "Take it, it might be important."

"Yes, Master." Xui listened to the call.

Confused, he looked at his master. "I have just got word from some people I know. They said that the guards let the two men go. One of them said that they would come back to destroy whoever poisoned his friend. Captain Quinn has come out of the lord's manor. His orders were not to kill the duo, but send them a message that the lord wants to meet with them," Xui said.

Eri's eyes went wide and then thinned as his fist tightened. "Call upon those loyal to us. I will offer twenty silvers for whoever kills one of them—fifty for whoever kills both of them and brings proof. We must not let these two corrupt the city lord's mind."

Rugrat had kept on running when they left Chonglu behind. Erik focused on healing his liver and kidneys. With flashes of healing his entire body, he couldn't focus on the fact that his body was dying from the inside. If he did, then he might give in to panic.

All he could do was deal with the problem at hand and disassociate what was happening in front of him under his Simple Organic Scan.

Rugrat found somewhere safe, pulling Erik off his shoulder and laying him on the ground.

"Get an IV and saline drip into me." Erik's face was white, with his veins turning from blue to black in places.

Rugrat didn't pause, quickly pulling out the gear. He found Erik's vein, put in the needle and set up the bag.

"Heal me, don't burn out," Erik said, every word forced and exhausting. "Gimme potions."

Rugrat pulled out his Stamina and Mana potion, tipping them into Erik's mouth as the latter was weak and fading fast. Rugrat used his healing spell on Erik, taking on some of the strain.

Erik focused on his liver and kidneys. The blood coming through was cleaner than what entered. It was slow, but now with Rugrat helping, its speed was increasing.

Erik could only focus on his kidneys and liver. The fear, the knowledge of how close he was to dying nearly sent him into a panic. It was hard to try to keep a cool head.

He noticed that it wasn't just Erik and Rugrat's healing at work. With healing his missing limbs, Erik's body was now naturally more resilient to damage; with the poison in his blood, his natural recovery was ignited.

The Stamina and Mana recovery potions that Rugrat had given him had run out. Erik's condition was still bad, but the black blood was slowly being cleared out by his liver and kidneys.

With Rugrat helping to keep the rest of his body functioning, Erik pushed on, just staying above Mana fatigue so he wouldn't have to endure the headaches and mental decline.

For two hours, they fought—healing spells against poison.

Erik had Rugrat alter the dosages of different chemicals and compounds added to the IV.

Finally there was no more damage. Instead, it stabilized. Erik was wheezing, his lips covered in caked blood, his entire body thin and pale as black veins showed.

"Dehydrated, starvation," Erik said to Rugrat.

Rugrat quickly pulled out another IV. It was hard to find Erik's veins in his arms, so Rugrat used his leg, giving him supplements to hydrate and give him the basic supplements he needed.

Erik and Rugrat continued to heal. They had never healed for this long before. The mental strain was intense as they both knew one mistake and Erik would be lost.

Erik's condition started to improve. The blood coming through his liver and kidneys was no longer filled with black poison and held a powerful vitality to it.

Erik felt as if his circulatory system was being reborn. A warm and powerful feeling traced through his body. His heartbeat increased in power, becoming deeper. Each beat shook Erik's body as blood flowed faster, the black blood being replaced with a deep red blood that seemed to brim with vitality.

Erik's color started to return as the black in his veins faded away and a natural red appeared.

After passing through his liver and then kidneys, there was no sign of the poison anymore.

His new blood was like rains upon a parched desert: his body drew it in and the previous damage started to fade away. Erik collapsed from the strain as a new strength entered his body.

25

A NEW DIRECTION

Erik woke slowly. His body felt stronger than ever before. There was still some remaining weakness from the dehydration and starvation he had gone through.

Rugrat moved to him. From his look, he hadn't slept all night, watching over Erik. "How you feeling?" Rugrat asked.

"A lot better." Erik checked over his body with a Simple Organic Scan. Instead of spreading poison, his body was getting stronger with the blood in his body, strengthening him internally.

"Scared me there for a bit," Rugrat said with a half-laugh.

"Don't worry, not getting rid of me that easily." Erik laughed.

His notifications symbol was blinking at him, drawing his attention.

Erik opened it up.

For tempering your blood, you have unlocked the quest: Body Cultivation

Quest: Body Cultivation
The path cultivating one's body is not easy. To stand at the top, one must forge their own path forward.
Requirements:
Reach Body Like Stone Level
Sub-requirements
Tempering of the Blood
Tempering of the Bones
Tempering of the Organs
Tempering of the Muscle
Tempering of the Skin
Rewards:
+3 to Strength
+3 to Agility
+3 to Stamina
+5 to Stamina Regeneration
+100,000 EXP

Through tempering your blood, you have found that your body heals at an increased rate. Your Stamina and Stamina Regeneration have also increased!
+1 to Stamina Regeneration
+1 to Stamina

Natural healing rate, like overall health, was a hidden stat and not something that people could quantify, or the system recognized. The only time that it was acknowledged was when someone's body's abilities took a leap upward, going through the stages of Body Like Stone, Body Like Iron, and so on.

You have reached Level 8
When you sleep next, you will be able to increase your attributes by: 5 points.

7,280/48,000 EXP till you reach Level 9

With Erik passing out due to exhaustion, his body hadn't acknowledged him as going to sleep, so the Experience didn't take effect and he didn't increase in overall level.

"Damn, how does anyone become a damn Body Cultivator when it's this hard?" Erik muttered to himself. With the Mana Gathering system, as long as he increased his Mana Regeneration then he was able to pass through the Vapor and Mist stage; in the Drop stage, he would need to compress his Mana slightly and the Core Compression stage would require him to use outside help or spells to control his Mana and form a Mana core.

With Body Cultivation, to just get to the first stage he needed to temper the different systems in his body—a total of five different systems. If going by how he had completed his blood tempering, Erik wasn't looking forward to the remaining temperings.

He dismissed the information and looked at Rugrat.

"So, what's the plan?" Rugrat asked. "Do we go back, kill the fuckers who targeted you?"

Rugrat's voice was casual but Erik knew he was serious.

"Not yet. There are some powerful people in the city and we still need to increase our strength." Thankfully they hadn't left anything behind as they had all of their gear stored in their storage rings. "Let's go to the Beast Mountains instead. We can increase our level and our skills, and build up our gold. There are many things we can find in the Beast Mountains to increase our strength and they don't care who we are."

Rugrat seemed to relax a bit. He had been tense ever since the previous day. Knowing that they weren't going right back into the fight brought relief.

"Let's move our camp, get some food and sleep. Then we'll head for the Wild Reaches Trading Outpost," Erik said.

Erik pulled the IVs out, storing them before digging into some of the rations and water they had. Satisfied, they cleared up everything and headed off.

They had both bought maps of the area so they knew the Beast Mountains region and the closest trading outpost that ringed the massive area.

They made camp and Erik took first watch. Rugrat quickly passed out as Erik surveyed the area.

He didn't know who had tried to kill him, but he would make sure that they wouldn't survive.

Domonos was sitting in a cafe with his people around him. The rest of the cafe had been cleared out. A man rushed up before taking a knee in front of Domonos.

"Young Lord, we have talked to different people around the city and tried to look for the two men but it has been hard to do so. Their clothing must have changed and they were wearing something similar to the people in Chonglu," the man reported.

Domonos frowned. He trusted his people to find out where the two people were. After all, it was just two nobodies; they had no status or position in Chonglu.

"Talk to the guards at the gate. Have them report to me if they see these two entering the city again." Domonos wasn't willing to chase after these two. The Willful Institute he had become a part of would be descending in the coming weeks to pick up the talents they had scouted and recruit more.

There was also some kind of competition that they had to temper their students that they brought but it hadn't been revealed to him what they did.

"Young Lord, there were two people who fled the city yesterday." A man beside Domonos stepped forward, speaking into his ear.

"Oh?" he said, showing faint interest.

"They were healing people in the market area. There had been one of them, but the second day there were two of them. They were attacked but killed the attacker before fleeing. One of them was heavily wounded. Many don't believe he would survive. The guards didn't stop them as they fled the city."

Domonos tapped his fingers against the armrest of his seat. It might very well be the people his youngest brother had talked about. To make the guards even fear from attacking them… *Was there something more?*

"Many of the people at the market said that when they were attacked, their aura was dominating, making many fear for their lives."

"They are nothing but weak pawns." Domonos dismissed them. He had heard that there was something going on with Lord Chonglu looking for healers. This might be the reason that the guards hadn't stopped them as they looked to flee.

"If they don't return, then we won't pursue them," Domonos said, dismissing the matter. He didn't have time to waste on these unimportant people and others seemed to want to kill them.

26

PATH TO BEAST MOUNTAINS

Erik and Rugrat headed from Chonglu City toward the Wild Reaches Trading Outpost through the forests, keeping clear of the roads and anyone who might be on them.

Their speed was much greater than before and they could run for longer easily.

They'd debated going back to their caches, but with the room in their storage rings, they wouldn't be able to collect everything, so they continued with what they had.

It was only when they were getting closer to the Wild Reaches Trading Outpost that they started to see people again.

They changed their clothes, wearing a different outfit. After what had happened with the Silaz trading house, they made sure to keep changes of clothes to hide their identity.

Wearing scarves to cover their mouths and a dark cloak, they looked like two bandits back on Earth.

No one who had seen them before would know who they were.

They joined the carts and people who were joining the main road.

Wild Reaches Trading Outpost was simply built, with large and powerful stone walls that showed signs of battle. Powerful weapons were affixed to the walls. Hard-looking men and women patrolled the walls. Their armor was uniform, but was worn based on the power it gave the wearer. These people, more than the clean-looking Chonglu guards, were those who had dealt with life-and-death battles again and again without hope of support and survived.

Moving to the gate, few people dared to yell out, paying their toll and moving into the city.

Erik and Rugrat paid their coinage.

"No killing in the city," the guard said, letting them through.

They passed through, getting their first view into the city.

It was roughly made, but all of the buildings were made from hard timbers and stone, looking like their own defensive forts.

The people were hardy and unkempt, looking as if they hadn't showered in weeks, but their weapons and armor were well maintained. They begrudgingly went about their day, selling their spoils to the various trading houses and merchants.

The bars attracted the greatest number of mercenaries, fighters, and traders.

There were different trading houses here that were looking for all kinds of goods, from monster cores, to monster meat, rare ingredients, even weapons and armor that one came across.

The Beast Mountains were not a peaceful place and there was a dark undertone to the city as people moved in groups and evaluated one another openly.

Erik and Rugrat moved through the streets. Using their rifles might attract too much attention. Most of the people here were high-level adventurers who shouldn't be underestimated. If they saw Erik and Rugrat's weapons and wanted them, as long as no one reported them, no one would know how Erik and Rugrat died.

Their first stop was a weapons store. It was one of the busiest, with people checking out the new wares. Weapons and armor were prized possessions. There were few stores in Chonglu City that could compare to their selection.

"Hello, can I help you?" a server came up and asked them.

"We're looking for bows," Erik said. Both of them had shot compound bows on Earth and had a few of them lying around.

They already had the Marksman skill so they didn't want to waste the effort they had put in already.

"Certainly. This way," the woman said, with a small smile, used to the blunt way that they spoke.

The floor had been broken up into different areas based on weapons.

She took them to a wall filled with bows. People were checking out the different items here.

There were no compound bows here; all of them were longbow or shortbow. Only a few were recurve. There were also some crude crossbows as well.

Rugrat looked them over, checking their stats and abilities.

Erik wasn't the best shot with a bow, so he focused on the shortbows. They required less strength to pull back on the bow string and their range was lower, but one could fire more arrows faster.

Rugrat went straight for the recurve bows. He'd used more crossbows before and the recurve bows, although being the most expensive, were also the most powerful.

Erik finally picked the best shortbow based on price and base damage.

Cold Whisper
Damage: 5 (piercing)
Weight: 3.2 kg
Durability: 89/100
Base Value: 1 Silver, 23 Coppers
Range: Short Range
Requires: Arrows

Just the bow by itself was worth nearly half a day's worth of healing people. Erik moved to the arrows, getting three different types.

Freezing Arrow
Damage: 2 (piercing) 1 (freezing)
Weight: 0.2 kg
Base Value: 5 Coppers
Attributes: Applies freeze damage on target for 15 seconds. Chance to paralyze.
Used with: Bow

Piercing Arrow
Damage: 6 (piercing)
Weight: 0.2 kg
Base Value: 9 Coppers
Attributes: Increases piercing damage.
Used with: Bow

Stun Arrow
Damage: 1 (piercing)
Weight: 0.2 kg
Base Value: 3 Coppers
Attributes: Applies shocking attack on target. Chance to stun.
Used with: Bow
The enchantments sounded very good and the merchant extolled their virtues but with them being of low quality and level they might annoy their targets more than do any true damage. Still, Erik and Rugrat thought that it would be best to test them out.

Finally, he grabbed some regular arrows as well.

Arrow (Basic)
Damage: 2 (piercing)
Weight: 0.2 kg
Base Value: 2 Coppers
Attributes: None.
Used with: Bow
Erik got ten piercing arrows, ten freezing arrows, thirty arrows (basic), and twenty stun arrows. With his bow, it came to four silver and two coppers with the weapons server bartering with him.

Rugrat got his recurve bow and a number of regular arrows; the special arrows were too expensive so he'd only have a handful of them.

Erik and Rugrat could only look at each other with pained smiles. They had been reduced to just thirty coppers remaining.

"You're new so you might not know—there's a request board that you can find near the eastern gate. It's in the eastern gathering square, which is a bit to the south of the eastern gate. People put up different offers for items that one might find out in the Beast Mountains," the server said.

"Thanks," Erik said.

"Just remember me when you make it big." She gave them a wink before getting back to work.

"Seems that every time we make money, we've spent it already," Rugrat complained as they walked out of the store, their new gear in their storage rings already.

"Everything has its price here," Erik said as they entered the eastern gathering square. Beyond it, there was a direct path to the eastern gate that led into the Beast Mountains itself.

People were all around, groups coming in and groups going out.

Those going out had a determined expression on their faces, while those coming in might display their biggest kills, earning jealous looks and glares from those who came back bloodied or missing people in their party who they had set out with.

There were massive signboards at the sides of the large open area. People put up requests or copied them down as they were heading out in the beast mountain range.

This second group were the veterans of the Beast Mountains, looking to get at least some small rewards on their trip into the wilderness.

Erik and Rugrat started to look over the different posters that littered the signboard. There were calls for materials, for different animals in various conditions. There were even requests for sightings on different beasts.

The posters that drew Erik's attention were those about the different plants and ingredients that one might be able to find in the Beast Mountains.

There were also the different animals that went for a high cost.

Rugrat collected information on the different ores and items that could be used for crafting and making of weapons.

"Looking for three people, need to be above level eight, ranged archer, or mage with at least five different destruction spells!"

"Looking for a tanker, must be level eight or higher!"

"Hunting for the black scaled Oek'sh, looking for three more party members. Bring your own poison potions. Level five or higher!"

People were forming groups or looking for groups here and there. There were a number of groups and guilds that had formed in this Beast Mountain Range to make more money and look out for one another.

There were even scouts going around, talking to people looking for a party, trying to recruit them.

Erik and Rugrat looked over it but they didn't pay any attention. If they were with a group, it was likely that they might reveal a secret when they were fighting.

Especially with Erik just getting stabbed in the neck by someone he thought was a patient, they were hesitant to be around others.

"I want to check out one more place before we leave," Erik said.

Rugrat followed him as they went back into the city and toward a store tucked away.

There were a number of high-level adventurers outside. All of them were respectful when they entered the store, looking around at everyone when they left as if looking out for trouble.

"Tommins Chemical Solutions?" Rugrat said, looking at the front of the building.

There were different plants and items in the window, but it was hard to see through the dirty glass.

Erik noticed that at the bottom of many of the ingredient request posters, this name had appeared.

"Let's check it out." Erik opened the door and a wave of heat and the smell of stored plants washed over him.

27
ALCHEMIST TOMMINS

Erik and Rugrat looked around the store. There were different viewing cases that held faintly glowing potions and powders contained in jade boxes. Placards were written out with the effects of each of the things on display.

Erik looked into one of the boxes, taking in a sharp breath.

> Name: **Unbridled Strength**
> Concoctions type: Powder
> Effects: Increase your overall strength stat by 3 points for 2 minutes. Go into Stamina fatigue for 10 minutes.
> Cost: 12 silvers, 45 coppers

That was more money than Erik had seen since coming to the Ten Realms. It was also one of the strongest effects he had ever seen. Increasing someone's stats by three points was incredible. That kind of power would allow someone to turn the tables on their opponent or win against an enemy at a higher level.

He looked over the shop. Different powders, a few potions, and ingredients were hung, sorted and stored around the place. It smelled of old wood and herbs, like a tea shop where the flavors have mixed together.

People moved in hushed reverence, calmly checking the store's wares.

A simple-looking man sat at the counter, resting his head on his hand as he tapped the cauldron on the table beside him, he was frowning, staring at the wall as if some great secret lay behind it. Or there was a new irritating stain on it.

Erik stepped towards the man.

"Recovery powders are on the right wall. The healing powders and potions are on the left wall," he didn't look up, his voice kind, but his tone telling Erik he had said such words till they were natural response.

Erik had glanced at the prices, while there were many people at other stores, the wares in this store were priced so high that few could purchase anything.

"Those formations, I don't know what they are, but they're damn powerful." Rugrat had learned a bit of formations and smithing, so his eyes picked up on the engraved runes and forms on the viewing cases.

"Sir, I saw your requests on the poster board. I was wondering if I might be able to get more information on these ingredients so that I won't bring you the wrong thing or damage them," Erik said in a respectful voice.

The man showed a note of surprise as he stopped tapping on the cauldron and looked up at Erik.

"A level eight fighter, but seems that you've got some brains as well." The man shrugged. "Well, if you can get me the ingredients, it doesn't matter much to me. Which items are you looking for?" There was a glint in the ordinary-looking man's eyes.

Erik and Rugrat could tell that he was anything but ordinary as he tried to mask his strength. His question was casual, but the man's eyes were locked onto Erik.

Erik knew that this was a test. "Wilderness Bane, Drakar Root, Holispun Feather, Moon Water, and Three-Colored Spirit Rose were the ones that I saw," Erik said.

"Seems that you're not just one of those people looking for a handout." The man smiled. "My name is Tommins. I hope you don't disappoint me." He pulled out a piece of paper and wrote down a list of different items before he pulled out an old book and put the list inside and threw it to Erik.

"If you learn this book and find at least five ingredients, then you might have some future as an alchemist." Tommins yawned.

Quest: Gathering Ingredients
Alchemist Tommins is looking for a number of ingredients for his various concoctions. The more you bring back, the greater the reward. Possible locations for the ingredients have been added to your map.
Requirements:
Find five ingredients Alchemist Tommins is looking for and deliver them to him.
Pass his test on the *Basic Alchemical Ingredients* book he has given you.
Rewards:
Based on your results
4,500 EXP

"Thanks you, Alchemist Tommins." Erik cupped his hands to the man.

Tommins nodded and went back to tapping on his cauldron.

Erik and Rugrat left the store. Erik looked at his map. There were a total of twenty-three locations marked on his map. They varied from large to small areas, some being just a few square meters and the largest being an area five hundred meters in diameter.

Still, it gave them places to go and look without wandering around the Beast Mountains for days, lost.

They quickly headed out of the city. They didn't want anyone to learn too much about them. They'd killed at least one person in Chonglu City. The city lord and his people might be after them, and they didn't know who was behind the poisoner.

Erik and Rugrat wanted to look at armor, but there simply wasn't any way for them to purchase it. Now they just had to try to make as much money as possible to upgrade their gear.

Exiting Wild Reaches Trading Outpost was as if they had entered another world.

The forests that they had walked through before had been large and seemed to stretch forever. Here there was a wildness to the forest. People seemed to hunch their shoulders as they moved forward. Powerful roars and animal calls could be heard in the distance; the sound of fighting could be faintly heard.

This wasn't a forest: it was a war zone, with the inhabitants clashing with one another to survive.

Erik and Rugrat looked at each other. It was similar to the pressure one would find themselves under when they entered a hostile country.

Everything was out to kill them and take their shit. Here there were no allies, only prey and predator. There was no knowing what powerful beasts and entities were to be found in the Beast Mountains.

They pulled out their bows and their quivers, moving into the forest toward one of the closest regions that Tommins's quest had marked.

Erik wanted to read the book but they didn't have time as they moved through the undergrowth.

People who were leaving the Wild Reaches Trading Outpost shot off in different directions, some having hunting grounds that they had scouted before, or looking for new ones.

Everyone here was looking to get that one score that they could make it big on and never have to enter the Beast Mountains ever again.

Erik and Rugrat looked out for them as they went off the path, making sure that no one followed them as people raced through the forest.

People showed off their agility, no longer needing to use the ground to move as they ran through the treetops with ease, or passed over the ground as if there weren't any obstacles in their path.

Erik and Rugrat continued on for an hour, their bows ready with an arrow notched, before they came across their first problem.

A shadow dropped from above as a burly creature dropped out of the tree, aiming to hit Rugrat.

"Rugrat!" Erik yelled out.

Rugrat threw himself to the side. He had the presence of mind to draw back his arrow and fire as he moved. The arrow slammed into the bear, throwing off its landing, letting out a pained howl.

Erik held his shot, moving to clear his line of sight. The creature let out a roar as it started to get up. Erik released his arrow. The stun effect cut off its howl abruptly as it twitched and missed its footing.

Rugrat's arrow had unerring accuracy as it pierced the creature's neck, sinking in halfway down the shaft.

Their attacks weren't strong to just kill the creature outright so they had to rack up continual wounds to bleed it out and wear it down.

Erik used a regular arrow, sticking it in the creature's back.

The creature howled. It was bleeding out of multiple spots, but nothing had been deep enough to kill it.

Erik used a piercing arrow; it went in through the creature's stomach and up into its chest.

The creature stiffened before it dropped. A tombstone appeared above its head.

"Sneaky fucker," Rugrat said.

Erik let out a sigh as Rugrat looted the creature. A white light appeared over his ring, showing that it had all gone into his storage ring automatically.

"Called a drop bear. Apparently, doesn't have a Mana core, but the meat and fur should be worth something. I got your regular arrow back." Rugrat waved his hand and passed it back to Erik. As long as they weren't broken, then it was possible to get one's arrows back.

Most of the enchanted arrows would be destroyed once they had been used up.

"Well, looks like things aren't going to be easy," Erik said, checking on his gains.

Skill: Marksman
Level: 19 (Novice)
No bonuses at this time. You must prove your skills first.

8,240/48,000 EXP till you reach Level 9

"You are fucking kidding me," Erik complained.

"What's up?" Rugrat asked.

"The amount of Experience I just got from that—it was less than five hundred," Erik complained.

"Well, it was a level six drop bear, dude. It was weaker than us, so the Experience just starts dropping," Rugrat reminded him.

"Oh, the sweet days of gloriously ascending levels," Erik lamented.

"Fuck, next thing you know, you'll be one of them weird poet types," Rugrat muttered.

They quickly set off again. They came across three more drop bears; one of them gave them a lower Mortal grade monster core. The others had only yielded meat and fur.

They checked their Experience and skill gains.

Rugrat, with his prior Experience, allowed him to increase his Marksman steadily. He had actually advanced into the Apprentice level and was headed toward Journeyman.

"So, what bonus and item did you get?" Erik asked.

"When I aim with my weapon, my eyes zoom, I guess?" Rugrat shrugged as he checked his storage ring. "I got a spell scroll. It allows me to buff the arrows I'm firing with an electric effect."

"Nice!" Erik said. Neither of these gains were small. With Rugrat's abilities, it would only increase his combat power. Erik was interested to see whether he could use the same spell on the rifles and firearms they had.

Skill: Marksman
Level: 20 (Novice)
No bonuses at this time. You must prove your skills first.

Erik's progress with the Marksman skill was much slower. He had messed around with bows but hadn't taken it on something serious. He was better than average but if he wanted to increase his power, he would need to spend a lot more time with it.

It was a little better than his Experience increase, which had slowed to a crawl because most of the things that they came across were a lower level than them.

9,650/48,000 EXP till you reach Level 9

Erik looked at the distance to the first location. They would reach it by the time night came around. There wasn't much room in their storage rings and they were realizing how weak their weapons were now.

If they used their rifles, they would be able to easily deal with everything that they had come across so far.

"Let's find somewhere we can sleep and then go to the location that Tommins gave us tomorrow," Rugrat said.

They headed off and found a cliff. Rugrat noticed something odd about it and they climbed up it a bit.

"Well, that's pretty grim," Rugrat said.

Erik was just going to ask what he meant as he made it into the cave. A skeleton faced the entrance to the cave.

They checked the cave. Everything was either useless or had been destroyed over time.

The only thing remaining was a gold brooch around the skeleton's neck and a storage ring on their finger.

Rugrat checked the broach, turning it over in his hand. He took the ring off as well and cut his finger, dripping some blood on the ring.

Once looted, the body started to slowly dissipate.

He smiled and then passed the ring to Erik, allowing him to see what was inside.

There were rations of water and food inside. Inside a storage ring, everything was placed in a kind of stasis, so food would never go bad. There was also a random assortment of meats, furs, and three different monster cores: two low grade Mortal cores and one mid-grade Mortal core.

There was also a casting staff and a selection of scrolls that had magical information. These books contained theory as well as a few spells. None of them were healing or did anything to help Erik. He tossed back the ring.

"What's with the broach?" Erik asked.

"I don't know, just a simple broach." Rugrat tossed it over.

"Well, anything can be a storage item." Erik dropped some blood onto the broach and looked inside. The area was over three meters square, putting it in as a Mortal Grade Major storage ring. It was worth three *gold* all by itself.

Erik was greeted by a body wearing armor still and all of their gear. There were also potions of Mana recovery, healing—ones that could also boost one's strength as well. All of the items were incredibly valuable, but that was the problem: they were worth too much. If he tried to take these anywhere to sell them they were more likely to end up dead than rich.

"What kind of person puts a body in a broach?" Erik asked.

"Huh? Wha-?" Rugrat looked at the body that appeared on the ground.

Erik threw the broach back to Rugrat as he looked at the man on the ground. The man looked as if he had died just minutes ago as his corpse hadn't aged in the storage ring.

Erik used Simple Organic Scan on the man, looking him over.

Unlike animals, people wouldn't disappear immediately if they were looted. It took up to three weeks, even if the body was looted, for it to disappear. Putting them in your storage ring meant that you didn't want their death to be discovered or you didn't have time to loot them and needed to run away.

Mortal grade major rings of holding had an ability that touched on something that the Earth grade storage rings could do as well: they could hold a storage ring inside of their storage space. This was one of the reasons that they were so prohibitively expensive. Although they were listed as a base price of three gold, they rarely went for anything less than seven gold.

Now, only one other storage item could be held in the Mortal major ring of holding, so it couldn't be holding another Mortal major ring of holding and then that was holding a storage ring and so on and so forth.

Rugrat was looking at the warrior's armor and his weapons, not the rings or the necklace around him. Erik looked at the rings. He had to cut himself again as his wound was already starting to heal itself.

With a few drops of blood, he covered the three different rings. Nothing happened with two of them, but the third did.

Erik quickly checked inside.

There were a number of powders inside; the warrior hadn't spent the money to get the more powerful potions.

There were also manuals on different fighting techniques, on smithing, and the upkeep of one's armor and weapons.

There were a few weapon ores as well as smithing tools to repair and maintain the armor.

Erik pulled the rings that didn't activate off the warrior's hand and looked at them.

Beyond limits
Weight: 0.1 kg
Charge: 73/100
Base Value: 2 Gold, 15 Silver, 7 Coppers
Slot: Takes up finger jewelry slot
Ability: Increase user's Stamina Regeneration by 10% (13 minutes left)

Greater Reaction
Weight: 0.1 kg
Base Value: 5 Gold, 43 Silver, 72 Coppers
Slot: Takes up finger jewelry slot
Ability: Increase user's Agility (+4)

The attributes and abilities of the two rings was stunning. The increased combat ability couldn't be matched in the First Realm.

"This armor looks like it's part of a set. Each piece gives the user an ability or enhancement, but with all of them together, the effects are multiplied. A 3% bonus of Strength on the legs will turn into 10% increase in Strength when one is wearing all of the pieces of armor," Rugrat said.

Rugrat touched it lovingly, as if it were the most beautiful thing he had ever seen.

"Well, I don't think he's going to be needing it anytime soon," Erik said.

Rugrat nodded and started to strip the man. The armor showed signs of being hit with magic. Melted metal, scarring and pitted as it was, would incite a war in the First Realm.

Erik pulled out the scroll he had found.

Simple Guide to Maintaining One's Journeyman-level Armor and Weapons.

"Heads up!" he yelled.

Rugrat looked over just as the scroll was coming over. With his increase in Agility, he caught it easily. He was about to shoot off an angry retort as the title of the scroll registered in his mind.

"What?" Rugrat sat down, forgetting about the armor in front of him as he started to look through the scroll.

It was a simple scroll, but here in the First Realm it was a treasure, allowing Rugrat to learn more about weapons and armor not normally found in the First Realm.

It had to be known that the armor in the First Realm could only reach the Novice level; the Second Realm, it would reach mid-Novice level, with some pieces in the Apprentice level.

The Third Realm would have different weapons and armors due to the realm's odd attributes compared to the other realms. In the Fourth Realm, the battlefield realm, one could find mid- to high-Journeyman level weapons and armors, with rare Expert armor appearing. Expert weapons and armor were enough to make the battlefield realm turn into a bloodbath with countless warrior sects and nations clashing over just one piece.

One's stats were the basis of their Strength: first, the power of their original stats; then what they got when leveling up; then the ultra-rare and hard quests that could increase one's stats. The Body Cultivation and Mana Gathering quests were these kinds of ultra-rare quests.

After that, it came down to one's weapons, armors, Alchemy concoctions, with skills and spells allowing them to draw greater power from their own bodies.

If someone in the First Realm was able to get a piece of Expert weaponry or armor, then the boost in their combat abilities would turn them into a god of the First Realm. Their strength couldn't be underestimated.

Erik could only shake his head bitterly at Rugrat's actions. It was understandable; he had only made a Novice smith and here he was looking at a manual talking about Journeyman-level armor.

If he could get some insights and knowledge from this simple manual, then it would be possible for him to increase his skill quickly and not waste his effort.

Erik held onto the ring, waiting for when Rugrat came back up to drop the rest of the items and information on him.

After all, there were a few maintenance kits and smithing tools inside the ring with ores that were incredibly hard to find in the First Realm.

The corner of his mouth lifted as he thought of what Rugrat's reaction might be.

He moved to the body and started to remove the armor. He stored the pieces away. Inside, he could see that there were complicated formations that were used to increase the power of the armor and the user's abilities.

It was truly not a simple set of armor.

There was a nasty wound on the warrior's neck where the last blow had landed, ending his life.

Erik was about to leave the body when he stopped. With a thought, he used his Simple Organic Scan spell and looked through the warrior's body, focusing on his body.

"I thought so," Erik muttered to himself, feeling a deep sense of excitement and anticipation.

The warrior had undergone Body Cultivation. His bones looked like polished jade and could be used for Apprentice-level weapons if someone were to refine them down. His blood had stilled in his veins, but Erik felt a sense of deep energy in them, no weaker than what he felt in his own veins.

As Erik's eyes looked through the man, searching out the secrets of Body Cultivation, he looked into the man's Mana channels.

Erik could only shake his head. The man's veins had clearly been altered; even now they were drawing in some Mana from the surrounding area. This was the power that came with altering one's body to increase their strength.

Clearly these Beast Mountains were not a simple place. There were many treasures and items to be found that weren't just in the bodies of high-leveled beasts and rare ingredients.

Erik moved the skeleton and body off to the side of the cave and sat down.

He pulled out the different manuals from the two. Most dealt with swordsmanship, using a shield, or casting high-leveled spells.

This information would be useful to others but Erik and Rugrat were walking down the path of a Marksman currently. Their biggest gains were from the two deceased's supporting Alchemy concoctions and their support manuals.

Erik pulled out another manual. It was a well-worn book but kept in good condition. Erik shook his head. Clearly this was a basic manual but to Erik it was an unmitigated treasure.

Basics of Mana Gathering: From Mana Drops to Core Compression.

28

MIDDAY MOSS

Erik closed the book in his hands gently, as if wary to damage the well-worn book. It quickly disappeared into his storage ring as he rubbed the ring, his gaze thoughtful.

There were thirteen Mana gates within one's body. Erik had always wondered where the fourteenth gate that was mentioned in the Mana gate-related quest came from. Now he understood.

The thirteen Mana gates created an array inside his body, all of them meeting up at the location of his core.

When someone's Mana Regeneration reached level fifty, then they would be able to compress a Mana core easily. If they had resources and aids, they could compress it earlier.

There was a third mythical possibility: once one opened all thirteen Mana gates, then there was a chance that they would be able to open their gate core.

All other compressed cores were simply called Mana cores. Once one compressed a core, they would open another gate according to the Mana gate quest—the elusive fourteenth gate.

If someone was able to open all fourteen gates, and open their Mana core, then they would undergo a Mana Rebirth, which would greatly increase their control and power over the natural Mana around them.

This was, however, legend and the information stopped at this point.

The main information talked about how one could move from the Vapor, Mist, and Drop stage, culminating in the Core Compression stage.

With these aids, one would be able to advance through Mana Gathering stages easier.

Erik turned his attention to his Mana system. His total Mana Regeneration was only at fifteen. He had five stat points to use when he went to sleep, but according to his plan, he would increase his Mana Regeneration by two.

It would take him to seventeen Mana Regeneration, close to the twenty to twenty-nine needed to advance into the Mist level.

With this manual, he was confident that he could compress his Mana enough to reach that stage. Once he did, then he could attempt to open another Mana gate. He felt that at his current strength, it would take a day to open the next Mana gate. He didn't have that time.

His reasoning was simple. The first gate took some six hours to open and the second nearly twelve. Based on this, it would probably take up to twenty-four hours for him to break open his fourth Mana gate.

If he was able to compress his Mana further, he felt that it was highly possible he could break open that next Mana gate in less than a day.

"It would be nice to have some of these Mana agglomerating pills or even some Mana Gathering powder," Erik complained. After reading about the different aids that were seen as common in whatever realm this mage came from, Erik could only sigh helplessly.

If he wanted those resources, he would need to make them himself, or find other ways to push forward.

If his healing abilities had been stronger, it would have been easier for him to heal himself. Instead of hanging onto life by just a thread, he would be able to easily conquer the poison and overcome his tempering of blood.

"With healing as a support, if I was able to find poisons for the different temperings, then I could advance through quicker."

But he didn't have the resources, so he would need to rely on his own efforts, skills, and abilities.

Erik pulled out a ration and started eating as the sun started to set. Rugrat was still reading over the entire maintenance scroll. He had rolled it out and was moving up and down, comparing the information and trying to gain greater insight. He was also noting down different important bits of information on his own pad of paper.

Erik took out the gift from Alchemist Tommins. The piece of paper with the different ingredients fell out. He checked his map and the marker listed as *Possible Midday Moss Location,* opening the general compendium on Alchemy ingredients and searching for midday moss.

Once he'd read through it, he checked the list of ingredients against the information in the book to gain a greater understanding on them.

Erik let out a short laugh. Many of these ingredients were rare, for the simple fact that they were hard to discern. Take the midday moss. It was a simple-looking moss that grew on Slastz rock, but it was only in the midday sun that someone was able to tell it was different from common moss.

Erik had gotten through a third of the book before he found himself unable to keep his eyes open. “You going to be up for a bit?” Erik asked.

“Yeah, I’ve got first watch.” Rugrat stood and rubbed his eyes.

“You might find some more useful things in there.” Erik tossed him the warrior’s ring.

Rugrat had a look inside as Erik pulled out his sleeping bag and quickly got ready for bed.

Rugrat started to pull out different items that were collected inside the ring.

Erik got into his sleeping bag and went to sleep, only to find a screen greeting him.

You have 5 attribute points to use.

He quickly distributed the points with one to Strength, Agility, and Stamina instead of Stamina Regeneration as he had gained one point from tempering his blood already.

The last two went straight into Mana Regeneration.

He confirmed his selection and looked on his new character sheet.

Character Sheet
Name: Erik West
Level: 8
Race: Human
Titles:
From the Grave
Strength: (Base 7) +6
130
Agility: (Base 6) +8
70
Stamina: (Base 10) +1
165
Mana: (Base 3) +0
30
Mana Regeneration (Base 3) +14
4.15/s
Stamina Regeneration: (Base 7) +11
4.35/s

Erik woke a few hours later and took over for Rugrat. They kept watch throughout the night. Sounds of fighting could be heard and alarms as creatures in the night snuck up on the sleeping adventurers or fought in the depths of the darkness.

Erik and Rugrat cleared up all of their gear in the morning, making ready to move. The cave had been an unexpected windfall.

They leapt out of the cave and headed for the marked area on their maps. They took their time as Erik waited for midday to come.

As the book said, there was a spot of moss that started to glow purple in the midday sun. Erik carefully peeled it back. A potent fragrance was released, making Erik's muscles relax and feel energized slightly.

Creatures in the area could smell the moss. Howls could be heard as they rushed to claim it.

Erik and Rugrat quickly headed for the next location on the map.

As they were running out, they caught the sight of an omagree. It was a mutated monster with four powerful lower limbs and pincers that it used to cut its enemies apart. It was covered in green chitin and looked similar to a praying mantis but about five times larger.

Erik and Rugrat split apart as the animal charged at them. They kept on running away from where the moss had been, which was quickly turning into a battleground for the surrounding animals whose territories bordered the moss's location.

They drew their bows and fired their arrows.

Rugrat's arrows glanced off the mantis while Erik's arrow missed completely, hitting a tree. He'd used one of his precious piercing arrows, so it cut cleanly through the side of the tree.

Erik could only pull out another arrow as the omagree skidded around, crashing into a tree to face the two who had run past it.

Rugrat's M40 appeared in his hands. He raised the rifle to his shoulder and fired in one fluid motion. Gray blood splattered over the area as the omagree let out a howl; half of its head was missing.

Rugrat was already working the bolt action on his rifle. As the omagree made to move forward, Rugrat fired again. His Strength and Agility made his action fluid and easy as the recoil barely affected his aim.

The omagree's cries were cut off as it dropped to the ground.

Erik was closest to the creature as its tombstone appeared. Erik took everything from the tombstone. The omagree faded away in light as Erik's new storage ring glowed, the items being deposited inside as they took off again. Rugrat found the casings for his two rounds and put them in his storage ring.

They ran on, not wanting to get caught up in the animals that were racing toward where the omagree had died, smelling blood.

The two figures flashed through the forest before they came to a riverside. They looked around for threats, getting their breathing back under control. Erik and Rugrat had escaped the animals fighting over the midday moss. They quickly checked their map and headed off in search of the next ingredient Tommins wanted.

"I hope that the reward is goddamn amazing," Rugrat said as they took off.

"Didn't you just make it to level nine?" Erik asked with a bit of jealousy. With killing the omagree, Rugrat had increased his Marksman and his Experience greatly, becoming a high-level Apprentice Marksman.

"Yeah, wish we could use our guns more," Rugrat said.

Erik grunted. Each round they used was another one that they couldn't make. They could reload them, but they only had a limited amount of gunpowder, bullets, and premade primers.

Erik opened up his notifications as his heart calmed down.

Skill: Alchemy
Level: 7 (Novice)
No bonuses at this time. You must prove your skills first.

10,700/48,000 EXP till you reach Level 9

29
SNATCHING YELLOW CREEPER

Erik and Rugrat were both frustrated that they couldn't defeat the omagree without Rugrat using his rifle.

There was nothing that they could do currently—their gear was too low ranked unless they chose to become a mage or warrior and use the gear that they had found with the skeleton and dead warrior. At that point, they would be hunted in the First Realm for those same items.

Screwed if they did—screwed if they didn't.

It only increased their drive to gain more power!

Their skills and their levels were too low. They needed to get into the Second Realm so that they might get access to more instructional manuals and resources.

They moved toward their next search zone. Instead of moving freely, they moved in stealth, stopping and listening to the forest as they moved, making sure that there was no one around.

Erik held up his fist as they came across a large striped panther lying on a log in the sun.

Erik pulled out his shortbow. He sighted on the panther and drew back one of his piercing arrows. His arm shook slightly, even with his high Strength stat. Erik took his time before releasing the arrow.

It struck the panther in the shoulder instead of its side but pierced deep into its body.

The panther lurched upward before drunkenly swaying and falling over to the side. A tombstone appeared above it.

Erik grimaced. He'd wanted to hit the panther in the side but his aim was off.

Rugrat patted him on the shoulder, sensing his frustration.

Erik lowered the bow, and Rugrat quickly moved forward to gather the loot.

"Minor Mortal core," Rugrat said.

"Nice," Erik said, not feeling all that motivated. Rugrat made using the bow look easy, while he was wasting precious piercing arrows all over the place.

Other than his rifle, Erik felt that his fighting skills didn't amount to much, being useless. He had been a combat medic; how would he still be one if he couldn't even fight the opponents in front of them?

He'd just be some rear echelon mother fucker twiddling his thumbs.

He checked on the notifications that had appeared with the death of the panther.

He didn't get a notification on getting a stealth attack anymore. It was added to the attack as a hidden mechanic.

A part of him wondered whether the panther would have died without the additional attack help.

Skill: Stealth
Level: 12 (Novice)
No bonuses at this time. You must prove your skills first.

Skill: Marksman
Level: 21 (Novice)
No bonuses at this time. You must prove your skills first.

32,000/48,000 EXP till you reach Level 9

Finally they reached their next search zone. The two of them separated to cover more ground faster. They stayed in stealth, looking for anything that might be a threat and the yellow creeper that Tommins was looking for.

Erik stopped as he saw that there was a hidden ravine in the search area. At the end of it there was a cave.

He used his binoculars to look inside. He could see a leopard almost the size of a van lying down. Its tail twitched from side to side, showing it was awake but didn't find anything interesting.

Erik was still as he looked at the animal. He quickly looked away and put the binoculars down. A cold sweat fell down his back. The leopard was lazing at the entrance to its den but the aura it gave off was no less than a level eleven creature.

From level nine to ten, there was a major jump. Instead of one just getting five extra Experience points, they would get ten and gain the ability to ascend to the Second Realm. Most of the creatures that were in the Ten Realms would automatically ascend, though there were a few that didn't do so.

This leopard appeared to be one of them.

Erik moved away, undiscovered by the leopard, before he continued his search, his heart beating rapidly. As he continued to search, he had a bad feeling in his gut.

He searched his half of the area before heading back to where he and Rugrat had broken apart.

"Did you find anything?" Erik asked.

"Nothing," Rugrat said. Seeing Erik's face sour, Rugrat let out a sigh.

"I think I might know where it is. In a level eleven leopard's den," Erik said slowly.

"Well, fuck."

"If we could draw it out, then we would be able to sneak in behind it and get to the creepers before escaping," Erik said.

"So, piss off another creature, bring it here to anger the leopard and draw it out, then go into its house, steal its yellow creeper and make off like gangbusters." Rugrat paused. "Actually it isn't the worst plan I've ever heard."

"Thanks. Your confidence is inspiring," Erik said dryly.

Rugrat shrugged as they broke down their roles. Rugrat would draw a beast close to entice the leopard into defending his territory. Erik, who knew more about the ingredient, would sneak into the leopard's lair, harvest the yellow creeper, and head back out to meet up with Rugrat.

They broke apart once again.

Erik was watching the ravine and the leopard's cave at the end of it. He made sure to stay downwind so that it wouldn't smell him. Time moved by slowly as he crouched there. The longer he was there, the greater chance of the leopard finding his position.

Finally there was a roar in the distance.

The leopard's head snapped up as it looked over at where the noise was coming from. A low growl was transmitted from its neck as it sensed the challenge to its home and territory.

There was another howl in the distance, closer this time.

The leopard let out a yell. The power contained within made Erik shake in fear.

The leopard's basic stats were impressive. The fact that it had become a level eleven existence only made it all the more terrifying. Countless other beasts must have fallen under its claws for it to gain that kind of power.

It lurched up to its feet as more howls rang back.

What the hell did Rugrat get? There sounds to be five creatures, not one!

Erik didn't have time as the leopard shot forward, causing the grass to lay low and stir up the dirt on the ground.

Erik stayed still. It was hard to not move as he gripped tighter on his rifle, not trusting his bow skills in the slightest.

The leopard rushed off into the distance.

Erik stayed low and moved forward. Checking the surroundings, he quickly disappeared down the ravine and into the cave.

He pulled out some moonstones. He only had a few of them as they had taken up the remainder of his coppers before they left Wild Reaches Trading Outpost.

He used the moonstone to look around. He heard a dripping noise in the depths of the cave. Following the noise, he came across a large pool with a creeper hanging along a wall and toward the water's edge.

It looked exactly how the ingredient book had described!

Erik saw another glow to the side, near a padded area where the leopard must sleep.

"Blood Vine, Gi Grass, Spiritual root of the Guyen tree," Erik muttered under his breath. There were ten to fifteen treasures hidden around the leopard's sleeping area. Erik didn't know many of them, but from what he did know, he knew that they were rare ingredients. Tommins might not have put them on the list, but he or the Blue Lotus might give them a good price for them.

Erik didn't immediately rush over to them, he needed to harvest the yellow creeper first.

He moved to the rockface that the creeper was on. He took out his knife and cut off some of the creeper.

A notification appeared in front of him.

Harvest Failed!

Erik looked at the macerated-looking yellow creeper that was slowly turning green in his hands.

You have gained yellow creeper pods (damaged)

Erik was about to store it away when he heard roaring in the distance.

A group of people appeared around the Chonglu Totem. An older and dignified-looking man flashed a badge to the guards, who could only bitterly bow their heads before the group headed away from the totem and toward the eastern gate of Chonglu City. Their gazes showed disdain for those around them, making people stand back from the streets.

"Who are they?" one of the passersby asked their friend.

"Those are the disciples from the Willful Institute. It's a sect with power based in the Second Realm. If not for the odd nature of the Third Realm and raging battlefield of the Fourth Realm, it's thought that they would be a power in the Third Realm," their friend replied.

"Why would they be in the First Realm?" the first person asked.

"Every few years, the sects from the Second Realm come to our Beast Mountains to have a contest. They send the mountain into uproar and pull out many resources from the mountain. I heard that they're even looking for a greater treasure," the friend responded.

"A greater treasure than those guarded by the beasts in the mountain?"

"The Beast Mountains has beasts that are a lot stronger than most beast-controlled areas in the Second Realm. It holds a great allure to sects and people from the first three realms. It is said that they are looking for a treasure that increases the strength of the beasts and allows the Beast Mountain to have such great natural treasures."

"Isn't the Third Realm filled with natural treasures though?"

"Yes, but the Third Realm is filled with powerful beasts, and has a strange environment. Wouldn't it be safer coming to the relatively tame First Realm?"

The people talked in hushed and respectful tones as this Willful Institute reached the city limits. Their speed shot up as they rushed off down the road toward the Beast Mountains.

"Why must we come to the First Realm, Elder Rei?" A proud-looking man with an arrogant demeanor asked the older man who was leading the group.

"If one does not face real battles in their life, then they will not gain any true achievements, Yan. You might be one of the strongest in the Willful sect's Eastern Division, but in the whole of the Ten Realms, you are but a frog in a well. To reach greater heights, you must increase not only your level, but your combat power." Elder Rei looked at this Yan with a cool gaze.

Yan lowered his head. A flash of embarrassment appeared on his face as he bowed slightly to hide the anger hidden deep in his eyes at the elder's cutting words. Feeling that they weren't accurate.

30
HARVESTING REWARDS

Harvest Failed!

Again, that merciless notification appeared.

"You fucking goddamn mother fucking creeper! I will harvest you if it's the last thing that I do!" Erik declared, kicking the wall.

He brandished his knife once again but he didn't attack the creepers again. Instead, he once again thought on what he had done with the two previous attempts and cross-checked it against what he remembered in the book.

He opened the book once again, muttering dark thoughts about the yellow creeper. After a few moments, he put it away and then looked at the yellow creeper.

"Defeated by a goddamn creeper. Thank God Rugrat isn't here," Erik grumbled as his blade moved, freeing the yellow creeper from the rock slowly. Then he got to the root buried in the wall. He used his knife and hand to gently pry the root from its home.

He finally pulled it all out from the recess. The base of the plant and the roots were easy to separate. If they were destroyed, then the potency would be lost as a best case, and it would be destroyed as a worse case.

Erik pulled it out and got a notification.

Skill: Alchemy
Level: 9 (Novice)
No bonuses at this time. You must prove your skills first.

Instead of the cold-blooded one from before, this one put a smile on his face.

Using what he had learned, he continued to harvest as much yellow creeper as he could reach.

There were only a few tufts left on the rock surface as he rushed over to the leopard's sleeping area. He cleared the area around the different ingredients and started to get to work, slowly extracting them from the ground.

He worked methodically, taking every precaution as the noises from outside of the ravine got quieter as the leopard finished off the animals Rugrat had lured into its territory.

Even as Erik knew that his time was running out, he didn't panic. He knew from the yellow creepers that panic would only lead to him failing to harvest the ingredients.

He didn't know what the ingredients were but seeing that they were around the leopard's sleeping area, he knew that they wouldn't be ordinary.

Sudden silence fell over the area as the leopard had defended its home. There were five different plants but Erik had already harvested four of them.

He grit his teeth; his knife moved slowly as he loosened the glowing bulbous plant from the ground. It was latched onto a collection of rocks with odd runes that surrounded a bone with runes engraved into it.

Erik pulled it all away from the ground and placed it into his storage ring.

With them all secured, Erik didn't dare to stick around. He rushed away from the cave and out of the ravine, toward where Rugrat and he were supposed to meet up.

He entered the area when a furious roar ripped through the forest.

"Time to get to running," Rugrat said, coming out of the underbrush.

Erik followed him out. They heard the noises of the leopard's growing anger, and they increased their speed as they didn't want to leave any sign behind.

The entire area seemed to be in fear as the king had gone into a rage. Creatures rushed to hide and others finished off their fights and lowered themselves to the ground to show that they weren't a threat.

Erik and Rugrat only increased their speed as they left the area.

They left the leopard's region behind, letting out a sigh as nighttime descended and darkness started to set in.

Erik felt odd, as if being watched. He put it off as just his fear as they looked for a place to stay.

After some searching, they climbed a set of trees and set up hammocks, securing them to the trees.

Rugrat took first watch as they ate rations, not wanting to light a fire in case they drew more attention. With each of the different search areas, they moved deeper into the Beast Mountains.

Erik quickly checked his gains from the day.

Skill: Stealth
Level: 16 (Novice)
No bonuses at this time. You must prove your skills first.
Skill: Alchemy
Level: 13 (Novice)
No bonuses at this time. You must prove your skills first.

32,000/48,000 EXP till you reach Level 9

His Alchemy skill had increased greatly, with his stealth jumping up as they'd evaded detection from the leopard.

Erik relaxed as he checked his Mana system. There looked to be less Mana in his veins as it was further compacted now. The power in that compressed vapor was much more terrifying than before.

Erik hoped that it would be what he needed to reach the Vapor stage. Then he could use the compressed Mana with the information that was contained in the manuals he had received to open another Mana gate.

It was a big undertaking but the rewards of doing so would put him well ahead of everyone else in the First Realm.

If people in the higher realms heard his thoughts, they would be shocked.

Erik settled his nerves down and started to circulate his Mana through his channels according to a rhythm written in the manual. It was slow at first but he increased its speed as time went on.

The effect was similar to a centrifugal system: the faster it moved in a certain path, the more compressed it would become.

Sweat started to fall down Erik's brow as he concentrated on circulating his Mana properly.

The vapor started to agglomerate as it was picked up in his Mana channels. As the circulations became faster, it started to congeal together, its power increasing step by step.

Finally Erik couldn't compress it anymore. His head felt as if it were going to burst as he needed to concentrate for so long.

The vapor underwent a change as it moved through his channels, still at great speeds but it was compressed into a new form.

A sense of power rushed through Erik's body as he let out a breath, nearly collapsing back into his hammock as notifications filled his vision.

He looked at them with a tired smile as power flooded his body.

Quest Completed: Mana Gathering Cultivation
The path of a Mana Gathering cultivator is not easy. To stand at the top, one must forge their own path forward.
Requirements:
Reach Mana Mist Level
Rewards:
+2 to Mana pool
+10,000 EXP
Quest: Mana Gathering Cultivation
The path of a Mana Gathering cultivator is not easy. To stand at the top, one must forge their own path forward.
Requirements:
Reach Mana Drop Level
Rewards:
+4 to Mana pool
+100,000 EXP

42,000/48,000 EXP till you reach Level 9

Erik went on to check on his stats to see how his character sheet might have changed.

Character Sheet
Name: Erik West
Level: 8
Race: Human
Titles:
From the Grave
Strength: (Base 7) +6
130
Agility: (Base 6) +8
70
Stamina: (Base 10) +1
165
Mana: (Base 5) +0
50
Mana Regeneration (Base 3) +14
4.15/s
Stamina Regeneration: (Base 7) +12
4.55/s

Seeing the rewards for reaching the Drop stage and his new stats, Erik felt a deep sense of satisfaction. The Mana Gathering system was much easier to develop than the Body Cultivation system, but both held their own power.

It would be easier to only walk down one path, but Erik didn't want to have regrets. He wanted to at least try out both systems. The worst that could happen was that he would fail to increase his power in one system but his overall strength would be greater than someone who had only attempted one system.

The other issue was that the energy required to train two systems would make him work two times harder compared to others, but the rewards would be much greater.

He didn't waver from his decision in the slightest as he quickly recovered.

Once again he calmed himself, ready to move onto the second part of his plan and attempt to open another Mana gate.

He gathered up his Mana. A new sense of power rushed through his body as he directed the Mana through his veins, concentrating on the Mana gate in the base of his right foot.

Erik's body shook as the sound of someone hitting a door rang through his mind.

Unseen by Erik, a pair of cold eyes looked through the trees at the two people in their hammocks.

A cold glint passed through these eyes as it sniffed the air, the scent from its lair the same as that on these two men.

31
COMPLICATIONS IN OPENING A MANA GATE

A roar cut through the night's quiet, startling Erik as his Mana spear hit the edge of his Mana gate. The rampant Mana rushed through his body and ravaged his foot.

He let out a cry as he started healing himself. His eyes snapped open. Cold fear ran through him. If one failed in opening their Mana gate, then it could be sealed forever, or they could suffer a backlash with the power ravaging their Mana channels.

Even the small backlash had nearly crippled his foot.

"Leopard!" Rugrat yelled, grabbing onto the tree next to him and jumping off as he pulled out his pistol, firing at the leopard.

"Shit." Erik tried to keep the flow of Mana going to his Mana gate. If it was stopped, then his gate would be sealed.

Erik pulled everything into his storage ring as he jumped for the tree as well.

The leopard tore through where Rugrat had been but missed and landed on another tree. Erik and Rugrat snapped off shots. The leopard's roars had a sense of pain in them. Their rounds had hit the creature but its natural defense meant that the bullets, although they'd done damage, weren't enough.

The leopard jumped off the tree and sailed toward Erik. He dropped from the tree, trying to keep the Mana flowing right as he slammed into the ground. He let out a groan as he landed on his feet and rolled. The Mana in his foot missed again, tearing apart his foot as he had to divert Mana to heal his foot.

The leopard didn't spare him another glance as it charged Rugrat, who had pulled out his personal rifle.

He was hit in the arm, his rifle spinning as his arm was opened up. "Fuck!" He tried to get away from the leopard but its claws were buried deep in his arm.

Erik fired into the leopard's back and unloaded his magazine. Rugrat finally got free, dropping to the ground below as Erik reloaded his pistol.

The leopard charged Rugrat again. Erik rushed forward, hitting the leopard in the side and pushing it away from Rugrat.

The leopard let out a growl as it turned on Erik. Its claws ripped into his chest, raking against his ribs as he screamed. Putting his pistol against the leopard's chest, he pulled the trigger again and again. The leopard's strength started to quickly leave it as it let out a roar. Knowing that it was about to die, it was going to take Erik out with it. Its head shot forward to rip out Erik's neck with his jaws.

A silenced rifle went off, hitting the leopard in the face. Its head sunk in partially as the light went out of its eyes. Its weight fell on Erik as he was stuck under it.

Rugrat hobbled over. He put his rifle away as a tombstone appeared above the leopard.

Its claws had ripped through Erik's chest. The damage to his body wasn't simple.

Rugrat's arm was in a bad way as well.

Erik couldn't move his hands and there was no space for him to pull out items from his storage ring. He focused on healing and attacking the Mana gate in his foot. With the strain and trying to keep himself from falling into Mana fatigue, he had to be extremely careful.

Rugrat struggled with the leopard before clicking on its tombstone and looting everything from it. It started to dissipate as Rugrat grunted. He could move the lightening load of the leopard. He got to work assessing Erik's wounds and started to pull out the priceless healing powders, using them on Erik's wounds.

"Fix yourself," Erik said.

"I'm using a healing spell already," Rugrat said,

Erik looked at Rugrat's arm. It was healing, albeit slowly, speaking to the damage it had gone through.

Erik let out a hiss as the powder went to work. A powerful healing energy went through his body, focused on the wounds. Quickly the wounds started to close up as the medicinal strength of the powder got into Erik's veins, healing his internal injuries.

He coughed up blood as he focused on opening his Mana gate. The strain on his body wasn't small. Thankfully, his tempered blood made his recovery much faster. Erik focused himself, feeling a jab in his side as painkiller flooded his system. He relaxed and the pain dimmed. But it became hard to focus the mind as he attacked the Mana gate.

Rugrat quickly pulled out a monster core. "Absorb this. It should give you the energy you need to open your Mana gate, or at least help out."

Erik took the monster core in his hand as an option appeared in front of him.

Monster Core
Do you wish to absorb this Lesser Mortal Grade monster core?
YES/NO
You will gain 5,000 EXP

Monster cores could be used for a great number of things. At their most basic level, one could craft powerful weapons, armor, and concoctions with them. They could also be used to recover one's Stamina and their Mana, and heal while increasing a person's Experience.

One could use monster cores again and again, but the power wasn't clean. After some time of absorbing the same monster cores, a person would gain a debuff, lowering the amount of Experience that they could gain.

It was a short-term solution to power. If one was to take more powerful monster cores or to have the resources to clear the debuff, then they could rapidly increase in power. This was something that the elites of certain sects and families could enjoy.

Some might call this the "pay to play" method, where one used money to increase their levels and abilities directly. It was, but that was the truth in the Ten Realms, strength ruled, so what if you abused the system a bit here and there?

The monster core cracked as the cloudy and dirty-looking core shattered. Threads of energy wrapped around Erik, being absorbed into his body. Erik felt his Experience increasing as the strength in his body surged.

Erik took direct control of the Mana in his body that had now stabilized. He drove it toward his Mana gate. His body shook as the final glow from the monster core was absorbed into Erik's body.

The sound of someone hammering against a gate filled Erik's body. Cracks started to form on the Mana gate. It was a proud edifice—unassailable—but here it was being worn down again and again.

Rugrat watched over Erik, retrieving his weapons as he looked for the spent brass. Most of it had been caught by his storage ring, but he couldn't waste one cartridge.

An hour and a half later, there was a breaking sound as the Mana in the area was stirred up. Threads of Mana were drawn into Erik's Mana gates as power flooded through his body.

Skill: Marksman
Level: 25 (Apprentice)
Long-range weapons are familiar in your hands. When aiming, you can zoom in x2.0.

Upon advancing into the Apprentice level of Marksman, you will be rewarded with one randomly selected item related to this skill.
You have received the Fine Arrows blueprint
+10,000 EXP

You have successfully opened 4 Mana gates.
+1 to Mana Pool

You have opened another Mana gate!
+1 to Mana Regeneration

Quest Updated: Opening the Fourteen Gates
Congratulations! You have opened your fourth Mana gate.
Requirements:
Clear all of your fourteen gates (4/14)
Rewards:
+1 to Mana Regeneration base stat
Undergo Mana Body Rebirth
1,400,000 EXP

You have reached Level 9
When you sleep next, you will be able to increase your attributes by: *5 points.*

13,750/64,000 EXP till you reach Level 10

Erik couldn't help but smile a bit. It had been a close call, but he had attained level nine, just one step away from becoming level ten, the threshold one needed to pass in order to ascend to the Second Realm.

His Marksman skill had also upgraded, giving him the benefit of increased magnification when aiming.

The hidden aspects of Marksman were also shown as his ability to shoot had increased steadily to the point where he could probably compete with the old Rugrat in terms of accuracy.

"Morning there, Sleeping Beauty. You good to go? We need to move," Rugrat said.

"Yeah." Erik got up.

Rugrat had changed his clothes and his wounds were healed with the combination of healing powder and his own healing spells.

"I thought that I would run a whole lot less once I got out," Rugrat complained as they took off into the night.

"Quit your whining. You're faster than anyone back on Earth," Erik said.

"I heard that you can get tamed beasts—wouldn't that be nicer?"

"Rugrat, the last time you had a 'good' idea, you made dinner for everyone on base and dosed it with so much hot sauce that even Rossy was left crying," Erik said.

"Well, I thought you could handle it," Rugrat complained.

"The bathrooms certainly couldn't. Do you know how painful one-ply is in a blue rocket that's so warm it's almost combustible from static when you have to run to the bathroom every ten minutes with forty other guys doing the hokey-pokey don't-let-me-crap-my-pants dance?"

"It was a good idea. It just didn't turn out that well. You guys also force-fed me the rest of it!"

"It took us four hours to find you and we had to keep switching out people or else they wouldn't be able to hold on!"

"Come on, that was pretty funny," Rugrat said.

Erik let out a tired laugh, knowing that there was no winning against Rugrat. He hid the smile that was forming at the corners of his mouth.

Rugrat let out a muffled curse as he tripped on something and fell down a small ravine. "Great. I wasn't looking for my exfoliating mud bath." Rugrat got out of the mud, flicking his hand to try to get some more of the mud off him. "Hopefully the next spell we can learn is night vision."

"Or a spell to clean or disinfect," Erik said, looking around.

"Oh, the things I would do for a shower," Rugrat said with a glow in his eyes.

Erik shivered slightly, not fully wanting to know what extent Rugrat would go to get a shower.

32

DEFINED ROLES

Erik hadn't seen anything like it before. Erik waited until the next day before he gave it over to Rugrat.

"A blueprint?" Rugrat said breathlessly.

"There something wrong with it?" Erik asked. It looked simple enough—a rough drawing with notations detailing the different size and makeup of the combined parts.

"Blueprints are really damn rare. They're also a big help in letting people understand how to build the item. Usually when you're crafting something, you need to figure out what you want, the shape the form, all the different parts required. Unless someone has told you what is needed or you have a blueprint.

"Using this, the materials are broken down. The way to put them together is also revealed. With this it's more like Lego than crafting, though you get a much better idea of how to craft the item," Rugrat said.

"So, basically a building guide for dummies." Erik grinned.

"Yes, in a way."

"Well, this any use to you?" Erik asked.

"No, but if we took it to the Blue Lotus or maybe a crafter who builds arrows, we can get a lot for it. We might even be able to trade for a blueprint that is actually useful for us."

"Take it. You know what to do with it more than me and I'm horrible with a bow," Erik said.

"Yeah, you ain't the best," Rugrat agreed.

"I think that I'm going to try to work to become a melee fighter," Erik said.

"You sure?" Rugrat looked at Erik with concern.

"Well, I've already been torn apart once. What is it to do it a few more times?" Erik laughed.

"Casual dismemberment—another sign that your friend has officially left the building," Rugrat said.

"Look, you're good at long range and if I give you Big Momma, then there's little that could stand up to you. I run crowd control. I hold them back—you pick them off. Otherwise we have what we had last night: the two of us trying to do the same thing and the enemy getting among us and tearing us apart."

Rugrat sunk into thought. Clearly he didn't want his friend jumping into the enemy's jaws so that he could get more time to set up his shots, but Erik made a valid point.

"If you go melee class, then we need to try to increase your Body Cultivation, get you some training manuals to increase the power you can pull from your body and display. Then you're taking all of the healing concoctions and increase your healing abilities," Rugrat said.

Erik was touched by how much his friend was looking out for him.

Finally for the first time they had nailed down their roles: Erik would be the healer and close range; Rugrat would be the long-range rogue type. They would both be able to heal as support, with Rugrat specializing in smithing while Erik would seek out more information on Alchemy. Erik was interested in it, but the information and resources here were too limited so Erik could only wait until he gained more knowledge.

"Well, then, our two biggest goals should be to get as much gold as possible and level up as fast as possible." Erik tossed Rugrat a petty Mortal grade monster core.

Rugrat looked up before sitting down, swallowing any words he might have said as the Mana core shattered and that rampant energy entered his body, strengthening it from the inside.

Erik stood guard, looking around the forest. Right now, potions and concoctions to increase the toughness of his body and go through the five temperings were incredibly hard to find.

If it's impossible to find easy ways to do it, then the other way was to use poison.

Erik checked through the broach once again, looking over the healing potions and other potions contained within.

The healing potions were incredibly powerful, so much that Erik wondered how people could die in the higher realms. With the potions, he was more confident about walking down the path of poisons to temper his body bit by bit.

A powerful fluctuation emerged from deep within Rugrat's body. He opened his eyes. The glow within made Erik shiver. It was as if he were looking at a slumbering beast, ready to attack at the slightest movement or confrontation.

Rugrat let out a slow breath.

"Congratulations on reaching level ten," Erik said.

"Thanks." Rugrat smiled.

"Want to take a nap and consolidate your gains? We've got the time."

"All right." Rugrat lay down against a log and closed his eyes.

Nothing happened for a few hours. Then, the breeze started to change as threads of energy from the First Realm were gathered into Rugrat's body. His entire body went through a transformation, becoming more powerful.

The energy continued to gather in Rugrat's body until there was a dull noise that sounded like an explosion. Rugrat's aura surged as he broke through the tenth level, becoming an existence that could enter the Second Realm.

The forest calmed down as Rugrat slowly woke up.

He opened and closed his hands, feeling the power contained within. A look of glee appeared on his face. "Damn! That's a fricking rush! Better than playing tag on the Fourth of July with Roman candles!"

"You have a very different idea of fun compared to normal people."

"You've never played Roman candle fights?"

"I did. Remember fricking Egypt's barracks? You fuckers came in, all Roman candles blazing, while I was asleep in my tent!"

"Oh yeah, I forgot about that," Rugrat said. "Good memories!"

"Maybe for some, you overgrown two-year-old!"

Erik and Rugrat joked around a bit before they started to make a plan for what they would do next.

First they'd scout out the next plots. They had been charging in every time and if they'd been taught anything, it was that sometimes having a plan was a good idea, or else they'd get their beauty sleep interrupted.

If there was an opportunity, they would take it to gather the different ingredients that Tommins desired. If they couldn't gather them as they moved into the Beast Mountains, they'd gather them on their way out.

So they set out again.

Rugrat and Erik searched for any signs of other predators in the area. The farther they went into the Beast Mountain Range, the more powerful the animals became. Thankfully, with Rugrat having upgraded his stats according to a level ten existence and with their weapons, they didn't have much to fear.

Still, they didn't purposely search out confrontations, choosing instead to use their stealth to close in on the different searching areas that were marked on their maps.

Rugrat threw glances over to Erik as they traveled. He was honestly alarmed at what Erik had said earlier. Taking on the role of tank meant he would be right in the fight, the most likely to be damaged, though Erik didn't seem worried in the slightest.

They'd both changed as they'd entered the Ten Realms. There were few opportunities to relax as they had found themselves in one situation or another.

Rugrat heard the sounds of rushing wind then crackling thunder and an explosion in the distance. He called a halt and used his rifle's scope to look at the area where the noise was coming from. He couldn't see anything clearly through the trees, but he could see the grand lights coming from the battle being fought.

"Looks like there's some kind of fight going on over there with people fighting it out," Rugrat said into Erik's ear.

Erik checked the map against the direction of the fighting. "It looks to be the location of the White Vein Spirit Grass. Maybe there are some people fighting over it."

"The power from the fight—I don't think that they're people from the First Realm, or if they are, they could have ascended some time ago." Rugrat's senses had increased. Although it was easy for him to tell how powerful people were below his level, he had a better feeling for judging the power level of those stronger than him.

A new heat rose in Erik's eyes. "Well, be a good a time as any to see how people in the higher realms and levels fight." Erik grinned.

Rugrat couldn't hide his own excitement. As long as they were just observing, they might increase their own fighting ability.

They moved through the forest slowly and quietly. As they got close enough to the fight to feel the remaining shock waves, they moved up into the trees. Tying themselves off to the trees, they used their scopes to look in on the fight.

There was a group of four people fighting against a three-headed snake. While a man and a woman stood back, observing them.

One of the snake's heads spat poison, another a flammable cloud, the third a lightning attack.

The snake's tail whipped around, leaving deep craters where it landed.

There were two more people standing on the tops of trees also watching the battle: a middle-aged woman who had a refined air about her and a man knelt on the tree, watching the battle with disinterest.

33
THREE-HEADED SNAKE

Erik turned his attention to the four who were actually fighting. They looked to be in their teens. They wore uniforms identical to the two people observing from the trees.

There was an archer, two casters, and a swordsman.

The archer was raining arrows down on the snake, aiming for its eyes, infuriating it and splitting its attention from the fire mage. It tried to spit out some more flammable gas, only to have a half dozen fire balls no bigger than a baseball fly toward its mouth.

"Fire Rain!"

The flammable cloud exploded, making the gas head reel back in pain as the other heads and the scales around the gas head were damaged.

The snake's tail shot forward. The swordsman let out a yell, "Stone Skin!" A gray aura rapidly covered his body and weapons as he braced his shield, taking the hit. Two deep trenches were created under his feet; the gray covering dimmed and then broke as the blunted power still sent him back five more feet before he regained his footing.

"Flame Sword Judgement!" The remaining caster unleashed a powerful flame-based skill. A spell formation appeared in the sky above the snake. All the heat in the surrounding areas was drawn into the spell formation that quickly turned red before a massive sword descended, shooting toward the snake.

The lightning head opened its mouth. A spell formation appeared as white lightning reached up into the heavens to meet the sword.

The poison head spat at the archer who was aiming for the lightning head.

The archer wasn't paying attention as the stream of poison shot out at him.

"Move!" the warrior yelled. The archer fired his arrow and looked around. Seeing the poison had reached him, he let out a scream as it landed on his thick armor, starting to eat its way through.

The archer was out of the fight; the other two had to redouble their efforts to keep the snake contained as the caster of the flame sword was fighting against the lightning head's power.

"Fire rain!"

"Molten armor buff!" The other caster chained spells together, distracting and blinding the two of the snake heads.

Red glowing buffs settled onto the warrior, his armor showing faint flames around the edges. He rushed forward, dodging the snake's tail, and he shot forward toward their heads, aiming for the lightning head.

The lightning head was still fighting with the massive fire sword. The other caster's face was pale as they poured in all their power to the great fire sword.

The lightning head could only stop its attack or be cut apart by the warrior.

"Flame steps!"

The warrior's foot glowed as he seemed to step on nothing and changed his direction.

"Cold Flame slash!"

Scales were separated from flesh as a bloody line appeared on the snake's neck. A sizzling noise could be heard as the warrior dropped to the ground, rolling awkwardly as his armor moved up and down with his deep breaths.

The Flame Sword Judgement had nothing in its path anymore. It shot down like an arrow released from a bow, cutting off the lightning head. The poison and flammable gas head yelled out in pain as they lurched forward at the caster who had launched the sword and dropped to her knee, all of her energy had left her.

The swordsman yelled out, but he was too far away. The other caster was just starting to pull together a spell. The archer had collected himself and fired an arrow at the snake but it struck the creature's scales, drawing its blood but not affecting it greatly.

The man on the trees made a gesture with his hand.

An arrow formed from flames appeared in front of the doomed caster and shot toward the flammable head.

As the head jerked backward at this powerful arrow, it pulled the main body with it, stopping the poison head up short.

The poison head spat at the caster.

"Fire projection!" the other caster yelled out. Their face rapidly paled as they drank a Mana potion with one hand as their other hand, in the center of a spell formation, unleashed a column of fire that burned the poison away, creating a disgusting stench.

Only a few drops landed on the immobilized caster on the ground, who yelled out in pain. Unlike melee types, this caster wasn't used to pain and she could only roll in pain, not looking to use her potions as she was stuck in a state of fear.

The woman said something to the man. Quickly he disappeared from the tree and he grabbed the two casters by their robes.

"Pull back!" he yelled at the warrior and archer, turning and running away from the battlefield. His fire arrow still chased the flammable head, pushing the snake back as it held its mouth closed, not wanting that arrow to enter its body.

The poison head spat at the arrow, weakening but not destroying it.

The four fighters left the area, the two remaining heads letting out angry hisses.

The man threw out his hand. "Fire arrow."

Another fire arrow shot out at the two heads, redirecting their attention.

The woman who had been watching walked off the tree. Flames appeared under her feet, slowing her momentum as she looked over right at Erik and Rugrat. Her eyes rested there before she looked away and ran off after the rest of her group.

"Do you think she saw us?" Erik asked in a hushed voice a few moments later.

"No, I just think she conveniently looked over as she saw a particularly nice tree," Rugrat said. "Yes, she damn well saw us, but I don't know how."

"Might be a spell that enhances one's senses?" Erik asked.

"Could be. I don't think that any of the others noticed us though." Rugrat looked to where the group had left and then toward the two snakes. The remainders of the arrows shot forward, hitting the snakes and making them cry out in pain. Their scales were broken and blood covered their bodies.

They hissed in the direction that the party had fled, but they didn't chase.

Monsters were powerful and strong and although they couldn't speak human tongues, they were smart. The more powerful the beast, the greater its intelligence.

"How the hell is there a level fifteen beast here?" Rugrat said.

"Fifteen?" Erik asked.

"Yeah, that lot were probably level thirteens or so. The lady and man watching must've been in the upper teens," Rugrat said.

"Great—a teenager can kick my ass. I'm starting to feel old," Erik said.

"Well, you're practically fucking ancient, so it's about time."

"You're four years younger!"

"Four years younger, less ancient. Full of vigor and energy. Don't worry, gramps. We all get old at some time," Rugrat commiserated.

"Come, tell me that when I'm not strapped to a tree." Erik swung at Rugrat, who was just two feet too far away.

"Ah, the senile ways. Don't worry—I'll find you a nice home."

"I'll find a nice home for my foot up your ass!" Erik said.

Rugrat shook his head at Erik's antics, knowing that he wouldn't hit him even if they were in striking range. "I'll go and check to make sure that they really left the area." Rugrat untied himself and dropped to the ground below.

Erik dropped with him. "If they are, then we might as well harvest this three-headed snake."

"I was thinking the same." Rugrat nodded.

"All right, we'll meet here. I'll watch it." Erik pulled out his map and pointed to a location.

Map Location shared to you, marked "Step off Point"

Rugrat checked the location and then put his map away.

"See you in a bit." Rugrat moved through the forest. His easygoing attitude faded away as he moved, listening for disturbances. He passed through easily, his skills as a scout sniper and the additional strengths that came with him leveling up in the Ten Realms displayed.

He passed undetected, circling the snake. One head licked its wounds; the other looked for any threats that might try to take advantage of its weakened state.

He checked the ground, finding the signs of the party's panicked exit. He followed it for some time but it was clear that the group had run off. The two more powerful users had guided them off deeper into the forest.

Rugrat stealthy climbed up a tree, checking the area once again. He didn't want them to sneak up on them when they were fighting the snake.

After assuring himself that they were gone, he headed back to Erik.

"We need to finish this thing off quickly. They might still get some Experience from attacking the snake once we kill it, so we have to get the hell out of here as fast as possible," Rugrat said.

They both needed to level up and the wounded high-level creature in front of them was their best chance to do it in a short period of time. Sure, it was dirty kill stealing, but this was no video game with a code of honor.

"Time for some snake killing." Erik nodded and pulled out his rifle. They looked at the unsuspecting snake still dealing with its wounds.

34
CLEANING UP BEHIND

"Did you find any of the White Vein Spirit Grass?" Rugrat asked.

Erik could only shake his head. "I think the greedy bastard might have it in its gut." Erik pointed to a location on the ground. There was a hole there, as if one of the snakes had eaten the ground.

"Mmm, dirt with a side of plant."

"We'll split up. I'll hit it from behind first, draw its attention and get it all riled up, then you shoot from cover, get our stealth attacks in. Then we just keep on shooting them till they drop," Erik said.

"You really wanted that White Vein Spirit Grass, huh?" Rugrat asked.

Erik didn't waste his energy in reply and started stealthing away.

Rugrat snorted and went his way.

Erik moved till he was behind the snake. He settled down into a good position, taking his time to aim properly. He waited a bit longer just in case Rugrat needed more time to set up.

Finally he lowered his eyes and looked through his sights. He pulled the trigger. The round hit the back of the snake's poison head, making it rock forward, nearly losing its balance as it was startled by the attack.

The poison head was dazed as the flammable head reared up.

Erik fired into the snake's back, making it turn.

Rugrat fired. His round entered a space under the snake's jaw and exited its head.

The snake let out a pained whistling noise as the poison head spat out in Erik's direction, getting the ground and the trees around him but not him. He was deeper in the forest, making it harder to see him.

The poison head now fully pointed in his direction; it was too easy.

Erik continued to pull his trigger again and again. The poison snake's head backed up as the rounds struck. The head dropped forward as Rugrat's fourth round landed, killing the flammable head.

The snake dropped forward. A tombstone appeared above it.

Erik moved away from the still dying vegetation in front of him. His storage ring on his trigger finger had been collecting the brass cartridges as they were ejected, leaving nothing behind.

Rugrat didn't have such a problem; he ran out, tapping on the tombstone marker and then on the air in front of him.

The snake's body started to disintegrate, including the lightning head.

Erik felt a heavy flow of power rush into his body before it built up and broke through a barrier within his body.

Erik didn't focus on this breakthrough much as he looked around the ground, looking for the White Vein Spirit Grass.

"Yeah, the grass is in its gut but it didn't digest it so it's half harvested," Rugrat said.

"Let's get moving." Erik was a bit relieved. They only needed to find five of Tommins's ingredients but Erik wanted to see what kind of rewards he would get for gathering them all.

"Huh?" The large swordsman looked at a screen in front of him.

Bai Hui, who was leading the group to temper them in real battles, looked over in question.

Xuyang Jaim was the one to answer her look. "We just got Experience for aiding in the death of the three-headed forest king snake."

She pursed her lips and looked at the rest of the party. Based on their condition, they wouldn't be good in a fight.

She had sensed two people watching their fight, but their auras hadn't been as powerful as the students she was protecting. She wasn't afraid of fighting them and had looked right at them to warn them off.

Hearing that they must have killed the three-headed forest king snake, she was in a bit of shock.

"It looks like their combat power is much greater than their normal strength," Bai Hui mused.

"Who?" Xuyang asked.

"It is no matter. At least we have gained something in this fight. Let us hurry to meet up with the rest of the sect. You should all know your faults." Her eyes moved over the party in front of her.

The cocky attitude they'd had upon entering the Beast Mountain Range had dimmed greatly.

It might only be the First Realm but the Beast Mountains had claimed many young fighters who didn't truly respect the danger of this monster-filled area.

They hung their heads, gripping their weapons or looking at the new uniforms they'd needed to put on as their old ones had been torn apart.

Seeing that look in their eyes, she waved for them to follow and to move deeper into the Beast Mountains. There would be more opportunities for them to fight before they met up with the older generation of their sects.

"Elder Oui, it has been a long time!" a large man said in a happy tone, a hint of coldness in his eyes.

"Elder Maurez, it has been a long time. I didn't know that you would be joining as a supervising elder at this Beast Mountains competition." Elder Oui, a skinny man, squinted as he forced a smile.

"So many old acquaintances. It should be good to see what the younger generation will do, seeing you are all gathered here." A dominating pressure passed over everyone as a man walked out of the forest onto the stage that appeared in the middle of the Beast Mountains Forest.

He had a gloating smile on his face as he looked over everyone.

"Elder Rei, it seems that you have broken through into the nineteenth level." Elder Maurez grit his teeth and bowed his head slightly to the other elder as he forced a smile.

"It is but a small matter. I was able to find a few lucky opponents in the northern reaches." Rei's eyes cut over to Elder Oui.

Elder Oui's eyes thinned. "Interesting. There were a few of our elders who went there to visit some old friends, but it seems that they have gone missing. Does Elder Rei know anything about this?"

"Seeing old friends, is it? Well, I hope that they were able to find them and have a good rest." Elder Rei laughed.

Elder Oui's eyes only thinned more, sensing the hidden meaning in Elder Rei's words.

After all, they were sent in search of a powerful Mana concentration. They had hoped to return with a medicinal ingredient or natural treasure, but they had never returned.

Elder Rei admitted to being in the area and his power had risen greatly.

There was no evidence that anything had happened, so Elder Oui could only let out a cold harrumph as more elders from the different sects and factions of the Second Realm that had become a part of the Beast Mountains trial emerged.

These elders ranged from level seventeen to nineteen. They were some of the strongest people in their sects, sent here to watch over the trial.

Only new disciples who were under level fifteen were able to compete in the Beast Mountains trial. First they would need to reach this stage by fighting or sneaking past the beasts. Once they reached this stage, then the elders would work together to open the path into the heart of the Beast Mountains.

Hidden in the depths of the Beast Mountains, there was actually a dungeon. A dungeon was a place hidden away from others, either built by the Ten Realms, or formed by people in the Ten Realms. These places could have great danger, but they could also hold great treasures.

The dungeon in the Beast Mountains was too hard for people in the First Realm to enter. It was only the people in the Second Realm who had the power and resources to open and compete in the Beast Mountains trial.

It was rumored that the Beast Mountains trial was built on a Mana vein and that the person who defeated the Beast Mountains trial would take control of the dungeon and the Mana vein underneath.

Of course, this was just a rumor. But if someone were able to take control of the dungeon, then not only would that person, but the entire sect behind them, increase in strength.

The dungeon gave birth to many powerful beasts, resources, and manuals. It could be opened whenever, but required a number of resources to do so.

"How many people do you think will make it to the third layer or higher?" Elder Oui asked a group of elders he had found. As one of the three most powerful elders in the gathering, many of them were willing to meet and talk with him. Becoming friends with him and the powerful Iron Spear sect could allow them to increase the standing in their own sect and even bridge an alliance to benefit both parties.

"There are many powerful new youths. One only has to look at Elder Oui's apprentice niece Julia. With her powerful attainments with the Iron Spear training manual and her strong body and ten Mana gates, she is sure to pass into the fifth—no, sixth level!" One spoke up.

Elder Oui smiled. After all, who didn't like being praised? "Niece Julia is wild in her ways, but she's done this old man proud."

"Does Elder Oui think that someone of the younger generation will make it into the eighth level?" another elder asked.

The ninth and tenth level hadn't been touched up to this point. There had been various attempts to reach these levels but they were incredibly difficult to crack. This made it a great place for people to temper their skills and grow in power.

35

GIVE A REDNECK NAPALM

Erik settled down in a place far away from where they'd killed the three-headed forest king snake.

Finally they had a chance to check out their gains.

Skill: Marksman
Level: 27 (Apprentice)
Long-range weapons are familiar in your hands. When aiming, you can zoom in x2.0.

Skill: Stealth
Level: 20 (Novice)
No bonuses at this time. You must prove your skills first.

15,075/64,000 EXP till you reach Level 10

Erik was more interested with the materials that had come with the snake.

He looked over the loot Rugrat had gathered.

1x Common Mortal Grade Monster Core
1x Petty Mortal Grade Monster Core (Lightning attribute)
1x Forest King Poison sac
1x Forest King Gas Sac
12x Three-Headed Forest King Snake Meat
5x Three-Headed Forest King Snake Tendons
3x Three-Headed Forest King Snake Fangs
6x Three-Headed Forest King Snake Skins
2x White Vein Spirit Grass

"We can probably sell the skins to an armorer, meat to a chef, tendons and fangs to a weapons shop, though the poison sac and gas sac we could use those," Erik said.

"Flame bombs—nothing like napalm in the morning!" Rugrat said in agreement.

"Can take the redneck out of the South, can't take the love of blowing shit up and setting it on fire out of the redneck," Erik muttered.

"Got that right!"

"I am *soo* excited for when you can start making firearms."

"I know! I've tinkered before a bit with them here and there, y'know." Rugrat tapped his nose and winked at Erik.

"There is literally no government left here to report you to and if I did tell them, they'd probably piss themselves and move their capital to get rid of your crazy ass."

"I wonder if I can get an achievement for that?" Rugrat actually looked as if he were thinking it through, which made Erik even more scared.

"All right, come on back down. I'll give you the flammable gas. Just try to make something that won't blow our fucking faces off," Erik stressed.

"Is singed eyebrows okay?"

Erik let out a pained sigh, the fight going out of his body. "Fine, fine! Just you're going to be throwing them every time then!"

"I knew I should have got that baseball bat." Rugrat groaned.

"Fire bombs and you want to hit them with a fucking baseball bat?" Erik nearly yelled before waving his hands, as if to get as far from this lunatic as possible. "Fine, right, okay, of course. For the love of all things holy, warn me when you start lobbing these things around."

"Will do!" Rugrat said with a pleased expression.

Erik looked right at Rugrat. "You're fucking insane."

Rugrat looked touched as he held his heart and bowed his legs, as if he were overly embarrassed. "Thank you. That's the nicest compliment you've given me!"

Erik promptly turned around and smacked his face into a tree. "Get. That. Image. Out. Of. My. Head!"

"And that, kids, is how Erik got brain damage." Rugrat walked off toward their next point.

Erik made some unintelligent noise.

"He was never the same after that!" Rugrat's words came out in a rush as he had to run to escape Erik's hands.

Erik looked over the poison sac that he'd placed in his own storage broach.

The sac was highly resistant to poison and it carried about three liters' worth of poison.

Rugrat was already experimenting with his sac. The contents of the sac were highly compressed; instead of being the gas that was shot out by the snakes, it was a liquid. Leading Rugrat along the path of making grenades while Erik's mind moved in another direction. From what he'd seen, the poison gas burned one's skin and affected their muscles. If he could find a way to use this poison, then he might have a chance of tempering his muscles and skin.

Then he would only need to temper his organs and his bones to reach Body Like Stone.

Since they were in a dangerous area, Erik put the poison sac away in his storage ring while Rugrat finished making his shrapnel and firebombs. The shrapnel bombs were filled with rocks and metal pieces; the firebombs had tape wrapped around holes. When throwing the firebomb, the liquid would turn into gas, being released out of the perforations before striking its target, where the match inside would be pulled against a piece of strike paper, igniting it.

Erik and Rugrat took a few slow days. They had spent a lot of time just running from place to place in the First Realm, so they spent it making different items, checking their gear, cleaning their weapons, and reading over the different information they had gathered and sharing it with each other.

Since they had talked about the roles that they wanted to take on, Rugrat now looked to improve his Mana system. Stealth spells, detection spells: this was the path that he wanted to walk down with ways to augment his weapons and their abilities.

As such, he had put eight of his attribute points of becoming a level ten existence into Mana Regeneration. He broke open two Mana gates in one night and was readying himself to open another, though it would probably take him at least half a day to do so.

The other two points went into increasing the size of his Mana pool. Rugrat was concentrating on Agility and Mana.

Rugrat would work with his rifle, aiming and firing with nothing in the chamber; they didn't have the rounds to waste. "Damn, I just want to get in front of a forge to test this all out," Rugrat complained on the second afternoon.

"I know. I just want to get some damn Alchemy formulas. If I have them and some information on techniques. I know that I'd be able to make some concoctions." Erik sighed along with Rugrat.

"I don't know how you haven't gone mad memorizing that Alchemy book," Rugrat said.

"I've got about half of it memorized now. I don't know, if something's interesting, you suck it up. Like how we know everything about weapons because we like them, but if someone asks us to do math tests we'd rather punch them in the face."

"Unless it's wind and range calculations, I ain't touching math," Rugrat said.

"Exactly. You find that stuff way more interesting and useful than any math could be."

"Well, on that note of things we need to do," Rugrat stood, "shall we go and check out that blue fennel?"

"Sounds good to me." Erik checked inside his storage ring. "We're going to need to pick up our supplies sooner rather than later. I've got eight mags left for my rifle, three for my pistol, and some twenty shells for my shotgun."

"Not even going to use the bow anymore?" Rugrat asked.

"You be the damn elf. I'll be a dwarf smashing things with my fists."

They walked through the forest easily. They'd got used to it over the few days they'd been there.

They'd also been observing this area for a while. At around mid-afternoon, the creature that hid in the fennel would leave to hunt. They checked that it wasn't hiding in the fennel and moved in.

Rugrat watched the area as Erik once again worked to pull the fennel out of the ground without destroying it.

They looked up to the sounds of movement. Erik increased his speed while Rugrat tapped his finger, ready to pull out his rifle in a moment's notice.

An angry-looking woman rushed from tree to tree, her speed impressing Rugrat, as she held a long metal spear in her hands. She didn't even seem to mind the weight as she ran onward.

"Erik," Rugrat said, having a bad feeling.

"Nearly done." Erik heard Rugrat's tone, so he sped up his efforts, nearly failing in harvesting it. Thankfully, it came free of the dirt without any issues. A strong medicinal scent was released before Erik stuffed it into his storage ring and the two made to run off.

A party of five people appeared in the forest. Their leader made them pause before he pointed in a direction. "Bring me that medicinal plant," he ordered imperiously, as if he were the ruler of this mountain.

The others shot off under his command.

"We've got company," Rugrat said.

They both increased their speed, breaking stealth as it was clear that they'd been discovered anyways. They shot off into the forest, alarming the four people following them.

"Our young master only wants to talk to you. Why don't you stay for a while?" One threw out a dart that pierced through a tree, missing Rugrat's head.

"Well, sounds like he's a right bitch, sending his dogs after us!" Rugrat shot back.

More darts whizzed through the air around him as he kept running.

"Their aim is worse than little Bobbins!" Rugrat yelled.

"Dude had one-inch thick glasses! How the fuck did he get past the recruiters?"

"I dunno!" Rugrat said.

"Must've eaten so many crayons he impressed the recruiter."

"Fuck you, man!"

Erik laughed his way through the jungle as they continued to be chased but the four behind them were catching up.

They rushed into a valley that thinned down.

"Nothing like the smell of napalm in the morning!" Erik yelled, pulling out a napalm bomb in his hand, ripping off the tape and throwing it.

Rugrat stepped off a wall and threw something from his storage ring. It left a trail of brown smoke behind it as he threw out two more.

"Fire in the hole, fuck." The homemade napalm bombs went off. The sludge stuck to the four pursuers and ignited as the rush of air being burnt threw Rugrat around, screaming. "Heeaad, fuck, rock!"

Erik grimaced as Rugrat smacked into a rock and rolled through the forest.

36

RAINING EXPERIENCE AND TREASURES

"I know that you might have been told to use your head more, but this is going a bit too far," Erik said as he healed up the cut on Rugrat's head and the brain bruise.

"Damn. That fucking hurt," Rugrat said.

Erik settled down. Seeing Rugrat was okay, he opened up his screens.

Skill: Stealth
Level: 21 (Novice)
No bonuses at this time. You must prove your skills first.

You have learned the skill: **Throwables**
Close-range and long-range weapons combining aim with the weapons at one's disposal, the throwable increases the range that one can throw at and the accuracy they do so.

Skill: Throwables
Level: 7 (Novice)
No bonuses at this time. You must prove your skills first.

You have reached Level 11
When you sleep next, you will be able to increase your attributes by: 20 points.

67,387/100,000 EXP till you reach Level 12

For killing an opponent 4 levels stronger than you, your Experience is increased by 300%

Erik laughed to himself as Rugrat read his own screen,

"Wait, how much Experience did you get?" Rugrat asked.

"Like two hundred thousand, you?"

"Like a hundred and fifty. Dammit, that level Experience increase is savage!" Rugrat said.

"Well, it's a lot harder to kill things above you in level."

"You were using *my* napalmers!" Rugrat deflated against the rock. "Damn, if I knew it would be that good to earn Experience, we should've gone for dumbasses long ago," Rugrat said. "What level are you?"

"Eleven, getting toward twelve," Erik said.

"Hah! Still on top, baby!" Rugrat pumped his fist in the air. "Twelve and proud!"

"Mental age?"

"Fuck you, too."

"Buy me dinner first, jeez!" Erik laughed. "I wonder why there are so many powerful people about? Think of the party that were fighting the snake, or that group we just ran into. All of them were a high level and they had good equipment."

Erik looked at the two new storage rings on his hand. He hadn't looked inside them yet.

"When I was working in the smithy, I heard a few people talking about how the Second Realm factions and sects come down and head to the Beast Mountains for something. Most people treat this as a forbidden ground. They treat it like a trial for their youngsters to increase in strength.

"The Beast Mountains gets all stirred up with it. Some of the people from the First Realm follow behind, collecting their waste as what's not valuable in the Second Realm is a priceless treasure here." Rugrat looked over to Erik as if to see what he was thinking.

"Well, I'm all about trying to gather some gold." Erik smiled. "They might be experts in their sects and factions but they're just hot-headed kids using their skills. Like damn second lieutenants, all squeaky and clean."

"Oh, they're so cute and new!" Rugrat laughed darkly.

"So what if they're a few levels above us? As long as we keep a low profile, only coming in after them, there shouldn't be an issue. If they want to fight, well, someone shouldn't be judged on just their level," Erik said.

"But first. Let me take a nap." Rugrat leaned back on the log as if to go to sleep.

"Rack monster."

"It is a skill and a talent," Rugrat said, not opening his eyes.

Erik nodded. Truly, the ability to sleep anywhere was a highly rated skill that Erik wished he was able to learn.

Erik took the time to look through the storage rings that they had acquired. There were different kinds of weapons, mostly of the Novice grade. Erik could only look forward to the riches that they would gain from selling all of them.

There were even a number of monster cores inside the storage rings; they weren't simple either.

Five of them were Grand Mortal grade monster cores, with one being a Fire Variant Mortal Grade Monster Core. Different variant cores could increase the price of the monster cores drastically, doubling or tripling the price that a Grand Mortal grade monster core would cost.

Erik started to organize the loot. Weapons were placed into one ring; cores joined them. Recovery concoctions were stored in the next. Finally, the highest quality cores, the best weapons and the manuals that were useful to Erik and Rugrat, were placed into the broach that he had taken from the mage in the cave.

Erik took his time to look through the gear. He took out a few pieces of armor. They were simple black bracers that were of the Apprentice level.

Cold Steel Arm Bracers
Defense: 27
Weight: 0.7 kg
Durability: 68/100
Base Value: 2 Gold, 5 Silver
Slot: Takes up forearm slot
Innate Effect: Resist cold damage 5pts
Requirement:
Strength 14
Agility 11

"Requirements?" Erik hadn't read anything about weapons or armor needing a requisite level or stat to be used, but now the glowing armor seemed to dim in his eyes. "Well, that's going to make things harder if we can't use some of it until we increase our stats." He even had the thought to use his newly acquired stats so that he would be able to wear this gear. He dismissed the thought. Just altering his stats to meet the needs of the weapons and armor would only make him weaker in the future.

"So, probably can't use half of this and it'll be hard as hell to sell because it's high-leveled." Erik could only sigh as he looked to the armored warrior. "Well, I don't think you'll be needing this anymore, sorry." Erik pulled out the cuirass from the dead warrior.

The armor was called the Golden Fox armor, the entire thing called the Golden Fox Set.

The stats were incredible when compared to the other gear.

Golden Fox Cuirass
Defense: 59
Weight: 45.3 kg
Charge: 23/100
Durability: 47/113
Base Value: 32 Gold, 17 Silver
Slot: Takes up chest slot
Enchanted Ability: Agility increases 2% per hit; can stack a total of 5 times
Innate Ability: Reduce magical attacks effect by 5%
This is a set item. When two or more set items are combined, the abilities of the set items will increase.
Requirement:
Agility 15
Strength 20

The problem was with how low the charge and health were. Erik didn't know how to charge the armor up more and would need to find out more information about it.

Also, when wearing the armor, it gave off a dull glow, showing that it was a Journeyman piece of armor.

An increase of 10% Agility would increase Erik's Agility from 70 to 77. It might not seem like much, but it would allow him to move on the openings he saw in a fight, allow him to have greater control over his weapons and increase his ability to dodge attacks. It couldn't be dismissed.

Erik put the cuirass away. If they were in a life-and-death fight, he would pull it out. Right now, it was more danger than it was a help.

He took out some simple boots. They were really rough compared to the ones that he was wearing but their stats weren't bad.

Diemar leather boots
Defense: 15
Weight: 0.5 kg
Durability: 78/100
Base Value: 17 Silver, 4 Coppers
Slot: Takes up foot slot
Innate Effect: Move quieter when in stealth
Requirements:
Agility 17
Mana 7

He had to sigh and put them next to Rugrat. With their abilities, they were better suited for him.

Most of the gear that the Willful Institute students had were items that had been given to them by the sect.

They'd found out where they had come from as they all had a manual containing the sect's rules and the emblem on most of their items and the manual were the same.

Erik might have killed them but he wasn't going to broadcast that to everyone.

He left those to the side. Maybe Rugrat would get some inspiration when pulling them apart.

Erik pulled out a pair of pants and a helmet to complete his hodgepodge collection.

The greaves were from the warrior again.

Golden Fox Greaves
Defense: 63
Weight: 5.7 kg
Charge: 37/100
Durability: 67/109
Base Value: 36 Gold, 13 Silver
Slot: Takes up leg slot
Enchantment: strength increases 4% (*5% when paired with Golden Fox Cuirass)*
Innate Effect: Reduce magical attacks effect by 3% (*4% when paired with Golden Fox Cuirass*)
This is a set item. When two or more set items are combined, the abilities of the set items will increase.
Requirements:
Strength 16
Agility: 21

The greaves were stronger than the cuirass as they'd taken less damage. When they were combined, their immediate strength didn't shoot up. Erik pulled out a helmet. Although its stats were high, it obstructed his view and he could only put it away when thinking of what it might be like if he shot his weapons while wearing it.

The boots weren't all that good and they weren't in the least bit comfortable compared to Erik's pair.

He turned to the last pile of items. His heart sped up as he got to the manuals and information books.

The four people had been disciples of the Willful Institute. Being students in their own right, they had myriad different training manuals. Not only did they have books that went more in-depth on the subject of Body Cultivation and the Mana Gathering systems, one had a book on the basics of Alchemy, another on formations, and another on smithing. Among these, there were various fighting manuals.

Erik opened up one of the manuals, reading the first page.

Throwing manual
With this manual, one will be able to exert greater force with their body when throwing items, increasing the damage of the throwable object, the distance traveled, and the accuracy at throwing.
Erik looked though the different manuals. They were mainly on training with swords. These manuals looked to increase the effect that a person would have with one given area.

So if it was with a blade, then increase the speed that they would draw with, the accuracy of their hits, the places that they should hit.

If it was archery, how one could use and work on different muscles, so that they were able to draw more strength out of their body without increasing their level.

"Basically, like any good training, the better you train, the more lethal you will become without having to make any big changes like get a whole new rifle if you've got the drills down." Erik put down the manual. "I just never thought of the specifics that might go into fighting with these kinds of weapons."

I just naturally thought that because they were blades and arrows that they weren't worth learning because I had a rifle.

Erik went through the manuals until he found one on hand-to-hand combat.

"Who the hell named this? Growling Tiger Elbow?" Erik could only frown at the title. "Damn. A plus for trying, but it just sounds like the writer was trying to make this sound mystical."

Shaking his head, Erik opened the manual.

37

USING MANA TO PUNCH?

Growling Tiger focuses on channeling one's inner energy (Mana) through one's channels, focusing the muscles and unleashing a powerful blow on your enemies.

A bunch of diagrams and explanations showed how one was supposed to move the Mana within their body and the movements in their muscles and body to drive as much power through their body to inflict the greatest damage on their target.

"Vicious little bastards." Erik sighed as he closed his eyes, studying the movement of power in his body and then tracing it through his Mana channels as the manual told him to.

Erik felt like some kind of ridiculous chicken as he threw his elbows out, as though he were in a football game.

Finally it went right as the timing between the movement of his arm and his Mana matched up. A rushing sound, similar to a growl, could be heard as Erik's arm moved much faster.

Erik felt the power that jumped upward, as it felt just right to him. He wasn't satisfied and moved to a tree. He elbowed it.

"Oh, shit, fucking funny bone! God damn!" After rubbing his funny bone and trying to heal it, which was having no effect, Erik finally got feeling back in his elbow.

He looked at the point of impact. There was a patch of the tree that no longer had any bark on it; otherwise the tree looked fine.

Erik changed his point of aim, remembering that *right* feeling. He practiced a few times, getting it down before he did it against the tree.

He hit the outside of the tree. The bark was cracked as the other side of the tree blew out in a spray of splinters.

Erik pushed on the small tree as it gave way and dropped on the ground. "Well, okay, that's kind of awesome." Erik looked at the destruction.

With the information in the book, it simply took what he had already, combined it together and used it in a different way to increase the overall power output he could display.

Erik continued to practice again and again, looking to improve his control until he could do it easily without needing to think about it too much. Mostly it was a lot of him smashing his elbow against trees and hissing out expletives as he struck his funny bone, again and again.

Power from the surrounding area started to gather. Threads of energy started to snake across the ground, entering Rugrat's body. His aura increased in power as he started to rise in level, his body undergoing changes.

It seemed like everything in a five-meter radius was sucked up into Rugrat's body.

"What the fuck's going on?" Rugrat asked blearily as he woke up. The power settled into his bones as he rose up. His bones cracked with new power as he reached out his hand.

"That's a rush." Rugrat moved his hands around as if he were grasping the very fabric of the space around him.

Rugrat looked up at Erik rubbing his elbow, his joy turning into a confused look. "What've you been up to?"

"Don't want to talk about it." Erik leaned against a tree and closed his eyes, willing the screen to appear.

Rugrat didn't even have time to say anything else as a screen appeared in Erik's mind.

You have 20 attribute points to use.

Erik was really feeling like he was being held back by his Mana pool. His healing spells from before didn't require all that much initial Mana to be cast and the output could be varied if he used more or less Mana.

Though it meant that his reserves were extremely low, if he got a stronger spell then he wouldn't be able to cast it based on his Mana pool. Also, it was a reserve that would allow him to pump out a lot of Mana in short bursts.

He placed seven points into Mana pool by itself, another four went into Mana Regeneration. Then three went into Agility and Strength; three more into Stamina Regeneration.

Erik looked over his character sheet.

Character Sheet
Name: Erik West
Level: 11
Race: Human
Titles:
From the Grave
Strength: (Base 7) +9
160
Agility: (Base 6) +11
85
Stamina: (Base 10) +1
165
Mana: (Base 6) +7
130
Mana Regeneration (Base 4) +18
5.15/s
Stamina Regeneration: (Base 7) +14
4.95/s

Erik felt the new energy flood into his body as it changed. Erik's eyes opened as he let out a breath. The air around him was disturbed with the power of his breath.

"Damn, it feels good to level up in the morning." Erik got to his feet, looking over to see Rugrat engrossed in his smithing manuals.

"So, what's the plan? You want to find out where these people are all going, or keep moving from place to place that Tommins has sent us?" Rugrat asked.

"I want to at least see what's going on. If we can get a few rewards, then that's even better. All of the stronger ingredients usually have some kind of beast or protector. With all of these high-level characters running about, it will be incredibly hard to try to lure beasts out of their homes," Erik said.

"I'm curious about what this Beast Mountains trial is all about as well," Rugrat agreed, putting away the manual. He was already wearing his own mismatched assortment of gear.

They didn't care how they looked, only that their gear was the strongest.

"You look like a goddamn hobo who went through a tannery," Erik said.

"You look like you're trying out for the movie *Gladiator* and you stepped in gold paint," Rugrat said.

"Touché," Erik said.

"You know what that means really?"

"No clue, but you've got to make something a little better than this when you can finally smith," Erik said.

"I haven't even learned the damn skill and you're putting an order in? What are you, an officer?"

Noises appeared in the distance. Erik and Rugrat heard them clearly. People were fighting and moving in their direction.

Erik and Rugrat dropped into stealth and moved away from their camp. Using their maps, they moved deeper into the Beast Mountains.

Elder Oui looked around. Still, he had not seen his niece even as other youths had made it to the platforms dotted around the Beast Mountains Range.

"Is something wrong, Elder Oui?" Elder Rei asked.

"Nothing, Elder Rei. I heard that your nephew Xi Yan has joined in on the competition?"

"Yes, though he likes to take his time. He will be here in time. I have faith." Elder Rei waved off any worries he might have.

"Elders, the formation is ready to accept Mana stones and monster cores," an array master elder said as he and a group of other elders had been watching the array that was embedded in the platform.

Quickly people started to organize themselves, breaking off their conversations. Those whose disciples hadn't appeared looked out into the Beast Mountains.

If they hadn't appeared, then they might be slow or they had run into some trouble. It wasn't uncommon for people to enter the Beast Mountains and not make it out alive, though this mostly happened once someone entered the actual dungeon, not while they were trying to get to it.

"The hell?" Rugrat said as a medallion popped out of the two storage rings that he had got from the people he'd used his napalm bombs on.

The medallion indicated direction. Rugrat looked over to Erik to see that he had two medallions floating in front of him as well.

"Shall we go and check it out?" Erik asked.

"Might as well," Rugrat said. They didn't go directly toward whatever the medallions were pointing at but went on an angle to make sure that they weren't going into some kind of ambush.

The Mana in the Beast Mountains was getting stirred up as people passed overhead, rushing toward where the medallion was pointing.

Erik and Rugrat made sure that no one saw them as groups met one another, getting into fights or fleeing from one another. It looked as if they had all come for the same thing, but they didn't want others to get it as well.

"All of them feel to be level thirteen and fourteen. Some are a little stronger, but I don't think that their combat capabilities are any less," Rugrat said.

"We've got to take some chances or else we won't get anywhere."

Rugrat looked at Erik. He could see that fire was back in Erik's eyes. It had scared him seeing how defeated Erik looked in that hospital bed. Since Erik had come to the Ten Realms, he didn't want to stay back; he wanted to move forward, looking to learn more and experience as much as possible.

So they moved closer to where the medallions were guiding them.

"What in the hell is going on here?" Rugrat said as a stage started to come into view, there were powerful fluctuations from the stage as well as the space in front of it as the air was distorting in front of the large group of people there.

Older people stood at the front of the stage. Youths who had been charging through the Beast Mountains stood behind them, watching as the elders pulled out Mana cores and glowing crystals, placing them into receptacles around the stage.

Erik and Rugrat's eyes glowed seeing all of that gold being poured out by these rich fellows as if it were nothing.

Runes and lines appeared on the ground of the stage, lighting up with power. The air before the stage seemed to consolidate as a faint tower appeared in front of the stage. It had ten floors that were covered in scenes of people fighting beasts. Each floor was fifteen meters tall.

The surrounding area shook as the tower seemed to connect with the stage. The tower's doors opened slowly, revealing a black abyss beyond.

38

RUN

"You know what those runes and lines mean?" Erik whispered to Rugrat.

"I've only looked at a book on the formations that are used in weapons—how the hell am I supposed to know what kind of formation or magical array would allow a fricking skyscraper to appear out of mid-air?" Rugrat said, stunned and excited by the possibilities of formations.

The youths, seeing that the door was open, took a second before the first person charged forward. It seemed to be what they were all waiting for. The elders watched on.

As soon as someone left the stage, they would disappear in a flash of light.

"A teleportation and illusion formation?" Rugrat muttered to himself, seemingly unsure.

Erik looked to the medallion that was pulling toward the tower.

"Damn you, Xi Yan!" A woman's voice yelled out from behind Erik and Rugrat, startling them both and making the elders on the stage stare over at them as well.

The woman with the steel spear appeared in the forest, charging for the stage.

"Who are those two?" an elder yelled out.

"They're not one of ours but they have the Willful Institute's medallions?" An elder said, looking to another man beside him.

"Kill them!" the man yelled.

If they ran back into the Beast Mountains, it would be hard for them to escape as the entire Beast Mountains had been subdued by these people. Behind them was the woman with the spear and the other half of the people they'd got their medallions from.

Erik and Rugrat only need to look at each other once before they burst out from the tree line.

Erik and Rugrat started running across the stage. The woman with the steel spear rushed past them. She gave them a sideways glance but didn't pay them anymore attention as she shot toward the tower's opening.

"Take this!" Erik tossed Rugrat a purple potion.

"How do they have potions?" someone yelled.

"Help the Willful Institute!" another person yelled.

Erik and Rugrat took the potion.

Potion of Speed
Quality: Common Mortal Grade
Type: Potion
Effects: Increase Agility by 40% for 30 seconds. Effect of second potion decreased by 60% if taken within 5 minutes.

Erik felt as if his body was *alive*. Power flooded his system as he was *launched* forward.

Erik and Rugrat laughed. They were like bullets from a gun. Their Agility increase allowed them not only increase how fast they could run, but their reaction times. Everything seemed to be moving slightly slower as their bodies were easier to move.

They dodged incoming spells and arrows as they overtook the woman with the steel spear, who had a look of shock on her face.

Their bodies' reaction time shot up, giving them the sort of control they had never had over their bodies as they could switch direction on a dime. It was as if they were swimming through the air instead of running across a stage.

Rugrat got hit with a spell on his side, spinning him away. But he quickly dodged a second hit and kept on his path. A dart found his leg, making him yell, but he kept running.

Erik was dealing with his own issues. He leapt high, missing a destructive bolt of Mana, and used his bracers to take on an arrow. If it was his original Agility, he wouldn't be able to move his arms that fast to intercept the arrow.

The momentum from the arrow sent him flying back. He hit the ground and twisted around as if dancing before he entered the opening of the tower, just as Rugrat stumbled into it.

Light appeared all around them as the stage disappeared and they fell onto another platform. It was much smaller—a ten-by-ten meter space—with a door in front of them.

They looked around for threats, but there was nothing in this open space.

"How you doing?" Rugrat moved to Erik, whose arm was missing.

"Well, I'm down an arm—can you grab it?" Erik said.

Rugrat picked up Erik's arm and pulled it over. Erik lined it up with his upper arm and put them together.

First he focused on the bone; he started to send just threads of Focused Heal just into the bone. The bone started to come together. In just seconds, it was healed good as new. Then Erik focused on the muscle tissue; again, he used just threads of healing energy in the muscles at the sight of the damage, rebuilding them rapidly. Then he moved to the nerves, the blood vessels, the organs, and the skin.

It took just a few minutes before he was fully repaired. As he was studying the effects of his handiwork, Rugrat was seeing to his own wounds.

Rugrat pulled the dart out of his leg and tossed it into a storage ring before he made to start healing.

The spell had hit Rugrat in the side, but he had been wearing his plate carrier. A chunk had been ripped out of it and the powerful blast crushed some ribs, but with healing spells he was fine. In less than a minute, Rugrat's side was repaired.

My Mana usage was much smaller the more focused, but the speed shot right up. It also felt different healing each different system. Erik looked over to Rugrat, who sat on the ground, his forehead covered in sweat from the pain of his shattered ribs moving back into place.

"If I was to start healing layer by layer, system by system, could that decrease the Mana needs, and increase the speed? Maybe the Focused and the Minor Heal Wounds are doing too much. When someone has a problem, you don't try to heal it all at once; you categorize and break it down. Stop the bleeding, the broken bone can wait, that cut on your hand isn't important now." Erik's eyes held a glow as he kept thinking.

"You lost your mind yet?" Rugrat asked, his voice strained as he drank from his water canteen.

"Thinking aloud." Erik's voice made it clear he wasn't actually paying attention to Rugrat's words.

"When using healing spells, it looks to heal *everything,* basically converts the Mana energy into an energy to assist the body in repairing itself, using Stamina, or food as a secondary fuel. Maybe with more Mana, or a better Mana usage, then there wouldn't be a need to strain someone's Stamina? Maybe you could actually heal them *and* up their Stamina at the same time? Now focus, and get back on track." Erik tapped his head.

Rugrat groaned as he finished healing Erik and moved to try to make his side not hurt as much.

Erik tossed him some Wraith's Touch salve to numb the pain.

"If you can heal the entire body in one go, why can't you heal just parts of it? Like if your body was a car—you could buy a new car, or you could just replace the parts. The actual physical parts might be special, but the resource costs wouldn't be."

"You know how much my smoke stacks cost me on my truck?" Rugrat complained. "You going to heal me up or what?"

"They might have cost a lot of money, but in resources, like steel, say it was necessary, much cheaper on resources than a whole new truck," Erik said, a shocked expression on his face as if he had just stepped through a new doorway. "This is the Ten Realms!" Erik laughed out loud. "I'm such a friggin' idiot!"

"I've been thinking of adapting *to* the Ten Realms, but what if I was to adapt the knowledge of the Ten Realms and Earth together? Like your idea of making weapons with smithing and formations. Ingenious! Medical science with Alchemy and healing! Oh fuck, we're cooking with jet fuel, ladies and gents! I've been thinking too low grade!" Erik waved his hands, finally seeing the light, a massive smile on his face.

"Well, that's nice and all. You going to heal me or can I do it?" Rugrat asked.

"I've got it. Let me help you get the vest off. I've got a plan."

Erik and Rugrat carefully got the vest off Rugrat, exposing the angry-looking wound.

Erik wasn't fazed by it as he pulled out his medical kit. He had Rugrat lie face down as he pulled out medical gloves and disinfected the wound with a spray.

Erik examined the wound with Simple Organic Scan. He could completely see what was happening in Rugrat's body, better than any MRI.

Erik used the Wraith's Touch salve, letting it soak into Rugrat's body. Rugrat let out a sigh as the pain seemed to disappear and he felt nothing.

Erik pulled out a clean scalpel and started to cut into Rugrat's back. He cleared away the dead cauterized tissue till he got to the live tissue.

He checked his watch and the time.

He placed his hands around the wound. Using his Simple Organic Scan, he started to focus on the different layers of the wound. Breaking it down even further, he started to rebuild the layer of fat, then the blood vessels, repairing the subcutaneous layer, then the dermis and finally the epidermis.

Erik physically watched the entire wound seal before his eyes in a matter of seconds.

Erik moved to Rugrat's arm, which he hadn't healed yet. He used Minor Wounds Heal on the area instead of the different systems and layers. His Mana output shot up. The wound was healing, but the cauterized old layer was proving to be in the way. Also the different layers were all greedily taking in the energy, wasting it.

The wound finally healed some time later. Erik looked at the time; it was a third more and he'd spent nearly twice the Mana.

He tapped Rugrat on the back and cleaned up.

"You look like you've figured something out," Rugrat said, waiting.

"Pretty much. The more focused, the better Minor Wounds Heal and Focused Heal is like a shotgun—hits a bit of everything, good to cover a wide area in short bursts, though it's not targeted. The more targeted you are with your spells, the greater effect you will have, like taking that shotgun and turning it into a sniper rifle," Erik said.

"Proceed through the doorway to enter the Beast Mountains trial," a powerful voice declared, coming from the doorway.

"Is there a time limit of how long we can be in here for?" Rugrat asked.

There wasn't any reply from the door.

"Guess there isn't." Rugrat shrugged. "You raise an interesting point, though."

Rugrat pulled out his notebook that he'd written SMITHING on the front.

After the speed potion wore off, they were both feeling haggard from running so much.

Seeing that the door didn't say anything else and nothing happened, Erik checked on his skills and Experience gain as he started to settle down.

72,687/100,000 EXP till you reach Level 12

Skill: Healer
Level: 43 (Apprentice)
You have become familiar with the body and the arts of repairing it. Healing spells now cost 5% less Mana.

Damn, showing my medical knowledge and healing spells together seems to have a multiplicative effect on increasing my skill level.

He started to read the Alchemy book Tommins had given him.

They sat there in silence, each deep in thought.

It wasn't until sometime later that Rugrat surfaced from his notebook.

"Don't you find it weird how used we've come to getting hurt now?"

Rugrat's words stopped Erik. His eyes couldn't help but dim as he thought of that hospital bed and waking up to the news that he didn't have legs or an arm anymore.

If this was on Earth, then it was likely he would have lost his arm just a few minutes ago. Instead of worrying, he dealt with the pain, even went so far as to get Rugrat to heal him, which was slower than him doing it himself to increase their Experience gain.

His first thought was that there was something wrong with them.

"Well, with healing, damage isn't permanent. In some cases, it can even increase your strength. Maybe it's like how people say that working out is harming your body and others embrace the growing pains of becoming stronger," Erik said.

"I guess that it is all mental," Rugrat said.

Erik and Rugrat took their time and checked their gear. They even pulled out their most powerful pieces, so that they could put them on at a moment's notice. They pitched a camp, not wanting to go into whatever was on the other side of the door unprepared and in less than their best condition.

The door continued to tell them to enter but Rugrat put his earplugs in and went to sleep as Erik kept watch.

"Beast Mountains Trial—wonder what that's all about." Erik just shrugged and leaned back on his rucksack, checking out the stage and doorway.

39
ENTERING THE BEAST MOUNTAINS TRIAL

Elder Rei and the different elders watched as the tower disappeared and the stage they were on started to dim.

Just a few hours after the trial had begun, youths started to appear on the stage. If they broke their medallion, then they would be sent out of the trial. If they didn't, then they would be lost to the trial. It was unknown how many geniuses had been lost to the trial so far.

"The first level is a sneak attack, with the other levels being about defeating creatures of the different attributes that grow increasingly stronger. It is no simple task to reach even the third level," one of the elders said.

The other elders all agreed as more and more people appeared.

Those in the first hour had made it to the first stage. They all knew enough to be ready for the first sneak attack on the grassland, but the second one, the creature was randomized. It was best to get a sneak attack on it and then kite it around, leading it with attacks until it was worn out and dead.

Similarly, with the following creatures, one had to work to maximize their attacks and minimize the energy expended.

This was the tenth time that the Beast Mountains trials had been opened and many knew of different tricks to increase their disciple's abilities. When someone left the Beast Mountains trial, they were given a score that they could purchase items with before they left.

In the third hour, people started to appear with Apprentice-leveled weapons. They were decent, but nothing that a sect of faction would care about.

In the sixth hour, people with high Apprentice-level weapons and mid-range Mortal fighting skills appeared.

Through to the tenth hour, people appeared with high Apprentice-leveled weapons, armors and concoctions, with high Mortal grade skills, proudly displaying off their goods.

It was in the thirteenth hour that people started to slow as they reached the sixth and seventh stages.

Did the idea that we come up with work? Elder Oui thought, worrying about his niece.

His eyes turned dark as he saw Xi Yan appear on the stage. The arrogant little boy looked angry but still walked toward his uncle without problem.

It wasn't hard for Elder Oui and the others to understand that Xi Yan had been chasing Julia Oui across the Beast Mountains to this location.

Xi Yan had only gone a few steps before his body shuddered under the murderous intent coming from Elder Oui.

Elder Rei lazily waved his sleeve, breaking Elder Oui's intent.

Xi Yan smirked at Elder Oui, as if looking down on him. Elder Oui hadn't ever wanted to kill one of the younger generation so badly.

"Excuse little Yan. He's rather abrupt in his pursuits. Love makes a man do many crazy things." Elder Rei laughed.

Elder Oui's anger only built, knowing that Xi Yan's interest was not in love but in lust.

Just as he thought that he wouldn't be able to hold it anymore, a person appeared on the stage, Julia Oui.

He saw Xi Yan look at her. His rage flared once again as he let out an attack, sending the boy sprawling.

"Watch where one's eyes go," Elder Oui said, moving to his niece.

"Elder Oui," Elder Rei said in a chastising way. He couldn't let his Willful sect nor his own blood relation take this kind of embarrassment.

"Elder Rei, you should know my temperament and resolve," Elder Oui said. His words sounded simple but there was a clear threat hidden within.

"The old should not interfere in the young's actions," Elder Rei warned.

"The young should know when to fight instead of hide behind their subordinates. I wonder why I see none." Elder Oui looked around.

Elder Rei gritted his teeth.

The blood is similar, using others as pawns to increase their own ability.

Julia Oui had already moved to her uncle.

Using a spell, she was able to talk to him without anyone else discovering it. "Instead of fighting the second beast, I snuck past it. Instead of seeing another beast, I saw a man, a man who saw everything." Julia shivered.

Elder Oui was shocked by her revelation. "We will talk about this later, somewhere that there aren't so many people."

Erik and Rugrat got up off the ground, packing their gear away.

Erik was now wearing the full Golden Fox armor, minus the helmet.

Golden Fox Cuirass
Defense: 59
Weight: 7.3 kg
Charge: 23/100
Health: 47/113
Base Value: 32 Gold, 17 Silver
Slot: Takes up chest slot
Enchanted Ability: Agility increases 2% per hit, can stack a total of 5 times (5% for a total of 12 times 4/5 Golden Fox Armor Set)
Innate Ability: Reduce magical attacks effect by 5% (12% 4/5 Golden Fox Armor Set)
This is a set item. When two or more set items are combined, the abilities of the set items will increase.

Golden Fox Greaves
Defense: 63
Weight: 5.7 kg
Charge: 37/100
Health: 67/109
Base Value: 36 Gold, 13 Silver
Slot: Takes up leg slot
Enchantment: strength increases 4% (5% when paired with Golden Fox Cuirass)
Innate Effect: Reduce magical attacks effect by 3% (5% 4/5 Golden Fox Armor Set)
This is a set item. When two or more set items are combined, the abilities of the set items will increase.

Golden Fox Gauntlets
Defense: 53
Weight: 3.2 kg
Charge: 21/100
Health: 31/109
Base Value: 27 Gold, 59 Silver
Slot: Takes up arm slot
Enchantment: strength increases 4% (10% 4/5 Golden Fox Armor Set)

Innate Effect: Reduce magical attacks effect by 3% (7% 4/5 Golden Fox Armor Set)
This is a set item. When two or more set items are combined, the abilities of the set items will increase.

Golden Fox Boots
Defense: 72
Weight: 1.8 kg
Charge: 73/100
Health: 77/107
Base Value: 31 Gold, 13 Silver
Slot: Takes up foot slot
Enchantment: Agility increases 4% (10% 4/5 Golden Fox Armor Set)
Innate Effect: Reduce magical attacks effect by 3% (7% 4/5 Golden Fox Armor Set)
This is a set item. When two or more set items are combined, the abilities of the set items will increase.

Erik felt his whole body had undergone an upgrade. His reaction time was almost the same as when he had taken the speed potion; his defense had a major upgrade and his strength made him feel invincible.

Erik punched forward, feeling the power rushing through his body as the formations inside the armor glowed, feeding him power.

The force of the punch threw Erik off-balance.

"Okay, damn," Erik said.

Rugrat watched from the side, wearing his "sneaking kit," as he called it. He looked like a cross between a sniper and a beggar with a woodland-looking archer headdress meant to help people blend into the environment around them, then a leather cuirass that had seen better days, fingerless gloves for his bow, trashed pants, and his runner shoe lookalike shoes.

Erik moved around to get used to the new power and the greater Agility.

Rugrat seemed to melt into the fabric of the square as he stayed absolutely still. Erik didn't even notice him as he worked to get greater control over his new attributes.

Finally Erik got the hang of it to the point that he felt confident moving forward.

He looked around for Rugrat, seeing him creeping around in a corner. "What the hell are you doing?" Erik asked.

"Grinding out my stealth skill and Experience." Rugrat shrugged. "As much fun as it is to see you fall all over the place, you want to go and see what is waiting for us inside this beast trial?"

"Proceed through the doorway to enter the Beast Mountains trial," a powerful voice declared, coming from the doorway.

"Not like we didn't hear it the first couple of dozen times," Rugrat said.

The two of them stepped forward to the door. The door started to open, revealing a grassland beyond.

Erik and Rugrat passed through the door, which quickly shut behind them, as if it were scared that they might go backward.

"I've never met two people who care more about preparing than actually doing the trial. Most of the others have already left!" The powerful voice seemed to take on a complaining tone as Erik and Rugrat looked at each other in confusion.

"Shit!" The voice disappeared as it seemed to realize it had done something wrong.

A creature in the grasslands jumped out at Erik and Rugrat's backs, giving them little time to react.

A rumbling roar could be heard inside Erik's body as he used Growling Tiger Elbow.

Rugrat moved to the side, trying to pull out his pistol, but Erik was already reacting.

Erik's elbow shot out, hitting the snake.

It exploded from the force on its body, covering Rugrat with the remainder.

"Not cool, dude. Not cool." Rugrat wiped some blood out of his massive headdress.

Erik tried to help him as another door descended.

"Only when you pass through the door will you have completed the trial." The voice returned again.

"Growling Tiger Elbow? What kind of made-up shit is that?" Rugrat asked.

"Well, it worked didn't it?" Erik asked.

Rugrat looked over himself. "Kind of," Rugrat grumbled.

Erik checked his information. There wasn't a tombstone to be found of the creature.

You have learned the skill: **Hand-to-Hand**
You like to fight up close and personal, using your fist against theirs. You don't need weapons as your hands are weapons.

Skill: Hand-to-Hand
Level: 7 (Novice)
No bonuses at this time. You must prove your skills first.

You have reached Level 12
When you sleep next, you will be able to increase your attributes by: 5 points.

24,437/120,000 EXP till you reach Level 13

"Damn, it's good to kill high-leveled creatures!" Erik said.

Rugrat cleaned himself off as best as he could before they moved toward the door. Once they got to it, the door opened. Waves of heat rushed over them as if they were standing in front of a blast furnace.

They dug their feet in and strained their eyes against the hot air, looking into the depths.

Inside they saw a slumbering creature. With its scales, size, and lizard-like appearance, it seemed like a dragon without the wings.

"Well, looks like there be dragons in these realms," Rugrat said in a pirate voice.

Erik wanted to smack him but held back. It certainly looked as if it were related to a dragon.

Maybe it's a dragonkin? Like how there are dogs—their ancestors are wolves, but they're just weaker versions. This one's like a twice removed on my mother's side, grandson from a dragon.

Erik couldn't help but grin. He felt the thrill of fear and excitement, knowing that there were dragons in the Ten Realms.

His smile dissipated as he studied the dragon kin. It might be a weaker version of a real dragon, but it still wasn't simple; it was certainly much stronger than him and Rugrat.

"Time to play chicken with a dragon," Erik said.

"Ohhh, I think I just got goose bumps," Rugrat said.

The dragon kin didn't notice the two idiots that had wandered into its home. Instead, it continued to lie on the ground, sleeping peacefully.

40
MAN IN MACHINE

Erik and Rugrat didn't move in directly; they moved off to the side and Erik lay down to sleep and put his attribute points to work.

You have 5 attribute points to use.

One in Strength, one in Agility, one in Mana pool, and Mana Regen and Stamina Regen.

Character Sheet
Name: Erik West
Level: 12
Race: Human
Titles:
From the Grave
Strength: (Base 7) +10
170
Agility: (Base 6) +12
90
Stamina: (Base 10) +1
165
Mana: (Base 6) +8
140
Mana Regeneration (Base 4) +19
5.35/s
Stamina Regeneration: (Base 7) +15
5.15/s

When Erik got up from where he was sleeping, he could feel the rush of new power in his body.

"All right, let's do this lava world shit," Erik said.

Rugrat got up from where he was. They looked over the terrain and discussed it with each other.

"Well, instead of facing it head on, why don't we just go around?" Rugrat asked.

"What?" Erik asked, a bit stunned that such words came from Rugrat's mouth, and also realizing that for once he was the one about to charge in and do something incredibly stupid.

"It's on its home turf—we're not. Maybe it'll have buffs for being in an environment that is a greater advantage to it. Mages using fire spells get buffs when they're in places of greater heat like volcanoes," Rugrat said.

Erik took a step back. He had been simply thinking about the Experience that they might gain, looking at the creature as the prize. If they were fighting every beast, then they'd get tired; they might gain Experience but there was no telling that they might win.

I'm wearing this armor and I might have increased a level but it doesn't mean that I am invincible. Far from it.

Erik took a moment to step back, looking at the situation differently.

"The voice said that we only need to get through the door on the other side," Erik said. Unlike the trial they had just passed, they could already see the door on the other side.

"Right, so if we can skirt around the outside, not wake it up, we should be able to get to the other side without any issues," Rugrat said.

"I'd say that it's worth a try."

They surveyed the area once again. Erik removed his Golden Fox armor and wore the best stealth gear Rugrat gave him.

They moved through the door slowly and carefully. It closed behind them quickly as they fought to adjust to the soaring temperatures. Both of them looked at the dragon kin as the door disappeared behind them.

There was no reaction from it as the door closed and then disappeared.

Erik followed Rugrat's lead as they moved around the outside of the map. They had to keep drinking water the entire time as they moved, crossing over lava flows and past hot gas pockets that would shoot up poisonous gas at random intervals.

It was slow work but Rugrat forged a path through it all, with Erik following.

They reached the other door. It opened to reveal a man sitting on a chair, with a desk in front of him. His eyes glowed as he looked down on Erik and Rugrat.

Erik and Rugrat moved through the door, ready to face any threats that they might find on the other side.

"You have successfully completed the first two stages of the Beast Mountains Trial. You have shown that in times of need, you will react without hesitation; instead of charging forth into a known battle, you are willing to meekly avoid it to save your energy. Now you must pass through the remaining three trials. Do you wish to continue as a team?" the man asked.

"Yes," Erik and Rugrat said at the same time, with no hesitation in their voices.

The man looked at them both. It was as if they stood before a veteran non-commissioned officer; there was nothing that they could hide. They stood up straighter, as if readying themselves for whatever trial was to come next.

What test had they gone through together and not had to suffer through until the end? They weren't going to just give up now.

Their fighting spirit was ignited. They were going to win this trial.

"Good." The man smiled as they disappeared.

Erik and Rugrat were covered in white light. Erik saw himself as a child, then growing up through elementary school, the high school, onto the army and training, the different war zones, the different people, the failed marriages, the lost experiences and time.

The pain and hell he had been through. Erik was panting, his emotions a jumble as the white faded away and he appeared in another space. Another flash of light appeared next to him as Rugrat was revealed. They nodded to each other and looked away, getting themselves focused and not wanting the other to see the tears and pain in their eyes.

"You have passed the test of character. Pick one of the workshop masters in front of you to judge your item. You can both attempt this trial or only one," the door voice said as they were looking at several men and women who looked at them with blank expressions.

Erik and Rugrat looked at each other.

"I'll give smithing a shot," Rugrat said.

"Sounds good to me." Erik wanted to be an alchemist but he hadn't ever tried it out before, only read about it. Rugrat, although he had only tried smithing out for a short period of time, knew much more of the basic working with metal than Erik knew of working with magical ingredients.

It was one thing to harvest them, another thing entirely if he was thinking about trying to make it.

"I'll do smithing," Rugrat said. All of the people went dim except one woman who stepped forward, looking at Rugrat and spitting on the floor.

"Well, this should be good," the woman said in a gravelly voice that came with working around smoke and hot metal for most of one's life.

"Can I ask questions?" Rugrat asked.

"Yes, you are free to do so," the woman replied.

"Any question related to smithing?" Rugrat asked.

Erik didn't know what the other was thinking but by the look in his eye, it wasn't simple.

"That's correct, as long as it pertains to the item you want to build," the smithing lady said.

"What if you aren't able to answer the question?" Rugrat asked.

"Then I'll freely admit you've passed." The woman laughed, not caring for Rugrat's words.

"Even if there was a time limit of, say, five minutes?" Rugrat asked.

"Even if there was a time limit of five minutes," the woman droned on. She seemed interested in Rugrat's mysterious words.

"Right, how do I build this?" Rugrat directly pulled out his pistol and displayed it to the woman.

The woman's smile stilled on her lips. Her brows came together and she moved forward.

Rugrat emptied the pistol, pulling out the magazine and storing the round in the chamber.

"No formations to add abilities, made from simple Mortal steel, multiple parts working together in different fashions. Could you take it apart for me?" the woman asked, intrigued.

"Sure." Rugrat quickly disassembled the pistol, putting the pieces on the ground.

"The workmanship on this is exquisite—few to no flaws. And the different processes to create these parts… There is specialized metal coating this cylinder here and there's exact grooving down it. Whoever made this must have spent hours to put all of these pieces together." The woman sighed.

"What if I was to tell you that this was made with a batch of weapons, hundreds of them, all of them the exact same," Rugrat said.

"What? That's impossible! It would take hundreds of people to make these and to do it the same way. That's not even in the realm of possible," she argued. Suddenly it was as if a bolt of lightning had gone off in her head. "You're a new arrival! You're not originally from the Ten Realms!"

She seemed to get excited and wary at the same time as she looked at them both closely again.

"Merrin." The door's voice seemed to remind her of the task at hand.

"Okay, so this, well, the main body you would need to cut out from Mortal steel, possibly even Earth steel. I'm talking about the basic version, that is. The parts would similarly be made with Earth grade steel, though you would need to shape it with different machines, from this here, to this." Merrin started to get into greater depth as Rugrat hung on every word, writing it all down.

Erik, seeing that they wouldn't be done anytime soon, sat down and got comfortable.

Rugrat went into a greater depth, talking about how one would form the ingot, refine it and then use that to form the pistol between them.

To Rugrat, it was as though he'd wandered into the damn candy store. Merrin talked about the processes that one might refine an ingot. Adding in different kinds of ingredients could actually increase the attributes of a normal steel ingot; this could, in turn, form the innate ability of the weapon. Certain ingredients were resistant to fire, some to ice or lightning and so on.

Then, from creating the ingot, one would have to then form it into their desired shape, or turn it into a sheet and then cut it to the needed shape.

The thing was that the Ten Realms didn't really have measurements. There were rules that were made when making certain things, but centimeters and meters were a foreign concept. When Rugrat told Merrin about it, she nodded, as if understanding it.

"When making complicated smaller machines, as you call them, then it would be necessary. We're building much larger items here, or one-offs. Even with blueprints, the final product isn't the exact same as the materials used and the shape that it comes out has been altered by the crafter.

"In nearly every crafting trade, secrets are only passed from master to disciple so that the information doesn't get out. Measurements, as you say—well, each crafter has their own, or they have to attune their senses to what their craft might need and they do it based on what they think."

It was Rugrat's turn to be thoughtful. They moved on to the barrel—made from one solid blank of stainless steel—and the processes—one might use tools or they could use spells—to alter the steel.

"Tools are used the most, but there are people who are capable of using magic to form metal to the needed requirements, though they're not as strong, I've found."

"Which will be able to hold the pressure the best?" Rugrat asked.

"Pressure?" Merrin asked.

Rugrat decided to put the pistol back together. "So, when I pull the trigger, the thing called a hammer moved forward." Rugrat pulled the trigger. "Now that would hit the primer, and ignite the gunpowder, firing the projectile or bullet." Rugrat pulled out a magazine and pointed to the parts of the round.

"Ah, it's like the Sha fighters! I knew it was similar!" Merrin smacked her knee.

"Sha fighters?" Erik asked, perking up from all of the boring smithy talk.

"Sha fighters use smithed weapons, like this, to fire projectiles through a combination of arrays and fire powder that their alchemists make. Their weapons are much cruder than yours, but I would think that they are stronger due to the formations and the fact that they use a stronger material to make their weapons!"

Finally they reached a stage where Merrin couldn't go any more as she didn't understand pressure, recoil, and how the Alchemy side of things worked.

"All right, you pass this stage. Damn thing's like a Sha weapon but instead of just firing one shot at a time, it should be able to fire multiple times," Merrin said, annoyed at being beaten, but excited by the weapon in front of her.

The door's voice sighed. "You've passed the fourth trial. You will now enter the fifth trial."

A white light enveloped them both.

41

NEW QUEST

Erik fell on his ass hard while Rugrat stumbled around a bit before he got back on his feet.

He looked around. They were outside of a simple-looking village. A one-hundred-meter area around the village had been cleared for farmland. The walls were simple, just two stories tall and made of mud, with nothing much to them.

People moved into the city, talking to one another. They didn't seem to find Rugrat and Erik's entrance out of the ordinary.

"For the next trial, you simply need to hold off five waves of beasts. As long as you both don't die, then you will win." The door voice disappeared again.

"I don't know about you but I really want to know who's actually behind that voice." Erik wiped off the dirt from his ass as he got up.

Screens appeared in front of them both.

Beast Mountains Trial
You have made it past the first four trials of the Beast Mountains. The trial ahead does not get easier. For this Quest, you will be seen as Lords by the people of Alva and gain control over the village building interface.
Requirements:
Survive the beast horde (5/5 Waves remaining)
Rewards:
Dependent upon results

"I feel like there's a lot not being said here," Erik said, looking at it all.

"You and me both. I thought that we were supposed to be fighting beasts every level?" Rugrat asked.

"Seems that we found the Easter egg inside the trial?" Erik looked toward the village and then the ground around it. "Well, we'd best go and meet the locals."

They started down the dirt road toward the village, passing farmers in their fields, working and talking to one another.

They got to the front gate. A guard looked them over and stepped forward. "State your business."

"Beast horde?" Rugrat asked.

Erik closed his mouth, shooting a look at Rugrat.

The guard's eyes went wide as he looked around to see that no one had heard what they'd said. "Are you the people sent to assist us in the defense of our village?" he asked in a low whisper.

Erik and Rugrat looked at each other before facing the guard.

"You could say that," Erik said.

"Please, please come and follow me." The guard quickly waved them forward and pulled them into the village.

The city seemed quiet and reserved. People greeted one another in the street. It seemed homely and easy as people went about their day.

"I have a feeling they haven't been told," Rugrat said.

Erik nodded. Based on how the guard had reacted and their attitudes, it didn't seem as if they knew of the coming beast horde.

The roads were simple packed dirt. There wasn't any drainage. Houses were made from a combination of wood and dirt with no stone buildings.

The guard led them to the largest building. It was two stories tall and looked over a square where people were looking to sell their wares.

They passed the guards who stood outside the building, passing people grouped together, bringing up their worries to the lord of the village.

They entered the private area of the residence and reached an office.

"Dani, these are the men sent to assist us against the beast horde," the guard said as he walked up to a secretary.

Her face was pale with the mention of the beast horde.

"I'll get Chief Blaze immediately." She quickly moved to the office door and disappeared inside.

The door opened a few moments later, with a large rough-looking man getting up from behind his desk. "Please come in," he said.

The guard moved aside as Erik and Rugrat moved into the room.

"Thank you for coming so quickly. My name is Blaze." The man came around the desk, quickly shaking both of their hands. He didn't look as though he had been able to get much sleep recently, based on his tired and broken appearance.

"It is no problem," Erik said.

"To defend the village, all of Alva's resources are at your disposal," he said without fanfare.

Title: Acting Lord of Alva
You've been given temporary command of Alva
You have gained control of the village building interface.
Grade: Petty Mortal (Can be upgraded)

Resources
Food: 500 Units
Stone: 50 Units
Wood: 80 Units
Gold: 3

Upkeep costs:
173 Units of Food per week
2 Silver per week

You have gained control of:
Store
Village Hall
Walls
Barracks
Granary
Smithy
Citizens: 181
Guards: 20

"All right, we need to know what the hell we're facing first." Erik looked to Rugrat.

"I can scout the area. Are there any hunters or people who know the surrounding forest?" Rugrat looked to Blaze.

"I can get a few of the people who are hunters in their free time organized." Blaze nodded.

"See if you can't get us some more food while you're out. The first wave is coming in two weeks. We've got enough food for three if we contribute some of our food. Blaze, can we harvest soon?" Erik asked.

"Unfortunately not. It'll be a week before we can start," Blaze said.

"All right, I need to have a closer look at the village, try to get an idea of what is going on," Erik said.

"Got it. Blaze, those hunters?" Rugrat asked.

"Come with me." Blaze led him out of the room.

Erik accessed his Land Holder interface to check the map. At the center of the village was the village square. The city was broken up into four areas. To the northwest was the storage area; this was filled with the granary and sheds to hold the different materials that they had harvested. To the southeast was a store and workshop area. This area melded into the residential area to the southwest. These were simple homes for the people of the village, from the farmers to those who worked inside the walls.

To the northeast was the barracks and smithy. Residential buildings also sprawled over this area as well.

Rough dirt roads went from the rough village square to the north, east, south, and west gates.

He walked out of the office, finding the guard who had led him there waiting for him.

"Mister Blaze told me to wait for you," the guard said.

"Good. We can walk and talk on our way to the store. What's your name?" Erik asked as he walked toward the exit.

"I'm Niemm," the guard said, happy to be of assistance.

"Good to meet you, Niemm. I'm Erik. Now, about your little village—I have some questions."

As Erik talked to Niemm, he got a rough idea of how strong the guards were in the little village. They were little more than hunters who had put on an emblem. They had some organization but it was more of a thrown-together militia than a true policing or military force. Their smith was of the Novice grade, spending most of his time repairing different tools and weapons for the guards.

Their water came from rain barrels and a large well off to the side of the village hall. A stream running nearby had been diverted to water the crops. The nearest village was a week away and most people wouldn't want to leave.

Erik reached the store finally. He moved the flap away and saw a woman putting away different goods.

The woman looked over at Erik, a look of interest appearing in her eyes. "Seems that something is wrong for someone so powerful to have entered our city," the woman said.

"Hello. I was wondering what things you have for sale?" Erik asked.

"I have a number of goods for sale personally, from grain to tools. You can use the sales interface to purchase auctioned items by other controlled villages and dungeons. However, you will need to pay a charge of five percent for each transaction." She pointed to the side.

Erik's eyes followed her hand, finding a glowing formation at the side of the counter. He moved over to it and a screen appeared before him, broken up into different categories.

He moved through weapons and armor. There wasn't just Novice armor—he could buy Expert armor if he wanted to! Though Erik didn't even know what a Sky grade Mana stone was.

He lowered his sights and moved through the different tabs. There were Alchemy ingredients but few recipes. The same went for smithing. The finished products were also much higher and although there was a buyout price, most things had a timer telling when the item would come to an end and the last bids would be placed. The numbers were changing as people bid on different things.

There was a section of the store labelled as Blueprint. People could buy blueprints for different buildings that they could create in their territories. It was like the fine arrow blueprint: someone could make it themselves if they had the know-how, or they could use the aid of the blueprint if they didn't know how to make the item.

Erik moved into the training manuals and technique books area, breaking it down into just technique books and then hand-to-hand combat.

The high-level books were rare. Each one of them was a treasure and few were willing to let them go. Normal manuals and simple training technique books were easily available and cheaper. Still, Erik didn't buy them. He needed to concentrate on saving the village first.

He went into the spell section of technique books. With the gold and silver he had gained from the dead people he had found, Erik only slightly winced as he paid the fifteen silver buyout price for the spell Plant Cultivation. With the 5%, Erik spent another seventy-five copper on the transfer fee.

The rune lit up and a flash of light appeared in front of Erik as a scroll appeared.

Erik grabbed it and rolled it open.

Technique Book: Plant Cultivation
Do you wish to activate this Technique book? Doing so will destroy this Technique book.
YES/NO

Yes. Runes appeared on the scroll as power was gathered together and focused. A ray of light shot out from the scroll and between Erik's brows. He closed his eyes. The scroll disappeared, as if caught alight by an invisible flame.

Information appeared in his mind as he understood how to cast Plant Cultivation.

Erik's head throbbed and he took his time opening his eyes.

Plant Cultivation
Novice
Speed up the growth of plants by aiding them with Mana.
Consumption of Mana based on plant type and growth.

Erik let out a breath. It had been incredibly hard for him to gain technique or information books in Chonglu. With the store here, it was as if he were staring at a gold mine.

Erik opened the store up once again and started to put different things he didn't need onto the store. Having cleared out his storage rings of everything he felt wasn't important, Erik dismissed the screen.

"I've received a notification of your items in the auction place. They'll be sold within two weeks or returned to you," the saleswoman said.

"Thank you. What's your name?" Erik asked.

"I'm Elise," she said with a small smile.

"Good to meet you, Elise. I'll probably be by sooner rather than later."

42

PREPARE FOR WAR

The next stop was the smithy.

Erik saw the smith sitting outside, puffing on his pipe as he watched the guards training in the yard and the people moving around the village. He seemed to have a simple and carefree life.

Erik knew that was about to change.

"Smith Taran!" Niemm called out.

"Hey-o." Taran waved at them as he got up. He frowned slightly as he looked at Erik. "You are the one in charge of the village now?"

"That's correct. I would like to ask you if you can make crossbows," Erik asked.

"Crossbows? I can, but I can only make one of them a day," Taran said, feeling the serious atmosphere that had descended.

"What are the components to the crossbow?" Erik asked.

"There are three components: the mechanism, the body, and the string," Taran said.

"How long would it take for you to make just the mechanism?"

"Just the mechanism? Well, I could make ten of them in a day."

"Good. Niemm, I want you to find people who would be able to carve the bodies for the crossbows, no less than ten per day. Get multiple people if need be, as well as people to do the same for the bow string and another group that will be in charge of putting all of the parts together," Erik said.

"Yes, sir," Niemm said.

"None of them have the expertise though!" Taran said, in a state of shock.

"Well, they will have to learn, won't they? We don't have much time and I want to get as many people with a crossbow as possible in the time that we do have," Erik said.

"So, there really is a threat to the city?" Taran tapped his pipe out on his leg.

"Yes," Erik said, not hiding anything.

"Then I will do my best to make as many mechanisms as possible," Taran promised.

"Good man. I'll make sure that you have all of the materials that you need."

Taran grunted and headed back into his smithy as he started to stoke the flames once again.

Erik moved to the barracks and looked over the guards there. They were level eight, with their commander being a level nine. If this was before Erik had left Chonglu City, he might think that meant something. Now, it wasn't much compared to the people and beasts he had gone up against.

Even if they were level twelves, up against a horde, they would need to fight against tens or hundreds each. It was hard to fight a few opponents, but fighting an army of them, they'd get overrun.

Still, they were much stronger than the level fours and fives that made up most of the village's population.

"Captain Glosil at your command." A thin man smacked his foot into the ground as he did his best to come to attention.

They might be lacking in skills, but they didn't seem useless. Erik looked over them all, analyzing them with the eyes of a man who had trained hundreds of soldiers throughout his life.

"Well, it looks like you're all that I have, so we'd damn well best make use of you!" Erik sank back into his role as instructor as he moved across the front of the ranks.

He pulled out a man's sword and examined it closely, seeing spots of rust. "Have you never heard of maintaining your weapon?" Erik's voice rose until it was a yell.

The guard nearly took a step backward. The man's mouth opened and tried to form words but he didn't know what to do.

"Do you *see* this!" Erik held up the blade and pointed to the faint rust on the blade.

"Yes, sir!"

Erik's eyes thinned but he didn't say anything. These guards didn't know any better.

"What is that?" he demanded.

"It's rust, sir!" the guard said in a panicked voice. His eyes darted around.

"They're not going to save you! Is this their weapon?"

"No?"

"Well, is it or isn't it?" Erik's voice rose into a roar once more.

"It's not!" The man shook now.

"Then it must be *yours*, is that correct?" Erik asked.

"Yes, sir!"

"Were you not taught to clean your weapon?"

"I was taught, sir!"

"Then I'd better never see this rust again in my life!" Erik yelled.

"Sir!" The man stood stiff, afraid to do anything.

Erik threw the sword to the side and moved down the line. All of the men were looking at Erik sideways out of the corner of their eyes, fear in their expression as he went through them, picking out the smallest flaw in their gear or the way that they were attired.

Erik finished and moved to the front once again. Their armor had been pulled apart, their weapons thrown, and they looked terrified and angry.

Erik restrained the smile that threatened to form on his face. *I might be able to make something out of them yet.*

"We have a week and a half until a beast horde arrives at Alva Village. The defense of this village, the defense of the people you care about, will be on your shoulders. There is nowhere to run and nowhere to hide. We will fight to defend this village with all that we have. There will be patrols out every night. There will be attacks on the animal hides in the area to reduce the number that can attack us and you will be a part of this. I hope to raise your levels and increase your fighting capabilities. Listen to me and I will turn you into soldiers." Erik looked at each and every one of them.

"I ask but one thing: carry out my orders. If you don't, then it might be your family, or your buddy, who will die and there is no room here for people who are not willing to follow my simple orders. If you do not think that you can be commanded by me or listen to my orders"—Erik waved to the door of the training courtyard—"there's the door."

The guards looked from the door to Erik.

"This will be the only chance I will give you. Leave now, or stay and fight." Erik's voice was no longer commanding, but calm.

Three of the guards moved for the door, taking off their leathers and gear, talking about the unfairness of it all and how Erik was overreacting.

Erik stopped Glosil, who was about to yell at them.

"Let them go," Erik said.

Another couldn't take it as they dropped their gear and rushed off.

"No one else?" Erik looked at them all.

Seeing none of them move, Erik clapped his hands. "All right, get your gear cleaned up and I want you to have all of your gear in order for tomorrow morning. Tomorrow we will assemble in the main courtyard outside of the village hall to speak to the people and tell them what is coming. During the day, you will be working with the farmers to help harvest the crops outside of the village. From there we will work on our defenses. Questions?"

"The crops haven't been fully grown yet—how can we harvest them? Why would we need them?" a guard asked.

"I have something to improve the rate that the plants grow. In a siege, the biggest factor over time is not how big your walls are. Instead, it is how much food and water you have inside the walls," Erik said and looked to another man with a question.

"I thought that the enemy was only coming in two weeks," the guard asked.

"They're supposed to be here in two weeks but the one thing you'll learn is the enemy, even if it's a damn beast, is never predictable," Erik said.

There were no more immediate questions, so Erik dismissed the men, including Niemm, and pulled Glosil over to his side to have a quiet talk.

"Let's take a tour of the walls," Erik said.

"Sir, for the guards earlier, I can only submit myself for punishment. As you saw, their abilities were weak and they were not keeping with a unit that should be ready for battle."

"This is a rural village and there are few threats around. It makes sense that things have slackened. We will have to make sure that they don't degrade further," Erik said seriously.

"Yes, sir." Glosil looked relieved, but Erik could see the shame underneath at his guards not being the best he believed they could be.

Erik didn't offer any more words. He needed someone else to push the guards as well.

"My plan is simple. We will look to pull the people into the village and I will be looking to the people in the village hall to organize that. You and your men will be focusing on training people on how to use crossbows, building new walls, creating layered defenses and traps in the farmlands. Each of your men will be in charge of five to ten of the villagers to create rotating defense teams when the actual fighting comes," Erik said as they made it to the wall. It was a simple construction of mud and straw.

"I will not let you down, sir," Glosil said, as the reality of the situation seemed to fall on his shoulders.

Erik knew that the true fear, the true weight wouldn't become real until they saw the first enemy.

"I hope not." Erik looked Glosil in the eyes before he looked over the wall. He smacked the wall in a few spots and pressed his hand on it.

Glosil frowned and winced as Erik moved down the wall toward the gates.

The guards stood taller and straighter as the two moved past them and to the outside of the wall, checking it over.

"I am sorry that the walls are not that thick, sir," Glosil said in a faint voice.

"Mud walls shouldn't be underestimated. I've seen them stand up to a Hellcat missile before," Erik said. "Once we harvest the wheat, we can use some of the straw to toughen up the mud and thicken up the walls. We'll need to thicken up any holes and have barriers to put behind the gates. Any modifications we make to the walls will have to depend on what Rugrat and the hunters find on their outing," Erik said, looking to the forest that surrounded the city.

43
THE HORDE

Rugrat moved through the forest easily. There weren't too many creatures in the surrounding area. Most of them were just rabbits and foxes. Rugrat didn't care as he moved through, killing them as they found them.

They disappeared off into his storage ring as he and the hunters moved deeper into the forest. Rugrat held up his hand, stopping the hunters from moving forward. They might know the area, but they weren't that quiet.

They only hunted on the side when they didn't have fields to look after in the day.

Rugrat moved off by himself, his bow down and ready.

There was a litter of boars. The creatures were grunting and making noises at one another as they rooted through the ground, trying to dig out some kind of food.

The farther Rugrat went into the forest, the less food he found.

Rugrat didn't directly attack the boars and moved back into the forest. Once there, he pulled out all the daggers that he and Erik had salvaged in their travels.

He found a long depression with plants in it.

He took the blades, secured them into the ground and bound them to logs so that they wouldn't move or be knocked over.

Rugrat hid them in the bushes.

"All right, I'm going to bring a bunch of boars through here. I'm going to position you. As soon as you see them cross this line," Rugrat used his boot to make a line in the dirt, "I want you to start shooting them with arrows."

The three hunters showed that they understood as Rugrat put them in hidden positions and then went off to where the litter of boars were.

He stood and drew on his arrow, sending it flying as it drilled through the front shoulder of one of the medium-sized boars.

The creature was only a level six, but its natural defense was really high. Still, they were just level six and Rugrat was level twelve with a bow and arrow to augment his base attack power.

The boar squealed and moved a few steps before it collapsed on its side.

The other boars looked around in alarm.

Rugrat didn't wait, drawing and firing his second arrow. It hit a boar, eliciting squeals, but not killing it outright.

The other boars were all gathering together.

"Hey, over here!" Rugrat yelled as he fired his third arrow, killing the boar.

The boars were tired and hungry, on the verge of losing their minds. Seeing Rugrat, they let out squeals and charged him.

Rugrat didn't try to fire another arrow and took off. He watched behind him, making sure that they were following as the remainder of the litter charged through the forest after him.

Rugrat led them into the depression that he'd rigged and fired an arrow back at them, more to anger them than try to kill. It flew over their heads as their pace only quickened.

Rugrat saw the bushes where he had hidden the blades. He jumped, missing the daggers, and kept on running. The boars continued to follow before letting out high-pitched, pained squeals. The daggers had opened them up from below, using their momentum against them.

Some made it past the blades with wounds but they weren't life-threatening. Arrows passed Rugrat, hitting the boars behind him, killing those that were still charging forward.

Rugrat jumped up the side of the defilade, turning and firing down at the boars. In just a few minutes, they killed the remainder of the litter.

The hunters came out from where they were hiding, looking at the boars with stunned looks. Then they opened their screens, letting out cheers as they had broken through bottlenecks in their levels.

They wouldn't fight the boars if they were at their level usually; these wounded and maimed boars were easy to kill under Rugrat's guidance.

"All right, collect the corpses. We'll clean them up when we get back to the village. We aren't done with scouting," Rugrat said, focusing them and silencing them.

They were still wary but they were excited now. As one increased in levels, it would be possible for them to gain a better position in life and be able to determine their own future. They collected up the bodies into their storage rings. Rugrat found that not many of them actually had storage rings, so he took the majority for himself and cleaned the daggers off before storing them.

They moved forward and killed three more litters of boars, racking up some fifty boars before Rugrat started to ignore them and move forward.

The hunters listened. They were pleased with their gains and wanted to keep on hunting boars, though their gains were diminishing. Rugrat was getting a hundred points or less per kill while the hunters were getting thousands in one shot. All of them were now level six and reaching for level seven. Rugrat was pleased in their increase of power but he still needed to know everything that they were fighting. They could kill boars all day long but they would run out of ammunition at some point.

Seeing the rewards that they could gain in following Rugrat, they listened to his every word and did their best to try to aid him. They avoided the groups of boars to find groups of wolves that ranged from level six to level eight, and then there were the panthers that roamed in small packs.

Rugrat halted everyone as he heard the sounds of a fight. The hunters all dispersed under his command. He moved forward to get a better look.

Well, that's not good.

Erik was staying at the City Hall, looking over the different reports he had got from Blaze, the village leader.

It wouldn't be the easiest to defend Alva, but Erik felt that it was possible.

Erik was sitting out front of the village hall when he saw Rugrat dismissing his hunters and moving to Erik.

"What are we looking at?" Erik pushed forward a beer.

Rugrat took a long drink before wiping his face with the back of his hand. "Looks like the creatures in the area grew in massive numbers, to the point that they've eaten the other materials in the area.

"First, we've got boars stripping the ground clean of any vegetation. They've grown in massive numbers, allowing the wolves that hunt them to have plenty of food and grow as well. Then there are the panthers that eat both of the other creatures and finally, the king beasts of the area—level nine and ten bad boys: bears, sabre tooth, even a few cougars." Rugrat sat in the seat opposite Erik.

"What do you think is going to happen?"

"Once the creatures get scared or hungry, then they'll either charge from the rear, the smell of blood startling those that are weaker, or the weak are going to charge forward, get wounded, either by us or naturally, then the smell of blood will entice the higher-level creatures," Rugrat said.

"Well, that sounds like a hell of a lot of fun," Erik surmised.

"How's things on the city side?" Rugrat asked.

"Guards are okay. Thinned them out some to get the ones who will stick around. I want you to take them out on patrol, get used to seeing the enemy, kill some, get them to a higher level."

"Great, more training." Rugrat shook his head. "The hunters are okay. They'll be decent and they're around level six, some level seven, so it'll be possible to use them to bolster up the people in the village."

"If possible, I want to get the guards ready to take out some villagers, get them to thin out the boars, increasing their level and confidence. You good taking over that side of things?" Erik asked.

"Shouldn't be a problem. Defenses?"

Erik pulled out a piece of paper. "We've got the city here. It's not big but lines of traps are going to be hard. Thankfully we're dealing with beasts so we can modify accordingly.

"First, I want to have a series of traps set up over dug-out pits with fresh meat at the traps. The boars are aggressive but they're not meat eaters. They'll move away from these places, or they'll go in the hole—doesn't matter much really.

"The second ring, I want to make obstacles, funnel the creatures down more—thinking sharpened stakes tied together. The next line will be inside bow range. I want to have deep pits with sharpened stakes. The final defense, I want small potholes all over the ground meant to break the creatures' ankles as they enter bow range. We hit them with bows and they have to amble forward, in too deep to get away easily." Erik tapped on his picture that now had four circles surrounding it.

Erik and Rugrat spent the night going over their plan. As their Stamina had increased, they didn't require much sleep. They grabbed a quick nap before the sun came up.

44

DIVISION OF TASKS

Blaze reported that the people for Erik's crossbow production were ready. Erik okayed the plan and they started working on crossbows that very morning.

Rugrat had also passed over his fine arrow blueprint reluctantly.

"Get this put into production as soon as possible," Erik said to Blaze.

"This..." Blaze took the blueprint as if it were a newborn child.

"The crossbows by themselves won't be that strong. Paired with arrows from this blueprint, we'll be able to increase their lethality," Erik said.

"This is too precious," Blaze argued, prepared to give it back.

Erik pushed it back to him. "We need to defend this village. If we're going to do so, we need to use everything at our disposal."

Blaze finally relented, looking at the two men with new eyes.

Next, Erik went to the store and accessed the store interface once again. He purchased several sound talismans and their additional consumable message scrolls.

It cleared out his remaining liquid cash, as he bought the two most expensive ones he could afford.

Sound Talisman
Allows one to send and receive messages over long distances.
Range: 1 km
For distances over 1km, you will need to use message scrolls in combination with the sound talisman.

He met up with Rugrat in the main square as people were gathering from the surrounding farmlands. Erik passed him a sound talisman and a number of message scrolls.

"Well, looks like this will solve the whole communication issue," Rugrat said. It looked like an armband and went on one's wrist.

"There are spells to communicate with one another but they only have a range of one kilometer," Erik said.

"What is with the damn metric system for everything?" Rugrat complained.

"Way of the world, and universe, I guess." Erik shrugged. He was used to it.

The villagers and farmers were all looking at the small stage in the square where Blaze stood, ready to talk to them.

He let out a whistle, the entire square becoming quiet. "I have been keeping something from you all," Blaze said. Everyone frowned and looked at him in question. "In a week and a half, a beast horde will descend on our village."

The crowd turned chaotic, starting to talk over one another as they began to panic.

A piercing whistle made them hold their heads and look to the stage once again.

"The surrounding cities and villages are too far away. We will not be able to get to them in the time that we have left. Thankfully, we are not alone!" Blaze pointed to Erik and Rugrat, who were beside the stage. "Hearing our plight, Erik and Rugrat were sent to aid us in our time of need. They have a plan for our village and a way for us to remain safe."

Blaze looked around the crowd. They had calmed down a bit.

"I have stepped down from my position as village leader and they have taken over to lead us through this time. Please let them explain their plan."

Blaze moved to the side as Erik and Rugrat moved up to the stage.

"The days ahead will not be easy, but if we work together and everyone plays their part then we will be able to weather the beast horde. Already we have seen what we are facing. We are making crossbows for our defenses and later today we will begin harvesting your fields so that we might have enough supplies to hold us through the siege. Everyone who is able to wield a weapon will be taught to do so.

"Rugrat here is in charge of taking groups out beyond the wall and training you in the use of the crossbow. He will be training the guards and then training all of you. I will be coordinating everything inside the village for its defense. If you have any questions, please see Blaze.

"This is not only a time of danger; it is a time of opportunity. Just look to the hunters in your ranks. Have you noticed the increase in power? All of them have made it to level six or seven in just one day of working with

Rugrat. It will be easy for all of you to do so as well. Alva Village will come out stronger after this all than we did going into it." Erik looked to them all. They were just scared people, farmers and simple workers who built Alva with their hard work and sweat, looking to expand into the wilderness. Now they found that the wilderness was coming for them in a terrifying manner.

"First, we must not let your crops go to waste. We will work to harvest everything that you've grown in the next few days. As this goes on, Rugrat will be looking to form militia groups. No one is exempt!" Erik said.

"What if you're crippled or weak?" an old person yelled out in the crowd.

"If you are weak, then there will be food to help you gain strength. If you are wounded or hurt, I will be healing people. It will be mandatory for everyone to come and see me for a check-up," Erik said.

A stunned noise went through the crowd and Blaze looked at Erik with surprise.

"Is he one of those famed alchemists or healers?"

"Why would someone skilled in healing come here to a doomed village?"

"I am a healer and a fighter," Erik said loudly, clearing up the small conversations. "I will also be looking to train people in first aid, the art of healing people or making sure that they survive long enough for me to take a look at them. This will not require magic, but simple supplies that we have in village," Erik said.

This stunned people even more.

"All right, everyone make a line. Once you've been looked over by myself and Rugrat, you are to meet with the guards, who will assign you a group that you will work with and fight beside," Erik said, ending the speech.

He stepped down from the stage as Rugrat stepped forward as well. Erik looked over the person in front of him: a middle-aged woman with a tired appearance. "First I'm going to see if you have any injuries, diagnose you so that I know if you will need to have anything healed," Erik said.

"O-okay," she said.

Erik took her wrist and sent his Simple Organic Scan through her body, checking her body.

"How long have you been pregnant for?" Erik asked as he examined her. The formation around his hand changed as he used Focused Heal on the woman's joints that were in bad condition and to her lower back, where she had multiple issues from hard labor.

She let out a sigh as the small aches and pain from her body started to go away and she stood up straighter, a bit of the tiredness in her expression dimming. "Pregnant?" she asked, confused.

Erik smiled. "Well, it looks like Alva will be welcoming a new resident in six more months." Erik pat her hand. "Since you're pregnant, you won't be placed on the front lines but we still need your help to make weapons and defenses."

"Yes," the woman said as the man beside her moved closer.

"Is what you said real, Sir Erik?" The man seemed to be stuck between shock and fear.

"It's just Erik and yes, it is. She'll be having a boy in six months." Erik looked at them both. It was clear that they were together.

"Dammit, Clevus," the woman said, tears in her eyes as she playfully hit her husband.

"Well, I can't do nothing but take responsibility." The man laughed as she hugged him.

The crowd congratulated the two and laughed with them. With the shocking news from earlier, hearing something good raised their spirits.

Erik smiled on as he looked to his next patient, examining them. He winced as he saw the man's fingers on one hand were all nubs.

The man pulled his hand back, trying to hide it away, but Erik's grip was firm.

"You want little nibblets on your hand or would you like fingers?" Erik asked.

"Fingers?" The man looked to be in rough shape. In a farming community, unless you could work and you had a complete body, you were useless.

"I'll take that as a yes. This won't be as easy to deal with. How are you with the sight of blood?" Erik asked. Everyone was watching as Erik and Rugrat worked on people.

Rugrat healed a man with a nasty cough and then a woman with severe migraines.

"You want to deal with the severe cases needing a rebuild; I'll do triage and check them over?" Rugrat said, looking to simplify the process.

"Okay, I'll work on them in the village hall," Erik said.

"Works." Rugrat nodded. "All right! Line up in front of me. I'll quickly look you over. I'll either give you a clean bill of health and send you to the guards, who will organize you and you'll be looked over later, or I'll send you to Erik in the village hall for any intensive kind of healing. Once I've checked everyone, the remaining people I'll work to heal myself," Rugrat said.

Erik made the man with the missing fingers follow him into the village hall. He took over an empty office and had the man lie on the desk.

"So what's your name?" Erik pulled out some Wraith's Touch salve, applying it to the man's hand.

"Storbon," the young man said simply.

"Okay, just look at the ceiling and I'm going to just work on your hand here." Erik pulled over a bucket and put it under the man's hand as he took out a knife, studying the man's hand.

"Will we really be okay against the beast horde?" the man asked Erik after a few moments.

"We will, if we work together." Erik checked Storbon's reaction as he slowly poked him with the knife. There was no reaction.

Erik went to work. First he put a tourniquet around Storbon's wrist, then he started to open the skin and then remove the infected or mangled remainder of the hand.

"Aren't the beasts really strong? I know my mom said that I should run away from the beasts in the mountain until I was stronger than them," Storbon said.

"Your mother sounds like a wise woman," Erik said, working quickly. Not having to worry about the damage he was doing, he quickly cut the hand back. Thankfully the enchanted blade was much better at cutting than any surgical blade he had used.

Using a sword to do surgery, oddity fact two hundred and thirty-nine being in the Ten Realms. If it works, then it ain't stupid no more.

"How strong are the beasts?" Storbon asked.

"The weakest, around level six, but then they can reach level ten," Erik said calmly as the blade went back into his storage ring.

Storbon sunk into thought.

The tourniquet had slowed the bleeding down as Erik started to reform the missing bones in the hand as well as the tendons to hold them in place. He built up the hand finger by finger, then went backward, focusing on regrowing the muscle overtop and finally the skin.

"I'm only level four. How can I fight against a level six creature?" Storbon said.

"Levels isn't everything. Trust in Rugrat, myself, and the guards. You're a strong young lad. If you follow what we say, then we can turn you into a soldier." Erik wiped sweat off his face, his hand covered in blood.

Storbon looked at Erik's hand in alarm and then at his own hand.

His face went white as a sheet as he saw a fully formed hand. Erik grinned and pulled off the tourniquet. Adding in a Minor Wounds Heal, the hand came alive as blood pumped into it and the tissues were revitalized.

"I can feel it, really feel it!" Tears appeared in Storbon's eyes.

Erik sat there and smiled. When he lost his limbs, he had been stuck in a pit of despair, but seeing Storbon fighting on, he felt bad for wallowing in his self-pity, and he could understand the feelings that Storbon displayed.

Erik helped Storbon up and to the door. Already there was a guard there, helping people.

"Thank you, Mister Erik!" Tears fell down Storbon's mud-stained face.

Erik smiled and smacked the man on the back. "You've fought this hard for most of your life already. I know there's a place for you in the Alva militia. Make sure you go report to the guards when the time comes. I want to see you on the wall beside me," Erik said.

"I will do as you say!" Storbon pulled himself up.

Erik sent him on his way and looked at his next patient. "Hello, Miss…?" Erik stretched out the word as a woman who was half bent over was waiting for him next. There was already a small line waiting for him.

"Louiez, Roska Louiez," the woman said in a hoarse voice.

Erik brought her into the room and looked over her injuries. "How did this happen?" Erik asked. The pain she must be in was incredible; she had multiple broken bones that had healed in the wrong way.

"Got kicked by a horse, left me all broken," she said.

Erik helped get her up onto the table and then looked through her body more thoroughly. His eyebrows rose in shock as he found something hidden in her broken body.

She had nine open Mana gates. This could explain how she had survived so far. If her wounds could be healed, then her strength would surge upward.

"All right, I'm going to put you to sleep, but once you wake up, you'll be much better," Erik said with a smile.

Roska looked up at him. She was a hard woman, unlike Storbon who had hope and optimism. She had lost that long ago.

Erik pulled out another concoction he had bought in Chonglu from the apothecaries, Winter's Sleep. He took out a drop and put it in Roska's mouth.

She swallowed it as Erik held her wrist, checking her pulse and examining what was happening inside her body, ready to act if anything went wrong with the drugs.

She lost consciousness. Erik saw that there were no complications and started to get to work.

He pulled out a blunt metal rod. He took out a blade. Making sure that there was no reaction to being stabbed, he healed the wound and put the blunt object to work, re-breaking the bone and putting it back into the correct position before fusing it together with Focused Heal.

Rugrat sat at the front of the line. He'd cleared out the worst cases, passing them to Erik. There were only four or five people who were in need of his care. A village out here in the middle of nowhere wasn't able to support many people who were heavily injured.

It was harsh, but a reality of being out here in the wilderness.

Colds and hidden issues were simple enough to heal with Rugrat's Focused Heal or Minor Heal Wounds. He simply poured in energy until the issue was resolved; it was simple but effective. Rugrat cycled through people, sending them to the guards, who organized people, sending some off to building groups that Blaze was organizing, to training groups that would be called up for training with crossbows in the coming days.

Most were grouped together but sent back to their farms to prepare to harvest their crops.

Rugrat finished healing those in his line and headed over to the barracks where the first three groups of people had begun training.

The groups were made up of ten people, for a total of eighteen groups. Three had been sent to help in making crossbows, arrows, or defensive instruments. Five had been dismissed back to their farms to harvest crops. Five were taken to the woods to gather wood. Three more groups were assigned to the guards to learn how to fight. The last twenty had been released back to their roles as their jobs were necessary to the running or management of the village, from the granaries, to the newly created kitchen staff, essentially support groups to take care of the storing and use of foodstuffs.

Each of the groups in training had three guards or hunters with them to show them how to use their crossbows.

As such the nearly two hundred villagers got to work.

Rugrat listened in on the lectures before grabbing onto his five-man scouting party that was made from hunters and guards. They all had their own weapons, thankfully.

Right now they had a total of twelve crossbows, including the seven that they had scrounged up from within the village.

"All right, everyone get in nice and close." Rugrat showed them a map of the city and the surrounding area. He pointed out where he wanted to patrol together and his aim to scout out the enemy and slim down the number of boars in the area. There were two hunters from the last day. Rugrat found that they were willing to learn and take orders from him yesterday; seeing their potential, he elected to bring them out again. One, to bolster the number of people who could handle themselves and two, to show off to the others how strong they could become if they listened and obeyed.

It seemed to have Rugrat's desired effect.

All of them paid attention before Rugrat checked their gear and then they headed off on their mission.

Rugrat looked over to the village hall as he was leaving. Erik was still working on the bad cases, but there were only three more people left to go.

It was time to build their foundation in Alva Village.

45
HARVEST

Erik came out of the village hall with his last patient. They thanked Erik profusely as they left.

The village seemed to be filled with energy as Blaze came over to Erik. He quickly updated Erik on everything that had happened while he was healing people.

"Good. Well, it's time that we looked into that harvest." Erik moved toward the village exit and the fields beyond.

Blaze followed him. They found people with tools sitting around and talking to one another casually.

"Well, let's begin!" Erik clapped his hands. He moved forward into the field. People moved around lazily.

"Does he think just because he commands it, he can make plants grow?"

"I heard only alchemists can do so," another said.

"These crops still need a month more to grow at least," another farmer opined.

Their voices weren't quiet and Erik easily heard them. He didn't grow angry; it was understandable that they were confused.

"Plant Cultivation," Erik said quietly. A spell formation appeared around him on the ground. It was simple compared to the Focused Heal and Minor Wounds Heal, but it was a much larger area of effect spell.

Erik closed his eyes as he focused on the Mana draining out of him to support the spell formation. He adjusted so that his expenditure matched up with his Mana Regeneration.

All around him, plants started to grow within the range of his Plant Cultivation spell.

Erik used what he knew from Focused Heal and Minor Wounds Heal. Plant Cultivation was a much simpler spell, but as he changed his thought process around the spell, actually changing the spell's framework, less of his power was wasted.

The speed of the plants' growth increased with Erik's smaller changes.

"Uh, when do I know they're ready for harvest?" Erik asked out loud. Sure, he knew the spell, but he wasn't a farmer nor did he know these plants.

The farmers, who had been looking at him slack-jawed, recovered quickly. It looked as though he wasn't some growing god.

"That should be good, if you want to move onto the next area!" Blaze said, the first to recover.

Erik moved forward. The Plant Cultivation spell was centered around him, so as he moved, he pulled it with him; with his footsteps, plants grew all around him.

"Would you be able to tell me about farming? The more I know about the plants, then I should be able to increase the speed they grow at."

Erik's words shocked the farmers slightly, but Blaze was starting to get used to expecting that nothing was simple with Erik or Rugrat.

"I'd be happy to help." Blaze looked to the farmers who had been lounging around. "Well, what are you looking at? Don't you know how to harvest crops?"

His words lit a fire under their ass as they were jolted into action.

"What do you wish to know about farming, Mister West?" Blaze asked.

"Might as well start from the beginning," Erik said seriously.

"From the very beginning, like clearing the fields?" Blaze questioned.

"Might as well. I'm going to be out here awhile and who knows what might help out," Erik said.

Blaze cleared his throat and organized his thoughts. He quickly told Erik how they cleared the land first, removing the trees and other vegetation. They would then burn the remainder down and till the fields, mixing the ashes in and taking out the rocks that were underneath.

Then they would plant their crops, making sure to water them. Then it was necessary to watch the weather: too much or too little of sun, water, or nutrients in the soil and the plants would wither and die.

Erik listened to it all as he looked over the plants and checked on his spell. He gained an understanding of how to tell when the plants were ready for harvest; he learned how to harvest them as well.

He was thankful that no one had seen him "harvesting" the different plants in the Beast Mountains. In the eyes of these farmers, let alone alchemists, it would be seen as sacrilege and a near thing that he didn't ruin the different ingredients.

The farmers might have been slow to react, but now, seeing Erik walking through the fields, leaving ready to harvest plants in his wake, they eagerly set to harvesting their crops.

It wasn't until the sun had set that Erik cancelled his Plant Cultivation spell.

He let out a tired sigh. The farmers were lagging behind. Even with them all working together, they weren't as fast as Erik was. "Finish up what you're working on and we can start fresh in the morning," Erik said.

This gained their agreement. Instead of seeing him as an outsider, they'd become closer to him as they saw him take the time to learn about how to be a farmer and worked with them to grow their crops.

If it wasn't for him, they would have lost the crops that they had worked on all growing season.

They cleared away the last of the food and brought it into village with them, passing it off to the people from the granary to clean up and store.

While Erik waited, he checked on the notifications that had appeared while he was working.

Skill: Healer
Level: 42 (Apprentice)
You have become familiar with the body and the arts of repairing it. Healing spells now cost 5% less Mana.

Skill: Alchemy
Level: 17 (Novice)
No bonuses at this time. You must prove your skills first.

21,497/120,000 EXP till you reach Level 13

Rugrat had dealt with the simple injuries; these would only give Erik a small amount of Experience gain as it was easy for him to deal with now. The more complicated the wound or process required to heal a person, the greater the rewards, allowing Erik to increase his Experience gain.

Growing plants with spells was also part of the Alchemy skill and had allowed him to gain a deeper understanding of the plants and alter the spell, reflecting in his increased knowledge and thus skill in Alchemy.

His Experience gain had truly reduced to a trickle. Fighting against stronger beasts and working with unlimited materials to increase one's skill were the fastest way to level up, but one needed to have the knowledge and ability to do so.

He could only sigh, knowing that his Experience gain was slowing down.

Still, he took it as a victory as he watched everyone gathering up the last load of harvested grain with smiles on their faces.

They headed back together. When they reached the village square, they could see people roasting large boar carcasses. These were the same boars that Rugrat had killed earlier.

Even Erik couldn't help but swallow in anticipation as he smelled the roasted meat.

Rugrat and his group returned from their adventure. Rugrat dismissed them as they mingled with the rest of the groups that had gone through training.

Meat was a rarity in Alva, high-level beast meat even more. It could give one bonuses depending on how well it was cooked.

Erik was looking forward to digging in.

People sat together around the tables and seats in the square. There was no platform and people mingled together, talking about what they had experienced. Rugrat's group talked of the boars they had fought and proudly told everyone of how their levels had increased. Some had made it to level seven and were advancing on to level eight; it was slower progress but it was only a matter of time to them.

Others talked of the crossbows, putting them together, and how to use them. Others about the harvesting of wood and the fields, or how they had formed the wood into odd, sharpened defensive objects.

Through this, everyone was able to see progress was being made; they were able to come together as a community.

"So what the hell is this? Some kind of simulation?" Rugrat asked.

"Hell if I know. You got any clues?" Erik asked.

"Nope. Seems real enough." Rugrat shrugged.

Erik pinched Rugrat.

"Ah crap! What was that for!"

"Wanted to make sure." Erik chewed on a piece of boar.

"Why did you pinch me? Shouldn't you have pinched yourself?" Rugrat complained.

"Nah, might hurt." Erik shrugged.

Rugrat looked as if he were going to club Erik with his boar leg when someone cleared their throat behind them.

They both turned around, as if nothing was out of the ordinary, Rugrat's arm still holding the boar leg high.

Standing before them was a simple-looking girl. Her face looked as though it was normally screwed up in a scowl but now she didn't know where to look as she wrung her hands.

"Roska," Erik said. It took him a moment to recognize the young woman in front of him. When she had come to him with her massive injuries, most would have given up on her; instead, he spent nearly three hours, working to rebuild her body. She still needed a few more treatments before she was fine, but the major damage had been dealt with.

"I told you to rest and eat." Erik's expression darkened. He had put a lot of work into healing her and her body needed nutrients to make up for the energy her body had expended.

She seemed to stiffen her resolve as she looked up at the two of them. "I want to be useful. I want to help you out, Mister West," she said in a strong voice.

Erik looked her over and saw the look in her eye. She wasn't to be denied. "Once you're healed and *only* then will we talk about what the future holds," Erik said.

Her potential to be a mage was incredibly high. It would be hard to find someone as strong as her within the Mortal realm with nine open Mana gates. Thankfully Rugrat had been able to gather a number of Mana cores from the boars. Erik could sell those off easily to the store and then use the funds to buy different spell manuals to increase Roska's fighting power.

It was Erik and Rugrat's hope to create a quick reaction force that could be used to bolster the village's defense when under pressure.

Although he had these avenues, Erik wouldn't pursue them unless he had complete faith in Roska. After all, he could buy better weapons and equipment instead of those costly spell technique scrolls and books.

"Rugrat, got another one for your patrol tomorrow," Erik said.

Rugrat lowered his boar leg bone and studied Roska. She tried to stand straighter, but her body was still broken in places.

"Still need some more healing," Rugrat commented.

"I'll heal her in the morning," Erik said.

"Will you be okay by the afternoon?" Rugrat asked Roska.

"Yes!" she said.

"Better be," Rugrat said.

"Eat and rest. You're going to need it," Erik warned.

"Thank you," she said before quickly moving away.

Rugrat looked to Erik.

"You want me to go easier on her?" Rugrat asked.

"You know the saying—the more you sweat in training, the less you bleed when the fight comes," Erik said.

"You got something planned?"

"Part of your quick reaction force if she's any good—maybe give you a new mage. She's got a ton of open Mana gates. She'd be an asset. Just need to see if she can listen to orders though," Erik said.

They ate in silence, looking over everyone in the village. They knew that it would be hard in the coming days, that they would be changed. This wasn't just about the quest anymore; these were honest and simple people who deserve their protection.

They'd put their all into making sure they could survive.

"I'm going to see if I can't crack some more of those Mana gates open before that time comes." Erik stood.

"So damn boring," Rugrat complained but he rose as well.

Erik shook his head, a grin on his face.

Erik got settled in the village hall, blocking off everything going on around him. He turned his attention to his body and Mana gates he had opened. Slowly he started to compress and guide the mist-like Mana through his Mana channels. It was much sturdier than the last time he had opened a Mana gate. At the same time his mana density had only increased. Still, he didn't rush to clash with the remaining Mana gate in his left foot that he'd targeted.

He took his time, compressing more and more, speeding up the rotation before he started to form the Mana and it passed through the main Mana channels in his legs, expanding them. They were like dried-out riverbeds accepting new rain. As the Mana rushed through and struck against the gate in his foot, a deep noise rang through Erik's body and he trembled.

Mana was drawn in from the surrounding area, drawn in through his four open Mana gates. They were like mountain springs: their energy rushed together, meeting up like a torrent as they were pulled in by the circulation in his Mana channels that compressed and sped up the mist before being diverted toward the Mana gate in his left foot.

Erik felt more in tune with the Ten Realms than ever before. The feeling of drawing in power from the Ten Realms to temper his Mana channels and his Mana gates was heady and intoxicating. Erik increased the speed of his circulations, pouring more attacks into his fifth Mana gate. Listening closely, one could hear the sound of wind even as the room was still; it was Mana being drawn through Erik's Mana gates.

An explosive noise sounded in Erik's body as his left foot's Mana gate broke down. Mana rushed in through the Mana gate, being drawn into the cycle of compression happening inside Erik's body.

Erik's eyes opened. The corners of his mouth lifted slowly as he called upon the Mana in his body and the ambient Mana entering his body. Suddenly multiple arrows of compressed Mana rushed from his center and into the Mana gate resting in his right elbow, eliciting a ringing noise like metal hitting metal.

"Break for me!" Erik yelled as his body started to glow, Mana tracing through his Mana channels. His Mana channels were forced open as he focused his entire body, his mind on breaking through the limits.

Erik's eyes closed, his eyebrows coming together as he fought. The slightest mistake and he would fail in opening his Mana gate, and it would be impossible to open it ever again.

Erik bared his teeth. He had walked through hell; he had lived in pain; he'd embraced it, turned it into strength. If there was an obstacle in his path, he would forge ahead. Life wasn't easy and this was a lesson he had learned long ago.

The Mana gate showed cracks and weaknesses. Erik started to laugh. This was living; this was victory! He was broken, a fucked-up soul. He fought for no other purpose than his brothers and sisters; he had fought because it was the only thing he knew how to do.

He lived for that drive, to go up against it all, to know that his actions had purpose—that was what made him feel alive! The Ten Realms wasn't a prison to him: it was a future, a new life that gave him a chance to do anything!

Challenges? Those were just more reasons for him to fight, to forge his own path ahead.

He had been passively living in the Ten Realms, but now as he struggled to increase his power, he started to know a truth. He started to think on the motto of the Ten Realms—fortune favors the strong. He wanted to rise to the limits of the Ten Realms, to touch upon godhood.

Wouldn't that be something. Even if I don't succeed, even if I get halfway and it's all game over, wouldn't it be one hell of a thing to have tried?

Erik's body seemed to inflate with the power circulating his body. His Mana channels were being torn up, showing signs of strain as he pushed past their limits.

His Mana channels were forced open wider.

His attacks increased again as he let out a low yell through his gritted teeth, holding up his arm and opening his hand.

A shatter noise rang through his body as a part of the Mana rushing through his body shot out of his hand, creating a bolt of pure Mana that struck the wall before him.

The wall exploded outward and debris rained down on the small street behind the village hall.

Erik was thrown back by the close explosion, going through the wall in the opposite direction and into the hallway.

Rugrat burst out of his door, shredding it as he looked to Erik.

Erik looked up from his hands in shock. "I can shoot Mana out of my hands!" Erik yelled.

Rugrat halted his movements. "You okay?"

"Yeah." Erik looked up at the hole in the corridor wall and the now nonexistent wall in his room as part of the roof collapsed. "Shit. That might not be so easy to fix."

Rugrat put away his gun and looked at the damage. "Yeah, this room's fucked."

Erik's adrenaline started to wear off as he discovered the pain he was in. The hidden power in his blood that had been brought out through tempering was already working to heal his internal injuries.

With enough time, with just my tempered blood, I would be able to recover completely.

Erik didn't need to rely on just his blood and sped up his recovery using his healing spells. He let out a sigh as the tears in his Mana channels were repaired, the rest of his body rapidly recovering from the bruises and minor cuts.

Erik noticed that Rugrat was looking at something through his busted wall with a displeased look on his face.

Erik got up and walked over to him, following his line of sight over to the barracks, where the guards were being pulled awake and organizing themselves.

Erik's joyous expression darkened as well, seeing just how fucked up they were.

"I'll go sort them out," Rugrat said.

"You need a hand?" Erik asked.

"You need to sleep and put those stat points to use."

"Right," Erik said.

Rugrat jumped out of Erik's room and landed on the ground, the three-meter drop not affecting him in the slightest as his body's strength and agility had surpassed any human's back on Earth.

Erik changed to another room and got comfortable in his sleeping bag. He opened up his notifications, a smile spreading across his face.

You have pushed your Mana channels past their limit and increased their overall capacity and ability.
+1

You have opened another Mana gate!
+2 to Mana Regeneration

You have successfully opened 6 Mana gates.
+1 to Mana Pool

Quest Updated: Opening the Fourteen Gates
Congratulations! You have opened your sixth Mana gate.
Requirements:
Clear all of your fourteen gates (6/14)
Rewards:
+1 to Mana Regeneration base stat
Undergo Mana Body Rebirth
1,400,000 EXP

You have learned the spell: **Mana Bolt**. Your spell book has been updated.

Mana Bolt
Shoot out a blast of Mana from your hands. Medium Range.
20 Mana per blast. Power and distance can be increased with higher Mana cost.

Erik's entire Mana system was drained but he could feel it trickling in through his Mana gates with even more power than before.

He was excited to test out the functions of Mana Bolt. It was his first ranged spell and the destructive force from blasting his wall apart and him backward left him excited.

Erik took a moment to focus his mind and think on his goals. "If I can increase my Stamina recovery, then I'll need less food and less sleep so that I can work more. If I increase my Mana Regeneration, I can then pop open another Mana gate, maybe two before the horde comes. I'll be able to heal more people if they're injured and speed up the rate that the fields can be harvested."

What about that poison? If I use that, then I might be able to at least temper my body some, getting closer to Body Like Stone. The biggest problem is balancing how much damage I can do to my body, while sustaining myself with healing spells, letting each system be destroyed before rebuilding them.

Erik sighed. He didn't want to waste the poison, but he didn't know what he could do. Too far and he would die; just enough and he would be able to increase the recovery ability and strength of his body explosively.

"Stamina and Mana Regeneration it is." Erik thought on his logic a few more times before shrugging. There might be a better idea, but that was what he had so far.

He closed his eyes as he heard Rugrat yelling in the distance.

You have 5 attribute points to use.

Character Sheet
Name: Erik West
Level: 12
Race: Human
Titles:
From the Grave
Land Holder (Temporary)
Strength: (Base 7) +11
180
Agility: (Base 6) +13
95
Stamina: (Base 10) +1
165
Mana: (Base 6) +9
150
Mana Regeneration (Base 6) +20
5.95/s
Stamina Regeneration: (Base 7) +16
5.35/s

46

PHASE ONE COMPLETE

Rugrat woke up early in the morning. He checked on Erik, who was still sleeping, before heading to the barracks.

He walked through the village and saw a boy running around the village. He had seen the boy sitting in a corner last night while everyone else was celebrating. He had been the one without any fingers and bad damage to his body from a life of labor; now he looked like a healthy young man filled with determination.

Rugrat diverted from his path to the barracks. "Wait up!" Rugrat called out.

The boy didn't seem to pay attention as Rugrat grumbled and had to jog to meet up with him.

"Heya!" he said as he ran next to the boy, shocking him and almost sending him sprawling.

"S-sorry, Mister Rugrat!" Storbon said, all jittery and scared, not knowing what to do.

"No worries." Rugrat smiled. "What's your name?"

"Storbon, sir," Storbon said, looking slightly panicked.

"At ease. I'm not here to yell at you." Rugrat laughed.

"I heard you with the guards last night." Storbon then looked embarrassed at what he'd said.

Rugrat's lips pinched together. "That was a different matter. There was a possible problem inside the village and they couldn't get themselves organized or ready. If we're going to make it through this coming battle, we need people who can get themselves sorted out and organized quickly. If I intend to train a group of soldiers, doesn't matter if they're a militia or God's given Marines, I'll damn well make sure that they're worthy of the uniform they wear," Rugrat growled.

The atmosphere was tense as Rugrat cleared his throat. "So why are you running around?"

"Mister West said that he wanted to see me on the wall beside him, but I'm not that strong so I wanted to get stronger," Storbon said.

He ain't even lying. Rugrat looked away, sinking into thought. "What group are you a part of right now?"

"I'm with the group that is chopping down wood," Storbon said.

"You trained with a crossbow yet?"

"No, sir." Storbon looked a bit awkward.

"What is it?"

"I don't mean no disrespect, but I'm not that good with anything ranged. But I'm good with things in close," Storbon said.

Rugrat frowned and then his face seemed to darken.

"I'm sorry, Mister Rugrat!" Storbon said, panicking.

"It's not your fault, boy. Actually, I should commend you. I never thought about the fact that the fighting might not just be long range. Dammit, Rugrat, you idiot." Rugrat hit his head.

Storbon looked confused.

"All right, so ideally we're going to engage the beast horde at range and there'll be nothing to reach the wall—all good, safe, and sound. The fact is that ain't going to happen. There will be breaks in the line and the beasts will get to the line. We're going to need people with close-range weapons to finish off the beasts that make it to the walls or over it. So, Storbon, you ever used a spear before?"

Erik woke up as light came in his new room's window. He felt energized, his whole body filled with energy as he got up.

His interface was flashing with a message symbol. When he had put on his sound talisman, the message icon had appeared, linking his interface and the talisman.

"Ran into Storbon this morning—put me on to something. So far we're only training people with crossbows. We're going to need people who can fight in close. Going to start training other groups of people with spears for close-range fighting. My plan is to train everyone with crossbows first so that they're able to weaken the beasts at range. I'm going to get the guards to pick out people who might be better suited for using spears. I'll teach some of the guards and then they can teach the recruits. I'm out to scout around with my new batch of guards. I'm taking Storbon as well. Looks like with him and Roska, we've got the start of a good quick reaction force if we can level and train them properly."

The recorded message ended and Erik recorded his own message to Blaze.

"I'll be out in the fields. Organize the farmers to start harvesting as soon as possible." Erik quickly set out and headed for the fields. The faster they harvested the fields, the sooner they'd be free to train with crossbows, or help build up the defenses that would go where the fields now lay.

A few people were waking up with the sun as Erik walked out of the gate. He looked over the guards. They looked as though they hadn't had much sleep but he could see changes in the way that they held themselves, no longer slouching and keeping an eye on the surrounding area.

He made it out into the surrounding fields and cast Plant Cultivation again. He didn't have Blaze there talking to him about the fields and the plants; instead, he had his memories and the information he had remembered.

The area of effect for his Plant Cultivation spell was larger than before and his pace was faster with the additional five attribute increase to his Mana Regeneration and his Mana pool's increase of twenty.

All around him, the field continued to grow and ripen. He messed up a few times as the plants weren't ripe enough or they were starting to falter because they'd grown too much. After some adjustments, he found his pace again and moved forward.

For three days, Erik worked in the fields to make the crops ripen. At night, he would heal people if they needed it. Erik would assist Rugrat in training the guards as needed.

Rugrat would train the guards in the morning before he took out a group to the forest to hunt boar. Then he would take another group in the afternoon, returning at night to train the guards once again.

The groups were rotated from training, to hunting, to working in the fields and chopping down wood.

Other set groups that weren't able to do physical labor, or were better suited for crafting, worked to create crossbows and defensive instruments, such as spikes, and hedgehogs, basically crossed wood that had been sharpened into spikes. There were also others who looked to the food of the village. All of the food was divided equally, each person having meat and grains to fuel their activities. Most of them probably hadn't eaten this well in a long time.

Rewards in the shape of salted meat were handed out to people for doing well in their training.

Erik stopped in mid-afternoon as he looked over the latest crops behind him.

In three days, he had walked through all of the farmland around Alva. All of the plants were ready to harvest.

The farmers were working quickly together to harvest it all and send it to the granary.

Seeing that he had time, Erik checked on his Land Holder interface.

Resources
Food: 2,371 Units
Stone: 50 Units
Wood: 230 Units
Gold: 8.389

With the harvest, their food levels had shot up; adding in the meat from the boars, they had plenty of food ready.

They had been harvesting wood since they started. As people increased in strength, then they were able to cut down and carry more trees per day. Stockpiles of wood were laid down outside the crafting workshops.

Rugrat had gone through and broken down the crafting into processes so assembly had increased in speed.

With the boars, they not only produced meat but monster cores that Rugrat sold at the store. A few of the items on auction had been bought out already but Erik was hopeful that more might be bought in the coming weeks.

Erik went to an area that had been marked off with stakes. This would be where the first defensive line would be located, with spaced-out pitfalls and traps with meat to entice the predators.

Erik took a stance and angled his right arm up. He directed Mana through his body, compressing and building it up. He accelerated it right out of the Mana gate in his hand. A bolt of blue Mana raged before it hit the ground. It touched the ground and exploded.

Erik ducked down as dirt rained over him. He looked over where the Mana bolt had landed. He looked at the crater and then back to his hand. Slowly he looked around to make sure no one else had seen his display.

"I'm a human grenade launcher, right." Erik put down his hand and walked to the crater. It was three feet wide and two deep.

After fifteen minutes, a group of guards moved to Erik with some of their trainees armed with crossbows.

Erik nodded as he watched them approaching.

They slowed down as the guard Niemm moved forward.

"Mister West, we heard a noise." He looked to the pit next to Erik.

"Good reaction! Smart, bringing some of the trainees to bolster your numbers. There is no need to worry. I was just testing something out," Erik assured them.

"Yes, Mister West," Niemm said.

"You can get back to training. I'm going to do some more testing." Erik moved off. He pulled more power and circulated it before shooting it out. Its trajectory wasn't straight and it arced, like a grenade launcher, as well.

The people watched as Erik blew another hole in the ground before examining it.

Niemm led his people back to the village to continue training.

Erik headed back after some more testing and moved over to where the crafters were working. Taran was working day and night to build more crossbow mechanisms. He had improved his failure rate and could make twelve a day now. The woodworkers and assembly teams had increased their production accordingly.

There was a total of seventeen groups, but only thirteen of these groups would see combat, requiring nearly one hundred and forty crossbows.

They had fifty crossbows in use already, and it would take eight days to make the remaining crossbows. Just two days short of when their quest said the beast horde would arrive.

Erik looked in and watched Taran at work. He didn't interrupt and left silently.

Rugrat has the theoretical knowledge. If I take over the afternoon group heading out into the woods, then he could focus on smithing—maybe working with Taran, get the basics down and share knowledge. They'd be able to increase the speed they work at. Might even have one of them making crossbows and one making spear heads.

Ever since Storbon had brought it up, Erik and Rugrat realized their oversight. Storbon was growing quickly under Rugrat's tutelage, and Roska applied herself to every job she had, looking to show off her ability.

Time that I adjusted my plans slightly.

Erik headed to the store. He found Elise there, salting meat and readying it for long-term storage. Although they had storage rings that could keep the meat fresh, they would still need to have a fire to cook it up properly. This wasn't ideal for the hunters if they went out for long periods of time, or if they needed food during the siege.

Erik wanted to be prepared for any occasion.

Meal packs were being organized so that at least everyone would have a few meals on them at all times.

"How can I help you today?" Elise asked as she worked with the meat and salt.

Erik was about to let her get back to work when he realized he hadn't asked a very important question. "What is the store—not like this physical place, but the interface and everything?" Erik had been rushing about and he hadn't thought of it.

"The store is something that only the leaders of a dungeon or a base can use, or they can give authority to people inside their city," she said simply.

"Dungeon or base leaders?" Erik asked.

"You are the acting base leader of this Alva Village. There are also people who control dungeons." Elise shrugged.

"They sell things between one another?" Erik asked.

"Yes. The auction isn't as good as if they were to sell to one another directly. Though it cuts down on the time that it takes to transfer things, across realms or between realms, albeit at a higher price," Elise said.

"So I can buy things from the Tenth Realm in the First Realm," Erik said.

"Yes, if you have the money to do so." Elise nodded.

It's a way for the leaders of these bases to sell off items that they don't need to gain riches. They can also use it to buy items that they desire. Some regions might have an abundance of one resource but be lacking in another, even across realms. Though there aren't that many things for sale, there's hundreds of thousands, but not millions or billions. Either the Ten Realms is smaller than I think, or most base leaders and dungeon bosses don't give access to their people. This makes sense; if they gave access, then it could cause chaos in their own city if there's a resource that they want to focus on gaining. It also gives the leaders more options to make money. Say there's an influx of items in their residence, then they can sell those items on the auction for a large profit.

He didn't waste any more time talking and went up to the auction platform.

First, he bought thirty simple shovels. Then he directly placed a bid for a healing powder auction that was ending soon.

He watched as the timer went down, having to increase his bid as someone beat him out.

Finally he won, at a bid of one silver and thirty-two copper per batch of powder, for a total of two hundred units deducting five gold, eighty silvers, and eighty coppers included in the transaction fee charged by the auction platform.

They appeared in Erik's storage ring directly as he winced. It had taken out over half of his accumulated gold.

Gold is gold. We can get it back, but lives can't be replaced. Erik looked over different sets of gear up for auction. He found a simple cuirass for sale.

Basic Leather Cuirass
Defense: 24
Weight: 5.3 kg
Health: 97/97
Base Value: 1 Silver, 23 Coppers
Slot: Takes up chest slot
Innate Ability: **Red Haze**. Upon killing 2 enemies within a 20s window, one's Strength will increase 1% and last for 30s. If user kills 1 more within 10s, then Strength will increase by 2%. Effect can be stacked up to 15%; will last 45s (will be renewed upon killing again).

It looked useful as hell and just what Erik needed. But the bids were actually around eighty coppers and there was still a day to go.

Erik took down the details and looked to Elise. "Does something seem to be wrong with this armor?" He showed Elise the information he copied down.

"It looks like Apprentice-level armor to me. That innate ability, Red Haze—I'm not sure what that's about. Sometimes innate abilities will be good, but they can have negative effects as well. I can get more information but that will cost three silver," she suggested.

Sometimes there were hidden effects with armor. The armor looked really good, but Erik had bought enough things online that he knew it was best to know everything about the item he was buying instead of getting it on impulse.

The armor was in bundles of ten. If he could secure this armor, then it might be possible to armor ten of the village's people.

He handed over the three silver. She used it to get a message scroll; using it with her sound talisman, she sent off the question.

Erik still had money left, but he didn't want to waste it.

"It might be some time till I get a response. As soon as I do, I'll let you know," Elise promised.

"Thanks." Erik headed out of the store. He didn't have anything better to do, so Erik used a shovel and stakes to outline the defensive lines. Now that the farmland had been cleared, he had a clear view from the city walls to the forest. It was time to move into the second phase of work: focusing on their defenses and their forces.

47

PATH OF THE SMITH

"That's about it!" Rugrat said in a happy voice as he patted Erik on the back. They'd been looking over a map that Rugrat had been updating and working to mark all of the positions of the different boar litters around the village.

Even though they had been hunting for three days straight, they could only kill some forty boars a day. There were hundreds if not thousands in the surrounding area and they were moving closer to the village every day.

Today it was Erik's turn to lead out a group to the forest. Rugrat was heading off to the smithy to learn more skills and help in building up arms for the village.

Erik could only shake his head and wave him off. "Go and play with your metal. Buy what you need from the auction house."

"Don't get lost! I don't want to have to come and find you!" Rugrat said.

Erik flipped him the bird.

Rugrat left the main village square; he followed the familiar path to the barracks and the attached smithy. He saw guards training the village folk. They were shaky, but they were improving quickly. These were, after all, lessons that could help them defend their homes.

He walked up to the smithy, where Taran was working on different crossbow mechanisms.

Rugrat waited until he had finished one before he cleared his throat.

Taran looked up with a frown on his face. His eyes caught Rugrat and his frown turned into a smile. "Got time for something other than hunting?"

"Erik told you?" Rugrat said.

"Yeah, let me know last night that you might be coming around to help me with the smithy." Taran stretched out his back. "So what do you know about smithing?"

"I have a good grasp of the concepts but I just haven't got any of the basics."

Taran nodded and waved Rugrat over. "In that case, I'll start simple. We'll make one of those spearheads first." Taran took an ingot of metal from the side and placed it into the burning coals. "Do you know what the stages of refining a weapon are?"

"First, sourcing the materials from the ores—where were they located, under what conditions did they appear. Then, refining the materials, combining them and tempering them with other items to increase their power, strength, durability, or innate abilities. Then there is the forming of the items—taking the refined materials and using different techniques to turn them into a finished and final product. This is broken down into shaping and tempering. Then if it is possible, the final stage is actually placing an array or formation on the weapon to give it further enchantments or abilities," Rugrat said.

Taran grunted in agreement. "This iron ingot here isn't anything special, but we're not making anything advanced, to be honest. What we need to focus on is heating up the iron so that we can forge it into what we want." Taran turned from heating the ore, then brought it out, using his tools and hammer to shape the metal, putting it back into the flames to keep it red-hot and then worked the steel again.

Rugrat watched as Taran formed the iron under his hammer. First he flattened out the ingot into a long strip, then he started folding the iron over at one side. Using a metal rod, he formed the socket of the spear, heating and hammering as needed.

Once that was finished, he moved to the actual spearhead, shaping it out and then hammering the edges. He let the spearhead cool and the red glow disappear before he tempered the spearhead, quenching it and pulling out the finished product.

Then he let it rest on some coals for its final tempering.

Rugrat watched Taran and thought on the information he had gained through the different books and scrolls he'd looted from the warrior's body and the bodies of the Willful Institute disciples.

Taran wiped some sweat off his forehead as he looked at Rugrat. "You think you've got the handle of it?"

"I've got some of it down," Rugrat said.

"Well, with smithing, one doesn't learn just through reading and watching—have a try."

Rugrat nodded and selected an ingot and started to warm it.

Taran started to heat up his own iron as he needed to work on more crossbow mechanisms.

Rugrat heated up the iron and pulled out a hammer he had looted from a Willful Institute disciple. He moved to one of the anvils and started hammering. With his strength, he was able to shape the metal faster than Taran.

He put it back in the furnace to keep it cherry-red. He focused on the metal and the rhythmic hammering as he and Taran worked.

He flattened out the iron and then started on the socket. He made it too thin and it failed. Rugrat put the iron into the furnace, to melt it down. He pulled out another iron ingot and started again.

Rugrat failed three more times before he was able to complete his first spearhead.

He studied it and put it to the side. Then he grabbed his first ingot and hammered it into the first shape he wanted; he started again. He finished his second spearhead and went to the third.

He stood in front of the furnace for a few seconds, reflecting on the failures that he'd had, the successes, then the final product. He pulled up his notepad that he had been writing on as he read through whatever manuals he had been able to read and his knowledge from Earth.

Rugrat pulled out the iron ingot and started on his next spearhead. He circulated the Mana in his body, directing it through the open Mana gate in his hand. His hammer glowed as his blow hit the iron, a bit of the Mana being absorbed into the iron.

That's it—that's the feeling I'm looking for!

Rugrat finished the spear and picked up the next iron ingot in a rush. His blows were powerful and sure; his eyes didn't move from the metal as he hammered on it. Red and blue sparks flew from his hammer as he worked, making Taran look over in shock.

Rugrat finished the spearhead in record time but he frowned, tempering it and putting it to the side as he worked on the next and the next.

Rugrat felt that he was *just* out of tune with the metal, as if there was a barrier between them. Unconsciously, he pushed more Mana into the metal. He was using Simple Organic Scan without knowing it after healing for so long.

As he worked, his mind worked through what he knew; it created an outline in his mind.

Rugrat moved to his seventh spearhead. All else in the world had faded away as he had turned into a forging machine.

He placed the iron ingot into the furnace, not noticing how the spell around his hand holding the tongs and the red-hot metal had changed.

A look of understanding and shock filled his mind as information seemed to explode in his mind. He could see the form of the iron, its very makeup. Rugrat perfectly tempered the iron, taking his time to understand this ability to see through the metal.

He placed it down on the anvil; his hammer blows rained down and the metal sang as a wide smile appeared on his face. Mana was stirred up in the air as it was forced through his body, through his tools, and into the iron. He was actually changing the composition of the iron slightly with the infusion of Mana.

A blue mist had appeared around the other spearheads, but now faint tracings of blue could be seen in the spearhead.

"Mana forger." Taran shook from shock as he watched Rugrat's gleeful expression. He had forgotten where he was as he watched Rugrat work.

Rugrat lost the concept of time as he continued to refine the spearhead and temper it completely. Finally, he put it down. Drained, he closed his eyes. It was as if he had opened a doorway, connecting the information in his mind to what he was doing before him.

Already the spearhead in front of him was an inferior product as he thought of ways to improve the iron ingot with different materials, reviewed what he had done wrong and what had gone right.

He didn't open his eyes for some time. When he did, he found the smithy was silent and Taran stared at him with shining eyes.

"Taran?" Rugrat asked, feeling something was off.

"A Mana forger—I didn't think that I would live to see the day!" Taran said quietly.

"Mana forger?" Rugrat asked.

"One who uses not only physical means to shape their metal but also Mana, able to call out deeper innate abilities in metal—in rare cases able to actually add formations, enchanting weapons," Taran said.

Rugrat hadn't heard of a Mana forger before.

Taran seemed to be stuck deep in thought as Rugrat checked on his notifications. Then it was his turn to look shocked.

He had made it to level nineteen in smithing; he'd only made it to level three before this! Also, he had learned the spell Simple Inorganic Scan.

"You mustn't waste your talent. I can't teach you anything here. You must fight to reach the Fourth Realm. It is the land of war and smiths," Taran said, but from his tone, it seemed he felt that such a task was incredibly hard.

"What else can I do?" Rugrat asked.

"You would need to find a Mana forging teacher, or technique books to increase your depth of knowledge," Taran said.

Rugrat's mind moved to the auction terminal. He wanted to see if anything was there, but he didn't want to waste their hard-earned gold on something that might not even help them in the coming fight.

"What are the advantages of the Mana forger?" Rugrat asked seriously.

"All I know is that they can create incredibly powerful items and even draw out greater strength from the items that they do make," Taran said, a sour expression on his face as he felt his information was lacking.

Rugrat nodded. He was interested and excited but now wasn't the time to be wasting gold on smithing technique books. As long as he could create spearheads and assist Taran, that would be enough.

Rugrat looked at some of the complete crossbow mechanisms. He walked over to them and put his hand on them. "Simple Inorganic Scan," he muttered. He was able to see into the mechanism, understanding its shape, form, and function.

After a few minutes, he stopped and looked up at Taran. "Would you be able to make a crossbow mechanism? I'd be interested in learning." Now that he had learned how to make spearheads, he wanted to learn to make more.

The crossbow's mechanism was simple, but it was smaller; the stresses were greater and it had to be exact or the crossbow would fail.

Rugrat watched as Taran worked. As he asked questions, Taran was stunned and he actually adjusted how he was working. With Rugrat and Taran talking as Taran worked, his process and speed improved.

Erik got back late from hunting and the groups dispersed. The people from the village had mixed emotions. Their levels had greatly increased, but then they had needed to kill tens of boars on their outing. Knowing that in the future that they would be up against hundreds of the beasts made everything all the more real for them.

Blaze met him as he was walking in.

"Good hunting?" Blaze asked.

"Not bad, just getting a hang of this thing," Erik showed his short bow, thankfully Rugrat had taken some time to show him how to be a better archer so he didn't look like a complete idiot in front of the hunting party.

Erik could see Blaze, the village leaders jealousy even if he hid it.

"You'll have to come out in the coming days when you're free," Erik smiled.

Blaze let out a dry laugh, rubbing his head as he'd been seen through.

"Sorry, it's just now I'm only a level eleven when I used to be the strongest in the town, now everyone else is catching up quickly!"

Erik nodded, working as the village's leader Blaze hadn't had much time to increase his overall level dealing with bureaucratic issues.

"What did you do before you were the villager's leader?" Erik asked.

Blaze seemed to be caught off guard by the question before he let out a laugh.

"I was one of the king's knights, I served for twelve long years, earning my right to create a camp. So I gathered some people, created a camp out here and built Alva as you see it now. Had to sell my horse and gear one year—the grain supply got too low."

Erik could see the pain in Blaze's eyes.

He could understand it, too. Blaze had been a warrior, a man to lead from the front, when he lost his armor and horse, he had lost that part of him. He'd become some guy behind a desk.

"Have you ever trained with a spear?" Erik asked.

"A spear?" Blaze looked confused but nodded. "It was one of the first weapons I learned as an infanteer. I lived with my spear for five years before I was able to become a cavalry squire."

"Good. I need someone to lead the spear squads. I want to build up three to five spear squads of ten people each. Their main purpose is to hold the walls at all costs and protect the archers led by Glosil," Erik said, looking at Blaze seriously.

He could see a fire in Blaze's eyes as one side of his mouth stretched into a bloody grin.

A cold smile appeared on Erik's face, a smile between warriors that only offered one thing: death to those who stood in their path.

Erik clapped Blaze's shoulder. "To be my man on the ground, I'm going to need someone to replace you in organizing all of the villagers," Erik said.

Blaze turned thoughtful, not answering immediately. Erik silently nodded to himself. Blaze might want to have the position leading the spear users, but he wasn't going to leave his previous position to have his previous efforts ruined.

"Elise," Blaze said after some deep thought.

Erik raised his eyebrow and indicated for Blaze to go on.

"She might just manage the store, but she's got a good mind for it. She's well connected to the people and has their respect. She's fair and kind, but crossing her is a bad idea. She's helped me out a time or two with planning out a few projects."

Erik hadn't spent that much time talking to Elise; he'd been off with one task or another, or just heading straight for the auction interface.

"Well, let's go and talk to Elise," Erik said.

"Also, the farmers should be done with their harvest midday tomorrow, and one of the woodworkers has expressed an interest to make a logging area. It will cost some resources and he will be removed from making crossbows, but it would increase the amount of wood we can cut," Blaze said.

"See to it," Erik said.

If I could find a technique manual to improve one's woodworking ability, then I could decrease the number of woodworkers on the weapons building side of things and then pull them for making buildings. I would feel much safer with woodworkers overseeing and working with the farmers to make the buildings. Less chance of it coming down like a pile of dominos.

They entered the store. Elise wiped her brow with the back of her arm as she looked up from the meat she was curing and readying for ration packs.

Seems like there's jerky everywhere I go. Not chili-flavored, though.

"Auction block?" She blew hair out of her face.

"Job recruitment!" Erik walked up to the table.

She frowned and looked from Erik to Blaze, as if trying to get a hint from them.

Erik tapped his hands on the counter as Blaze grinned.

"So, want to manage the village?" Erik asked.

"What?" She looked at Erik as if he had grown a third head.

"Well, Blaze here will be creating a spear unit and I am in need of a boss lady to get this village on the right track. I was told that you would be the right person to talk to." Erik watched her closely. Although it was Blaze's recommendation, Erik couldn't let such a key part of the village's development be ignored or fall through.

"You're serious, aren't you?" Elise said.

Erik simply nodded as Elise pursed her lips, thinking.

"I'm not going to lie. I'm not thrilled with the idea of taking over the role and I have a few conditions," Elise warned.

"Duly noted," Erik said.

"Good. Then I'm going to need helpers. No offense, but Blaze was making a dog's breakfast of this, trying to manage it all. I want to break down the operations of the village on the civilian side even more. I want Jasper to manage the resources and their storage—grain, wood, stone, food—as well as meal preparation—morning, midday, and evening meals and creating rations in their time off. Also, I want him to have twenty people, not just ten. Taran will be in charge of making weapons; he'll appoint someone to attend meetings." Elise saw Erik and Blaze wince. "Every day, I want to have a meeting with all of the leaders. You two, Rugrat, Glosil, Jasper, Taran, and I will attend to go over everything that has happened in the day. If you agree to this, then I'll agree to the position."

"Done," Erik said as fast as possible, not willing to let her get away.

Blaze scratched his head. Compared to Elise's management skills, he was truly lacking,

Erik pulled out a notepad he had been working on, flipping through the pages.

Breakdown= 17 groups+ 2 guard groups (190 people) (9 unable to work)
Groups- Activity
3-Weapons/arrows/defensive items
5-Farmers Harvesting
5-Logging
1-Food/Storage
3-Training/hunting

2-Guards

"Elise, I want you to focus on building projects. The first to be completed will be the logging camp to assist the loggers. I want you to use people from the harvesting groups once they've harvested all of the crops. One group will be sent to assist Jasper. One second." Erik opened up the auction marketplace and went to blueprints.

1000 Gold Village Hall
100 Gold Barracks II
100 Gold Workshop II
10 Gold Smithy I
100 Gold Store II
10 Gold Stone Mine II
100 Gold Ore Mine II
10 Gold Farm I
10 Gold Warehouse I
10 Gold Wall
10 Gold Watchtower I
100 Mana cornerstones (Earth grade) Teleportation Array I

If he had the gold for it, he could buy any of them. The Village Hall could be bought, but it couldn't be built until the village had certain buildings within its domain and a certain population base. He could build a smithy, but unless he had a smith, or he trained one, then it would be useless.

He wasn't just held back by these buildings; he could build whatever he wanted. Erik wanted to build badly, but he took a minute before rushing forward.

Defensive lines—sure, we need them, but not immediate concern. Need to build up the basics of the village. We aren't going to rely on the walls but on people. Food, sorted. Water, need to put some measures in to make sure that we have enough. We've got the well and people have rain water barrels but we need to make sure that's sustainable. If I was able to get a purification spell, I could get Roska to purify the water; then we wouldn't have sewage and wastewater. I could talk about health and safety while people are eating; that way, we could keep down infections and diseases. Bathing is low on these people's priority, but it would keep down disease and increase people's morale, having a hot shower. Shelter, we need to make sure that everyone has good sleeping quarters. Clean out that sprawling mess, clear up the roads to the walls. Then get watchtowers up to give us an early warning. That will require people.

Erik flipped to the auction side of things and looked through spells.

Purification
Novice
Purify water you are touching
Consumption of Mana based on amount of water purifying.
Bid: 7 Silver, 35 Copper
Time: 1 day, 17 hours, 23 minutes
Buyout: 12 Silver, 79 Copper

Erik bought it directly and looked to crafting technique manuals. He looked at an architect technique manual but it was in the range of fifty gold. He could only shake his head and move onto the next best.

He moved to the crafting and then woodworking section. The big-name Expert Woodworkers technique guides and other straightforward titled manuals had been bought up. Erik reduced his overall buyout amount, limiting the number of books as they became more obscure.

Most people want the general guide and pass by; if one was to look at the basics, the key points, then those would be the greatest influence.

Erik's thinking was based on how his general spells were less effective and cost more in Mana than when he targeted his Focused Heal as much as possible. Like a machine: if you only had to build one thing, you didn't need to be a master of that machine, just the master of making that one part.

Basics of joining
Apprentice
Learn Apprentice-grade woodworking skills. Focused on: Joining, Load-bearing joints.

Bid: 4 Silver, 35 Copper
Time: 3 days, 9 hours, 21 minutes
Buyout: 6 Silver, 37 Copper

Wood Carving
Novice
Simple guide on working with complex and fine carvings

Bid: 1 Silver, 72 Copper
Time: 13 hours, 59 minutes
Buyout: 4 Silver, 11 Copper

Hope I don't fuck this up.

Erik bought them both, watching as his gold dropped again. It came to nearly thirty silver altogether which, although it was expensive, Erik could still chalk it up as a test. Not including the new monster cores that he had gathered in the hunt, the village had eight gold, four silver, and seventy-three copper, though Erik and Rugrat were holding onto the strongest monster cores, selling off the excess.

The villagers grumbled about having to hand them over to Erik and Rugrat but they were happy enough with the levels and seeing their combat capabilities, they had been stifled.

Erik closed the auction, organizing his thoughts

Erik nodded to himself and looked to Blaze and Elise, coming to a decision.

He outlined his plan from showers, to tents and new buildings to watch towers and defenses.

"Since we don't have the numbers, we're going to have to make it up with quality." Erik pulled out the technique books for woodworkers.

"This book on joining is for whoever is the best you think for construction, designing, and leading the construction teams. I want them to look into building a watchtower. Here are the specifics." Erik passed her a note on what the watchtower would do and some technical drawings to build from. "The woodworking technique manual is to increase the woodworker's ability to do fine and detailed work, and I hope it helps them increase the speed that they can create crossbows and spears. Questions?"

Elise and Blaze were looking at the technique manuals and Erik, clearly a bit stunned.

"All right then. We will have your first official meeting of the Alva council tomorrow night. Make sure that everyone knows their appointments. Also, keep an eye out for people with potential. Blaze, I need people for that quick reaction force. Elise, make sure that you and the new heads that you've assigned pass me a list of promising people. At the meeting, we can talk about them, see if we can give them the best environment to grow their skills. The stronger they are, the stronger *we* are," Erik said, trying to drive home the point to them.

Blaze and Elise stood straighter; their faces hardened, accepting their roles and showing their determination to do their best.

"Understood," they replied.

Erik looked deep into their eyes, feeling as if he had made the right decision.

"See you at dinner. Blaze, best you talk to Glosil about your new position and discuss it with Rugrat—they have the best handle on the military side of things." With that, Erik left the store, leaving them behind in stunned silence.

Elise and Blaze's eyes turned back to the counter where Erik had put the two technique manuals. They both knew how such things would be expensive. Most people would hold onto them forever, not letting them go; to not only give them away, but to give to Elise to pass onto her candidates showed Erik's trust in her. It also provided a test for her to look for the person most deserving of the manual.

"He said that he wanted lists of people we recommend," Elise said, as if just realizing his parting words.

"Yeah." Blaze nodded, a heavy expression on his face.

"Do you think he would give them technique manuals as well?" Elise had known Erik for a few days but it was in passing; Blaze had been next to him from nearly the moment he walked through the gates.

"Rugrat and Erik aren't like other lords or fighters. I don't think he even understands what he's just done right now. He also said to me one time, money is money, but it can't buy lives—what use is having all this money if you can't protect the people around you?"

They fell into silence, sinking into their own thoughts.

Elise stored the manuals in her storage ring. "Right, well, I've got work to do."

Blaze grunted in agreement, the two of them moving with purposeful strides.

48

ORGANIZING ALVA VILLAGE

That night, Erik sat in his new room. The Mana around him shifted. He had waited for three days to let his body stabilize, but now he was focused on opening his seventh Mana gate, located in his left elbow.

Sounds like arrows striking a metal wall rang through his body. It was harder than ever before, but Erik didn't falter in his attacks as he sat there.

As the sun started to rise the next day, Erik's body glowed with power once again. His open Mana gates were visible as his sealed Mana gates shook. The gate in his elbow showed crack lines before it exploded outward. The Mana that rushed out like stampeding horses was drawn back in, as if being called back by their master.

Erik's Mana rushed through his Mana channels. With the rush of energy from his new Mana gate, the compression in his channels reached new heights as the mist slammed together. A shining blue drop appeared at the very center of Erik's body, in his dantian.

It seemed to ignite the Mana in his body and in the room. Erik felt his dantian growing larger as more Mana was drawn into his body than ever before. Energy from the Ten Realms shot into his body. He shook with energy before it disappeared.

Erik slumped as weariness fell over him.

Quest Completed: Mana Gathering Cultivation
The path of a Mana Gathering cultivator is not easy. To stand at the top, one must forge their own path forward.
Requirements:
Reach Mana Drop Level
Rewards:
+4 to Mana pool
+100,000 EXP

You have opened another Mana gate!
+1 to Mana Regeneration

Quest Updated: Opening the Fourteen Gates
Congratulations! You have opened your eighth Mana gate.
Requirements:
Clear all of your fourteen gates (8/14)
Rewards:
+1 to Mana Regeneration base stat
Undergo Mana Body Rebirth
1,400,000 EXP

You have reached Level 13
When you sleep next, you will be able to increase your attributes by: 5 points.

5,341/140,000 EXP till you reach Level 14

Quest: Mana Gathering Cultivation
The path of a Mana Gathering cultivator is not easy. To stand at the top, one must forge their own path forward.
Requirements:
Form Mana Core
Rewards:
+10 to Mana pool
+1,000,000 EXP

Erik closed his eyes to be greeted by a familiar sight.

You have 5 attribute points to use.

Increase Mana systems or look to increase my Stamina? If I increase my Mana, I'd have more spells for longer, but if I increase my Stamina then I can work for longer and help build up the village faster.
Two to Stamina Regeneration and three to Stamina pool. I need to use that snake poison in the coming days to temper my body.
Erik put in his points and watched as his character sheet took an impressive leap.

Character Sheet
Name: Erik West
Level: 13
Race: Human
Titles:
From the Grave
Land Holder (Temporary)
Strength: (Base 7) +11
180
Agility: (Base 6) +13
95

Stamina: (Base 10) +7
255
Mana: (Base 6) +11
170
Mana Regeneration (Base 8) +21
6.55/s
Stamina Regeneration: (Base 7) +20
6.15/s

As he slept, Alva Village underwent a number of changes as Blaze, Glosil, and Elise recruited Jasper and Taran, passing on his orders and working to build a plan for the people in Alva Village. Elise passed out the technique books to the man who was helping with the logging camp and a replacement in the workshops.

Erik woke the next day, power flooding through his body. His strength had increased in leaps and bounds while he'd been in Alva Village due to the different items that he had acquired and using them tactically, chaining them together to assist in leveling up another system or completing a quest.

I've basically improved my Mana system to its limit. I'll try to open another Mana gate tonight. Once I can't open any more, then I can try tempering my body with the snake poison. The higher my ability with my Mana system, then the strength of my healing spells will increase so I can temper multiple systems.

Erik wasn't simply looking to do one system at a time, but use them to increase the power of the other.

Rugrat woke up at the same time, conditioning from their time in the military.

Erik felt the power rolling off Rugrat.

"Damn, did you compress another drop in your dantian?" Erik asked.

"Yep, two drops." Rugrat circulated his power. Blue Mana channels, much more powerful than Erik's, appeared.

"Show-off," Erik muttered.

"Well, that's the joy of only focusing on one strengthening system, not both of them. I might know some first aid but I don't have the confidence to temper my body like you. I can help you temper your body, though."

"Tomorrow or the day after," Erik said, feeling the shot of adrenaline and the nervousness in his stomach. Tempering his body wasn't simple and the threat of death was always hanging over his head with it.

They walked down from their rooms and to the square. The food and storage groups had already set up breakfast and were serving people who had woken up early to carry out different tasks. Erik and Rugrat got some food from the servers and dug in.

Elise was also up. She looked tired but there was a glow in her eyes as she walked over. "I got some information on that armor. Red Haze not only boosts one's combat capability, it makes them highly aggressive and likely to attack anything in their path. The more someone kills when wearing the armor, the greater their fighting ability becomes. But if they stop fighting, then they will be extremely tired."

Her words were alarming but Erik thought on the armor. Its stats were really too good.

"Is there a way to overcome it, like through training?" Rugrat asked, overhearing them.

Erik looked at Elise.

"It blurs the mind. If you were able to train them to the point where they listen to only one's orders, I don't see why not." She didn't sound truly confident, but she didn't shoot it down right away.

Erik and Rugrat looked at each other.

"The spear groups aren't going to like us," Rugrat said.

"The stats are really good. If we train them properly, turn them into soldiers who live to follow commands…" Erik shrugged, not needing to say anymore.

"Break them down and build them back up. Going to be hell to do it in just a week," Rugrat said.

"Did Blaze pick all of the people for his spear groups?" Erik asked Elise.

"He and Glosil figured it all out last night," she confirmed.

"We do a crash course on crossbows for those who are to be part of the spear unit. Then take them hunting, raise them all up to level six by tonight, have Blaze leading them on the hunting trips, instill their confidence in him." Erik looked at Rugrat, the two of them wholly focused.

"Wake them up after five hours of rest and get them training, from dawn to dusk, till they drop—pick them up with healing spells and get them going again. We're going to have a lot of them drop," Rugrat said.

"Create four groups—we break them." Erik's words were cold, with no room for failure. These people would be their last line of defense. They would have to step up to the wall and hold, no matter what. If they fell, the village fell.

Elise shivered, looking at the two men. It was now that she was reminded that they weren't just leaders; they were fighters underneath it all.

"Equip them with the armor—take them out hunting. We'll watch over them, see how they react. If it works, we get more; if it doesn't, we look for something else."

"I'll update Glosil and Blaze, then put a bid on the armor on my way to the barracks," Rugrat said, using his sound talisman to send messages.

"What's the water situation?" Erik asked Elise, shovelling down food quickly.

"We've got enough water to last for two weeks, between the wells and all of the rain barrels."

"Okay, here are the plans for the showers and washrooms. Everyone in the village is to use it. No one is allowed to just pee or crap in the street," Erik said severely.

Elise winced at his crude ways and looked at the design. It was simple but effective, and also through purification spells, they'd reclaim a great amount of water that would have been lost. Once the fight started, they wouldn't be able to go to the springs or lakes to get water.

Erik was preparing to defend for months, not weeks.

"Something wrong?" Erik asked as he ate, Elise still staring at the plans.

"This—it removes our waste and it retains so much water, also greatly improving our hygiene situation and morale." Elise looked at the simple sketch.

"Any of the people not working at the logging camp, I want them working on this. I'm hoping that tonight or tomorrow morning, we'll be able to shower. Break them up into shifts if you need to, sending half to recover and then work tonight," Erik said.

"I'll see to it," Elise promised. "Also, the guards went through the residential area last night while on patrol and did up a report on different residences. I hope to get that sorted out by tomorrow night. The man who came up with the logging camp plan is working on making designs for the watchtowers. He should have something tonight. If I have people free, what should I do with them?"

Preparing ahead where she can, without wasting time or resources. Looks like Blaze picked well.

"If you have people free, get them started on digging up the fourth defensive layer." Erik pulled out his plan for the layered defense around the village.

"The dirt and clay is to be dumped at the wall. Once there's enough material, using mud reinforced with straw, I want to repair the main wall and increase its strength." Erik pointed out the planned defenses, from bait traps, the sharpened hedgehogs, and obstacles to funnel the beast horde into pits filled with sharpened stakes and then potholes.

"When did you plan this out?" Elise looked at it all and the steps listed down the side, using the materials from making the defenses and harvesting the crops, to greatly reinforce the wall.

"The first day." Erik looked to Rugrat, who nodded, draining his bowl of soup with a slurp.

"All right, I'm off hunting with Blaze," Rugrat said.

"All right, I'll start building the defenses. I'll make one of each so that you have examples to show your people," Erik said.

"Understood," Elise said.

"Tonight I'll talk about first aid, the showers, and hygiene to everyone at dinner," Erik said.

"Do you want to do that tomorrow and I can talk about construction tonight?" Rugrat asked. "Worked on a few sites when I was younger."

"Elise?" Erik asked.

"Construction would be best," Elise said.

"We'll do that, then talk about hygiene and the showers tomorrow morning so people know how to use them and why they're using them," Erik said.

"Sounds good." Rugrat got up and took his bowls to the kitchen staff.

Erik did the same, Elise trailing behind, writing down his orders.

49
IMPRINTING

Blaze looked at the new batch of trainees. Thankfully, there were just eighteen potential spear candidates who had not reached level six already. He had been with Rugrat, sizing them up and looking to show off his skills and increase his level. Against level eight and nine boars, nothing was his opponent; with every spear slash and stab, he reaped lives. He didn't take one step back and everything was killed within two or three swipes of his spear.

As they walked back to village, he could hear them talking to one another.

"Did you see leader Blaze's spear technique?"

"How fierce was that? Is he even human?"

"I wish I was able to do that!"

Blaze hid the smile that threatened to appear on his face as they made it back to the village.

They passed a number of pits and defenses that had been put together. Erik's examples had been created and the logging camp had been finished, with the people not needed there copying Erik's examples and building up the four-layered defensive lines all the way back to the village's wall.

They would have been more of a hindrance than help in making the showering and bathroom installation.

Blaze saw the cleared area where the building was supposed to be placed. People were bringing in lumber under the guidance of Shi Wanshu, the woodworker Elise had put in charge of designing the different structures Erik had ordered.

The homes had also been organized, some being torn down to clear up roads. The new clean and orderly streets allowed one to quickly pass through the area and they could actually fit in more houses, reducing the cluttering around the barracks to the northwest.

They headed for the barracks, where Erik and a new batch of trainees were waiting.

"Consolidate your gains tonight. Tomorrow we'll begin training." Blaze dismissed the group that he had headed out with in the morning.

They dispersed, dropping off their weapons at the barracks. Rugrat nodded to Blaze and he headed off toward the smithy.

"Captain Blaze, good to see you. I'll be scouting ahead, if you want to take command of this group?" Erik asked.

"Yes, sir," Blaze said, knowing that Erik was establishing a chain of command, with him leading the others. It would make things easier in the coming days to establish it now.

They already thought of him as a leader; now he would impress this into them personally.

Rugrat's hammer stopped mid-swing, as he started to realize something: he could see through his hammer. He released the hammer but he could still see it in his mind. It was as if an imprint had been made in his mind.

His brows were pinched together as he pulled out a sword. He closed his eyes as he traced out the sword with his Simple Inorganic Scan. He built up an image of the sword in his mind. With a simple thought, he flickered from the imprint of the sword and the hammer.

He took out other weapons and tools in the shop, imprinting them on his mind.

It wasn't long before he had imprinted all of the tools and items in his storage ring and in the smithy into his mind.

Rugrat stood there with his eyes closed as he looked at the imprints from the different weapons and items that had passed through his hands.

He compared and evaluated them. He didn't know the full techniques of how they were made; all he could sense was their makeup and appearance. Based on this, he was still able to see similarities and it allowed him to finally apply some of the knowledge that he had accrued against the different objects he was seeing.

He could also see how the Mana he injected, subconsciously, into the weapons he was making allowed their power to increase. Without even thinking about it, he would circulate the Mana in his body, condensing it, like he would to open his Mana gates.

Erik might be at eight Mana gates, but Rugrat had opened eleven. His every action seemed to draw in Mana. To him, it was no different than using his muscles.

Rugrat frowned as he looked to clear his mind. He thought on the compound bows and crossbows from Earth. He thought on their gears. He drew a few pictures. Taran looked over but he didn't say anything as Rugrat continued to close his eyes, picturing them and writing down as much information as possible.

"String, tension on the tendons, springs," Rugrat muttered to himself, trying to inspire more thoughts.

Soon, he ran out of things to write down. He gathered everything and left the workshop. Finding a cart, he put his hands on the leaf springs under the cart and took in that information. Then he went to the storage area, moving to the pulleys that were used to move different objects.

He headed off to find Shi Wanshu.

"Mister Rugrat, can I help you?" Shi Wanshu was a burly-looking man with bright-brown eyes.

"Pulley systems—do you have a drawing of one?" Rugrat asked.

Shi Wanshu pulled out a picture and gave it to Rugrat.

He muttered to himself and wrote something on a notepad. He passed it back and walked off, gathering odd looks as he compared the different pieces of paper.

He went back to the workshops and talked to a lady who worked with the tendons.

After some time, he went to an empty desk in the workshop. Papers were littered around him as he started to make individual drawings of different components.

He grabbed one of the completed crossbows and put it on his workbench. There was a stirrup to make it easier to string one's bow, but it still wasn't that fast.

Rugrat went and grabbed two hooks and a length of metal. He put the hooks on the bowstring and using the leverage of the metal, easily drew the bowstring back.

He did this another five times before he put the string with hooks and metal down. He started to pull on the string with just his bare hands. It was much harder and slower as his hands were starting to hurt after doing it five times.

A woman in the shop who was watching him closely ordered people to get more hooks and string to make the assists and get more lengths of metal.

Rugrat made a note on his papers and then grabbed some pulleys and put them on the sides of the bow. He bit his lower lip in thought, comparing his drawings against the crossbow.

He left quickly, taking his notes.

He saw that people were gathering rope and hooks. He went to the woman organizing things and dropped off a page of information. "Modify the bows that you can—make multiple lines with the hooks," Rugrat said.

With that, he headed back to the smithy. He grabbed a crossbow that hadn't had a bowstring put on it yet on his way out.

Taran was there working on a crossbow as Rugrat worked on a piece of metal. He built what looked like a leaf spring but with notches in it.

He worked it according to a template he had drawn out. Then he created two ridged pulleys and smoothed out the pulleys.

He pulled off the old bow arms on the crossbow and put on the new ones with the pulleys. He fought with the tendons, finally getting them looped to one another. He then strung the bow and wiped his brow.

He looked at his new creation with a proud expression.

He grabbed his reloading assist system he'd built and went out of the smithy into the archery range.

Glosil frowned when he saw the new contraption in Rugrat's hands. His eyes bulged out at seeing Rugrat's reloading assist. The way that the leaves for the bow bent backward was alarming.

Rugrat raised it to his shoulder and fired. The arrow shot straight and true. Just hearing it, one could tell that the power was much greater than the original crossbow's.

"Hah! Pulleys, mother fuckers! Enough pulleys and levers, and you can move the world!" Rugrat shook his head and looked at the bow in his hands with a smile.

It was more complicated than the original crossbow, needing a new front assembly that had to be flexible and not brittle, and having a pulley system that was precise took time to smooth down perfectly.

The draw weight on the bow had nearly tripled, though.

"It's going to take longer to make them. I can get Taran to make the trigger assembly, then I'll make the leaves of the crossbow and the pulleys, break it up and increase our speed." Rugrat went back to the workshop and showed Taran his new weapon.

"So, do we change the ones we've already made or just make them in this style now and then work backward?" Taran asked.

"Leave what we have—at least they're weapons. The lever loading assist will already increase their rate of fire a lot. We can give the updated ones to the best shots and then go through updating the other bows afterward," Rugrat said. "Also, I was looking at different weapons and it seemed as if I could almost remember everything about them as soon as I had a good understanding of them?"

"Imprinting—it's a hard skill to learn." Taran nodded. "Basically, there are two ways to do it: use a technique book with the imprints of a lot of different items, though those would cost more money than you'd see in one lifetime because it's like giving someone tens of blueprints at once. The other is to become extremely familiar with a weapon. I can make simple swords for the guards easily because I've got it imprinted. You've never learned this? It's like using a spell, it will become easier and easier."

Rugrat went silent. This wasn't like back on Earth. It seemed that as he learned items, an internal codex remembered them for him; he could perfectly recall all of the tools in the shop, then all of his spells.

He didn't realize how strange that was until now.

Domonos stood at the gate, looking toward the Beast Mountains.

He'd received word that the Willful Institute had finished whatever they were attending and were heading to Chonglu to depart through the totem.

Domonos knew how dominating they were and had made sure to pay the guards before to make sure that there were no issues.

Wren might be the one inheriting the Silaz trading house, but Domonos wanted to make sure that their position was secure.

Thinking on this, his thoughts turned to the two men who had shamed his brother Wren. Strength was everything in the Ten Realms. He needed to make an example out of them, or if they were indeed stronger, make reparations. Wren might have to throw away his reputation, but if they could keep or grow their position, Domonos wouldn't hesitate to force his brother.

There was a cough from a covered carriage next to Domonos.

He turned to the covered carriage. "Little sister, you should've stayed at home," he said in a quiet voice.

"Big brother doesn't know when he'll be back, so I want to be around you until you have to leave," a soft voice complained childishly.

Domonos could only laugh. He might be the strongest in the Silaz family, but the core, the heart of the Silaz trading house was his little sister Qin. All of his brothers and father used her as inspiration to grow the business and their strength more, to try to find something that could help or heal little Qin'er.

That was why Wren's gift of premium monster cores was so well received: it allowed Domonos the capital to increase his position, by gifting it to people he had come into contact with in the Willful Institute.

Domonos gripped his fist tighter. If they had to bankrupt the entire Silaz trading house, they would do so for Qin'er.

Domonos saw a group, wearing the same uniform and crest on their chest, appear in the distance. *So fast,* Domonos thought, controlling his expression as he saw the people from the Willful Institute coming closer.

They reached the gate, not caring about the line.

Domonos bowed to them. The group slowed as one of the elders slowed, nodding at Domonos, seemingly pleased with his disposition.

"Not bad," he assessed. "We will be leaving for the institute promptly."

"Yes, Elder Rei," Domonos said.

"Oh, do you know these two men?" Elder Rei showed a crystal that had a picture of Rugrat and Erik captured on it.

Domonos fought to control his expression. *It's them!*

"I don't." Domonos shook his head, bowing again to hide his expression. "This lowly one is lacking."

"It's not your fault. Come, we'll go to the Willful Institute directly. Say your good-byes in five minutes." Elder Rei received the crystal and headed for the totem with the group of other Willful Institute people.

Domonos nodded and quickly moved to his sister's carriage, his mind abuzz.

If he was able to survive the Black Blood poison, then they must be actual healers! The healing houses must feel threatened at losing patronage and business. If we were able to get them to look at little Qin'er, maybe they could help.

"Little Qin, listen to your brother," Domonos said as he lifted the curtain. He saw the tears in her eyes but he didn't have time for words of comfort.

"Brother Wren is to make peace with the two back there. They're real healers—they might be able to help you." Domonos made sure that she understood everything.

"Qin'er will tell Father and brother Wren."

"Good girl," Domonos said. A harsh emotion rose in the back of his throat. He cleared his throat and pinched her cheek. "Big brother has to go now." Domonos smiled as tears fell down her cheeks.

He didn't have more time as he left the carriage and ran to catch up with the Willful Institute people.

50
VILLAGE MEETING

Rugrat felt determination in his very bones and excitement. He had a catalogue of weapons in his mind. He still hadn't built up the skills he needed to make them all, but from them he could draw inspiration and find solutions to the issues he had.

He stopped himself from diving right in as he looked at Taran and frowned.

"Something wrong?" Taran asked, confused by the change in Rugrat's appearance.

"Just that Erik and I have been idiots." Rugrat quickly left the smithy and headed for the store. Elise was out dealing with the village, so Rugrat went right to the auction interface and went to the smithing manuals area.

He spent nearly two gold before he left the interface and headed back to the smithy.

Taran was working on trigger assemblies when he returned. Taran finished off, wiping his brow as he looked at Rugrat.

"Take the night off and use these." Rugrat passed Taran four different technique books on smithing.

Taran took in a sharp breath, seeing them all. He had heard of how Erik had taken out two technique books, but they were on small subjects and they were given to two different people. Rugrat was giving him four books in one go.

As much as he wanted to accept them, this kind of wealth wasn't easy to come across. "I can't accept these," Taran said.

"You've been working as hard as anyone here and you're our only true smith. I'm only just learning the techniques and while I've got a bunch of ideas, you're the core of the weapons workshop. You haven't asked for anything and kept working, even though these crossbows probably don't increase your Experience anymore." Rugrat could see that his words were right on the money. As someone made an item, the first time they would get a lot of Experience; for making it higher quality and showing a progression in their smithing ability, they could again earn a bunch of Experience. After a while, doing the same job, there wasn't much more Experience to be made.

"Among the crafters in Alva Village, you've been worked the most and our entire plan relies on you. The stronger you are, the better our weapons and the more we can make," Rugrat said.

Taran could see that Rugrat wasn't going to let this go. He slowly put his hand on the books, as if verifying that they were real.

"Well, they ain't much use if you don't use them. Hopefully we can raise you up to an Apprentice, maybe even a Journeyman smith before the fight," Rugrat said.

Taran's body shook as he looked up at Rugrat.

"I've got a few ideas that might be able to help you." Rugrat put down the manuals that he had received on top of the technique books.

Taran looked as if he had lost his soul, stunned by the resources and information that Rugrat was giving him.

Rugrat took out a notepad, the one that he had started writing on as he got different questions, putting down facts that he had confirmed and answering questions that he had come up with. "Read over this and the manuals. Once you've done so, use the technique manuals—maybe they'll be able to answer the questions you have." Rugrat passed the book over.

Taran looked at the book and up to Rugrat. Slowly he took the book from Rugrat, as if it were a treasure.

He stood upright and looked right at Rugrat. "I, Taran Choi, swear my allegiance to you, Rugrat, and Mister West. If you are ever in need of my services, I will not hesitate to serve you. I so swear an oath to the Ten Realms."

A powerful blue light descended from the Ten Realms, examining Taran. Then it shot outward, one hitting Rugrat and the other passing through walls and buildings.

Rugrat was greeted by a screen in his vision.

Taran Choi has sworn his allegiance to you. If he breaks his oath, then the Ten Realms will punish him.

Rugrat's eyes went wide, before he waved the screen away. He put his hand on Taran's shoulder, a smile on his face. He couldn't express his thoughts and feelings. "Erik and I will do our best to make sure that we do not disappoint your oath," Rugrat promised.

Taran bowed his head, gruffly clearing his throat. "You lead, I'll follow."

Rugrat clapped his shoulder again. "Good man." Rugrat stood a bit taller. He would do all he could to make sure that he did his best by Taran. "Now go and train."

Taran nodded and collected up the different items. There was no need to stand on ceremony anymore.

After Taran left, Rugrat headed over to the training ground, where he found Captain Glosil.

"What was that bow you used? The power was incredible and that loading system was much easier to use than our hands," Glosil said.

"I'll have the new loading system to you soon. That new crossbow is a modernized version. Make sure to pick out the very best shots for them." Rugrat pulled out another book and held it to Glosil. "Use this and train well."

Glosil took the book and opened it. He found a screen in front of him. His jaw dropped and others looked over. Glosil recovered a few moments later. He could only see Rugrat's back as he walked into the smithy once again.

Rugrat got a call request from Erik.

"What happened? I got a notification about Taran making an oath?" Erik asked.

"I gave him a bunch of books on smithing techniques. He was pretty moved by it, so he made an oath to both of us," Rugrat explained.

"I'm an idiot. I didn't think to give him manuals." Erik sighed.

"I'm right there with you. With the meeting tonight, we'll need to talk to everyone and see what they're lacking. We can buff up the leaders with technique books to make up for deficits in their abilities, then raise the strength of the people by tactically increasing the pillars of the community, increasing our overall strength. About the gold?" Rugrat said.

Although they were both strong and determined men in their own right, Rugrat was younger than Erik and he had looked up to the other man, who had taught him and acted like Rugrat's older brother. Both of them respected the other's opinion, but Erik had unconsciously taken over the leadership position in the relationship in most ways. If they were dealing with a situation, Erik would turn to Rugrat without hesitation; one man couldn't do everything by himself.

Rugrat was feeling guilty spending that much gold.

"Don't worry. With what I estimate, we should be able to make another twenty gold in the next couple of days as the different sales run out. Raising our strength is more important. If you can, see about learning more about formations, arrays, and enchantments. If we can add enchantments to our bullets, then we'll be able to gain another increase in power, or we can upgrade people's weapons," Erik said.

"Increase the strength at the base to push everyone higher," Rugrat said.

"Right."

"Okay, I'll go back to the store and spend some more to try to learn enchantments. Don't forget to get more healing spells and Alchemy books," Rugrat said.

"I'll do my best, but healing and Alchemy books are expensive in their own right as most of them come from the Third Realm and higher," Erik said, sounding bitter. "I'll try to get some more healing spells, then I can use those to assist in the tempering."

Rugrat's gut tightened; he'd forgotten how Erik still wanted to temper his body tomorrow. "Right."

"Okay, see you at the meeting." Erik cut the connection.

Rugrat went to the store again. If one was watching, they'd see light illuminating the inside of the store and dissipating a few seconds later.

After it happened a few more times, Rugrat wandered out of the store, his eyes glowing. He had to use the wall to support himself.

He stumbled back to the forge, muttering to himself before he pulled out a pen and paper. He started recording information, writing on the paper, then sketched out something on his hammer with chalk. Looking to the anvil, he started tracing on it, too.

Rugrat's mind teetered between exhaustion and creative explosion as inspiration struck him.

He didn't notice when Erik entered the smithy, or when he left.

Elise, Glosil, Jasper, and Blaze were sitting at the table when Erik met up with them.

"The other two won't be coming." Erik sat down with a bowl of food. "Now, these are for you guys." Erik tossed out books to them all. These were different manuals or pieces of paper that he had written out things on.

"I gave more to Rugrat to pass over to Taran."

Blaze opened up the piece of paper. Shock showed on his face as he saw that it was a training plan, from beginning to end, about using spears.

Glosil got a written document from Erik about the strengths and weaknesses of the defenses, defensive tactics as well as information on archery.

Jasper got information on different ways to prepare and serve food to make it last longer and different systems to make it easier for his people to handle their jobs. He also gave Jasper two storage rings.

He gave Elise pen, paper, and a list of his priorities, as well as technique books to increase people's abilities in different areas.

Between the different goods, the technique books, even after hearing or seeing Erik passing out technique books, this was alarming.

"You are all pillars of Alva Village. Taran included, even though he's not here," This got a few smiles. "You have been working as hard as anyone else. Your levels might not have increased but it is my aim to increase your skills and abilities." Erik looked to them all. "Do you have those recommendation lists?"

They pulled out pieces of paper and he collected them.

Erik looked them over and then pulled out a pen. He wrote a few things on the paper and then tucked them away. "Glosil, after the meeting, come with me to the auction store. I'll give the manuals to you and you can disperse them."

"I will not let you down, sir." Glosil stood, hitting his chest and lowering his head in salute, happy to do something to repay the gratitude he felt toward Erik.

Erik nodded, saluting back with his hand against his heart. "Now, I want a report from you all: Elise, then Jasper before Glosil and Blaze." Erik looked to Elise.

She cleared her throat and made to stand.

"We won't have time for that. Also, for these meetings, we can do them while eating. We don't have much time to spare. Have you all eaten?" Erik looked to them.

Seeing their reactions, he looked over to the serving ladies. "Could I get four meals for these boneheads?"

"Yes, Mister West!" the server said excitedly.

"Thank you." He smiled and looked to the sheepish foursome. He grabbed his bread and his spoon, waving for Elise to start as he began eating.

"The logging camp has been started. The shelters are undergoing renovations and should be complete by midday next morning. The shower building's foundations have been laid. The underground clay storage tanks have been created and filled. Building can start tomorrow morning when people wake up—hope to be done by midday. Mister Wanshu has taken the technique book and is working on developing watchtowers based off of the technical drawings you made. He says that he will need more wood workers, but he said that they could be built in three days."

"Do you have the plans?"

"I don't have plans; he'll make them as he goes," Elise said.

Erik frowned but waved her on.

"There was an excess of people working on the project, so I had them start working on the defenses. I don't want to have to switch the people out who are working on the shower so progress is quick; the same for the watchtowers. I have made sure that the crews have all done the crossbow course and have reached level seven. With their increase in power, they're much faster," Elise said, finished.

"All right, at these meetings, it is our goal to improve on what we have. Nothing is meant personally unless you've messed up in your role," Erik said, making sure that his words weren't taken in the wrong way.

"Shi Wanshu is to make plans for the watchtower. There shall be only one plan. The parts will be made before reaching the site, then assembled on location. There will be one group making the parts and another that will assemble them together. They will use the measurement systems that I have given them. This means less time trying to make multiple plans and blueprints; also, moving from one tower to another, our people won't have to get acquainted with each one of them.

"Second, we don't need to sleep as much with the increase in Stamina Regeneration. As there are patrols on the walls and roaming groups of guards, we can start incorporating shift work into the day. There can be a crew working from midnight to midday and another from midday till midnight. We will have fires so that everyone can see. Also, it will mean that we have half of the city awake at any given time, ready to react to any threat and make sure that there is not a break in progress. Our people are stronger;

they have greater Stamina regenerations. Good plan with not switching out the crews so we don't have to familiarize them with the project each time."

Elise winced but nodded her head.

"I want those showers finished for tomorrow morning if possible," Erik said, his statement also a question.

Elise took a moment before nodding. "It's possible."

"Good. Make sure that we don't take on too much. We can't have our people burning out unless it's for training purposes." Erik paused as the server came over with food, putting it in front of everyone.

"On the food and supplies side, we have plenty of wood. With the logging camp up and running, they're able to clean up the incoming lumber, making it easier to store. We have enough food for four months. We have rations for everyone in the city for four days—breakfast, lunch, and dinner. If possible, I want to get a book of recipes so that the cooking staff might find new ways to prepare and store food for the rations and increase the effects of the beast meat's recovery abilities. With the storage rings, I want to make pots of stew and other meals. In the storage rings, they will remain warm and not spoil. We do not have enough cauldrons for that, though."

"I can get you some small storage rings just meant for soup, cooking it up and hold it in one storage ring. Then, when needed, can just have someone running around with the storage ring, pouring out soup, stew, and hot tea when needed," Erik said.

It was a much more expensive method, but it solved multiple problems in one shot.

"Also, use the larger storage ring—go and gather water from the nearby lake, and pour it into the storage tanks that are being built for the showers and the well," Erik said.

"Yes, sir." Jasper nodded. This was his first time meeting Erik and he looked to be a bit overwhelmed by it.

Erik was cleaning up his bowl with the bread as Glosil started.

"We have trained everyone, except for forty people, in the use of crossbows. Nine groups have gone hunting beyond the walls; the majority have now reached level seven. The combination of in-field experience and training has been good. With improved loading techniques and the new bow type Rugrat has come up with, our rate of fire will greatly increase. We've got two thousand arrows. Still, I believe we will need many more arrows to survive the coming conflict—ammunition is used at an incredible rate. I have made a list of thirty people who are the best shots in the groups so far and show promise worthy of the newer crossbows," Glosil said.

"Good. I want the guardsmen to work in groups of two to take more people out of the city and go on hunting trips, so it's not just Rugrat and me. This will increase the speed that people level up and slim down the numbers we're facing. The guards will be in charge of taking out groups to gain Experience. I want to get everyone to level seven. I want to have refresher courses on crossbows, but otherwise we will look to developing our core military groups, the sharpshooters, and the spearwielders. Rugrat and I will take out the crossbow sharpshooter groups that already have some levels and work to make them stronger. We'll be attacking the wolf groups," Erik said. "When the time for battle comes, I want them to be intermixed with the regular forces to pass on their knowledge and boost their strength."

Glosil nodded, showing his understanding.

Blaze was next. "All of the spear-wielding candidates have already been sent to sleep. They are in the temporary housing along the northwest wall. I will be studying the plan that you gave me tonight. I might need help in the coming days to manage the spearwielders," Blaze said.

"Understood. For now, the guards who are part of the training unit—make them the officers and backbone of the different units. Rugrat and I will be there to assist periodically, switching off with you. Our aim is to break them first, to tear down everything, to make them forget about their body, about their needs, and build them up to be a unit, a single mechanism that lives, breathes, and dies together. Right now they're nothing but fodder, but we'll turn them into heavy infantry."

"Sir." Blaze saluted.

"Five of your best from the heavy infantry and crossbow units will be used to form the quick reaction force that I will personally lead. Rugrat will be in an overwatch position. Elise, your people will be his reloaders," Erik said.

"Reloaders?" Elise asked.

Erik smiled and his entire aura changed, making the others shiver.

"Trust me, anything that comes into range of Rugrat won't last long." Erik's smile faded as he looked down the long tables that were set up in the main square. People were sitting down and eating, relaxing from their day's labors.

"Do you want to give out the announcement of the shifts, or do you want me to say it after I do a presentation on first aid?" Erik asked Elise.

It took her a moment to recover from Erik's sudden change. "After the first aid," she said, clearing her throat.

"Okay." Erik stood. "Rugrat will talk tomorrow, but I think that Taran and he will be indisposed for the next few days. However, their production speed and quality might see a great increase."

The others nodded, glancing at their storage devices where they held the manuals he had passed out.

"Anything else? Questions?" Erik asked.

"What about the children?" Elise asked.

"Right now, they're working in the workshops or they're being tended in a nursery run by your staff, right?" Erik asked.

Elise nodded.

"I don't want to put them in more danger. When the fighting starts, they'll be held in the Village Hall," Erik said. "Anything else?"

They looked to one another but they didn't say anything.

"All right, time to get my teacher hat on." Erik stood and passed over his bowls to the servers. Then he went up on stage. The villagers all looked at him, seeing that he wanted to say something.

"Hiya, everyone." Erik waved to them all. Conversations died down as Erik grabbed a box and sat on it, looking out at everyone. "You can all keep eating. I'm just here for your dinner entertainment and to teach you a few things about health." He cleared his throat. Everyone was eating but they moved to get a better view of him.

"As you all know, healers are people who use magic and spells to heal people. There are also alchemists who can make medicines to help people. I am here to tell you that there are people who can heal others and they don't need to be alchemists or healers. What I want to talk about is Minor Heal Wounds and first aid. Minor Heal Wounds are ways to keep yourself and your family members from getting sick. First aid is used to help people if they're wounded. In this coming fight, people will be wounded, so listen up—this lesson might save the person's life on your right and left." Erik was used to soldiers joking around after these words. In this situation, where most of them had seen the enemy that were training up, they were quiet as they looked to their neighbors and then to him with greater focus.

"Okay, so first, let's talk about germs."

51

BREAKING THE NINTH, CHALLENGING THE TENTH

Jasper pulled out a writing kit and he jotted down notes as Erik spoke. His lesson seemed to resound within Jasper's mind.

"People need to wash their hands or else they might get the germs on their hands into the food they're making. This way, you will get an infection or disease and it could lead to you being sick or dying. I know that a lot of you had to go to the bathroom a lot and there was vomiting when I got here. This is food poisoning. Clean your hands, use clean tools on your food, and don't cut different types of meat with the same knife. Otherwise, I'll let you sit on that toilet for three days," Erik said.

Jasper could feel that Erik wasn't lying. Seeing as he was in charge of food, he felt more than one set of eyes fall on him.

"Not having good habits when you're eating is one thing—needing to bathe is another. Right now there is a public shower being created for everyone. Everyone will be allowed one shower a day to clean yourself. The cleaner you are, the less likely you are to get something nasty."

Jasper and everyone in Alva had seen how a cold could kill and a cut could turn rancid; now they knew those were infections where their body was rotting away.

"Also, there will be a bathroom facility. There will be two more created in the northwest and southeast districts. Use them. You go for a piss in the night or a dump, use them; otherwise, you're going to get others sick. If you do that, then you're more of a problem than the hordes at our door. We need to look after one another inside these walls. If we don't, the beast horde won't even need to finish us off." Erik's words were cutting, making people look away in embarrassment.

"All right, those are general health rules to keep everyone safe from getting an infection or some kind of disease. Now, first aid."

Jasper listened to Erik, wrapped up in his words, knowing that this might be some of the most important information he had ever heard.

Erik called up people, talking about their body, demonstrating what to do if they had broken a limb, if their breathing had stopped.

People ate their food numbly, focused on Erik's words. This kind of information was unlike anything they had heard before.

I wonder if I would be able to get this information from anywhere but the royal colleges or the different sects? None of them would be willing to give this information out for free. The tuition for the royal colleges is in tens of silvers for just a few lessons. Jasper shook his head. Truly, Rugrat and Erik couldn't be compared to others he had met before.

Erik cleared his throat and drank some water as he dismissed his latest volunteer. Everyone was looking at him as if he were telling them the most interesting story in the world.

"All right, that's all I have time for now. There will be more lessons coming in the next couple of days. It's my hope that with them you'll be able to gain at least some information that will be useful to you all." Erik let that sink in. "Also, most of you have gone through some rapid increases in levels, which has allowed you a greater Stamina Regeneration. You can do more, longer, on less food and sleep. Don't worry, we're not cutting your food, but the fact is that since you don't need to sleep as long, we can advance our own defenses and the abilities of Alva Village. We don't have time to waste. Now, the first job I want to complete is the building of the showers and the bathrooms across the village. I want to make sure that no one falls ill and that everyone is in the best condition possible."

Erik's voice was softer. He had come to know these people over the last couple of days; he'd harvested with them, hunted with them, eaten meals with them, and become a part of their community. He might be here to complete a quest, but he'd become a part of Alva Village.

"The department heads will have work rotas for you. Together, Alva will survive." Erik turned and left the stage. It was a somber atmosphere as they thought on his words. Those who were done with their food went over to see the department heads.

Erik moved to the Village Hall. He got comfortable and turned his vision inward. He focused in on his Mana system.

His Mana circulated through his Mana channels, moving from his Mana gates. It was compressed and refined before reaching his dantian, where it was thickest. He looked at the two drops of Mana that rested there. They stood opposite each other, like bratty children in a fight. Erik could feel the power that was pooled within them. They looked like calm drops of pure blue water, but he knew that they could erupt with power.

Erik's mind moved through his Mana channels, checking on his Mana gates. One had turned into eight. It had been a fight to reach this point.

Erik moved his hand. When he focused, he could feel the Mana in the air move slightly according to his movements, as if fish in water, interested by the strange movement.

He felt a slight resonance with the air as he remembered Rugrat's words when he opened his tenth Mana gate. *"You think that you're powerful now—just wait until you reach past the tenth Mana gate. It's like you become a lord of Mana."* Erik remembered the shine in his eyes, the look of intoxication.

Erik's hand made a fist. He felt the Mana and the blood moving through his arm, the power that was hidden within.

"Ten Mana gates, huh?" Erik got comfortable as the air around him shook slightly. If one was to strain their eyes, they'd see blue mist appeared around his open Mana gates: one at the back of his skull, one in each of his hands, his feet, his knees, and right elbow. The power seemed to resonate with his body, the two accepting each other.

Erik's control had reached new heights, and with Rugrat forging the path ahead, he had told Erik the secrets he had discovered.

Erik's Mana channels expanded as a deep rumbling like the gathering of a thunderstorm sounded from within his body.

Erik didn't create spears of Mana; he gathered it together, and spun it, creating a tornado of rampant Mana, a Mana drill.

He knew that opening his ninth Mana gate would be no simple task. Moving neither fast nor slowly, the drill was refined, creating a system powered by the compressed Mana in his system. The drill focused it further, taking incredible control as Erik gritted his teeth.

The Mana drill moved through his Mana channels. Rushing would make it lose power, so slowly it passed through, reaching the site of his ninth Mana gate. Erik focused on the Mana gate. It no longer looked like stone, like the others; it had a silver sheen to it, like polished steel hidden under debris.

He drove forward. The Mana drill slammed into the Mana gate. There was a screeching noise as it gained purchase. The drill's speed slowed and Erik's veins popped out. He drew in more power, forcing the drill against the Mana gate.

The Mana gate's surface was cleaned off under the attack, revealing the spotted Mana gate underneath. It was an iron door, stopping one from advancing.

The drill's progress was slow but measurable.

Erik sat there, his Mana channels sticking out. It seemed as though the world breathed with him, faint Mana mist trickling through his open Mana gates.

It was monotonous and straining.

If you think just because it's boring and repetitive, I'll stop, you're mistaken. Erik stared at that Mana gate, his determination increasing the power of the drill.

Pain tells me I'm alive! Erik yelled in his mind, sinking into the training that had taken him through war zones across Earth. His will would not be broken.

Time slipped by as the Mana gate showed weaknesses. The drill made it farther as Erik altered it, increasing its strength.

His body was under incredible stress, but Erik had learned to deal with pain and discomfort long ago. To him, they tempered his determination as he pressed forward for more, to show he wouldn't be defeated, to show he was the best.

The Mana gate made a shrieking noise, like metal being bent inward. The Mana gate gave way, its fight over.

The rush of Mana ran rampant through Erik's arm, aiming to rush out of his hand.

Erik reversed the draw of the Mana. "I'm not done yet!" He opened his eyes. He used the rush of fresh Mana coming in through the newly opened gate and closed his hand; power threw the Mana drill back to where it had come from. Erik circulated it through his Mana, faster and faster as his eyes located his next target: his tenth Mana gate.

"You are mine!" Erik yelled out. His Mana channels lit up with power as the Mana drill circulating his Mana channels shot up through his Mana channels like a bullet.

The Mana drill connected with his tenth Mana gate.

A resounding boom shook Erik and made the air around him shake.

52
MANA LORD

Erik was covered in sweat. The air around him seemed to have become stagnant as spurts of Mana were drawn into his body.

He had simply been straining his Mana systems for so long, he was on the verge of collapsing.

That steel-like Mana gate stood there, its surface scarred and showing signs of strain. But it seemed resilient, standing tall despite all else.

Erik needed more power. If he failed, then his tenth Mana gate would be sealed and it would be even harder for him to break through. He might have to dismiss breaking through it until he had three drops of Mana.

Drops of Mana? What if I didn't compress them but made them expand?

A crazy idea filled Erik's mind. Reaching the level of forming Mana drops was a massive undertaking; if he was to decompress them, he would be taking a step backward.

Erik was determined and he had faith that he would be able to reform them.

A crazy expression appeared on his face, his hair wild and his clothes stuck to him with sweat. "Form!" he yelled, slamming his hands together.

He pressed the Mana gates in his hands together as he pressed his feet together, aligning his Mana system and closing off four gates to the outside world.

Mana moved from his dantian through his left leg, up his right leg, through Mana channels to his left arm, and down through to his right hand. There it would go through his arm and reach the Mana gate where his spine and skull intersected.

Erik formed Mana into shapes again, a shape he was only too familiar with. The Mana turned into bullets. They weren't aimed at his tenth gate yet, just circulating his system—one at first, then two, and three, with more being created, adding to his Mana channels. Their speed increased with every circulation.

He drained the ambient Mana from within his body. Just as his body felt as if it were about to burst, Erik laughed.

"Fire!" With his command, he no longer circulated the Mana bullets but directed them toward the tenth Mana gate.

The effect of the compressed Mana drop decompressing was like gunpowder going off in a round. The Mana drill and the Mana bullets shot forward. A rushing noise filled Erik's body as his Mana system was being torn apart under the stress.

The Mana bullets were like rounds from a machine gun hitting the exact same spot. The tenth Mana gate had no time to recover as tens of rounds slammed into it. Cracks formed as it put up a good fight.

It wasn't enough.

The Mana bullets had done their damage as they broke through the tenth gate.

Erik relaxed his control; the bullets' control over his Mana system disappeared. Erik fell backward, fainting.

His tenth Mana gate gave away fully. Erik's entire body seemed to resonate on an entirely new level. The energy of the world resonated with him. A rush of invisible power shot out from Erik's body as if messengers rushing to tell the world of the birth of a new lord.

Meanwhile, in the smithy, Rugrat's eyes cleared for a second as he looked toward the Village Hall. That invisible wave of power was visible to him, his Mana gates resonating with that power.

He shook his head. "Looks like he broke through his tenth Mana gate."

A thought crossed his mind as he started to chuckle. It grew into a laugh as he twirled his hammer and slammed it into the metal on the anvil. "Very well! You're not the only one who wants to increase his power!" Rugrat's voice was filled with power, resounding through the smithy, his hammer blows strong and fast, but precise. His competitive spirit was ignited. How was he going to let his friend beat him in strength?

Rugrat bent down to his work with greater determination.

No one else felt the disturbance.

Erik remained on the ground. His Mana system was torn apart, but as he rested, the powerful recovery ability of his tempered blood worked to heal his body. His wounds were severe, but with a bit of healing magic and his body's recovery ability Erik was starting to see the benefits of his body cultivation combined with healing magic.

Storbon woke up, looking at the door as a guard walked in, an angry look on his face.

Storbon reached for his hand. Finding his fingers there, he was comforted. Still, he looked around the barracks quickly. When he hadn't had a hand, he was used to people looking at him with derision and spitting on him, thinking of him as a waste of resources in Alva Village. He didn't feel that animosity anymore, but it was hard to forget.

"What are you doing? Do you think this is a vacation! Get your asses up!" the guard yelled, kicking the nearest bunk.

People were stunned awake, looking at the guard.

"Get dressed and on the training grounds! Move it!"

People started grabbing clothes and ambling about, drawing the ire of the guard.

"Don't you know how to get dressed? Too slow—out!"

Storbon slept in his clothes and was rushing to the door.

The guard went through, using his club to "motivate" people to hurry up.

Storbon saw that the other three barracks were being drained of people as guards moved through the ranks.

In the parade square, Rugrat stood with his hands behind his back, wearing armor. It was well worn, but it had been cared for meticulously. He looked at what was happening without feeling. His expression was unreadable as guards continued to usher people out.

"Get in one of the squares!" another guard yelled.

Storbon saw the squares that were carved into the dirt and quickly stepped into one. A few others were as fast as him. Anyone who seemed to be lagging was met by the guards' clubs.

It wasn't long until people in different states of undress were lined up in the squares.

Everyone looked at Rugrat, but he hadn't moved once. A look of shame mixed with disgust appeared on Rugrat's face.

Storbon's stomach dropped.

"I'm supposed to train you to be heavy infantry. Do you know what I see?"

No one said anything, the square eerily silent compared to the yelling and shrieks from before. The guards seemed to take the disappointment personally, their expressions darkening further as some people in the grid squares shook in fear.

"I see a bunch of failures. I see a bunch of people who will *break* instead of hold the line!" Rugrat's voice rose until it shook their already tense nerves.

Storbon felt as if he were going to throw up. He wanted to be useful; he wanted to do Mister West proud. He was determined to prove Rugrat wrong; he wasn't a failure!

"When you're ready to admit you're a failure, ring that bell." Rugrat pointed to a bell that stood off to the side. "I want everyone here, in this group and in the city, to know that you don't have what it takes to be in the heavy infantry."

Rugrat let those words sink in as people's eyes were drawn to the bell, each making their own decisions.

Storbon gripped his fists tighter. His eyes moved from the bell to Rugrat. He didn't need a bell.

Rugrat's hand dropped slowly. "Get them out of my sight. Next time I see them, they best at least look like they're worth a damn." Rugrat turned and left as the guards started yelling.

"All right, you're going to learn how to march! Then it's off for a haircut and a shave and shower. You will be clean every morning before parade. You will not relieve yourself anywhere but the bathrooms. We don't accept dirty street scum here. If you don't know how to keep yourself clean, how will you look after a weapon or your armor?" Guard Niemm barked. "Watch closely! I will not repeat myself!"

Niemm showed how to march. Storbon tried to follow and do the same. Still, the guards, seeing them all messed up, used their clubs to get them into proper form.

Someone dropped to the ground, trying to protect themselves as they started crying.

The clubs stopped as a guard moved to him. "What are you on the ground for? Do you think the Earth god is going to help you! Ring the bell! The bell is your only way to escape me, boy! Ring it! Make that bell your new god! Do it!" The man continued to cry on the ground as the guard yelled at him, not even hitting him. His words were more painful than any beating.

"Get up!" The guard hauled the man to his feet. He was a level twelve while the recruit was a level seven; to the guard, it was like picking up a child. "Get into formation!" He pushed the man back into place.

The man was still crying, the guards picking on him, but he continued on. Eventually the guards harassed others.

The bell rang out. The first had already left.

He was taken off to the side and to the guard captain's quarters.

Storbon wondered how many more would ring the bell that day.

Erik awoke to the ringing of bells. He rose from the floor and let out a sharp breath. Pain flared up in his body. Erik used healing spells and he started to rebuild his body.

It was still dark.

"Whistles are meant for if there is a beast attack—the bell, spear training?" Erik muttered.

He cleared up the confusion. Looking toward the barracks, he could hear the sounds of yelling. The heavy infantry unit had started training.

Erik's body was repairing, much faster than normal. The Mana in his body was purer, so his recovery higher. His every movement seemed to resonate with the Mana around with him; instead of creating a slight disturbance, he gained a much higher command over it.

Erik opened his notifications.

You have opened another Mana gate!
+2 to Mana Regeneration

Quest Updated: Opening the Fourteen Gates
Congratulations! You have opened your tenth Mana gate.

Requirements:
Clear all of your fourteen gates (10/14)
Rewards:
+1 to Mana Regeneration base stat
Undergo Mana Body Rebirth
1,400,000 EXP

You have successfully opened 9 Mana gates.
+2 to Mana Pool

You have successfully opened 10 Mana gates.
Hidden Reward: Gain Title: Mana Lord

Title: Mana Lord
Your Mana control has increased greatly.
The strength of your spells has increased by 10%. Your Mana Regeneration increased by 10%

Erik's eyes bulged as he quickly pulled up his character sheet.

Character Sheet
Name: Erik West
Level: 13
Race: Human
Titles:
From the Grave
Land Holder (Temporary)
Mana Lord
Strength: (Base 7) +11
180
Agility: (Base 6) +13
85
Stamina: (Base 12) +4
210
Mana: (Base 6) +11
170
Mana Regeneration (Base 10) +21
10.05/s
Stamina Regeneration: (Base 7) +20
6.15/s

"Hubba hubba." Erik looked at it, feeling like an excited little kid getting a present. "This must be the hidden effect Rugrat was talking about," Erik said. "While one can increase their overall Mana Regeneration with the attribute gain at every level, they don't gain these hidden benefits. No wonder Rugrat feels different. The little bastard got a ten percent increase in his overall Mana Regeneration!"

It was a much bigger change than just increasing one's attributes. When Erik leveled up, then his increase would be even greater. For someone focusing on a Mana-based build, this was gold raining from the heavens.

"No wonder Rugrat was so confident that I would make it through my tempering. The little bastard was holding this back." Erik shook his head. He'd need to get Rugrat back in some way later on but for now he was too happy with his gains.

It felt incredible, but his smile paused as he looked toward his dantian. There was only one drop there now. He had used the other to open his tenth Mana gate. Still, with enough time, he knew he'd be able to reform it.

"With the later Mana gates, to open them, I might need to directly use the Mana drops to clash with them. I'll have to ask Rugrat," Erik said.

He took another tour of his inner body, checking his body and Mana system. His Mana gates no longer looked like stone but instead had spots of silver.

Erik stood. His bones seemed to crack, giving him a refreshing feeling. He felt revitalized. Then he took a deep breath in and nearly choked.

"Oh God." Erik's eyes teared up a bit as he realized how awful he smelled.

He found a layer of grime on his skin. "Wait, the showers should be done by now!" Erik said.

He moved to the window and saw that the shower block was complete. He saw lights in the other districts as people were working to build bathrooms.

Erik quickly left the Village Hall and went to the showers. He looked over the building. There was a note on the wall, telling people how to act and use the showers.

Erik went inside and found the showers there. He turned one on; it was cold, but the water was refreshing and clean. He didn't care. He jumped in and washed off the grime, quickly jumping out to wash off and back in, dancing around as he had a brisk but fruitful shower.

He was shivering by the end but he felt a lot better after he had his first shower since arriving in the Ten Realms. "It's all about the little things." Erik got dressed and walked outside, warming up even though the sun hadn't come over the horizon.

Seeing he had some time, Erik thought about going and seeing Rugrat, but a thought hit him.

"I've wanted to adapt the growling elbow technique. Since I've got some time, I should try that out instead of bugging Rugrat. If he needs me, he can message me, and Blaze should be fine in training the heavy infantry."

Erik headed off toward the storage area, where there weren't any lights on. He found an empty area that had plenty of room for him to move around in.

Erik threw a few elbows. A growling noise came from his body as Mana was directed through his body before he unleashed it.

He did it a few more times, imprinting it all on his mind.

Then he tried to do the same thing with his right knee. It took a few tries but then a growling could be heard as he struck out. The dust around him was disturbed once again. He did it again and again until he had a complete grasp of it. Then he did it with his other knee. It got easier each time.

He didn't feel the least bit tired as he controlled his breathing.

The growling elbow basically compresses and expands the Mana in my Mana channels to increase the power of each blow. It's almost how muscles and tendons expand and contract to allow movement.

Erik had an idea. Instead of moving onward, he threw a few elbows, tracing the different muscles, tendons, and systems that he used in moving his elbow. Then he started to trace it and move his Mana according to that expanding and contracting. It went on for ten minutes. There was no roaring, but Erik's body glowed with Mana slightly as the wind was stirred up violently.

His elbow shot out. The power had increased greatly, but it was completely silent now.

Erik's eyes remained closed as he started to move through different fighting positions. He traced out the different body systems that were working together, building up a greater image in his mind. It was much more in-depth knowledge than he had even cared to understand about the human body when he was being taught to be a medic.

That was theoretical; with this, he could see a direct use and benefit from learning it.

Erik's body started to glow. The power in his body increased as his physical and Mana systems worked together. It was not a simple increase of one plus one, but a multiplicative effect.

Erik stopped sometime later, letting out a hiss as he retracted his Mana. Fighting this way, he burnt a lot of Mana in a short period of time. It also had a toll on his body. Mana, after all, was a form of powerful energy. His body could accept a certain amount into specialized systems, but too much for too long and the other systems that were not meant to handle Mana started to sustain injuries and fail.

Erik could heal himself, but then his Mana usage would soar.

Although Erik wished he had been able to do more, the gains he'd made weren't simple.

"Well, I guess I should call it the Mana amplification fighting technique. When I temper my body, it should be able to handle more Mana running through it, allowing me to use it for longer and decreasing the Mana needed. Also, my base Strength and Agility should increase." Erik clenched his fist. Slight blue tracings could be seen inside his fist if one was to look closely.

He released it as the sun started to fall on Alva Village.

He heard yelling over at the barracks and moved to check on it. Erik didn't go inside the barracks but went on the wall to look inside.

He could see four groups of people who were being marched around the barrack's training area. Guards were yelling out orders and correcting people.

There was a group that was lined up. The village's barber shaved off their beards and cut their hair down to military regulation.

There was still a long way to go. Erik watched without being seen, unconsciously entering stealth, as he viewed the different groups.

One was coming back from the showers, to get issued their kit; another was heading off; another was at the barber's; and the last was getting their group to march properly. There was not a second to be lost and even marching to the showers was an opportunity to learn.

Erik knew that it wouldn't be easy on them and that a number of people would probably fall out. Right now they didn't have time for feelings; if they left, then Blaze would talk to them before they left. But if they were here, there was no mercy waiting for them.

Erik could hear ringing from the smithy as he went down to the barracks.

"Sa-lute!" the guards yelled out. Clearly Blaze had been teaching them more than just marching and how to use different weapons. He'd only had them two days but he'd whipped the guards up enough so that they were a few days ahead of the recruits. Thankfully they didn't need as much sleep so they could be trained and train at the same time.

The guard slammed his fist to his chest. Erik returned the salute as the guard leader yelled out, "Eyes front!"

The trainees were all confused as the guard walked away. As soon as Erik stepped into the smithy, he could hear the guard going off on them.

"Don't you know how to salute! What kind of useless creatures are you!" the guard yelled out, berating them and forcing them to complete some repetitive and hellish task.

Erik was greeted by Rugrat and Taran's backs as they worked at their anvils. There was a feverish movement to their actions. It was as if they had to work right now or else they would never be able to get it back.

Erik didn't say anything as he looked at the drawings over one wall, the lines on Rugrat's hammer and his anvil.

There was a pile of pulleys, new bow arms, reload assists, and trigger mechanisms off to one side.

Erik was a little alarmed at the number of them—over forty sat there. With a glance, Erik could see that the worst ones were at the bottom with the better ones appearing at the top. They were all the same parts, but their quality increased each time.

Not wanting to disturb them, Erik collected the parts and quickly left. He found one of the guards as he left. "Make sure that Rugrat and Taran aren't disturbed, and make sure to bring them their meals," Erik said.

"Sir." The guard saluted.

"Is there something else?" Erik asked, sensing more from the guard.

"Are they…increasing their skill level?" The guard was embarrassed to be caught, but their interest won out.

"I think so," Erik said.

"Understood, sir." The guard's expression became serious in the blink of an eye. If their smiths were able to increase in skill level, then their equipment might improve greatly as well!

53
BUILD

Rugrat looked up from what he had been working on. After he had talked to the trainees, he had gone back into the smithy again. Taran had arrived as soon as he woke up. The two of them had talked for only a short period of time before they got to work. They would glance over at each other's works, gaining inspiration as they poured out all of their effort.

They held nothing back as they broke past their limits.

The furnace burned red-hot as their hammers struck metal continuously. The very building was stirred up as Experience was drawn in from all around, increasing the strength of their bodies.

Rugrat had felt Taran break through a number of bottlenecks as he accumulated more Experience and his skill level shot up.

Rugrat was empowered in this situation. They didn't need to talk as their minds resonated with each other toward a singular goal, to push the limits of their smithing knowledge.

Rugrat looked around. He felt as if he were forgetting something. His tired brain started to turn over; as he was about to go back to work, he realized that the sun was coming up. It was time for breakfast. He looked over to the side, where there was a note left behind by Erik.

"When was he in here?" Rugrat questioned, starting to realize how concentrated he had been on proving or disproving the ideas he had. He picked up the note and read it.

"Ah shit!" Rugrat put down his hammer and rushed off out of the smithy. Taran didn't even look up, his eyes glowing as his hammer made the metal sing.

Rugrat stored his gear. It wasn't long until he reached the square where people were eating. The spear groups had been served earlier, the village talking about them as Rugrat cleared his throat and moved to the stage.

"Morning, everyone. I'm here to talk to you about construction, at least the different stages of it and things you should keep in mind when building anything," Rugrat said.

This gained everyone's attention. Erik's information had opened up a new world to them but Rugrat's was something that they could see and they had knowledge of.

He talked about the basics, the need for a good foundation or base, the need to have load-bearing supports, different kinds of roofs and their use.

He opened up the floor for questions. The different people who had built homes came up with myriad ones.

To Rugrat, they were all basic, or he could at least give them a general outline. He poured out everything that he had, holding nothing back.

A lot of thoughtful people wrote down notes. They'd heard of the rewards that the department heads were passing out to those people who were able to do something that could benefit the village.

There was much to do and there were people who wanted to show off their talent. If they could grab the eyes of one of these people, they might go from Earth to heaven in a single step.

Rugrat's talk came to an end as people started to go off to work. He turned to leave the stage and found Erik standing there.

Rugrat scratched his head awkwardly. "Sorry I'm late," he muttered.

"Way to keep the Mana Lord from me," Erik said under his breath.

Rugrat looked stunned before he laughed. "Well, I wanted to leave at least some kinds of secrets from you. So how did you open it?" Rugrat asked, genuinely interested. That was also the other reason he hadn't told Erik about what happened when someone opened up ten Mana gates; he wanted to see how Erik would open it.

He was ahead, but only by one Mana gate. It had been incredibly hard for him to get to this point and he wasn't going to try to open the next Mana gate until he had the power that came with leveling up again.

Erik told him in detail what he had done, shocking Rugrat.

"Damn, you're competitive." Rugrat sunk into thought. It was actually ingenious, but it put a massive strain on one's body.

"So how did you open your tenth and eleventh Mana gate?" Erik asked.

"Okay, well, I used a drop of my Mana. I took it from my dantian and then I slowly pressed it into the Mana gate. The gate absorbs energy, as we know, so basically I pumped so much energy into that sucker it popped. With the influx, I was able to condense another drop of Mana. I only opened one in a concentrated push. The eleventh one cost me two Mana drops to open and I could only recover one drop—took me a few days to compress another one."

"Smart," Erik said. It didn't put as much strain on Rugrat's body and although it was a slower process, it was more stable.

"You going to try to open another one?" Rugrat asked.

"I think that if I can temper my body, then it'll be easier for me to open more gates in the future," Erik said.

Rugrat nodded and started yawning.

"You get back to the smithy. I'll take people out hunting today," Erik said.

Rugrat was about to argue but thinking about the smithy and the work he still wanted to complete, he just nodded sheepishly.

Glosil could only look over bitterly at the heavy infantry units. Since this morning, they had been grilled all day long.

He had been working with the latest group of villagers to be trained with the crossbows. These would be the last groups to come through the basic training. After this, they would focus on raising their own crossbow sharpshooting group. Most of them were hunters or previous guards.

The heavy infantry groups were being marched out of the barracks, leaving it in relative peace for the day. They would learn how to fight as a unit.

They didn't have time to mess around, so Erik and his people would be acting as spotters and scouts for Blaze, sending groups of boars at the groups of heavy infantry.

This would allow them to grind levels. They'd switch out, taking on waves and waves of boars.

It was hellish training, but they didn't have time to be nice.

Seeing that they didn't need sleep, when night came, they would be carrying on what the day groups had started: digging and building up the layered defenses around the village.

This would get them to understand defensive positions and the lay of the land. It could also build up their strength and get them used to the new gear that they had been issued.

Glosil's eyes turned to the guard units that were getting ready. There were two guardsmen to ten people. Erik had set off earlier with the advanced group that were meant to be the elite crossbow groups. They needed to go farther to penetrate the boar line and try to hunt down packs of wolves. Glosil was afraid for them, but he knew that Erik had hidden his strength so far.

The groups and the guards were looking to him, ready to go. They were a mix of emotions. The ones who hadn't done this before were scared and nervous; those that had done it a few times were more relaxed, apprehensive as they had a realistic view of how things could go wrong but assured in their own skills.

"Good hunting. See you back for the midday meal," Glosil said.

The guards saluted as the newest village hunters looked on awkwardly, unsure of what to do. They moved out toward the gates and onto the wilds beyond.

Glosil heard people training in the back of the barracks and saw people finishing off the public bathrooms across the city.

The forest was being cut back still to fulfill their need for continuous lumber. Watchtowers were planned out and the wall reinforced and cleaned up so it was a true defensive structure.

The whole city had been changed dramatically from what it was before. It was now a well-oiled machine, more military camp than village. He could only shake his head.

The power of these people—any of them could become main figures in a powerful city in the area.

None of them thought to leave; this was their home and they had grown closer, working together and suffering through the same hardships as they got together to eat and to build.

They could see how their village had grown. They had a sense of pride that had been bred into their bones.

People talked of the showers; they talked of the building on the walls, the logging camp, and the weapons coming from the smithy.

Glosil felt deep pride looking at them all. He had been brought to the village, a man kicked out of a noble's family because he had helped a lady who the young master of the house had attacked.

He did his duty, but he didn't feel connected to the village. He felt cut off from everyone, but this training—the need for his time and the demands on him—reminded him of when he had been in the royal army, a time when he had purpose, he had meaning.

Even then the army had bred him to be a fighter. They had built up his body, but they hadn't educated his mind. A technique book would be seen as a waste on him, but Erik and Rugrat had given him *three* such books meant to improve his understanding of tactics, how to use his troops more effectively.

He didn't look forward to battle, but he felt that they were ready for it.

He felt the new power within his body. He had finally broken through and reached level eleven. Following Rugrat and Erik, it felt as if anything was possible.

Even Blaze has come to accept them.

They weren't the best leaders, but they looked after their people first and it showed.

A message came from Blaze, shared to Glosil, Erik, and Rugrat.

"Heavy infantry units are moving into position. Starting them on drills right now," Blaze said.

"Has everyone been issued healing powder?" Erik asked.

"Yes," Blaze said, sounding torn.

"Good. Review with them what will happen if they or the person beside them is wounded." Erik's voice was cold.

"Yes, sir." Blaze might have hang-ups but Erik's words were law in Alva Village.

Glosil could only grimace, feeling sorry for those heavy infantry groups.

They were only armed with spears, and some had to share one between the different groups as Rugrat and Taran were still building more.

They weren't allowed to wear their armor as it might bring on the Red Haze and mess everything up. If the boars got in close, then they'd get hurt and badly. Erik could save them, Glosil had faith, but those wounds might leave scars that weren't only physical.

54
BLADE SECTION

"Your friend is injured to your side!" Blaze yelled out.

"Inform the second line, continue to fight, don't be distracted!" the heavy infantry groups yelled out in response.

"Hu-ah!" Niemm yelled out.

"Hah!" Their spears shot out into the space ahead before rushing back.

The guards carried out the same actions, though they were wearing full training gear, unlike the trainees, who were dressed in simple clothes that would lie under their armor.

Blaze could already see the deadness in their eyes, the blankness that came as one resigned themselves to their fate, forgot about what they were doing and only did what they needed to do. It was in this state that soldiers were made.

Their bodies were trembling as they were stuck in a half squat, their legs straining.

"You are injured!" Blaze yelled.

"Move to the rear, do first aid!"

"Chaaaange ranks!" Niemm barked.

The heavy infantry on the front stood and snapped to the side, their spears up as the second rank moved through the gap.

"Hah!" Their spears thrust out again as the second rank became the first. It was their turn to squat and hold their spears out as the old first rank cycled to the rear of the formation. The ranks behind turned sideways to let them pass and then snapped to face forward, their spears ready over the front ranks, creating greater depth and more spears to hit the oncoming enemy.

Niemm looked to Blaze and he waved for him to go on.

"Faaace right!" Niemm barked. The right corner of the group stayed where they were as the left side moved forward to create a block facing the right.

"What the fuck was that? Are you a fucking caterpillar? You are a *formation*! Move as one! What do you think—you're special or something?" Niemm barked.

"Faaace left!"

The left stayed and the right moved, looking even more messed up.

"You're in the rear rank and there are wounded—what do you do?"

"Treat according to first aid!"

"First aid stages?"

"Check the scene! Check if they're responsive! Check if they're bleeding!"

Blaze's eyes fell on a few people who had been slow at responding. The guards moved in, yelling at them and demanding medical questions out of them as Niemm continued to make them face right and left.

"They're non-responsive, what do you do?" Blaze demanded.

"Check for wounds, treat as needed!"

"When treating someone, whose medical kit do you use?"

"Theirs first and then yours!"

"Someone is bleeding, what do you need to do?" Blaze asked. Even he had burned this information into his mind. Erik had given him a full manual on first aid, with a simplified guide specific to what the heavy infantry might need.

It was simple, but it could save a life.

"Pour powder on the wound, seal with a bandage!"

"Someone is critical, what do you do?" Blaze yelled.

"Hu-ah!"

"Hah!" Their spears lashed out again. Those without spears had sharpened wooden poles that would be turned into spears.

"Move to the rear, they will be collected!"

This continued on until midday.

"Halt!" Blaze yelled out, standing up and slamming the butt of his spear against the ground. The people working in the logging camp and those working on the defenses glanced over, looking at them all.

"Sergeants, break them down into groups—food and water. Let's see how they fight against pigs," Blaze said.

The guards, who had been renamed sergeants, moved to their groups, talking to them all. Two were on guard duty; the others sat down, pulling off their packs and downing water and food rations. None of them were allowed to use their storage rings. It made things harder on them, but the more discomfort they embraced now, the less it would affect them later on.

They sat with their cuirasses that were lying on the ground. They huddled together; the sergeants and Blaze moved away out of earshot as they sat down for their meal too.

Away from the recruits, their angry expressions disappeared and the men underneath the uniform appeared as they took off their helmets. They were covered in sweat and tired, but they weren't about to show weakness in front of their men.

"Fuck, don't think the sun could get any warmer." Sergeant Chun shifted his shoulders inside his armor, to try to get some air circulation going on.

"My wife's always wanted me to lose a few pounds." Sergeant Yi grinned.

The others laughed as they ate the simple rations. They were actually better than the meals they had every night. Having decent food while training was something that seemed to revive the soul.

"You think they're ready?" Blaze looked to the sergeants.

The jovial mood from before turned contemplative. For the last week, they had done nothing but learn from Rugrat and Erik, been trained and trained others.

They'd grown in that week. Blaze had brought most of them from the army with him and with the training, they had not only kicked away the old cobwebs but they had exceeded their abilities in their prime.

"No, but I think I'm going soft on them. What other choice do we have but to push them?" Sergeant Niemm said.

The other sergeants continued to eat but showed signs of agreement.

"We've also got a group of sharpshooters watching over us and Erik," Sergeant Chun said. "Even if they're wounded, as long as they make it to Erik, I think they'll be fine."

The other sergeants all agreed.

Blaze nodded and dug into his food. "All right, so what do you think of the people in your groups?"

"Simms's son Rafe is good," Sergeant Yi said.

"You seen Storbon? That kid might have been weak, but now—" Niemm looked up from his food. "That kid's got potential—damn tiger in human clothing."

Blaze grimaced as he looked over. Even though Storbon was one of the best, he was still ostracized in his group. He was someone who was seen as a waste in the village not that long ago.

Blaze could see a greatness in him, someone who could easily become a sergeant, his power rivalling others.

He needed cohesive units as fast as possible. Although he might be powerful in the heavy infantry, if he was part of the quick reaction force under Rugrat and Erik, his strength would soar.

Blaze's eyes hardened. "Seems like they still haven't learned how to be a unit." Anger colored his words.

The sergeants looked over to the heavy infantry groups. Storbon was eating, checking over his armor and then his spear while the rest were just eating numbly.

The other sergeants' expressions fell. A coldness entered their eyes as they looked at the different groups, seeing more isolation as people were separated out.

They were all heavy infantry; all of them were as strong as their weakest, seeing clear separation and exclusion.

The trainees looked up from their meals. The sun seemed to have disappeared as a cold sweat ran down their backs.

Storbon had been checking on his gear and eating as fast as possible. It was a practice that was now bred into him. Not knowing where his next meal might come from, he never let any crumb go.

The sergeants looked over at everyone. Their anger influenced the very air as everyone looked down, trying to not draw their ire. Even the strongest among them, who might be proud in front of their fellow trainees, didn't try to go up against the sergeants.

"Five minutes!" Blaze yelled out.

People stuffed food and water into their mouths rapidly.

The sergeants headed over, wearing their gear and spears. "Form up!"

They had learned to form up quickly and moved into position.

The sergeants came around, collecting the armor. Then they were marched toward the forest.

Storbon gripped his spear tighter.

A man to Storbon's side tripped him up, sending him sprawling.

"Storbon, on your feet!" Sergeant Yi yelled, coming over, anger written on his features.

Storbon could see the man who had tripped him smirking. He didn't know why the man had done it—because he was angry and wanted to lash out, or because he didn't like Storbon.

Storbon gritted his teeth. He just wanted to prove himself to Erik. He didn't care about the past, but these others were petty.

An arrow came out of nowhere, cutting the man's cheek.

Everyone went silent as a hidden aura erupted.

"Blade." Erik's voice passed through the formation. Even the sergeant's faces paled before they turned into cold anger, focused on the man who had tripped Storbon.

Blaze's sound talisman lit up before he walked over to the man holding a spear. His face was emotionless as he ripped the spear from the shaking man's grasp. With a backhand slap, he sent the man flying to the side.

Spitting blood and teeth, the man looked up at the rest of the unit.

Blaze looked away, as if he didn't exist anymore. He looked at the heavy infantry group. "Sergeant Niemm!" he yelled out.

"Sir!" Sergeant Niemm moved up to stand in front of Blaze.

"I asked you to raise a bunch of heavy infantry. You rose a group of blades, it seems! Not one of your people moved to help a fellow trainee, nor say anything about how one of their own attacked him." Blaze's voice became louder and louder. His powerful aura, over two times the strength of the trainees', made them shake with fear.

Storbon, who had recovered his position, bore up under that pressure.

The entire group was looking at the man on the ground holding his broken face with coldness in their eyes or looking down in shame.

"A heavy infantry formation falls together or they fall apart. Trainee Yoros likes to stab everyone in the back, so your unit will be named Blades. You will be at the front because I don't trust you to be in the rear anymore!" Blaze threw out four stretchers.

"Blade section, you will be in charge of these stretchers. Every failure you have, every time you drop it unless to change out carriers, weight will be added! Go and get four rocks the size of a man's head from the roadside! Sergeant Niemm, I hope you are able to redeem this group of blades!"

With that, Blaze turned away.

"Move it, you fucking useless blades!" Niemm roared. "Form into groups of two! Storbon, you're with me!" Niemm barked.

So the Blades section was formed as the other sections did everything they could to not be noticed.

"Sergeant Chun, Sergeant Yi, collect a stretcher for each of your sections!" Blaze yelled as he marched up the sections, dropping off stretchers.

Stones were gathered and put on the stretchers. Two people grabbed the poles, putting their spears on the stretchers. Once they were all ready, Blaze nodded.

"You will be in charge of switching off with one another—the sergeants won't, to make up for their mistakes and inability to teach you lot!" Blaze yelled.

The man on the side of the road looked around, fear and confusion in his face.

"What do I do?" the man asked, his face all messed up.

"Get back into position!" Niemm barked.

Everyone looked at him with daggers.

"In the heavy infantry, we are one! One of us fucks up, we all fuck up. Punishment will not be on just one person, but on everyone."

Niemm's words were meant for everyone as they carried on on their path.

Erik moved with his group, as the heavy infantry marched through the forests. They were in charge of making sure that nothing snuck up on them.

Erik opened up a channel. "Roska, have your group bring in the boars."

"Sir."

Erik had kept an eye on Roska, having her concentrate on increasing her Mana abilities. At the same time, Erik had her train with a crossbow. She was now fully recovered from her previous injuries.

Erik wanted her to earn what she gained. She worked as hard or harder than everyone else. She purified the water of the city and she read all of the manuals Erik had given her. He had taught her to create Mana bullets and Mana bolts as well. For firepower, she was one of the strongest in Alva Village. Erik let her discover her own path. He wanted her to develop her own path of magic.

His was based around strengthening his body, and using it to increase his melee abilities; it was easier for him to understand and use.

Erik signalled to the hunters. They had all reached level ten now. Their stealth abilities and marksmen were among the best. They climbed up into different perches, looking out over the heavy infantry groups.

"Boars!" a sentry outside of the formation yelled.

The groups started to panic.

"Blades, stretchers down. Form up to face the enemy. Section Two and Three, move to the left; Section Four to the right of the Blades!" Blaze snapped out. The sergeant corralled them, quickly getting them into position.

Everyone was nervous as they could see the boars. Still, they got into position, albeit hastily.

"Brace!" Sergeant Niemm barked. The front rank braced themselves and their spears while the second rank pushed their spears over, making a wall of spears.

The boars let out their squeals as they rushed forward.

They met the first spears; the heavy infantry let out grunts as they took the full kinetic force of the boars.

The second and third lines were there to support them and strengthen them, like a rugby scrum, spreading the weight and holding them steady.

Three of the boars impaled themselves, with one getting through, driving its tusks into a man's leg.

He let out a scream as the people behind and on either side finished off the boar.

"Man is wounded!" Sergeant Chun yelled out.

"Pull him to the rear!" the trainees yelled out, pulling the man back as the second rank man moved up into his position and someone from the third rank took his place as others looked to the wounded man, using their healing powder and their bandages.

All of the boars were now dead.

The man's pained yelling was dying down as the powder went to work, putting him back together.

"Next wave," Erik said to the scouts as they lured in five more boars from the same direction. Erik and the hunters sat in the trees, watching the heavy infantry, unnoticed.

55
RAPID GROWTH

Five boars had increased to ten, and then fifteen and twenty.

There wasn't much space between the attacks and they seemed to be endless. The heavy infantry had wounded: eight were being tended to, and those who had been injured early on were back on the line.

There was no time for them to relax or take a break.

Storbon took a hit to the side. He felt something break inside his body as a spear shot out, killing the boar. Storbon cut his side and put on a stick bandage with healing powder.

It started to fuse the bone back together as he got up and back on the line. He was in pain, but he didn't want to let that take him out of the fight. As they had fought, walls, associations—all of it fell away. They were heavy infantry; it didn't matter what they did before, or who they had been before. Even the sergeants were part of them.

They didn't fight for themselves; they fought for one another. Storbon didn't even realize it—it came naturally.

"Second rank, advance!" Blaze called out.

Storbon stabbed out with the first rank and then went sideways, trusting the first rank completely as they charged forward, killing those in front of them.

"Hah!" Spears shot out, coming back bloody as the first line moved to the rear.

"Get some food and water into you!" Blaze yelled. He was holding down one of the flanks by himself. His spear was covered in blood, as was his armor. Each sweep and stab gravely injured the boars, directly clashing with them. He was some kind of war god.

Storbon numbly took out food from his pack. As he ate the dried beast meat or the prepared meals, his energy quickly came back. The rations had been specially made to recover Stamina.

The boars were their whetstone. All across the line, the front was fighting, the second recovering as fast as possible to get back into the fight.

Now everyone was stuffing food into their faces, having none of the pride from before. They had hard eyes and looks. They were drained but now their training showed results directly.

"Third rank! Move to the left flank, form up two lines. Sergeant Yi, take command!" Blaze called out.

Storbon stuffed food into his face and put the rest away as he grabbed his spear, moving with the rest of the third rank.

If they were slow, then the others might get hurt. There was no one out here to help them; they had to rely on themselves. They were all the same; it could be them on that line later.

They moved into two lines. Yi positioned them, calling the boars that came from the flank and directing them into the main body of the heavy infantry unit.

Storbon didn't even notice as his levels continued to increase. With all of them working together, the entire group was sharing Experience gain.

The sergeants and the heavy infantry were using their storage items to recover the boars, but there was a thick smell of blood in the area.

"Wolves are on their way," Roska informed Erik.

"Archers, move out to the flanks of the heavy infantry. Wear down the boars. Main target is the wolves," Erik said. This was no longer time for them to hold back.

He jumped from the tree and landed next to Blaze, firing his crossbow. It took a boar in the eye, dropping it to the ground. His Marksman skills had increased rapidly to forty-one, closing in on becoming a Journeyman Marksman. When increasing his skill, it became easier to use his ranged weapons. He'd already passed the skill that Rugrat had as a trained sniper. Rugrat, on the other hand, was terrifying with anything ranged.

"Wolves are coming in," Erik said to Blaze.

"Shit." Blaze looked at the line.

Erik reloaded his crossbow with ease and shot another boar, taking it down before it speared someone on the line in the gut. "Archers will assist. I'll be in reserve if there's a need. Time we saw what they're made of."

Blaze grit his teeth and cut down two more boars. "We need close-range weapons. Spears are good at distance, but if there are enough numbers and they get in close, we're screwed."

Erik studied the battlefield. Blaze was right. "You'll have them tomorrow, and spears," Erik promised, firing again and taking down another boar. "Form up ten across and four lines deep."

"Understood." Blaze cleared his throat. "Blade section, up front, ten men across. Second, third, and fourth section, behind!"

With the archers, the rush of the boars was stopped. They could hear the howls of wolves coming closer.

The heavy infantry followed their orders. If they were slow, they would mess it up for everyone.

The four lines formed. The sergeants checked on everyone as powder was applied to minor wounds and people drank water and shoved food into their faces. They had been fighting for hours and it was already late afternoon.

Erik checked on the archers, making sure that they were in good positions. He let Glosil and Rugrat know what was going on as Blaze personally went through his lines, checking on people.

Erik moved to the badly wounded. He didn't need long to heal them fully. They looked at him in shock, as if he were some wraith that had come out of nowhere. Their sergeants got them back on the line and the heavy infantry's morale shot up. They had thought that they were alone, but Erik and the archers had been watching over them the entire time.

Erik checked that the archers found good positions flanking or behind the heavy infantry. He shuffled them so that they would direct the battle and the wolves.

He left his two best scouts out ahead of the battle and Roska appeared beside him.

"Make sure every spell counts. Stay behind the heavy infantry and cut off the wolves from flanking the heavy infantry. Only use Mana Bolt when I tell you to and never go below twenty percent Mana unless it's life or death," Erik said.

"Understood," she said simply. Her hand picked at the side of her pants.

"Don't worry, you've got this," Erik said, seeing her nerves.

She gave him a small sheepish smile. He knew how rare a thing it was and couldn't help but smile back as a wolf charged out of the forest. Arrows took it down. Those who had fired reloaded with their new levers built into the butt of their crossbows. Three more wolves jumped over its corpse. They were cut down again, but more were coming. They moved in erratic patterns. They were much smarter than the boars, with an alpha wolf leading them.

Crossbows fired again and again while they thinned and directed the wolves. They weren't able to stop them all.

Erik fired his modified crossbow. Each arrow took down a wolf as he calmly looked over the battlefield.

"Brace!" Blaze yelled, taking direct command of the heavy infantry.

The first two lines met the wolves with spears, taking the full force.

"Hu-ah!" Niemm called out on the front line with his section.

"Hah!" The first and second line withdrew their spears and stabbed forward again, the action no longer conscious at this time.

Wolves let out yells as they were stopped by the spears, their hides turning bloody.

The archers worked to reduce the pressure on the heavy infantry and guide the wolves.

"We've got two more wolf groups coming in," one of the scouts still out in the forest said.

"Use the leopard scat—that should deter the other wolf groups," Erik said.

"Understood!"

"Second rank, advance!" Blaze yelled out. The first line returned to the rear as the second pushed forward, taking their place.

Wounded looked after themselves, or by other members of the heavy infantry. Erik healed up those in the worst condition.

The wolves weren't dumb and they were trying to circle the heavy infantry, or get in low at their ankles.

Erik and the archers had to focus on driving the wolves away from the flanks.

I just can't shoot fast enough with this. Erik put the crossbow back into his storage ring and threw up both of his hands. He circulated Mana through his body faster and faster, compressing it into bullets. As he looked ahead, his vision zoomed in.

Looks like this counts as Marksman skill in the Ten Realms.

Erik had only thought of this; he hadn't tried it out before. Finally, he directed the small Mana bullets through his Mana channels, down his arms and out the tips of his fingers.

Small Mana bullets shot out of his hand. When they struck the wolves, they went off like firecrackers. Based on where they hit, they would kill the wolves instantly or leave them with serious injuries.

Quickly the situation changed as Erik stopped firing with both fingers and concentrated on his right finger, increasing his accuracy.

Wolves died in droves. Three full packs had been drawn in by the smell of blood, some fifty wolves.

The groups set into a rhythm, the heavy infantry being changed out on the frontline and resting at the rear before they moved to the front again. The archers tried to reduce the threat while Erik guided the wolves toward the heavy infantry and stopped them from flanking.

Erik put down his hands as he looked over the battlefield.

"Hu-ah!

"Hah!" The last wolf's pained howls were cut off abruptly.

The heavy infantry stood there, waiting for their next order as the archers reloaded and looked over the area for anything that was moving.

"Anything else coming?" Erik asked the two scouts quickly.

"Nothing. It looks like the leopard scat worked."

"Keep an eye out for more," Erik said.

"Understood."

The channel was cut as Erik looked to Blaze.

"Gather up all of the corpses. We need to head back to the village," Erik said.

"Yes, sir!" Blaze got his people organized. They swept the battlefield, clearing away all of the animal corpses.

Erik treated everyone who had bad injuries. No one had died and the medical training made it so that anyone badly wounded had got back to Erik for him to heal.

Everything was cleared up and the archers tossed out leopard scat. Even if the area smelled bloody, the lower-level creatures would be scared back and the higher-leveled creatures didn't come this close to the village yet.

The heavy infantry was formed up and they quick marched back to the village. They were dead tired, but their every action was completely different from how it had been in the morning. They reacted to every command as fast as possible. They looked out for one another as well.

The sergeants didn't have to yell much and they seemed to be part of the sections now. They'd gained every person's respect.

The whole force moved away from the forest as night was coming in. It wasn't long until they had left the forest behind and they were walking through the cleared fields.

Erik checked the different groups working in the fields, expanding the layered defenses. There were nearly no crews working on reinforcing the walls anymore. With the new shifts, work didn't stop in Alva Village.

They didn't have much time left until the beast horde was unleashed on the village. Erik could even see one watchtower had been built and another was underway.

The spear unit's clothes were tattered; blood stained the cuts in their shirts and pants. They stood proud, not caring of their appearance as they moved forward.

"Two and Three section, break for dinner and get cleaned up. Blade section, Fourth section, we will be assisting in building the defenses of the village."

Erik and his archers moved toward the city as Blaze saw to the administration of the heavy infantry units.

Their day hadn't ended yet. With their current ability, they didn't need more than six hours of rest to recover fully.

Erik took the time to view the notifications that had appeared.

Skill: Marksman
Level: 43 (Apprentice)
Long-range weapons are familiar in your hands. When aiming you can zoom in x2.0

Skill: Stealth
Level: 25 (Apprentice)
When in stealth, your senses are sharpened by 5%

Upon advancing into the Apprentice level of Stealth, you will be rewarded with one randomly selected item related to this skill.
You have received the spell book: **Silence**
+10,000 EXP

97,481/140,000 EXP till you reach Level 14

Nearly all of the heavy infantry had been raised up to become level nines. The sergeants were closing in on level twelve. Erik was still behind. He had focused on increasing his Mana system and his Body Cultivation but although they gave rewards, it wasn't enough Experience to become a level fourteen existence. Fighting creatures that were below his level was incredibly easy. The level eight boars only gave him some two hundred and fifty Experience; the level six heavy infantry earned nearly seventeen thousand Experience.

When they were all fighting as a group, the person who got the kill got the most Experience but the overall group also got partial Experience, allowing everyone to grow rapidly.

The archers he'd taken out were now all level eleven. It would be incredibly hard for them to make it much higher unless they directly fought only wolves.

Now they would become part of the village teams, helping to speed up the work on the defensive features. They would also take up patrols, easing the strain on the guards who had been turned into sergeants for the Alva defense force.

Also, with their greater knowledge, they could help to improve the general population's combat capabilities with crossbows.

Erik wanted to diffuse the effects as much as possible. The more people talked and shared, the stronger they would be as a whole.

Erik made it back into the city. He dismissed the fighters with him and told them to report to Elise in the morning.

They understood. Although they might like being fighters, they knew that Alva Village needed builders as much as it needed fighters right now.

Erik went to go and find Glosil.

He was overseeing the second watchtower being erected.

They were simple structures. Stairs led to a raised platform, with a wooden wall facing out with a simple wood roof on top.

Storage bracelets were hung up on the post to the rear of the hut. In it, people could find a whistle, arrows, and spare bows as well as rations and healing powder.

Erik and Rugrat could take more of a backseat as the five pillars of Alva Village took over running the day-to-day of the village.

"Looks like you've been busy since I was gone," Erik said.

"I heard that you ran into some trouble," Glosil said.

"Yeah, thankfully the archer team knew how to handle themselves because we'd been out hunting wolves this morning, but we separated them out from the pack and killed a few, not dealt with entire packs. The heavy infantry did well—took a beating but they've got strength to them." Erik looked out at the two sections who had put down their kit and were now working to dig out defensive potholes and traps in what were once fields.

A few of the heavy infantry were patrolling the area, looking for threats in case something came up on them.

Erik felt a disturbance in the air. He looked over toward the Village Hall. "Did Rugrat go back to the Village Hall to rest?"

"Yes, he did. Sorry for not reporting sooner."

"No worries. He didn't send me a message—he must've been wiped." Erik's voice dropped lower so Glosil could barely hear. "Little bastard reached level fifteen, looks like."

Erik turned thoughtful, wondering just how much Rugrat had increased his smithing. He had been out on more patrols than Erik, but with the small Experience gain, it must have been down to the increases in smithing, his Marksman or stealth.

Erik's expression sobered as he rubbed his storage ring, as if sensing the snake poison sac that rested within.

"Hello, you little money grabbing formation," Erik said, addressing the auction platform.

With sales made through the platform, he had raised another three gold, just paying for the previous losses.

Erik pulled out a chair and sat. He looked over the list of different people. There was information on what they did and the paths they wanted to pursue. He couldn't give them all books but for some of them, he had information or items that would be able to help them.

Slowly he made notations beside each name, filling up the pages.

He opened up the auction platform, placing bids on different manuals and technique books, buying out some fully.

He then moved to the weapons section. First he browsed shields. When he selected it, he could "view" it: a version of him appeared with the weapon or item next to him. Erik checked out the size and build of the shield.

He went through a few different types. Once he found what he wanted and they had enough, he bought a group of fifty square shields priced at three silver each.

Then he moved over to the weapons, getting a single-handed sword. It went for four silver each but there were batches of thirty.

Just the weapons came to nearly three gold; the manuals and technique books had come to three gold. Erik used the remaining gold he had to buy healing potions and powders, draining all of his savings. In the next three days, his auctions would be completed and he could expect more gold to come back to him.

Erik shut down the interface, looking at the items in his different storage rings.

With a sigh, he headed for the main square where dinner was being served. He found the different leaders and a tired-looking Taran sitting there, waiting for him with food.

Erik grabbed his own meal and joined them. He transferred over the different goods to them. They all got different books with their list detailing which items were to go to whom.

Then Erik passed Jasper the healing potions and powders; the shields and swords were given to Blaze and he gave the excess over to Glosil.

Blaze gave out a report on the condition of the heavy infantry, Glosil on the last of the training and the training that the specially picked archers would be undergoing to increase their levels.

Everyone else had been trained at least with the crossbow and were working to build up the defenses or cutting down more lumber.

People were putting their all into their work and it showed. Morale was high and the people were confident. The showers and bathrooms were being used properly, dealing with the waste of the city.

"Most think that they've died and moved into a noble household," Jasper joked. The others smiled and grinned.

Bathing with warm water wasn't something that they were used to, let alone doing it every day, nor were they used to having beast meat in their meals and being given healing powders and potions in case of emergency.

"Well, for the next couple of days, we won't be able to get anymore manuals and books. Currently we don't have any more gold remaining," Erik said.

This got shocked looks but they seemed to understand. They had been spending so much on books it only made sense that it would run out at some time.

Rugrat appeared and wandered over to the eating line. After retrieving his dinner, he made his way to the stage. He looked as if he'd just woken up as he hid a yawn.

"All right, so construction, first from my lesson." Rugrat cocked his head to the side, going back through his memories. "This morning, do you have any questions?"

People started raising their hands and Rugrat went one by one, trying to help them out as much as possible. As he talked, the meeting with the department heads for Alva Village started to come to a close.

"So, Taran, how about those spears and crossbows?" Erik asked. The others were all interested too, wanting to know just what level his ability had reached.

"If it was just me, then mid-Apprentice grade. With Rugrat's help, I can make mainly mid-Apprentice grade, with the occasional high-Apprentice grade weapons," Taran said with a tired but proud smile.

The others all congratulated him as Erik showed a pleased smile. With better equipment, they could increase their attack power, increasing their combat ability even without increasing their overall level.

"Okay, also, tonight I will be attempting to temper my body. I don't know how long it will take or what the effects will be. Rugrat will be assisting me, but depending on how long it takes, we both might not be of much use tomorrow," Erik said.

"If it's okay with you, I'd want to post a few guards at the Village Hall. That way you're not disturbed," Glosil said.

Erik paused before nodding. "I'll agree to it."

The others didn't look pleased that Erik was going to try to temper his body but they didn't raise any other concerns.

Erik headed back to the Village Hall after the meeting.

He sat down and pulled out the forest snake sack. It was still full and there must have been two or so liters of liquid held inside still.

Erik moved to the bath in the Village Hall. He pulled out the forest snake's scales and laid them down inside the tub. The scales were unaffected by the poison, so they were the best material.

Erik poured in hot water he'd taken from the showers; being in his storage ring, it hadn't cooled yet.

Rugrat knocked on the door a few minutes later.

"Come on in." Erik's guts twisted in nervousness.

"Look at you—just like taking a bath, right!" Rugrat laughed.

Erik laughed but his heart wasn't in it. They both knew that it would be much more than that.

"All right, so the plan is that I will get in and you'll monitor me and release the poison slowly. First it will attack my skin, then my muscles and finally reaching into my organs. I will be using Minor Wounds Heal to increase my regenerative abilities. I will be using Wraith's Touch salve on my neck. It numbs the nerves so I won't feel anything below my head. Make sure to monitor me and if anything happens, use Minor Wounds Heal to help my regenerative ability." Erik pulled out an IV bag. It had a pink, on the border of red, color to it.

"What did you add to it?" Rugrat asked.

"I took saline solution, mixed it with healing powder and injected it into the IV. It shouldn't create any problems." Erik pulled out another three needles. "These are weak Novice-grade healing potions. If things are going badly, use these in the IV to boost my healing ability. If that doesn't work, inject it straight into my neck."

"Your body is going to be in the bath. How will you hook up an IV?" Rugrat asked.

"You'll hook it up, and it's going to go into my neck."

Rugrat's head recoiled back, his lips pressed together. He looked like an offended lama. "Dat's fucked."

"Thanks for the confidence boost," Erik muttered. "Fucking support lama."

"Who's a lama—*you're* a lama!"

Erik put the items on a table and put the IV bag on a stand next to the tub.

Rugrat took his time, checking everything and then moving to the IV. He put on gloves and sanitized Erik's neck as he had Erik sit down in the tub and look at the ceiling. His hands were steady as he inserted the needle. Blood appeared as he advanced it a bit more, seating the catheter properly. He taped it down, removing the needle and attaching the IV tube before taping that down as well.

Rugrat checked everything once again.

"Good?" Erik asked.

"Good," Rugrat said. There was no playing left.

"Thanks, Rugrat." Erik had a rare moment of vulnerability. His brother had been the reason he was here, the reason he hadn't taken his life back on Earth. His debt to Rugrat wasn't simple.

"Anytime, brother." Rugrat pat Erik's shoulder. There was no need for complicated words between them.

Erik let out a shaky breath before he pulled out the snake poison sac and handed it to Rugrat.

Rugrat put it to the side and applied Wraith's Touch around Erik's neck.

Erik had a moment of fear as the feeling of nothingness returned. It was the same as when he had lost his limbs in Africa. He took deep breaths as Rugrat let some of the snake poison enter the water.

They waited as the poison diffused through the water. It started attacking Erik's skin, burning it. Erik didn't feel anything and just watched as he started using his Minor Wounds Heal spell.

Rugrat could see what Erik was seeing, one hand on Erik's head, the other on the poison sac. Slowly, he increased the dosage.

The poison was more of an acid than poison. It broke down Erik's skin, and then moved through to his veins. His tempered blood fought back, but this was a much stronger poison than anything it had dealt with before.

Erik decreased his Minor Wounds Heal. He didn't want to heal too much too fast, otherwise the poison might not go through his entire system.

The poison moved through his muscles. Erik's body slumped; still, he held off from pouring out all of his Mana in healing.

The poison moved to his organs.

His entire body was shutting down now.

Erik found it hard to concentrate as his brain was being deprived.

Rugrat increased the poison concentration and used Focused Heal on Erik's brain, clearing his thoughts and allowing him to function fully.

Rugrat put the poison sac away.

Erik's entire body was now falling apart below the neck. The water turned red as his muscles and skin were dissolved. Erik's face showed strange fluctuations.

Rugrat opened up the IV. The healing solution entered Erik's neck and started to move through his body.

Erik didn't hold back anymore as a healing spell formation appeared on his forehead.

His body was trying to fight back against the poison. It was like building levees in the midst of a flood, trying to slow a flood that was already happening.

Rugrat focused on maintaining Erik's brain, keeping him conscious. He grabbed a needle filled with healing potion; he had it inserted into the IV drip assembly, ready to push the plunger at a moment's notice.

Erik started to panic as he saw that nothing was happening with his healing spell and the regeneration powder solution.

Thankfully, he didn't feel the pain as he concentrated his mind, eliminating the random thoughts. *Fight, mother fucker, fight! You going to let some kind of poison kill you?*

Erik used a burst of healing power. His entire body was coming apart; the water was fizzing slightly and colored red with blood.

The Mana in the room was stirred up under the two's draw.

Rugrat changed spells, using Minor Wounds Heal to assist Erik. Rugrat let out a low grunt. His eyes flashed as his Mana channels lit up. Erik might be a Mana Lord, but Rugrat was like a duke, able to move an army with a single word.

Power rushed into Erik's body. His body started showing concentrated signs of fighting back. Every time he advanced slightly, the virulent poison would destroy it.

Erik's body was in a state of rebirth, trying to advance and being destroyed. Each time it regrew, it would become stronger, evolving to fight the poison.

Rugrat couldn't hold off any longer and injected the needle of healing solution into the IV drip.

The pink saline solution took on a deeper red appearance as Erik's body increased the speed that it was destroyed and rebuilt.

Rugrat grabbed another needle, ready to act as he watched.

The room was whipped up into a frenzy as threads of Mana could be seen, drawn in through the Mana gates of the duo.

The Mana in a thirty-meter radius was stirred up as those passing the Village Hall backed away, feeling uncomfortable.

Erik and Rugrat might not be moving but they were fighting one of the hardest battles in their lives, with Erik's life on the line.

There was no time for them to care about what was happening around them.

Finally, Erik's body wasn't being torn apart anymore and was actually stabilizing. It wasn't regrowing, but it wasn't being destroyed anymore.

Rugrat was surprised at the tenacity of Erik's body. His tempered blood and heart acted as the framework for the rest of his body. With each beat of his heart, the vitality of his body started to increase.

Erik's organs that had failed long ago started to show signs of life. It wasn't sudden, but an incredibly slow progression. Still, Rugrat watched, not letting his concentration waver in the slightest, not putting down the needle filled with healing potion.

As Erik's body started to recover, one could sense power coming from within his organs and his muscles.

Erik's body had been destroyed and healed continuously, going through countless cycles of rebirth. Each time, his organs, skin, and muscles were tempered and their impurities removed. He seemed to become closer to the Ten Realms as threads of golden energy from the Ten Realms entered his body.

Rugrat and Erik worked throughout the night.

Rugrat could tell that Erik would be completely changed.

Erik's recovery ability took a leap upward as he fell into unconsciousness, the mental and physical strain too much for his mind and body to handle anymore.

Rugrat continued to heal and watch over Erik.

Finally, Erik's body fully recovered, sitting in that highly concentrated poison that could no longer affect him.

Rugrat used a storage ring to gather the poison water up. He hauled Erik out of the tub, checking his vitals again.

Erik's body was fine. He had just sunk into a deep sleep from the strain.

Rugrat pulled out the IV and picked him up. "Well, at least the extra strength makes it easier to carry you." Rugrat threw him unceremoniously over his shoulder and dropped Erik off in his bed, checking him again.

Rugrat paused for a minute and then pulled out the needle with a healing potion. He put it in Erik's neck and injected it. "Better safe than sorry," Rugrat said, feeling light-headed and nauseous. "Damn, that hurts worse than that second-hand tequila from Columbia."

He went back to his room and collapsed.

While Erik was recovering, Rugrat wasn't sitting idly by.

There was a muffled explosion as the room he was in exploded.

"Do you think that there will be anything left of the Village Hall by the end of this all?" one of the guards watching over the Village Hall asked.

"Nope," Blaze replied.

"I figured it out!" Rugrat yelled as he waved the dust away.

"Is it safe to come in?" Blaze yelled through the door.

"Yes! Come in!" Rugrat said.

Blaze entered the room to see pure destruction. A table had been turned into splinters; the windows were blown out and people could be heard in the street.

Rugrat, on the other hand, was studying a green gas inside a clear container.

"Making something new?" Blaze asked with a nervous laugh.

"Bombs, Blaze—making bombs!" Rugrat said. "I had the densities all wrong. It's really kind of a coincidence that they went off against that Willful Institute bunch." Rugrat half muttered the last part to himself.

"Huh?" Blaze asked.

"While we have defenses in place, we should always have a plan ready for when everything goes to shit, one filled with explosives and destruction. Hopefully, in the future, Erik will make different explosive substances that I can use, but for now I've got basically pure bomb fuel from a three-headed snake that Erik and I killed. In high densities, it will create a flame that will stick to a person and not go out until all of the fuel is consumed. Not even water will fully stop it. Though, when it's aerosolized, with a simple spark, it makes a nice pop!" Rugrat waved around, indicating the room.

Blaze couldn't help his laugh at the simple "pop."

"Now, if I could find a mechanism to spread the flammable liquid over a large area and then spark it, do that all around the defenses we have in one go, welcome to thermobaric weapons," Rugrat said, losing himself in thought.

"Some kind of explosive charge to aerosolize, then another to set it off. Hard—don't have the materials. Mechanical solution? Mortars? Create a tube underground, someone pulls on a string, triggers the crossbow, the bolt attached to a container shoots upward. When leaving the tube, have a claw pull off a covering; the container starts dispersing the flammable material. Disperses the liquid turned to gas all over the place. Pull a second string that is connected to containers with pressurized gas. Just like the one I made. That should send off the liquid that was dispersed first." Rugrat paused, his eyes moving back and forth as if picturing the device he was thinking of.

Blaze didn't know why, but he felt distinctly *less* safe after hearing Rugrat's plan.

56

NOTHING TO DO BUT WORK

Rugrat might have gone to sleep exhausted but when he woke up just a few hours later, he was filled with energy. *I wonder what Erik will say when he finds out that every time one opens a Mana gate above ten, their Mana Lord title will be upgraded?*

Rugrat got up and went to check on Erik. He was fine but he was still out cold. Seeing that there was nothing to do but let him rest, Rugrat left the building and went to the main square.

Some people were returning home after completing their shift; others were waking up and getting their meals before heading off to work.

Rugrat detoured to the showers quickly before heading back to the main square.

He saw that Glosil, Elise, Jasper, and Taran were all there. Sergeant Niemm was also at the table; Blaze must have been off training the heavy infantry.

Rugrat didn't like having to be the leader, but as his friend was down and he was the other leader of Alva Village, he grabbed his breakfast and moved to join them. "Erik's going to be out for some time," Rugrat said. "How's the village?"

The others nodded and organized their thoughts.

"We should be done building the watchtowers in four more days. After that, everything will be focused on creating more defenses. With our current group numbers, not including the heavy infantry, we will be able to complete the defenses in another week. With them, four days, even less if we use the people from the logging camps," Elise reported.

It was coming down to the wire now. It was the seventh day since Erik and Rugrat had arrived. A lot had happened in that time, but Erik and Rugrat wanted the city to be ready for attacks by the ninth day. It looked as if they would be late, unless they gave up on the logging camp.

"Break the logging camp. Everything is to be collected and the groups will be put onto construction and building defenses," Rugrat said.

"Yes, sir," Elise said.

"We have enough rations for everyone for three weeks now. We have twelve warm meals prepared ahead of time as well. With water and food supplies, we should be able to hold out for four months," Jasper reported.

"Good. Keep up the good work," Rugrat commended.

"We'll have spears for everyone by day's end. We'll have twenty of the modified crossbows as well, with enough regular crossbows for everyone able to fight," Taran said. Rugrat already knew the situation with the weapons but the others didn't.

Rugrat and Taran's techniques had greatly improved over the last two days and nights. For them, it was much easier to create Novice weapons and armor; they even modified older weapons to increase their attack power and abilities.

"It is my aim to make Apprentice-level crossbows and spears moving forward, to cut down on costs. This will mean melting down older weapons," Taran said.

Everyone congratulated Taran on the new skill increase to Apprentice Smith before continuing.

"The guards have basically all become sergeants for the Alva Village protection force. Those who have showed promise among the archers have been termed sharpshooters and taken on an active role, patrolling the walls and the streets, being stationed in the completed watchtowers. When they are not on patrol, they are scouting the forests, killing more boars," Glosil said. Now that the groundwork had been laid for the archery units, there wasn't much more need for him to do anything but provide an early warning system for the village.

"Captain Blaze is working with the heavy infantry, teaching them how to use their swords and shields. They will be training all of today. Tomorrow, he wants to take them out, patrolling in the forest and use the sharpshooters to lure in beasts. So far, we've lost seven trainees who have quit," Sergeant Niemm said.

"I want fourteen people who have a good grasp of first aid. It doesn't matter their role—all I want is for them to be willing to learn. The plan is to turn them into medics like Erik so that everyone else can focus on the battle, or pass wounded over to them. They'll heal them up and get them back in action," Rugrat said.

The others broke into discussion. Rugrat had some ideas on who he wanted, but he let them break it down; they knew what was happening in their different groups.

Rugrat was working in the smithy again when someone knocked on the door.

"The medic trainees are here," a sergeant said.

"Thanks." Rugrat finished up what he was working on and then headed out to look at the fourteen people. They came from all walks of life.

"All right, so, in this job, you're going to see a lot of people wounded and you're going to put them back together. Is everyone okay with blood and some nasty-ass injuries?" Rugrat asked.

A few people turned pale.

"That's no problem. If you're not good with that, go back to your work parties and have your leaders send over new people," Rugrat said.

Five people left. Rugrat was a bit disappointed that the leaders hadn't truly vetted their people.

"I will not be teaching you healing spells, or how to be an alchemist. I will be teaching you how to use needle and thread, bandages and tourniquets, different ways to apply healing powder, healing solutions as well as in-depth methods you can use to save a life. Let's get started." Rugrat clapped his hands together.

"Swords!" Blaze yelled out.

The spears in the heavy infantry's hands disappeared and their swords and shields appeared. They braced their shields and stabbed forward with their swords. "Hah!"

Dust rose from their feet. They'd thoroughly trampled the ground, their actions sending out a wave of air.

Since they had rested last night, they'd increased their levels in one shot. Their combined power couldn't be compared to before.

Fighting with a sword was more complicated than a spear but Blaze had broken it down, using a mix of tactics from his time in the army and what Erik had suggested to him, something about Romans and hoplites.

Blaze looked over the groups with approval. Their reactions were better: they didn't pause in carrying out their orders; they didn't care who was beside them; and, although they still had close friends, they all interacted with one another.

They'd formed a brotherhood in the last few days.

Blaze could see the strength that was emerging from these farmers and he was excited.

He looked over as he saw Rugrat and the sharpshooter group moving through the fields. Erik had slept for two days now; his heart twitched, nervous for the changes that Erik had gone through. Rugrat assured him that Erik was fine, but not seeing him for so long after the strange happenings from the Village Hall a few nights ago didn't make it easy for Blaze to calm his heart.

"Recover!" Sergeant Niemm yelled out as the sharpshooters in their armor made from boar hides looked at the heavy infantry. Their eyes seemed to be challenging the other group.

The heavy infantry didn't even look at them, as if they weren't worth looking at.

Blaze smirked slightly. It looked as though a small rivalry had started between the two groups.

"Ready?" Rugrat asked. Although everyone had crossbows, he had created a bow with pulleys, like the modified crossbows, and a composite metal. It was even stronger than the crossbow in strength; matched with Rugrat's added marksmen skill and speed, he was tens of times faster with his bow and just as deadly as those with the modified crossbows.

"Ready," Blaze confirmed.

"All right." Rugrat waved off some of the archers. He had spent yesterday and the morning working with the group to be medics; the rest of his time, he had been teaching the sharpshooters everything he knew from being a sniper.

They would go ahead to scout out the forest then guide the boars back to the heavy infantry. First, they would use the boars to test their abilities and techniques. They would even try to move while under attack; it was much harder but it showed their skill.

They would go through transitions from spears to swords. Although they expected boars, there was also the possibility of wolves being attracted to the battle like they had been before.

Blaze and Rugrat even planned on it, wanting to surprise and get the heavy infantry to react.

Rugrat had brought two of the medics in training with him as well to deal with any severe injuries.

"Prepare to move out!" Blaze yelled. The heavy infantry sections got organized. Blade section had been allowed to regain their title as Section One. All of them had the same haircut, was freshly shaved, and wore the same armor and weapons. There was no difference between them now.

Blaze was proud of how far they had come.

As they marched toward the forest, his eyes turned dark, knowing of the threats that hid in those trees.

57

HEAVY INFANTRY ARMOR

Erik slowly opened his eyes. It was dark outside his window.

He stretched, feeling his bones pop and crack. He felt a pulling sensation. Finding an IV needle, he pulled it out.

Feeling refreshed and a bit hungry he opened and closed his hand, finding the feeling odd, it felt harder, but it didn't appear any different.

He felt power moving through his muscles; his entire body contained an explosive energy that just wanted to escape. It felt as if he was even stronger than when he was in his prime.

He took his time to review his notifications.

Quest: Body Cultivation
The path cultivating one's body is not easy. To stand at the top, one must forge their own path forward.
Requirements:
Reach Body Like Stone Level
Sub-requirements
Tempering of the Blood
Tempering of the Bones
Tempering of the Organs
Tempering of the Muscles
Tempering of the Skin
Rewards:
+3 to Strength
+3 to Agility
+3 to Stamina
+5 to Stamina Regeneration
+100,000 EXP

You have successfully tempered your Muscles!
+4 to Agility
+5 to Strength

You have successfully tempered your Organs
+4 to Stamina
+5 to Stamina Regeneration

Erik's body shook as he saw the massive increases to his attributes. This wasn't just increasing one stat—this was as if he had leveled up four times!

He hadn't gotten a notification when he had tempered his blood and he didn't get one now when he tempered his skin.

One's recovery ability wasn't calculated in their stats, nor was the strength of their body, as one's body wouldn't recall how many health potions they had or the armor. It was increases that increased their combat strength but not overall level or attributes.

Erik looked into his character sheet.

Character Sheet
Name: Erik West
Level: 13
Race: Human
Titles:
From the Grave
Land Holder (Temporary)
Mana Lord
Strength: (Base 12) +11
230
Agility: (Base 10) +13
115
Stamina: (Base 16) +4
300
Mana: (Base 6) +11
170
Mana Regeneration (Base 10) +21
10.05/s
Stamina Regeneration: (Base: 12) +20
7.15/s

The increases were added to his base stat instead of his modifier. Erik took his time. He felt refreshed as he examined his body.

Seeing that there was nothing wrong, he adjusted to his newfound strength and agility. As much as he wanted to show off his strength, he knew that it was a mistake and a quick way to look like an idiot.

Sometime later, the sun still had to come up as he heard Rugrat moving to his door.

Rugrat opened the door, rubbing his tired face. He stopped his hand, looking at Erik. "You're awake?" Rugrat asked, waking up in a second. "It's about time!"

Erik laughed, seeing Rugrat's face lit up with a smile. "Wait, about time? How long have I been out?"

"It's the tenth day since we've been in Alva Village," Rugrat said.

"I was out for three days?" Erik asked in alarm.

"About," Rugrat said.

Erik munched on food and looked to the IV. It was green in color. It must've been some kind of Stamina Regeneration powder or potion.

Back on Earth, someone who had slept for three days would be starving and dehydrated, but Erik only felt as if he'd missed a meal.

"What's been going on since I've been out?" Erik turned serious. They had four days left, according to the voice from the Beast Mountains trials.

It felt as though it were a lifetime ago that they had appeared outside of Alva Village.

"The three sharpshooter sections have been stepped up—went through, trained them up. Picked out five for your quick reaction force, then the rest are helping out with work on the defenses, or on the walls acting as patrols.

"We've pulled everyone from the logging camp and broke it down. All of the heavy infantry are trained with their spears, swords, and shields. They've all broken through level ten and are helping with the defenses now. I've trained some twenty medics since you've been out—got five of them to deal with greater problems and got them some healing manuals. I checked on the local population, healed any issues that were left. Blaze has four people from the heavy infantry he gave to me and I've been cross training with the archers I picked for the quick reaction force." Rugrat looked up, searching for anything he might have forgotten.

"Oh! I don't have any idea what kind of mage Roska is. She's not related to an element, or enchanting or crafting really," Rugrat said.

"Did you get a testing stone?" Erik asked.

"Nope! They're fifty silver each."

"How much did we make from the auctions?"

"Umm." Rugrat opened up his interface. "The hell?"

"Around twenty to thirty gold?" Erik asked aloud.

"Thirty-three," Rugrat said.

Erik shook his head. He'd put the items up for sale and it looked as though Rugrat hadn't been paying attention to them at all.

"Get the testing stone. We can use it on Roska and a few others. We can try to get some spells. Also, this is for you." Erik took out the silence spell scroll and he gave it over to Rugrat.

"What is this?"

"It's a new spell. It'll silence anything that you cast it on."

"Anything?" Rugrat asked.

"I think so. I didn't check it out fully." Erik shrugged.

"Where did you get this from?"

"I got it when I gained my Apprentice level in stealth."

"Why are you giving this to me? Couldn't you use it?" Rugrat pushed it away.

"I'm aiming to go more melee and healer style. I could do with ranged healing spells, but I don't think that me sneaking around is going to be all that useful. Whereas you, working on making rifles, getting that sneak modifier is going to hurt our enemies a lot more," Erik said.

Rugrat was hesitant but he put it away after some time. "So, plan moving forward?"

"What are you thinking?" Erik asked. Rugrat had been awake these last few days, so he knew the situation better.

"We keep doing what we're doing—build up our defenses, improve on our weapons, level up as we can, promote people to grow in their own skills and ways," Rugrat said.

It wasn't a crazy plan, but they didn't know what was going to happen in the coming days. They couldn't mess around.

If they went crazy with training, then everyone might be tired when they needed to fight.

If they let them all off, then they might not be focused when the time came.

"Increase the amount of food that they get. We'll raise up their morale and give them some more free time to enjoy their higher levels," Erik said. They'd been working so hard for so long, everyone needed to blow off some steam.

It took Erik a half day to recover. He joined in on the evening meeting. Rugrat was talking with Glosil on techniques one could use with their crossbow.

Today was the last day of training for the heavy infantry, so they got the night off, with extra food and a few beers. Most of them devoured their food and beer, talking in groups at the tables.

Erik and Rugrat shared a look as they saw how they acted. It was as if they were back in any military cafeteria in the United States.

The groups went off to play games, or get some sleep or see their families.

They were different from before, not only in appearance but how they acted. Erik wondered what they'd be like with a few more weeks of training, higher-leveled enemies to fight, and better gear.

It sent a sort of thrill through him, the kind he had when a new unit passed through training and headed out to gain specialization. They had the groundwork, but with time and the right tools, they would become powerful veterans.

Everything was as Rugrat had explained.

Rugrat excused himself and headed back to the smithy.

Rugrat had made dozens of weapons while Erik had been asleep.

"I think that his skill level must be in the Apprentice level, but with the different ideas and practices he has, some of his works can rival Journeyman-leveled items. I think with the right materials, some more information, and maybe discussions with Journeyman smiths, he'd be able to advance greatly. He's only just started on his path," Taran said. Erik could see the glow in his eyes and the excitement there. His path ahead was no longer blocked and he was pushing his own boundaries as well.

At different tables in their off hours, people were talking to one another, not only discussing what had happened in the day, but also improving their own knowledge through discussion. Jasper was in charge of a new department, the library, that held a number of manuals that they had purchased from the auction. People were allowed to read them there and make notes but they couldn't take them away.

Erik sipped on his weak wine and sat beside Taran. The others were off dealing with one issue or another.

"Do you know anywhere that has libraries?" Erik asked.

"Sure, some of the lords and ladies do on their estates. Maybe a few cultivation manuals that have been handed down through the generations. Kings and Queens, they'll have them. Though they wouldn't be willing to give them out to the general population unless they have an uprising," Taran said seriously.

Taran saw Erik's confused expression and could only frown to himself.

"I've meant to ask something for some time," Taran said in a low voice so that no one else could hear him.

Erik indicated for him to continue.

"You and Rugrat. Are you really sent here by the king?" Taran asked.

Erik tapped his cup in thought, thinking of Taran as a man and what was to come. *He swore to follow Rugrat and me, even when he had doubts about our identity. If I don't trust him with the truth, can I trust anyone else?*

"No, we're not," Erik said.

Taran seemed to sink into thought, a dark expression on his face. "Do you think that the king might order someone to help us?" Taran asked bluntly.

"I don't know, but I don't think so. Blaze sent word weeks ago. If they used their horses, they should have been here a week ago."

Taran looked away at the ground, lost to his own thoughts.

Erik let him be.

Taran took some time to recover, clearing his throat and drinking some water. "There are a few reasons people don't have libraries. One—the books are all treasures and they cost a lot to buy. They also need to have people managing them, so this is a large cost to any leader. The second is that the Ten Realms is based on the fact that the strong make the rules and the weak abide.

"To become strong, one needs backing, resources and information. If the people don't have that information, then it makes it much harder for them to increase in level and turn into a threat to the rulers. Who would make a system that puts them out of power?"

Erik nodded slowly. An idea started to form in his mind, but he dismissed it. Right now he didn't need to plan anything beyond defending Alva Village. Everything else would come later.

Erik and Taran sat there, looking over the village square. People who were on later shifts started up their work while others gathered with their families. There were a few people off to the side. Kids were playing and greeting their parents who had been working all day.

Erik stood. It was time he started to train.

58
OATHBREAKER

Erik left the village square and went to the barracks. It was quiet as the sergeants were either asleep, with their families, or on patrol of the village walls.

One could hear Rugrat still working away in the smithy.

Erik stretched out before he moved to do squats, burpees, and sit-ups. He went through one hundred of each with little to no fatigue. It felt like more of a warm-up as he stood up and started punching and kicking. It had been a long time since he had done a class on close combat fighting techniques.

He took his time through the different movements, going through them again and again. The more he moved, the more he remembered, the memories buried deep in his muscles.

After he felt he had a handle on it, he started to incorporate the Mana fighting techniques, using Mana in concert with his muscles to increase his striking power.

The strain was less on his body than it had been before and he could increase the amount of Mana channeled through his body and the duration he could do it for.

Erik then started to incorporate the Mana bullet spell into his close quarters fighting, shooting at the archery targets. He limited the power greatly so it wouldn't make enough noise to wake those sleeping.

"It's painful just watching you," Rugrat said from the door of the smithy as he rolled up his sleeves, showing the tattoo sleeves that ran up both of his arms.

A simple bow appeared in one hand as he pulled out a quiver of failed arrows and put them over his shoulder.

"What you thinking?" Erik asked warily, facing Rugrat.

"Bit of arrow skeet. I'll shoot arrows at you, you destroy them or dodge them?" Rugrat said.

"This doesn't sound like a…" Erik didn't finish what he was saying as Rugrat strung an arrow and fired at Erik.

Erik advanced toward Rugrat. The arrow hit his shoulder, missing his head. It made him wince, but it would have cut another person, leaving them with a deep bone bruise, maybe even a break.

Erik had no time to stop as Rugrat had already fired his second arrow.

Erik threw out his fist. The rush of air threw the arrow off target slightly as it sailed past. Erik grimaced; he wanted to destroy the arrow.

He threw out his fists, trying to break the arrows that were coming at his body. Erik grunted if they struck his body, opening him up for more attacks. After twenty arrows, he had pushed five to the side and he had failed to destroy a single one. The others had all hit him.

Rugrat had another arrow on his bow, ready to fire as he looked at Erik.

"Come on," Erik said.

Being able to alter the direction of arrows with just the power in his body, it was incredible, certainly not something that was possible back on Earth. Erik was determined to destroy the arrows in flight.

Some karate shit, maybe even catch a fly with chopsticks!

Erik didn't have any more time as Rugrat started moving through the barracks, shooting arrows at him. Erik not only had to fight back and try to hit the arrows so they wouldn't hit him; he had to keep on moving to adjust to the new attacks.

He was surprised by Rugrat's ability.

Rugrat paused another twenty arrows later. Erik's breathing was more forced but he was still filled with energy, his Stamina recovering quickly.

"You're level fifteen," Erik accused.

"Yeah, made a breakthrough a few days ago." Rugrat smiled unapologetically.

Erik was happy for his friend, but he felt that he was falling behind further and further. Rugrat had been able to find someone to talk about his craft with; he had also been able to find plenty of supplies to work with. Erik needed either wounded people or information manuals and technique books.

He wasn't going to start hurting people and heal them up. The Ten Realms system wasn't stupid and gave little to no Experience to people for healing themselves or others who they had hurt on purpose.

If it was someone they intended to hurt and then healed afterward, it was a different story. The Ten Realms wasn't like a video game in that respect;

it seemed to read everyone's intentions instead of making judgements based on its settings.

Right now, Erik was increasing his ability in hand-to-hand; because he didn't use it against anyone or anything, he didn't gain any Experience.

This was like how Rugrat had studied different smithing manuals and information that they had collected in the Beast Mountains. Once he had access to a smithy and gained a basic understanding, his skill had shot upward.

It was like when someone took a class: they would learn tons of information, but it was only at the end when there was a test would they get a final grade on it. The test could also show them what they didn't understand and draw attention to those areas so that they might do better in later tests.

"All right, let's see what you've got," Erik said.

Rugrat fired an arrow as Erik fought back, the two of them using the other to hone their skills.

Unseen by them both was Glosil and Sergeant Niemm. They had been checking on the different patrols and checking on the village. When they returned to the barracks, they stood at the entrance of the barracks, watching as Erik used his fists to fight against Rugrat's rain of arrows. They moved almost too fast to be seen with the human eye and Rugrat's speed at drawing and firing had reached an unreal level.

Glosil and Niemm didn't say a thing, stock-still as they watched the two.

Niemm realized something, his heart shaking. "Are they *smiling*?"

Glosil nodded. "For some people, proving their skill and improving it—there is nothing greater in the Ten Realms. It looks like Erik and Rugrat are pitting their skills up against each other, using the other to improve while also showing off their abilities. To them, there is the threat of damage, but it allows them to get as close to a real fight as possible without a fatal threat."

"Why do I have the feeling that we haven't seen their full capabilities yet?" Niemm asked.

The two of them watched as Erik started to hit more and more of the arrows out of the air, his fists actually making contact with them now as the shafts exploded.

Erik let out a laugh, working harder to make the arrows explode.

Rugrat continued to move, making it harder for Erik to dodge or stop the arrows. The two of them started to reveal more of their abilities, creating a terrifying display.

Rugrat showed no signs of stopping.

Erik started to adjust the amount of power he put out as the fight continued on. His attacks were concentrated and gauged, looking to use just enough power to destroy the arrows and move his body instead of wasting it all in a few explosive movements.

Glosil watched as Erik's speed decreased, but his movements flowed from one to the next, turning graceful and making him seem like a tree in the wind instead of a shield turning to face the enemy.

Rugrat's movements became cleaner and had less wasted effort to increase the speed that he could fire. He even started firing without aiming, using different techniques to alter the arrows' path so that they were harder to defend against.

Occasionally an arrow would hit Erik, or Erik would destroy an arrow.

Rugrat paused some time later, the two of them breathing heavily now. Rugrat had reached for another arrow but there weren't any left.

"Again!" Erik said. Even as he was breathing heavy, there was a fire in his eyes, a look of excitement.

Rugrat pulled out another quiver. He took a second and then started firing at Erik, faster than before. It was as if they had surpassed their previous limits! In the face of challenging each other, they wanted to fight as much as possible.

Niemm and Glosil looked to each other with bitter expressions. They had thought that their fighting strength wasn't bad, but seeing these two, they felt that they had a long way to go.

Who would be insane enough to fire arrows at their friend? Or try to destroy them in the air and then laugh about it? Are our training methods just not that good? Niemm kept watching, unconsciously moving his hands and altering his stance to try to gain an understanding of their movements and learn from their fight.

Blaze felt something was wrong. He sat up in his bed as a notification screen appeared in front of his vision.

> **Oathbreaker**
> Lord Salyn has broken his oath and no longer swears to protect and care for Alva Village.
> Alva Village is now a free village.

Blaze looked at the information. "He broke his oath, removing Alva Village from his protection, but he sent Erik and Rugrat? That doesn't make sense."

59
WHO ARE YOU?

Erik and Rugrat were left sweating and panting as Rugrat lowered his bow, looking around at the barracks that had tens of arrows lying around.

"Well, this is going to suck to clean up," Rugrat said.

"Just like cleaning up brass on the range." Erik started to pick up the arrows. A few of them were still serviceable, but most of them were useless. "Talking about rounds, you made any more advancements with the bullet engraving?"

"I've got a lot of theory and I've made some simple enchantments on arrowheads. I think that it would be possible for me to put it on bullets as well. I don't know what it would do to them and I don't want to have to pull apart our good rounds to experiment on them," Rugrat said. "When we get the extra rounds from the cache, I'll have to do some trials."

"What can the enchanted arrows do?" Erik asked.

"Increased piercing, basically the same effect you had on your arrows. Then I've got silence and stun, though I've focused on the first as the silence and stun ones are only really good against people."

The two of them continued to clean up the barracks. Niemm and Glosil entered some time later. Seeing them at work and not wanting to be pulled into it, the two of them sped up and went to their rooms.

"Were they watching us training?" Rugrat asked.

"What does it matter if they did or didn't?" Erik asked.

Rugrat shrugged. Erik made a good point.

"You've got to stop favoring that back foot. I know you broke it ten years ago but time to get over it. You're still jumpy on it and we both know that it's been totally healed by now," Rugrat said.

The two of them started to critique each other and offer advice, even if the other didn't want it. If they knew their failures, then they could find a way to fix it.

Blaze didn't sleep much that night, his mind filled with questions. He waited out front of the Village Hall.

Erik and Rugrat appeared before the sun was coming up.

"Blaze, is there a problem?" Erik asked as they saw him waiting for them.

"I wanted to ask you," Blaze looked at them both, knowing that his next words might change everything that he knew about them, "who sent you?"

Erik and Rugrat looked to each other and then back to Blaze.

"I know that it wasn't Lord Salyn. Last night, when I was sleeping, I got a notification. He broke his oath and left us to fend for ourselves." Blaze couldn't hold back the anger in his voice.

"Let's take a seat," Erik said. They moved to what had been Blaze's office, sitting on the chairs there.

"We're not from Lord Salyn. To be honest, we were teleported here. We don't know why or even how, or what the purpose of us being here is. We entered the village knowing that you would be attacked by a beast horde and that there would be five waves of the beast horde attacking the village. Other than Niemm, you were the first person we met from Alva Village. The rest you know," Erik said.

Blaze was quiet for some time. Neither Erik nor Rugrat could read his thoughts.

"Are you only helping us because of the trial?" Blaze asked.

He saw the look of pain on Erik and Rugrat's expressions before they shook their heads in the negative.

Blaze felt guilt for asking such a question after seeing all the time and resources they had put into Alva Village, but it was a question that had to be asked.

"Salyn, that spineless fuck," Blaze growled. "He was the one who told me not to tell the people and to wait for reinforcements. Did he just want to make sure that the entire village was destroyed so that he wouldn't have to deal with the refugees?" Blaze slammed his hand into the desk. He didn't control his strength, breaking it.

It was some time before Rugrat cleared his throat. "So, just like want to know—we cool, man?"

Erik looked up at the ceiling, letting out a sigh as a part of his soul seemed to leave him before looking at Rugrat.

"Not like you weren't thinking it. We just going to all sit here and mourn the death of a crappy old desk?" Rugrat pointed at the remains on the ground. "'Twas a valiant desk, but it will also be valiant firewood."

"We're good," Blaze said. "If it wasn't for you two, we wouldn't be ready for the beast horde. We'd all be cooped up and not know what was coming. We sure as hell wouldn't have archers and heavy infantry, or defensive lines," Blaze said, the other two focusing on him. "You might not be the help that I asked for, but you're the ones who came and did everything in your power for Alva Village. I wouldn't be able to kick you out of the city." Blaze let out a humorless laugh, his eyes serious. "You lead, I'll follow. I swear on the Ten Realms."

Power appeared in the room as screens appeared in front of Erik and Rugrat.

> Blaze Steel has sworn to follow you into battle as long as he agrees to your orders. If he does not agree with your orders, then this oath will be annulled.
> If he breaks his oath, then the Ten Realms will punish him.

"I swear on the Ten Realms that I will not break faith with you. I will do my best for the greater good of Alva Village. I swear on the Ten Realms," Erik said.

"Beat me to it," Rugrat complained as the power of the Ten Realms was activated once again.

Blaze seemed to relax, returning to his normal personality as Erik and Rugrat both made oaths to him, backed by the Ten Realms.

"What do you want to tell the people?" Erik put the decision in Blaze's hands; he was the lord of the village, after all.

Blaze let out a heavy sigh. The decision wasn't to be taken lightly. "If I tell them, there might be problems in the battle that is to come. We don't need more confusion and people's minds wandering in the fight. Once the battle is over, then we can let them know," Blaze said.

Erik and Rugrat nodded, accepting his decision.

"Well, time for some damn food then!" Rugrat said.

Storbon was working with the people who were part of the QRF. They all lived together and unlike the heavy infantry or the sharpshooters, they didn't go home every night; they lived in the barracks.

They had personal lessons from Glosil, Blaze, Rugrat, and Erik. They also had access to dozens of foundational manuals on all different kinds of skills.

They patrolled the village and hunted down the beasts, but the rest of the day they trained, fighting one another, working in the different industries of Alva Village to increase their skills. All of them pushed themselves to the limit.

"Have you noticed how much Alva has grown in just two weeks?" Storbon asked Yao Meng.

Meng let out a short laugh as they walked the village walls. "Yeah, I don't think that any of the nearby villages have the same strength as us now. A city where the citizens are on average level seven, the trained fighting forces around level ten, sergeants at eleven. Captain Blaze and Glosil are fourteen and twelve, though Erik and Rugrat are thirteen and fifteen."

"The amount of resources that they've used on us to raise us up to eleven and twelve, surely Erik and Rugrat could have increased their own level by leaps and bounds," Storbon said.

The two of them fell into a silence as they continued to patrol the wall.

"Yeah, they're nothing like I would think people at higher levels would be. Those stronger figures are always hoarding their resources and not wanting to share with others, only caring about their own path." Meng's voice had a hint of anger.

"Well, now we're those people," Storbon said.

"Yeah, never thought that I would be able to make it to level ten so I can ascend to the Second Realm," Meng said honestly.

Storbon paused as his eyes thinned. The morning sun was coming up soon but something seemed to make him wary.

Meng looked to his friend and then scanned the distance. "You see something?" Meng asked after a few seconds, gripping his crossbow tighter.

Storbon shushed him and pointed where he heard noises from.

There was a rustling at the edges of the defensive area. It had been built up; the first three lines had been completed and the last line was being worked on. It would take a few more days until it was completed.

A squeal cut through the night. The two raised their crossbows, ready to fire at the noise.

Storbon could see that one of the boars that had been in the forest had charged out and impaled itself on one of the defensive spikes.

The squeal led to the rest of the litter rushing out of the forest as wolves that must have been chasing them let out howls.

Meng grabbed his whistle and blew on it.

Across the village, people woke up with dread in their hearts.

People pulled on their clothes and grabbed their weapons, heading to their different rally points. They had been trained continuously over the last two weeks; for them, it was imprinted on their minds.

The archery with their sharpshooter component moved to the walls as the heavy infantry formed up at the village square, ready to be deployed to the walls and bolster them as was needed.

Erik and Rugrat were having breakfast in the village square when they heard the whistle. They pulled their weapons from their storage rings, rushing off in different directions: Erik toward where the whistle was coming from, Rugrat to the Village Hall and the watchtower that had been put on the top of it.

From there, he could look over the entirety of Alva Village and see the defensive works beyond.

Erik was halfway to the wall when Rugrat contacted him, Blaze, and Glosil.

"Looks like we've got some coming in from the south side, a couple litters of pigs and wolves chasing them. Fifty pigs, twenty wolves—looks like more are coming. I can't see much in this low light."

"Everyone do what we trained; have the heavy infantry and QRF ready to move out. Rugrat, you're in charge of placement. Glosil, I want you watching the north. If they come in from another direction, I want to know," Erik said.

"Understood," Rugrat said.

"On my way," Glosil said.

I hope that we're ready for this, Erik thought. It looked like the beast horde had come early. It was the eleventh day since they had reached Alva Village.

60
FIRST WAVE

Erik reached the wall. With two large jumps, he was at the top, looking out over the layered defenses and the first wave. The boars had grown from a mere fifty to some two hundred. Wolves poured out from the forest. Smelling the blood from the boars, the half-starved beasts were sent into a frenzy.

Alva Village had spent their time thinning out the numbers of boars. It was one of the reasons that they had been able to quickly raise their level. It had also led to the wolves and other beasts finding that they didn't have enough food to eat.

Erik looked over the wall at the incoming boars. There wasn't anything he could do but watch; they were out of crossbow range at this point.

Instead of focusing on the boars that had appeared, he looked into the forest and looked to see whether there were any more boars coming out of the trees.

Storbon and Yao Meng ran over to Erik, their crossbows ready.

Erik glanced over at them and then continued to look over the battlefield.

"What do you want us to do, sir?" Storbon asked. The two of them saluted.

"No need to salute now that the battle has started. If the enemy saw that, then they would look to kill me to screw up our chain of command," Erik said in a calm voice as he studied how the boars were running into the first layer of defenses and the traps.

They ran forward blindly, stepping on top of the flimsy coverings and dropping into the spike-filled pit. Squeals came from the pits as the wolves behind them weren't able to stop themselves and fell in as well.

"Yes, sir," Storbon said.

"Report to the sergeants of the archery groups. Make sure that they know the situation. I want to have them spaced out along the wall and make sure that they keep an eye out for any other breaks in the tree line," Erik said.

"Sir!" Storbon and Yao Meng said at the same time, stopping themselves from saluting at the last minute. They turned on their heels and rushed off to meet the archery groups that were moving up to the wall.

Erik contacted Rugrat. "How are things looking from up there?"

"I've got clear sight all around the village. We've got waves coming in from several different directions. If north was the twelve o'clock, we've got groups coming in from the five till eight movement, at the one to two. I've pushed out the first group of archers, and held back eight groups. I've got the cooks making up food. They'll feed the people who are holding in the village square. As we rotate people out, we can get them fed," Rugrat said.

"Sounds good to me. I—" Erik didn't get out his next word as there was a howl from within the forest. A massive wolf walked out of the trees. Around him were all different kinds of elites. Their eyes were on the boars but they showed greater intelligence than the first group that had rushed forward.

The other wolves all seemed to pause what they were doing, looking to the wolf king for permission.

"That's one ugly damn mutt," Erik said.

"I don't know—I'm a dog guy," Rugrat said.

"You got it sighted?"

"Yup, ready to go when you need it," Rugrat confirmed.

"Hold off. We'll bleed them a bit—time that our people got some experience with holding the walls," Erik said.

"Got it. I'll keep my eyes peeled for any other groups."

The wolf king let out a roar. The forest seemed to boil as squeals filled the air. Boars rushed out of the tree line as wolves rushed out. The true first wave had begun.

Erik could feel the nervousness of everyone on the wall. "Hold your fire." His calm voice cut through the air as people gripped their weapons tighter. "Breathe. Let them come to us. No sense in shooting at them before they get into range."

The sharpshooters and sergeants of the different archer groups looked over their people.

The wolves had made it through the first line of defenses in places. The second defenses were meant to injure and push the beasts into killing corridors.

They got packed together, running straight toward the village's walls.

Like fish in a barrel.

"Prepare to fire!" Erik yelled out.

Everyone checked their weapons and sighted their targets as the sergeants picked out areas for them to aim at.

The beasts threw one another off, cutting themselves on the spiked defenses.

Erik saw the beasts come into range. "Fire!" he yelled.

The archers fired, raining down arrows on the beasts the beasts howled in pain as they were cut down.

The archers had trained again and again, but training and combat were very different things. Many were stunned with the effectiveness of massed fire.

"Do you think we have all morning!? Reload!" Sergeants yelled out instructions to their people, motivating them and pushing them to be faster.

"Fire in groups! Sergeants, you have fire control!" Erik ordered as he fired on a beast. It crumpled under the powerful arrow and he loaded another arrow with quick, precise actions, looking up and over the wall.

There looks to be a lot of them but we've got plenty of people and crossbows. As long as we have ammunition and there's not a big jump in numbers, we should be able to bleed them white.

Erik quickly looked over the situation as he loaded an arrow, sighted a wolf and fired. It crumpled as Erik reloaded once again.

Now that they were into the rhythm of things, death came quickly for these beasts.

"We've got incoming at the ten o'clock." Rugrat's voice sounded in Erik's ear. "Just wolves. It looks like the wolf king is directing them. They're trying to come in quietly."

Erik frowned. This showed that the beast horde had some tactics. Dealing with beasts was one thing; dealing with smart beasts was another thing totally.

"Archers will bring them under fire as soon as they get into range."

"Got it," Erik said.

Across the battlefield, arrows continued to fall like a black rain on top of the beasts, whittling down their numbers. More were coming out of the forests, seemingly endless as they pushed around the areas they'd made progress, finding new routes to the walls.

So it went on for twenty minutes. The wolf king seemed to be annoyed as it pawed the ground and let out another howl.

The wolves seemed to resist for a second before they began to turn back.

"Take the wolf king," Erik said.

"On it," Rugrat said.

Erik heard the familiar crack of a rifle. Others looked around in shock as the wolf king was hit in the chest, dropping to the ground in a pool of blood.

The other wolves all looked around in alarm. They didn't know what had happened, but they seemed to realize that the noise had come from the village.

Their retreat was cancelled as the elites rushed forward as well; the wolves charged forward again.

"Bring up three of the archer groups; have them on the five to six o'clock wall," Erik ordered Blaze, who was still in the village square.

"On their way!" Blaze said.

The village wasn't all that big and the archers quickly crossed the distance. The archers on the wall were pressured but with the reinforcements, they once again pushed the wolves back.

"Sharpshooters, target the elites," Erik ordered.

Armed with the advanced crossbows and with their higher Marksman skill, the sharpshooters quickly brought down a large number of elites.

They were the fastest and strongest; without them, the wolves were being torn apart.

After ten minutes, the wolves broke and started to flee, seeing the losses. Even if they were feeling the loss of their wolf king, they weren't willing to just throw all of their lives away.

The crossbows slowed their rate of fire as the wolves got out of range. Finally the sergeants started to stop them from shooting.

Jasper's people came around with arrows and food.

People reloaded and ate their meals, their hands still shaking. The peaceful morning was broken—the beast horde had arrived.

The pits were opened, with many beasts falling into them. The killing corridors that had been created with different obstacles were filled with bodies.

They hadn't made it to the third layer of defenses.

We need to patch the hole in our defenses to the west. "Have the heavy infantry prepare to move out and clear the battlefield," Erik ordered Blaze.

"Will move two groups to the southern gate, with another moving to the eastern," Blaze replied.

"See to it." Erik wasn't jealous of the men doing the task. They'd need to pull down the wolf carcasses so that they wouldn't affect the defenses and make it easier for those that attacked later.

Erik felt as though dozens of eyes watched him from the forest. Erik looked back, tapping his finger on the side of the crossbow.

A screen appeared in Erik's vision.

Quest Updated: Beast Mountains Trial
Requirements:
Defeat the beast horde (4/5 Waves remaining)
Rewards:
Dependent upon results

"It's just started," Erik muttered.

61

WELCOMING THE HORDE

Blaze had trained in the royal army for decades. Although it looked as though it was a system meant to work together, it was more the guards than the actual soldiers who had the best cooperation.

Everyone joined the army to gain skills and levels; there wasn't a lack of people wanting to join. It might be bloody and people died, but it was one of the fastest ways to increase one's power and reach higher, even touching the boundary of the higher realms.

When he had trained the heavy infantry, he thought that as soon as the battle started that they would break apart, simply wanting to get as many merits as possible and increase their own power. Everyone was looking to make their own legends and the military was filled with wild and ambitious people.

Well, most militaries. The Alva Village people had been turned into soldiers. With their grim faces, they were ready to go into battle, waiting for their orders. Now that they were sent to clean up the battlefield, they didn't complain and understood that their actions, which seemed simple, helped the whole.

Blaze felt great pride looking on them and the people of Alva Village. They were closer than ever before, putting the group ahead of the individual.

I wonder how much stronger we will be once everyone is working together? Once all of their forces were deployed to the walls, he was interested to see how things would go.

As the heavy infantry left the southern gate, they looked to the archers. They had been simple farmers and village folk; now they were steely-eyed watchers, looking out for the heavy infantry and ready to fight again.

The heavy infantry dispersed into pairs. Using their storage rings, they were able to clear up the tens of wolves and boars, returning the defenses to how they were.

Blaze could feel that something was happening in the forest but he didn't know what. He worked with his people to speed up how fast they cleared the area and then pulled back to the village.

The heavy infantry passed off the full storage rings to the quartermaster division being run by Jasper. Rugrat had renamed it a few days ago, finding that the name suited the group better.

They took all of the storage rings. Most of the meat was ruined but they could still use the tendons and other parts, though it would be much harder to separate them.

Roska came over to them, a strange look on her face. She walked up to Blaze. Roska had been badly wounded at an early age, abandoned by her family as they moved to another village. He felt sorry for the girl and wanted to help her but she was determined to do things on her own.

Now she was no longer wounded and although she wasn't immensely powerful, her reserved air and the way she analyzed things made Blaze feel that she would quickly surpass him in ability.

"May I have one of the corpses?" Roska asked.

Blaze opened his mouth to reply and then closed it. He waved his hand; a boar appeared on the ground.

Roska didn't care about the blood or the dead beast's wounds as she put her hands on it. A magical circle appeared around her hands. The spell formation flashed with bright light.

The boar split apart, creating a row of pieces. One was bones, another tendons, another the meat; the skin was pulled from the boar and the organs neatly arranged.

The blood splashed on the ground. The rest of the meat had little blood on them.

"What is that?" Jasper, who was nearby, asked in a husky voice. Cleaning and storing the meats and materials took a lot of time, but Roska had separated it all in just a single spell.

Roska didn't answer right away. A screen appeared in front of her. A hint of a smile showed on her face as she dismissed it. She looked around, noticing everyone staring at her. Her expression turned cold once again.

"It's a spell called Separation. It breaks down the target into its components. It can only be used on dead bodies and inanimate objects. More Mana is required to break apart stronger weapons, and if they're in use, then the Mana requirement increases quickly," Roska said.

Blaze let out a short laugh.

Roska looked at him in question.

"Looks like Jasper is going to want to steal you. Also, it's funny—no one would share the effects of their spell with everyone," Blaze said.

"Did I do something wrong?" Roska asked.

"Nothing at all—just showed me something I haven't seen before," Blaze said with approval, looking to his people. "All right, let's get a move on back to the village square!"

"Before you go, take these." Jasper held out a sack to Blaze.

Blaze frowned but looked inside the bag. "What am I supposed to do with these monster cores?"

"Use them." A grin slowly spread across Jasper's face.

"What?"

"Erik and Rugrat kept back a bunch of the monster cores. There are mainly Common Mortal grade monster cores but there are a few Greater Mortal grade monster cores. The Commons will give you five thousand Experience when using them and refill your Stamina, Mana, and increase the speed that you heal. The Common will give you ten thousand Experience, with greater effects. One should use the Lesser core and then the Common core. Once I have some more, I'll send out more of the Common monster cores. Erik and Rugrat wanted to wait in giving these to everyone so that they pushed hard to increase their levels as much as possible on their own. With these, it will allow people to break through their bottlenecks right before they fight. It would be best to hold back on using them right away. That way, people can use them to get back into the fight. The more cores of the same grade you use, the less effective they will be. After the first use, they'll go from giving you five thousand Experience to giving you two thousand. And by the fourth use, they'll practically give you nothing," Jasper said.

"Been reading up on them?" Blaze asked.

"Something like that." Jasper pulled out another sack. "These are healing supplies to be given out to your people."

Blaze accepted the items. "Anything else?"

"Nope!" Jasper turned and look to Roska. "Would you be able to help us out, Miss Roska?"

Blaze smiled and signalled to his sergeants.

The troops moved out, leaving their items with Jasper.

Roska had more than enough corpses to test out her new spell on.

Rugrat sat in the watchtower. His rifle rested in his arms as he looked over the village. He was eating his ration as he scanned for threats.

Work crews were coming back from the west side. The entire village had nearly poured out to finish the defenses.

"Feel a lot safer with everything patched up now," Rugrat said through his sound transmission device.

"You're bored again," Erik said.

"Well, sitting in a watchtower like *Saving Private Ryan* ain't exactly the most entertaining thing to do," Rugrat complained. He could hear people filing through the village square, getting their breakfast as they came off the wall, working in shifts to relieve those who had been on the wall since the first wave.

Seeing everything move efficiently, Rugrat couldn't help but feel satisfied.

"I think I have movement in the northwest," Glosil said.

Rugrat put his food away and scanned the area quickly before using the scope on his rifle to look over the forest. The trees in the distance were moving and the movements were getting closer.

"Yeah, looks like we have incoming," Rugrat said.

"I've got movements over here," Erik said.

Other reports of the trees moving came in as archers were moved up to the walls and the gates were checked.

In a rush, beasts appeared around the village. The leading beasts let out their howls and roars. The bushes and trees were shaken as their numbers swelled.

Erik used a whistle, bringing Alva Village on alert. "Archers, fire on the sergeants' orders!" Erik yelled.

The pits were used once again as the beasts dropped into the spikes. This wave was much larger than the previous one. Even if they wanted to try to dodge, they couldn't as the pits started to fill up and they were impaled on defenses. The obstacles broke the horde up and packed them in tighter.

The archers couldn't miss as their arrows cut the beasts down like wheat before a scythe.

Rugrat looked out for strong beasts like the wolf king—those were his targets.

There were hundreds of beasts and they had been starved to the point of insanity.

"We've got some panthers!" Rugrat called out as he saw fights break out at the rear of the horde as beasts, smelling nothing but blood and driven wild by the charge, attacked one another. The panthers might not have numbers on their side but they had the strength.

Rugrat silently willed them on. Them killing one another meant less pressure for the people on the wall to face.

Rugrat checked the magazines on his chest rig. He didn't have that many rounds left. Erik had given him his rifle magazines as well, leaving him only with his shotgun and pistol ammunition.

Even with the panthers in play, Rugrat didn't fire. Instead, he continued to scan, looking for the areas that seemed to be more controlled.

"Time to earn that pay." Rugrat sighted a large wolf that was coming out of the forest. The magazine in his gun glowed as he used the spell explosive shot. It gave the projectile an explosive attribute where it would explode when hitting its target.

Rugrat was a little nervous, scared that it would cause the round to explode within his rifle.

He pulled the trigger. The round cut across the open area, hitting the wolf. It went off with a muffled explosion. The wolf was killed instantly. It was still intact, telling of how tough its body was.

The lower-leveled wolves around it were even slightly wounded.

Rugrat let out a shaky breath. If he had used normal rounds, it would have wounded the wolves, but killing them with one hit wasn't a sure thing.

Well, looks like I haven't blown up yet.

He cast the spell again, buffing the next round as he found another wolf. He fired again. The crack of his rifle meant the death of another elite as arrows continued to cut down the charging wolves.

Although they were killing tens of beasts, there were hundreds in the wave.

It wasn't a glorious fight but one where they needed to wear down the other side to win.

New roars could be heard in the distance as the waves of wolves started to slow and more panthers entered the battlefield. Alva Village was now surrounded by a sea of beasts.

Rugrat saw the flash of power as Erik used Mana Bolt. It arched over the defenses and landed among the beasts.

The Mana bolt went off as other ranged spells were used. There weren't many people who had gone the path of mage. Erik and Rugrat had basically picked out those with the most open Mana gates as they had a greater natural advantage.

Now they started to show off their power, thinning down the incoming numbers as they launched spells into the beast horde. The dazzling display of magical firepower was similar to machine guns and artillery.

Rugrat needed to take a minute to gather himself and ignore the sights and sounds.

Alva was starting to use their trump cards.

62

CONTINUOUS WAVE

Erik had turned into a human grenade launcher as he kept firing Mana bolt after Mana bolt. He took a break as Mana fatigue started to set in.

He slowed down. The beast horde had made it to the third layer of defenses, the spike pits. Most fell to the sharpened sticks; although others were able to clear them, they broke their ankles in the final layer of defense, turning into easy targets.

"Deploy all but two heavy infantry units to reinforce the eastern side," Erik said. All of the archers were on the walls now. There were no breaks. Even with their constant arrow rain, the beasts were getting closer.

The wolves fought well together, but they weren't as powerful as the panthers, whose individual strength was the same as the elites of the wolves.

They were able to evade some of the obstacles and traps but under the press of bodies, their movement was restricted.

The panthers and wolves didn't like one another, but their initial fighting had stopped as they went all out to try to defeat the humans.

Erik reloaded and fired with easy movements.

Rugrat stood in the middle watchtower. As targets were called out, he would drop them. Up there, he controlled the whole of Alva Village.

Erik felt the Mana coursing through his veins as the beast horde broke through from the third line of defense and moved to the final.

"Heavy infantry, prepare to defend!" Erik called out. "Blaze, use your people as you see fit."

"Sir!"

The heavy infantry readied their spears, spacing out and ready to fend off the beasts.

A spell formation appeared on Erik's finger. He fired Mana bullets; with the beasts in so close, he didn't need to rely on the AOE effects of the Mana bolt.

Erik's reaction speed had increased past human limitations with his increased Agility. Each bullet cost twelve Mana, just shy of his regeneration rate of 10.05 Mana per second.

So he could fire a Mana bullet nearly every second, combining his Marksman skill and his high Agility.

Erik wasn't simply killing the beast horde; he started to push them back in his area. Blue rounds shot out from his right finger, one after another. Each bullet ended a beast's life.

The speed couldn't be compared to the archers, who had to fight to reload between each shot. On average, they could fire eight to ten per minute. Over one hundred and twenty archers—that wasn't anything simple. As the beasts got in close, they were tired and bloodied. Their speed usually wasn't that good as most of them had broken their ankles or hurt themselves in some fashion.

The archers started to fire by themselves. Just like with Erik, they didn't need to saturate an area with arrows to try to kill a few. At less than one hundred meters, they picked out their own targets, their lethality and the number of deaths they caused only climbing.

It won't be enough. Erik knew that although tens of the beasts would die, they still didn't have a high enough rate of fire.

"Spears!" Sergeant Niemm yelled out. Other heavy infantry groups put their crossbows away and grabbed their spears.

"Push them back!" Niemm yelled as the beast horde crashed into the walls of Alva Village.

Erik's heart tightened. The beasts didn't have long-range attacks, so there was no threat with them far out. In close and at melee range, they were stronger than the people of Alva Village. This was where injuries and deaths could happen.

A roar came off from the side. Erik looked over as he saw trees being uprooted.

Several rhinos appeared, being chased by panther elites.

If they charge forward, they'll mess up our defenses and might even crack the wall!

"On me!" Erik said, contacting the quick reaction force.

They quickly gathered together and ran for the section of wall in front of the charging rhinos. Arrows stuck out of them, but it wasn't enough to kill or slow them.

Rugrat's buffed bullet hit a rhino in the face, taking out its eyes. It turned to the side, its horn piercing the companion next to it.

"Illusion spells! Get them to run into the other beasts!" Erik yelled.

Two mages specializing in illusion spells started their incantations, power rushing toward them. Two magical circles appeared in the sky above the rhinos. They slowly solidified before a stream of ancient runes shot out of them, falling on three rhinos.

The rhinos looked dazed as they turned away from the group. They hit others on the way out; they complained in pain before they charged into the other beasts that were trying to push through the defensive lines.

The mages looked tired, their energy drained.

Erik gritted his teeth and started to run. "Cover me! Use your monster cores!" Erik said these words as he jumped off the wall. He ran straight toward the beast horde. All of the beasts seemed to sense him, trying to catch him.

Erik's heart was in his chest but now he had made his decision, he would stick with it. He increased the speed that he fired his Mana bullets, allowing him to cut a path through the beasts.

Rugrat, seeing his friend rushing into danger, opened up on the panther elites behind the rhinos.

Erik could no longer support firing his Mana bullets or else he would run into Mana fatigue. He let out a yell as he sidestepped a wolf lunging at him. Erik hit the beast in the side with a sickening crunch, caving in their ribs and side.

Holy shit!

Erik didn't have any time to think on his newfound strength before reactions took over. He pushed on, clearing a path with his fists and kicks.

"By the gods." Storbon fired his bow. It was faster to shoot than the crossbow and with his high Strength stat, he hit with enough force to kill the beasts in one or two hits.

The quick reaction force thought that they would be like heroes, forging ahead in this fight, but it was unlike anything they had seen before. They were all terrified and they knew that it was their job to be in the worst of it.

Right now, they only felt like side characters as Erik charged into the fight, leaving broken bodies behind him. His speed and strength were actually higher than the beasts'!

It was like an adult dealing with children—they simply couldn't fight back. It was only the numbers of the beasts that slowed Erik down.

"Move!" Erik yelled out in frustration. His entire body glowed blue as Mana formed on his fist. The Mana on his fist exploded, throwing the beasts away.

Storbon could see that Erik was injured but it cleared him a path as he jumped, clearing obstacles and getting into the areas that weren't filled with beasts.

He was getting out of the quick reaction force's range; only the mages could support him now.

Storbon saw Roska, who was waving her hand and muttering an incantation. Arrows drifted from the quiver at her side into a magical formation. They tore through the air, firing at a rate that was even higher than Erik's Mana bullet.

She attacked the rhinos and the panthers around them.

An unlucky rhino had its mouth open when an arrow shot through it, killing it from the inside.

I need to increase my strength! Storbon focused on what he was doing instead of what the others were up to.

Erik jumped back into the fight. There were seven rhinos left. Two spell formations appeared in the skies, the illusion mages casting their magic once again.

Two more rhinos charged into the surrounding panthers that had been attacking them. They didn't seem to feel pain as they crashed into the beasts around the defenses.

"Then there was five," Erik muttered to himself as panthers that had been trying to charge the defenses now turned their eyes on him.

They lunged toward him.

Erik jumped between them, kicking one as he was in mid-air while infusing his body with Mana. The kick's explosive power crushed the panther's shoulder and side. Erik used the momentum to push him to the side, avoiding the other's attack and moving him closer to the rhinos. They were nearly at the defenses.

Erik channeled Mana into his body, increasing the power he could display. He was unstoppable. He hissed in pain as he took hit after hit, not willing to waste time fighting if it slowed him.

The elites around the rhinos let out warning growls and looked to attack him.

Erik pulled out his pistol and it barked. Normal rounds wouldn't be able to kill these elites, but these were enchanted by Rugrat, greatly increasing their lethality.

They were crude but with the natural strength of the bullet and with the enchantment, even a small increase was a big change.

In his hands, the pistol was almost as fast as a machine gun. The surrounding panthers were left in shock as their elites dropped as if they had run into a wall.

Erik didn't have any faith in the bullets being able to end the rhinos.

How to fight rhinos—stand right in front of their charge. This was a great idea.

Regardless of his own realizations, he couldn't just let them charge forward.

Erik ran at the nearest rhino, coming in on an angle. The rhino, seeing him charging, let out a roar as it lowered its horned head to take on Erik.

Erik pumped his body with power as he sidestepped. His body arched as he moved his body to get as much power into his attack.

Erik's body let out a quiet but powerful roar that made one's hair stand on end. It connected with the side of the rhino. Its power wasn't in blunt force, but in the Mana he had injected into the rhino's body.

The rhino coughed out blood and went down in the dust. Its internals had been largely destroyed.

Erik let out a yell. Channeling that much power through his body had led to him greatly injuring his leg. He could see the stress fractures as he used Focused Heal. He could only grit his teeth and run for the next rhino.

He launched himself forward, holding a spear.

He actually went past the level four rhino, making it half-turn to try to face him. Erik thrust his spear into the stomach of the rhino and up into its chest cavity.

The spear was torn from Erik's hands by the powerful rhino's movements. The rhino was howling in pain as it tried to dislodge the spear; it would only drive it in further.

Another dropped as Rugrat's blunt round hit it in the side. The strength of the round was turned into blunt impact energy. As piercing enchantments focused the cutting power of the rounds, the blunt enchantments would convert all of the energy into kinetic force on impact, spreading it out laterally.

Not knowing if this would be enough, Rugrat had also buffed the round with explosive shot.

With the power of the round, it was as if a grenade had gone off.

"Why didn't you use those rounds earlier?" Erik demanded.

"I only have three of them!" Rugrat said as the rhino closest to the defenses died.

Erik rushed another. He jumped over one rhino and dove toward the one on the other side. Again he pulled all of the power within his body as he coated his fist in Mana.

He struck out at the rhino's side. Its head and shoulders were too strong to penetrate and the skin was as tough as armor. Erik's only course of action was to do so much internal damage that it was fatal to his target.

The Mana on his hand went off in an explosion before he struck the side of the rhino. It let out a mournful wail as Erik let out a muffled scream when his hand broke.

He didn't have time to stop as Rugrat took out another. Erik cried out as a panther came out from behind the rhinos and sliced at Erik's back; his claws caught onto Erik's neck, sticking in the top of his armor.

Erik shook around, trying to get rid of the panther as others rushed at him. Erik jumped on the ground, trying to flatten it as he fired a Mana bolt at the three nearest, destroying them. He grabbed his pistol, putting it against the panther's head and pulling the trigger.

He yelled out as the recoil from the gun jarred his broken arm. He threw the body off as another lurched for his throat, its mouth open.

Erik moved to the side, getting scratched on his face as he launched his uninjured arm into the panther. The panther went back in the direction it had come. Erik was using Minor Wounds Heal. His Mana was low and his body was beaten up from the fighting and channeling Mana through himself for so long.

He couldn't fight for much longer. The remaining rhino used his tusk, driving into the defenses and ripping open a new path.

The horde followed it as everyone focused their fire on it.

Erik started running for the wall. He drank down some healing solution to save his Mana. *If I stay out here much longer, then the beasts will kill me.*

The rhino made it to the third layer of defenses, its body covered in cuts and scars before it impaled itself on one of the half-buried wooden spikes in the ground.

The other rhinos, under the direction of the illusion mages, had caused mayhem in the beast horde. The numbers had thinned down and although there were still some beasts coming from the forest, it wasn't a full-on sea of beasts like before.

On the wall, the heavy infantry were using their spears to fend off the beasts. They were highly effective, not willing to back down in the slightest, but there just wasn't enough for them to be everywhere.

People fired their crossbows point-blank while others dropped rolling wood, basically logs that had been tied up on the wall, crushing anything that was below.

Erik was now running back through the beasts. The healing potion was working but his body was in bad condition.

He punched with his good arm as he shot Mana bullets with the busted-up one. *Hurts like a mother fucker!*

He had to circulate the Mana in his body to fire the Mana bullets. The disturbance in his arm, even if it wasn't recoil, was enough to make him wince in pain.

"We've got beast kings entering the fight!" Glosil yelled out.

"Fuck, that's ugly! Got something that has the body of a lion, a scorpion tail, and a bird's head," Rugrat said.

"Catarai—they're nasty little bastards. They taunt with their tail and launch attacks with their paws and beak. Their stinger contains a powerful paralytic," Blaze said.

"Well, I hope that it's allergic to lead," Rugrat said as Erik heard his rifle firing.

Three wolves stepped out of the forest. Their size was impressive, no smaller than a horse, and they gave off a powerful feel. They all had manes and the other creatures seemed to treat them as if they were royalty, moving around them so that they weren't disturbed.

The big wolves moved in a pack, the one with the longest mane in front as the other two moved beside it, ready to fight on his command.

A massive gorilla charged out, smashing his fists into the ground as a group of other gorillas came behind him. They started hooting as they charged forward at the walls, in a group.

Erik increased his speed, unleashing the full strength of his body. It was as though he flew across the ground; he didn't have time to rest.

He pulled out a monster core. "Time to party!" Erik yelled as the monster core broke in his hand.

63
SWORDS AND SHIELDS

"Rugrat!" Erik yelled. His voice rose in alarm as he ran. A screen appeared in front of him as he gripped the Common Mortal grade monster core.

> **Monster Core**
> Do you wish to absorb this Common Mortal Grade monster core?
> *YES/NO*
> You will gain 10,000 EXP

"On my way to you! Quick reaction force, move to the eastern side and engage the beast elites there! All forces, move up to the walls! Blaze, I want the heavy infantry ready to fall back on the village square if needed. Elise, start putting the inter-village blockades up!" Rugrat yelled.

Yes. Erik's thoughts were rewarded with a golden light as the power around him was disturbed. Energies from all around increased their flow as Erik's wounds healed at an accelerated rate. The pain from overusing Mana fell away as his Stamina and Mana regenerated quickly.

Erik didn't let it go to waste and he ran at full speed. A wolf rushed his side. Erik turned, punched it and sent it flying back. His hand came up to fire a Mana bolt into a group of panthers. He jumped into the sky to avoid a blockade. The ground underneath him lit up with Mana bolts that streamed from his hands, leaving a swathe of destruction below. He dropped to the ground, rolling and coming up. His two hands were covered in magic circles as he ran through the dust, firing Mana bullets as fast as a machine gun. The lines of Mana could be clearly seen in the daylight—twin streams cutting down anything in their path.

"Shit!" Erik yelled as he saw the Mana bolts hit a post with a purple piece of cloth.

A massive explosion went off and Erik was tossed to the side. He rolled and got back up. Getting his feet under him, he charged forward at the ape group. The smoke and dust around him was stirred up in his path as he jumped over the crater where the marker had been.

"Did you just set off my explosive?" Rugrat asked.

"I think so!" Erik yelled back.

"Don't do that!" Rugrat yelled. Erik saw Rugrat's massive build on the top of the village's walls. He was no longer using the M40 but had his personal rifle.

The sound of shots rang out as Rugrat ran and shot at the same time, covering Erik and thinning out the beasts.

Erik let out a yell as he jumped over spike pits. He saw the incoming gorillas. With their powerful forearms, they smashed the defenses away. They were much smarter and their strength was incredible.

All around the village, it was a state of chaos. The walls were being attacked; the panthers and wolves there dug their claws into the walls and tried to climb up. Here and there, they topped the wall. There just weren't enough defenders to cover the entire wall.

The first casualties were being treated and rushed back from the front lines.

"Blow the IEDs!" Erik yelled.

They'd built the improvised explosive devices from the three-headed forest king snake gas sac and other compounds Rugrat had played with.

The people of Alva Village on the wall reached down and grabbed onto seemingly simple ropes and pulled on them.

Arrows shot into the air; some failed to deploy as there were obstacles in the way. Those that shot into the air carried ceramic jars filled with holes. They sped off into the sky.

Erik jumped into the air, tossing healing powder into his mouth.

The second rope was pulled. Small explosions went off all around the village that bloomed into a massive explosion as Rugrat's thermobaric weapons were set off.

Alva Village was hidden under explosions and rolling thunder as the beast horde was ripped apart. Their defenses were obliterated but they'd taken out two-thirds of the horde.

Erik was buffeted around. He used healing spells as he was hit with flying debris. His fatigue was coming back as the strength from the monster core was dissipating. He hit the ground awkwardly, twisting his foot, and slammed into the ground. He pushed himself up. He was slower now, feeling his injuries.

He looked around at the beasts that were recovering. Those closest to the wall were better than those still stuck in the defenses. The wooden spikes and barricades had turned into shrapnel, tearing them apart.

Erik took out a sword, finishing off a few close-by beasts as he oriented himself.

He could hear Rugrat firing over the dull ring in his ears from the pressure wave. His eyes found the gorilla band. They were covered in blood now and they had lost some of their numbers. But they seemed even more determined as they let out angry war cries as they rushed the walls.

The lead gorilla slammed against the wall, cracking it. It was only made of mud and it couldn't stand up to the powerful gorilla elite's hit.

"Prepare to move back from where the gorillas are attacking! They're getting through the wall!" Erik yelled. He tried to run and limp his way toward them; the Focused Heal worked on his foot, getting him to run once again in a short period.

"Where are the quick reaction force?" Erik demanded.

"They're fighting off a group of panther elites," Rugrat yelled back.

"We've got a breach in the northeastern sector!" Glosil yelled out over the command channel.

"Blaze, have the heavy infantry take up the rearguard. Start retreating back into the village square!" Erik hoped it was the right decision. The walls were the greatest obstacle against the beast horde. If they tried to hold it too long, they would be cut off from one another and unable to retreat in strength.

"Yes, sir!" Blaze said.

There was movement on the wall as groups prepared to retreat back into the village. People were taking their monster cores, using that extra power to rally themselves.

Rugrat jumped off the wall and back into the village.

Erik fired his pistol at the gorillas. It hurt them, but they still continued on.

Erik adjusted his aim, going for the head, and started to drop more of them. He paused his steps, not wanting to get too close. With their brute strength, not even Erik was sure he would be able to fight them one-on-one.

A section of wall was destroyed. Dust flew up away from it as people could be heard yelling on the other side of the wall.

The gorillas started to charge forward and widen the gap, only to be cut down by rounds buffed with explosive shot.

Rugrat was holding the other side, giving people time to evacuate.

Erik saw other beasts making it over the walls and into the village. There must have been some five hundred of them still remaining.

He felt despair, fear that they wouldn't make it but he had to bury it—he needed to fight!

With the expanding breach and even with Erik and Rugrat firing on them, the gorillas were making headway. They were tough bastards and didn't always go down with one round, taking three or four each. Erik fired and reloaded as fast as possible until there were no more magazines left in his storage ring.

He had to move as some of the beasts that hadn't made it into the village were rushing him. He had to look to surviving as he fought across the crater-pitted wasteland that the exterior of Alva had been turned into.

The walls were breached and there were beasts inside the walls.

Sergeant Niemm watched as archers and people from Alva Village weaved around the heavy infantry, running up the main road toward the village square.

Archers were set up on rooftops and different elevated positions so they could provide support and plunging fire right into their enemies' teeth.

With the archers leaving the walls, the beasts didn't have any obstacles in their paths as they dug their claws into the mud walls and pulled themselves over.

The larger beasts directly attacked the walls, opening up holes and flooding through. The beast numbers inside the walls swarmed.

"Ready!" Niemm yelled out as he saw panthers turning around the corner and rushing up the main street toward the heavy infantry.

The archers fired, cutting down the leading beasts. The heavy infantry were silent. Niemm had gone straight to swords and shields. Their spears were more liable to break than kill the beasts; with their shields, they could reinforce one another's strength and their swords—being of a higher quality and made from metal, not wood—were stronger and less likely to be pulled away by a beast.

The sounds of fighting could be heard, the noises from different spells going off as Rugrat's rifle fired again and again.

Sergeants called out behind them, organizing the archers and their fire zones. They watched the beasts getting closer, running over the bodies of their fallen.

"Heavy infantry! What do we do?" Niemm asked.

"We stand!" They replied as one, their voices resonating inside the shield wall.

"What do we not do?"

"We do not break!" They all replied and gripped their weapons tighter. The lingering doubts and fear in their minds cleared.

"I am proud to stand with you all today. We might not last till tomorrow, but we will not break! We will stand together!" Niemm yelled, feeling his throat close up with emotion.

"Hah!" They slammed the sides of their blades against their shields in salute and agreement.

"Here they come!" Niemm said as the first beast reached the shield wall. The wolf was covered in wounds and had two arrows sticking out of it as it charged at the shield wall. The wall recoiled slightly, but they backed one another up, taking the impact as those under the beast stabbed outward.

"Hah!" Their clean blades cut into the open underside of the wolf as it tried to climb over them.

"Hu-ah!" Niemm yelled out as the shields bashed the wolf corpse away. More beasts rushed them now as blades shot out once again.

"Hah!"

They fell into a rhythm, using their shields to bash, their swords to kill.

A red haze started to appear around them, the effect of the armor Erik had procured for them.

Niemm felt himself losing control, leaving him with only his reactions.

"Hu-ah!" Shields slammed into the beasts, pushing them back and opening them up.

"Hah!" Swords came out as one, wounding and deadly.

"Watch those blades!" Niemm barked, seeing people extending to get an attack to land. They corrected, only hitting within their reach and not overextending.

As more beasts came, the lines were getting inundated with bodies and the press of attacks. They held, relying on one another to not break.

Their aura was undergoing a change. The beasts had a slight hint of fear in their eyes as the red haze around the group started to increase, their strength being bolstered.

"Second rank! Prepare to move forward. First rank, prepare to move to the rear!" Niemm yelled out, organizing everyone. "Change!"

"Hu-ah!"

"Hah!"

The first rank turned; the second rushed into the gap, taking up their position.

"Hu-ah!"

"Hah!"

Niemm could see the arrows thinning out the beasts but it wasn't enough.

The first rank were bloodied, tending to their wounds by rote response. There was a dullness to their eyes as that red haze continued to build up around them all.

I think the armor affects others with the blood haze effect.

Niemm could feel the draw to destroy, the heady feeling as his power increased when he killed or the slight increase in the red haze when someone killed around him.

It was a drug, making him crave to kill more, to gain more strength, to become a god-like power.

You will not fail them! Niemm yelled inside of his head, gathering his thoughts.

Someone screamed out as their arm was cut up by a panther's claws. Those on either side covered them as they were pulled back and another stepped up into their position.

"Prepare to fall back!" Niemm yelled, putting emphasis on his words, making it a clear order. He knew that they were being affected by the red haze. They looked as though they wanted to argue but then, seeing Sergeant Niemm, they closed their mouths.

"Fall back!" Niemm said.

"Hu-ah!" The shields opened up some space, knocking back the forward beasts.

The first line took a step back, the second line making sure that the first line didn't step on anything that might make them lose their footing.

The archers adjusted their positions but continued to fire down on the beasts; in the enclosed spaces, they couldn't miss.

Sharpshooters aimed for elites and the most powerful beasts, weakening or killing them before they engaged the heavy infantry.

The heavy infantry started to methodically fall back, leaving the street covered in bodies.

64
FALLING BACK?

Glosil was coordinating with the different archery groups that were all pulling back into the center of the city.

"We're moving back," Roska reported as she and the quick reaction force had dealt with the two king-ranked beasts they'd been tasked with.

"Move to assist Blaze," Glosil said.

As Blaze was coordinating the heavy infantry, he didn't have time to check out the overall situation. Erik and Rugrat were still on the wall and among the beasts, killing as many of them as possible.

If the king-ranked beasts were to make it into the city, they would smash through the heavy infantry defenses.

They had to be stopped no matter what.

Erik and Rugrat were the only ones who could go toe-to-toe with them. The quick reaction force made up of elites still needed ten people to kill just two king-ranked beasts.

Glosil was on top of the Village Hall, using the binoculars in the watchtower to see what was going on. He saw a commotion on a rooftop. A group of panthers had climbed a house and hit the archers who were using the roof as their firing position.

"Sergeant Shi! Assist Sergeant Flo!"

"Sir!"

The archery sergeant turned his attention to the fellow groups, worried. Three people had been cut down by the panthers; the remaining three on the roof were in a panic as they jumped off the roof.

Sergeant Shi's people had just reloaded, thankfully, and at this distance, it was hard for them to miss. Three of the four panthers were killed outright.

The final panther dropped onto the group. Glosil's heart stopped. With the panther inside their defenses, they could get in behind the heavy infantry and tear them apart, or get to the archers who weren't well suited for close-range combat.

"Medics, I need you to take out the panther in the southwestern sector! Sergeant Flo's people are on top of the Yui family home. There are wounded among them," Glosil said.

"Yes, sir." Sergeant Mi of the medics organized his people. The medics were prized possessions. They had the greatest armor and close-in weapons as they ran from fight to fight, supporting the different groups and getting people back on their feet.

After the quick reaction force, they were the strongest group.

Glosil didn't want to use them to fight, but he didn't have anyone else he could pull from as the quick reaction force were fighting their way back to the village square.

He could see the heavy infantry units were just fifty meters away from the village square, that distance reducing slowly but surely.

"Archers! Watch your area—already we've had beasts breaking through our lines of defense and attacking other groups," Glosil warned.

There were holes showing in their defenses, but now there were less than two hundred beasts inside the village. The problem was that they were all elites.

Even the advanced crossbows weren't able to kill them in just a few hits. The worst conditions were those for the heavy infantry as they directly clashed with the elites.

A red haze and bloody smell seemed to come off them. They didn't seem to feel pain, even as they were pushed to the rear with massive injuries. As soon as the medic released them, they'd step back up to the line, ready to go again.

Glosil felt a chill when he looked into their eyes, their blank stares as they'd pushed beyond Stamina fatigue, reaching a new state that surpassed their limits. He understood the hellish training that they had gone through now. Even with everything, they had their reactions.

"I think one of the panthers is evolving in the northeastern sector!"

Glosil looked over as he saw a panther, growing in size. Its power flowed out, giving off a stifling pressure. *Sneaky bastard. This must be the panther king. He hid in the ranks, moving like one of the regular panthers just to show himself at the last moment!*

The panther grew until it was the size of a horse. Blue lines appeared on its body as the air around it became dense with Mana.

"Mana beast," Glosil said breathlessly.

The panther let out a roar. The lines along its body glowed as energy seemed to flow around it. A magic circle appeared in front of its mouth. A ray of Mana shot out, hitting the heavy infantry line.

Three of the soldiers were knocked down, their fates unknown.

"Quick reaction force!" Glosil yelled out, feeling his panic rise. They weren't ready for something like this.

Another magic circle appeared under its feet as a yellow glow fell over the panther's body, increasing its strength.

Glosil hadn't seen it before, but he knew what it was. One of the terrifying abilities of Mana beasts was their ability to use Mana. This gave them ranged attacks and could be used to buff their stats and abilities greatly.

Erik and Rugrat's Affinity for Mana had increased as they became Mana lords. With the disturbance created by the Mana panther, they looked over in alarm.

The gorillas had made it into the village and they were pushing hard; it was difficult to push them back. There was simply too many of them and it was impossible to one-shot them.

It took four or five good hits on their vitals to take them out; that was some twenty grievous injuries. Their natural defenses and strength were high, as was their reaction speed.

Cracks were showing on Erik's Golden Fox armor from the hits he'd taken.

Rugrat knew that he was hurting and near the end of his abilities. He was deep into Stamina and Mana fatigue. Rugrat was using his sneak to get the attack modifier, but with so many, it was hard for him to sneak off.

"What's that?" Rugrat yelled over the sound transmission device.

"A Mana beast panther!" Glosil said. The normally disciplined guard captain's voice shook.

"It's level fifteen!" Blaze confirmed.

Do we try to fight off the gorillas or move to the Mana beast and kill it?

"We're on our way. Get the quick reaction force to hold off the gorillas. They're breaking through the houses. If they aren't stopped then they're going to break through the barricades that we made in the different sectors." Erik fired at the gorillas.

Rugrat started to run for the Mana panther's location. He didn't need anyone to tell him where it was as the disturbance in the natural surrounding Mana was like a beacon to him.

Erik was right behind him. It only took them a few minutes to get to where the Mana beast was.

Screams greeted them as they came across the Mana beast plunging its claws into a heavy infantry soldier who was still slashing at the beast's leg.

The entire section had been torn apart by the Mana beast. The other beasts with it were rushing forward into the archers who were behind them.

Rugrat buffed his rounds with explosive shot. He switched to full auto on his personal rifle, unloading into the Mana beast.

It was thrown backward under the unrelenting assault.

"You help the archers and pull the heavy infantry back together!" Rugrat said.

Erik dodged through the fighting and grabbed two heavy infantry who were around the Mana beast. Rugrat altered his aim to not hit Erik.

Erik got clear with the wounded: one over his shoulder, the other held in his left hand as he charged the beasts.

With Rugrat's Strength stat, his rifle, even at full auto, didn't shift its point of aim. The sound of shattering glass could be heard.

The golden-like aura around the Mana beast shattered as Rugrat dropped his old magazine and slapped in a new one, his speed hard to follow as there was barely any time between reloading.

Rugrat stepped forward. Other beasts, seeing him attack their leader, rushed to kill him.

Rugrat flipped to semi-auto once again. To him, they were all moving too slow. The rounds knocked them back as he fired with his right hand. A grenade appeared in his left from his storage ring and he threw it out underneath the Mana beast.

The grenades went off. Rugrat turned to the side; debris rained down on him as he turned back and fired at the Mana beast again. It had turned a powerful and dominating beast into a bloodied and burnt-looking weakling.

Erik helped ease the pressure on the heavy infantry. They took their monster cores to recover faster; the worst were placed with the medics as they charged forward. Erik led them as they attacked the beasts directly.

The red haze around them made the beasts scared to fight them. They didn't seem to worry about injuries as they only wanted to kill more.

Sensing the danger to their rear, the beasts started to face the heavy infantry. The archers pulled back. Combat medics and other heavy infantry who had been pulled from other sections rushed forward. Their shields slammed down as their swords slashed outward.

They didn't fall back anymore but pushed forward—forward to meet the beasts, forward to rescue their fellow heavy infantry members.

The Mana beast dropped to the side. With the piercing enchanted runes buffed with explosive shot, its side had been torn apart.

It didn't sense Rugrat and Erik before they attacked. Rugrat hadn't paused in his shooting, pushing the beast back. It had lost its momentum and the pain made it unable to do anything but accept the damage.

Although it was a level fifteen beast, so was Rugrat. Instead of using his magic to attack, he used it to buff his rounds. Each one had the force of a grenade launcher.

Nothing would have been able to survive such an onslaught, but the Mana beast's recovery ability was much greater than anything back on Earth.

The panther finally dropped to the ground, its body broken. Half of its head was gone, showing skull underneath.

Panthers relied on their speed, not their tough hides like the gorillas.

Rugrat reloaded and fired at the panther's skull. A tombstone appeared above it.

Rugrat turned and looked to the other beasts. They had fought with renewed vigor, seeing their king enter the battlefield. Now, seeing that it had fallen, they were scared.

Rugrat started firing on them, no longer caring about holding back his Mana. In two or three shots, he was able to kill a creature.

I've only got two magazines left. Rugrat could only grit his teeth and keep going.

Suddenly, the beasts stopped trying to fight and started to flee. The remaining elites and kings let out calls. Grouping together, the beasts started to pull back out of the village. Once they were past the walls, they ran back toward the forest.

The people of Alva Village used their crossbows, chasing them with arrows, bleeding as many as possible.

Rugrat pulled out his bow and started firing on them as they retreated. Now it was the people of Alva chasing and charging them.

They made it beyond the wall. The day had worn on and it was already late afternoon. Some beasts fell into the craters, others into the defenses. Only a few made it back into the forest.

Rugrat stood at the edge of a breach. He nocked a new arrow, looking around, expecting to see a target, looking for the next threat.

Details started to enter his mind: some of the wooden defenses on fire, the beasts' parts across the ground, the rubble at his feet, the people around him.

The yells behind him.

"Archers, on the walls!" Erik yelled out before falling into a fit of coughing as he dropped to a knee.

Rugrat felt a wave of exhaustion fall over him as well. He took out his Common grade monster core and absorbed it. The flow of power allowed him to clear his mind.

"Start patching up the breaches! See to the wounded! Wounded are to report to the Village Hall!" Rugrat called out.

Erik pulled out a healing solution and drank it, his body covered in big and small wounds.

They were tired from fighting all day but they worked together.

Rugrat could only grimace as he saw human bodies among the beasts, no longer moving. He opened up the last notification. His whole body relaxed, seeing that screen.

Quest Completed: Beast Mountains Trial
Requirements:
Survive the beast horde (0/5 Waves remaining)
Rewards:
Title: Dungeon Master
Control over Beast Mountains Dungeon
+100,000 EXP
Teleportation scroll (location locked)

Erik picked himself up, using the wall beside him. His face had blood on it; his armor on his legs and arms had broken long ago. His eyes were hooded, drained of his energy, but still he was able to stand. "See to the village. I'll check on the wounded."

"Got it." Rugrat held out three Mana recovery potions.

Erik took them and headed for the Village Hall, where the sounds of pain could be heard.

Rugrat checked his rifle and moved to the wall, checking on the different people there. *Dungeon Master? I wonder what that means.*

65
AFTERMATH

Erik's entire body hurt. It was different from muscle pain; it was the feeling of his Mana channels being strained past their limits repeatedly.

Still, he bent to his work.

Deal with it, West! Erik yelled inside his head as he used Focused Heal on the artery he was holding. The artery closed as Erik used more Focused Heal on the woman's bone marrow to promote the creation of blood.

"She's going to need liquids. Next." Erik didn't know how long he had been doing this. He must've seen two dozen patients, from the worst of just breaths away from death, to those who had complicated wounds that required too much healing powder or potion to fix.

"There's no one else." Elise sounded tired, not only physically but mentally.

Erik made a noise of acknowledgement before he turned around. He found a chair and slumped into it. He pulled off his gloves and sent them into his storage ring.

He held his face in his hands. The need for sleep called out for him, but he didn't give in as he took a deep breath, using it to sit up and look around the village square.

The people under Elise's command were working as extra hands to help the medics.

Jasper's people had brought over all of their healing supplies and tended to those who had been healed, giving them food to eat.

Those on the walls were eating their prepared rations. There was no movement from the forest but it looked as though they had scared off everything in the remaining area. With all of the beasts killed, there were more than enough resources for the remaining beasts to live off of.

Forces that weren't on the wall ate and cleared up the city. The northwest sector was a hive of activity as beast corpses and Mana cores were recovered.

Erik's vision was swimming from the lack of sleep. His eyes felt gritty and raw. He took out a canteen and took a drink of water. "How many did we lose?"

Elise looked at him. The dead expression in her eyes left no need to ask anything else. "Seventeen." Elise took a breath afterward. She had to force the word out or else it would get stuck in her throat.

Erik could see her expression twist, the guilt and loss. Everyone knew one another in Alva Village.

Erik didn't say anything.

The silence stretched as those dark emotions turned in their stomachs.

"Erik, you need to get some sleep. You've been working nonstop all afternoon and night. Let us take it on now. We've stabilized everyone just need to be monitored, with enough food and time they'll recover," Elise said.

Erik's tired brain wanted to argue, to say that he wanted to keep on going, that he could keep on going.

Though he knew from her look that he would be more trouble than use. "Okay." He rose from his seat slowly. His eyebrows pinched together at the headache mixed with head rush that seemed to crush his brain.

Erik took a few seconds to stabilize himself before he headed off toward the Village Hall. He moved to his room. He pulled his armor off and dropped it to the side. He laid down on his air mattress and sleeping bag. He half pulled the open part of his sleeping bag over himself before he passed out.

He'd taken himself to the edge of Mana and Stamina fatigue, but his mind cleared slightly as a new screen appeared in front of him.

You have 15 attribute points to use.

Erik was slightly startled by this but it made sense. A part of him just wanted to throw it into his character sheet.

After a few moments, he got himself back under control. He might be tired and depressed with how everything had gone, but if he just easily threw away his stat points, he would regret it.

All right, so what do I do? I could power level up my combat abilities, my straight Strength, Stamina, Agility, and Stamina Regeneration. This would make my combat ability soar, though I would be at the same stage in trying to open more Mana gates. Also, there is no guarantee that I would be able to temper my bones. I might need to rely on just potions, which are expensive, instead of my own healing ability.

Like this, Erik dismissed putting all of his stats into increasing his body's Strength and Agility.

I could go full Mana, increase my Mana pool. It's been lagging behind and I can up my Mana Regeneration. I could get it to maybe twelve Mana per second—I could fire my weakest Mana bullets every second, so sixty rounds per minute. I could also use the increased Mana Regeneration and Mana pool to create more Mana drops and attack my Mana gates, creating a multiplicative effect of increasing my Strength, not just once like I would with increasing the strength of my body. Also, I could use my healing spells to support myself when tempering my body, allowing me to increase my body's strength.

The other option is to split my stats between them all. Up to now, I've been putting my stats in based on the situation. I haven't really had a plan for it.

He sunk into thought.

What is my biggest problem right now? Where do I get most of my Strength from? It's not from just right up punching people; it's only with the growling tiger that I modified that I was able to get the strength to kill those different creatures. Combining magic and body together to be more powerful allows me to implement greater power. If I cultivate my Mana system and then use outside sources to temper my body, that would allow me to increase the power of both systems and have a multiplicative effect on my Strength. I'm already beating Rugrat out in Strength and Agility when I was level thirteen and he was level fifteen. He has to watch what he does, moving to longer range while I'm going to close range.

What if every time I leveled up, I was to put one point into Strength, one into Agility and Stamina Regeneration, with the last two into Mana Regeneration. The higher the Mana Regeneration, the more I can temper my body because I can cast a healing spell for longer. The Stamina Regeneration will mean I can eat and sleep less while also fighting for longer in a fight. Strength and Agility are good because the body tempering system doesn't seem to be simple at all. The Mana system allows me to gain points for opening Mana gates and for compressing the Mana in my body. This is easier than enduring the pain that comes with tempering one's body.

If I was to only have the stat points, this would be a dumb idea as I would have no strengths, but combined with increasing my Mana Gathering system and Body Cultivation, I'll be able to take the benefits of both.

Erik was determined now.

He placed three points each into Strength, Agility, and Stamina Regeneration, and then six into Mana Regeneration.

Character Sheet
Name: Erik West
Level: 15
Race: Human
Titles:
From the Grave
Mana Lord
Dungeon Master
Strength: (Base 12) +14
260
Agility: (Base 10) +16
130
Stamina: (Base 16) +4
300
Mana: (Base 6) +11
170
Mana Regeneration (Base 10) +27
11.85/s
Stamina Regeneration: (Base 12) +23
7.75/s

Land Holder disappeared. What the hell is Dungeon Master? I need to check my notifications when I wake up. Erik's vision went to black.

Jasper returned from handing out food. The storage sector in the northwest had been turned into a processing center for the animal corpses.

Crews were moving through the city, collecting up the animals and dumping them for Jasper and his people to deal with.

For the corpses that were too damaged, they simply accessed their tombstone and took the useful components and separated them to be stored in the storage warehouses.

Those still in good condition were handed over to the butchers, who would clean the animals out, separating them more thoroughly. If they were elites or high-ranked beasts, they were put in storage rings for Roska to separate.

There were thousands of beasts, making it a complicated and hard task.

Seeing the mounds of supplies and his people working, Jasper was still in shock. He didn't know how they had survived.

"How are things?" Elise said as she saw Jasper.

"Busy." Jasper saw another group wave their storage rings, making more corpses appear in the storage area. They simply didn't have the room in their storage rings to hold the sheer amount of supplies.

"The others want to have a meeting in an hour," she said.

"Okay, I'll be there," Jasper said.

"Make sure that your people get some rest," Elise warned.

"I'll do my best, but we might need more help if we want to keep most of the meat and other useful parts of the beasts," Jasper said. Simply put, there was just too much for them to do.

"I'll see if I can find some people to help out," Elise promised before she headed off to her next task.

Jasper moved forward to help out his people in organizing the beasts, breaking them down. With the supplies they'd gain out of this, it was more money than anyone had ever seen in Alva Village.

Jasper might have been excited at any other time; right now, he just wanted to deal with it as fast as possible. Friends and people he knew had died in the battle. It was hard to take any joy from making a gold coin.

Jasper got lost in organizing where people should drop off the different corpses they brought. He would work with the broken bodies to activate the tombstones and dump the collected items in the right collection points. They had run out of storage space in their rings and items long ago.

When it was time for the meeting, he headed over to the village square.

With Erik's healing spells and the medics' use of healing solutions, potions, and bandages, most of those who had been injured had been sent home to rest.

Others were still there, eating and drinking as the healing had been so intense that their Stamina was now lacking.

Jasper thanked the server as he took his meal and went to the table. The smell of the thick stew and bread was heavenly.

Blaze and Elise were there already. They greeted one another with looks and continued eating. All of them were hungry.

"Sorry I'm late." Glosil sat down.

"Where's Rugrat?" Elise asked Blaze.

"There's something I need to talk to you all before talking to Rugrat and Erik." Blaze's face turned grave.

The others looked at him with curious gazes and frowns.

Blaze took a deep breath and told them about how Lord Salyn had broken his oath with the people of Alva Village, how Erik and Rugrat had come here and been given a quest.

"So they defended Alva Village because of a quest?" Jasper asked.

"Why didn't they tell us?" Glosil asked.

"They had our trust and we didn't block them in planning out the defense of the village. If you were in their shoes, would you have corrected my assumption?"

The others fell silent, each of them with complicated expressions and feelings.

"So, other than the quest that told them to survive the beast horde…" Elise said.

Everyone looked to her. She had become the leader of the little village, stepping into her role fully.

"Right," Blaze said.

"There was no need for them to defend and help us survive. They just needed to make it through. They used all of their resources to increase our strength. You might not know this, but they put their own goods up for sale so that they could fuel the advancement of our people. I don't really care where they came from or why they came—they were there for us in our darkest hour. Do you remember what they promised you when they entered Alva?" Elise looked right at Blaze.

"Alva Village will come out stronger," Blaze said.

Elise blew out a dismissive breath. "Fuck Lord Salyn. The reason we're here is because of Erik and Rugrat. I'd say they're our real lords."

If this had been before, her words would be a sort of blasphemy. Now it was an accepted fact.

"So what do we do now?" Glosil asked. "Do we follow them? Will they let us? What happens if Lord Salyn comes here and sees the village is still standing and we're all over level ten? Will everyone move to the Second Realm?"

These questions didn't find answers as they all looked at their cooling stew.

"It's not something that we need to figure out right now. The first thing we need to do is let the people of Alva Village know the truth about Erik and Rugrat. Personally, I'm going to follow them if they are willing," Blaze said.

The others agreed.

Jasper had seen Erik and Rugrat perform what were nothing less than miracles. He wanted to see just what they could do in the future.

66

GAINS

Erik's eyes opened slowly as light started to come into his room. He could hear the noises of people going to breakfast, their voices low. He could feel the heaviness in the air.

Seventeen.

Erik slowly pushed himself up. He sat there for some time, just needing to collect his thoughts.

He saw his exclamation mark notification flashing at him.

Needing a distraction from his thoughts, Erik opened his notifications.

Skill: Marksman
Level: 39 (Apprentice)
Long-range weapons are familiar in your hands. When aiming, you can zoom in x2.0.

Skill: Hand-to-Hand
Level: 26 (Apprentice)
Attacks cost 20% less Stamina

Upon advancing into the Apprentice level of Hand-to-Hand, you will be rewarded with one randomly selected item related to this skill.
You have received the One Finger Beats Fist Technique Book
+10,000 EXP

Skill: Healer
Level: 47 (Apprentice)
You have become familiar with the body and the arts of repairing it. Healing spells now cost 5% less Mana.

Upon advancing into the Apprentice level of Healer, you will be rewarded with one randomly selected item related to this skill.
You have received Ranged Heal-Simple
+100,000 EXP

Quest Completed: Beast Mountains Trial
Requirements:
Defeat the beast horde (0/5 Waves remaining)
Rewards:
Title: Dungeon Master
Control over Beast Mountains Dungeon
+100,000 EXP
Teleportation scroll (location locked)

Title: Dungeon Master
You've become the master of a dungeon
You have gained control of the Dungeon building interface.
Grade: Grand Mortal (Can be upgraded) (Must visit Dungeon to take control)

Resources
Food: 0 Units
Stone: 700 Units
Mana: 1200
Gold: 0

Upkeep costs per day:
1 Mana

You have gained control of:
Dungeon Core (Sleeping)
Alchemy workshop
Beast Stables
Smithy
Citizens: 1
Guards: 0
Vzztpssht: 41
Beasts: 214

Erik looked over the information but he didn't really know what it all meant. It was like the information he had got when he and Rugrat had become the acting lords of Alva Village.

You have reached Level 15
When you sleep next, you will be able to increase your attributes by: 0 points.

Must be zero because I already used them last night to increase my stats.

56,534/195,000 EXP till you reach Level 16

Even with the killing of thousands of beasts, even if they were shared over the people in Alva Village, Erik had killed dozens by himself and it had only allowed him to level up two times.

"One really needs to advance in the realms if they want to increase their rank." Erik felt as though he had dried out all of his avenues in the First Realm.

It was hard to nearly impossible for him to gain the Experience he wanted. Killing most creatures in the First Realm would give him just a few pitiful hundred Experience. The resources weren't enough to support increasing his skills; even the technique books and manuals only covered the basics, allowing one to gain an understanding, but finding it hard to advance.

We must go to the Second Realm when we can to increase our level.

Erik's thoughts turned toward Chonglu City. His expression hardened. *There are still things that we need to look after first.*

When he gripped his fist, an explosive energy filled his body. Now he might be able to defeat those rhinos with just his fists and feet instead of needing to enhance his body with Mana.

With this thought, Erik opened up his storage broach. Inside was the ranged heal spell scroll and the One Finger Beats Fist technique book.

He checked his different storage devices but wasn't able to find the teleportation scroll. "Rugrat and I did the quest—he probably has it." Erik pulled out the two new items he had gained.

Technique Book: Ranged Heal-Simple
Do you wish to activate this Technique book? Doing so will destroy this Technique book.
YES/NO

"Yes." With Erik's word, the scroll started to disintegrate and a white light shot between Erik's brows.

He closed his eyes as information flooded his mind. In just a few seconds, he knew everything contained within the scroll and how to use the spell.

You have learned the spell: **Ranged Heal-Simple**. Your spell book has been updated.

"Ranged heal," Erik said. A green Mana circle appeared around his hand. It looked more complicated than his other healing spells as a green ball of water formed and shot out. It hit the wall; like a water balloon, it exploded but other than a wet stain, nothing happened.

"It'll take me some time to be able to insta cast," Erik said. Learning the spell was one thing, but it took repeated uses and a deeper understanding before it could become his spell.

It was as though he had read the back of the book: he had an idea of what it was about, but it was only when he read the book that he would be able to make deeper connections and greater understandings, making the book his.

"With this, I can heal Rugrat even if we're apart. I need to look into spells more. There are a lot of them but so far I've only been able to make Mana Bolt and Mana Bullet on my own. If I can understand them, I might be able to make new spells that suit my different way of healing."

Erik put those thoughts to the back of his mind. The world of magic was a large one. He had a basic understanding of different practices, but for the large part, he used the spell technique books to gain spells.

Although it would be nice to make more spells himself, he didn't know how much or how little work it would take.

Erik assessed the small headache he had from using the first technique book and opened the second.

Technique Book: One Finger Beats Fist
Do you wish to activate this Technique book? Doing so will destroy this Technique book.
YES/NO

"Yes," Erik said.

The pages started to flip in the book; energy built up before shooting between Erik's brows again. This stream lasted longer before the light dissipated and the book closed with a bang. Erik waved his hand and the book turned to dust.

He let out a cold breath and pinched the bridge of his nose, rubbing it between his fingers.

"That wasn't as fun." Images filled Erik's mind. A woman stood on a field; she held up a fist, but after a second, she raised her index finger. She pushed her finger forward. It seemed simple but Erik could see the rapid movement in the air around her finger.

The scene changed. The woman was now older, more refined, as she still thrust out with her finger. The seasons changed as the woman grew older, executing that same finger technique. With each scene, the air moved differently as she gained insight and greater understanding to her movements.

Finally, she stood opposite a man with a gloating smile. He wore purple robes that might have looked tranquil on another person but did nothing to soften his eyes.

The woman stood there, poised and uncaring, her gaze cold.

It was a match; the stands were blurry and the area around the two was hard to see.

The man launched himself forward, his feet leaving craters on the tiles.

Erik's eyes widened at this explosive power; he could sense the power of the man. "Body Like Stone? Maybe even higher? Body Like Iron?" Erik's words disappeared into a shocked whisper. He found it hard to follow the man's movements as he crossed the arena in just a few seconds.

Flame appeared in the man's eyes and lit up his fists. His muscles glowed with power as he unleashed a powerful strike, holding nothing back.

His face held a smirk as the woman repeated the same strike that Erik had seen hundreds—no, thousands—of times.

Power condensed and formed on the woman's finger. There was no rushing air like before, but a small distortion in the air.

Fist met finger. The powerful and dominating-looking man's flames were snuffed out mercilessly. His arm broke.

The rush of air made the woman's clothes billow around them. Her finger stretched out to meet her opponent's fist. He was blown to the side like a puppet that had been yanked back by the puppeteer.

Slowly, she lowered her finger.

He had used brute strength while she had focused and controlled that strength, striking at his weakness. The woman's eyes seemed to find Erik's.

A cold sweat fell down his back. He felt powerless beneath that gaze, as if a mortal looking to a god. All of his secrets seemed to be revealed.

"Interesting." This one word was simple but it seemed to be able to command the Ten Realms.

Erik opened his eyes, back in his room. The information in his mind seemed to explode, imprinting into his very body and soul.

Before, it would have taken him months to learn the technique. Now, he could feel part of the woman's own thoughts and ideas; with these, it would be much easier for him to learn.

It was some time before he was able to recover from it all.

"I thought that when using technique books, people would just immediately know the spell or technique. Some of them are more guides than they are the answers. It will take longer to understand and those who use them might not ever understand them in their lifetime. Though if someone uses this with their own knowledge, they could create a technique that is better suited for them and can display more power."

It was a blessing and a curse: one would only get the most out of it if it was best suited for them. If it wasn't, then it would be wasted.

"I haven't even scratched the surface of the Ten Realms." Erik let out a small snort and a smile. He still had a long way to go.

67
TELEPORT SCROLL

Rugrat woke up before midday. He felt the flow of power through his body as he had broken through into the sixteenth level.

He opened his hand. A scroll appeared in it, the teleportation scroll.

There was a metal clasp on it. Gold lines and deep-blue jade shimmered in the light.

Opening the scroll fully revealed a highly complex magical circle.

Teleportation Scroll (location locked)
Using this scroll, one will be teleported to the locked location. The teleportation circle will have a radius of one hundred meters.
Location: **Beast Mountains Dungeon**
Do you wish to activate?
YES/NO

Rugrat closed the scroll once again. A thoughtful look appeared on his face. He checked his sound transmission device, seeing that there was a message waiting for him.

"Hey Rugrat, you get that teleport scroll thing and did you get a new title called Dungeon Master? It seems that it might be linked to this quest we completed. Is the beast trial actually a dungeon? Send me a message when you wake up."

Rugrat called Erik.

"What's up? I'm near the south gate checking out the wall. Haven't seen anything since yesterday. Everyone is down to twenty-five percent—everyone needs some sleep. It looks like there are going to be a lot of level increases," Erik said.

"Did you see the thing about dungeon master?" Rugrat asked.

"Seems like you did, too. I think that this trial was to become dungeon masters or whatever the hell that means. The teleport scroll, where is it locked to?"

"Beast Mountains Dungeon," Rugrat said, confirming everything that Erik had just said.

"Looks like our time here has come to an end." Erik's voice sounded carefree but Rugrat could see through it. After all, coming to Alva Village, they had found somewhere they felt comfortable. It wasn't Earth or back home, but it was somewhere they could be themselves and not have to worry.

"Well, the teleport scroll has a radius of one hundred meters," Rugrat said. "Right now, the people of Alva Village don't have a connection to anyone else. They were abandoned by Lord Salyn. What if we were to offer to bring them back to the Beast Mountains? From there, they could go where they wanted with resources if they needed."

"All right, but I also want to learn more about this whole dungeon master thing. Does it mean we control the dungeon, own it?"

"Well, I talked to Elise and some of the people in the village who might have known, but none of them seemed to. Maybe we'll find out something when we get there?"

"More teleporting. All right, we'll ask them if they want to come."

Roska wiped the sweat off her brow as she looked at the next pile of goods that her helpers were picking through and storing in different storage rings. The most valuable items were shifted into storage rings. Anything that was less valuable would be removed and placed into the storage huts.

The heavy infantry sections watched the walls while the rest of the village dealt with the aftermath.

Last night they had ceremonies for those who had fallen; in the dying sunlight, they'd collected their tombstones and laid them to rest in the ground. After a few weeks, there wouldn't even be bones left behind.

Roska hadn't felt much about being someone from Alva Village before. She just thought of it as the place that her family had abandoned her. Now, with the way people treated her, the warmth she found with everyone, she felt defensive of them, as if she wanted to protect them too.

All of them had gone through great changes. Roska was no different. She was now level thirteen, reaching for level fourteen. Being only in her mid-twenties, she was seen as a genius in the First Realm.

She looked over at the commotion at the gate. People were crowding around as Rugrat and a number of the archers entered the village.

Everyone was interested in the situation going on in the surrounding forest, but immediately Roska saw that Rugrat and the other archers had a bunch of small beasts tied up with rope that they were pulling along.

These little cubs mewled and snarled at the humans, but their actions were lacking the ferociousness of their parents that had attacked the city. They looked adorable and even Roska had a hard time associating them with their parents. Each of them had jet-black fur and yellow eyes.

Rugrat and the others continued into the city.

"Why did they bring back so many panther cubs?" one of the helpers asked Roska.

Roska shook her head. She didn't know herself.

"I heard that there are people who can rear animals and tame them to do their bidding, even contracts that beasts can make with humans, allowing them to work together," the other helper said.

Roska and the other man looked at him.

He scratched his head, a bit embarrassed. "When I was a boy, I raised some farm animals. My parents told me such things. They came from one of the big cities with Captain Blaze," he said.

Roska and the other man nodded. City people were exposed to more information.

"Do you think that Mister Erik and Rugrat will leave Alva Village?" the man who had talked on beast taming asked Roska.

The other looked over in interest.

"I do not know." Roska wouldn't admit it, but her heart tightened hearing these words. Erik had given her back her life and he'd helped to teach her; Rugrat had spent time to teach her how to better direct her spells and think of new ways to utilize them.

Everything she had now, she owed to them.

Her debt to them was too great. She wanted to follow them. Alva Village had protected her from the beasts beyond the walls when she had been hurt; now that she was recovered, she wanted to see beyond the walls and into the world.

Her eyes shone as the corner of her mouth twitched slightly, her heart captured by that wanderlust.

"Maybe we'll find out tonight at the meeting. They want everyone to attend," the other man said as they returned to work.

Glosil looked at Jasper and Elise nearby, sharing a look of common knowledge. They were nervous for Rugrat and Erik, as well as what they might say.

Erik had reached level fifteen. Rugrat had reached level sixteen but was close to level seventeen. Without any conscious thought, their auras seemed to disappear, no longer war gods, but two ordinary guys. None of the Alva Village people would look at them the same—the power that they had displayed, putting their lives on the line. If they said that they were the second strongest, no one would say they were the first.

Blaze cleared his voice. He was on top of the stage and Erik and Rugrat were behind him. Their faces didn't show any emotion. To Glosil, it was as if they were two men standing up for their execution, ready for it to go wrong at a moment's notice.

Everyone settled down and looked to him.

"Together, we have made it past the beast horde. We have survived and come out stronger than ever before. We have made sacrifices; we have lost loved ones. Though we are here today due to those sacrifices that must not and will not be forgotten." Blaze received a round of nods as he looked to Rugrat and Erik.

"Rugrat and Erik came to us in a time of need. They came, using their own resources and knowledge to assist us. They did this because they felt it was the right thing to do. They were not under orders to come here. In fact, Lord Salyn told me to keep the truth from you all, that he would send aid. Before the battle to protect our village started, I was notified that he had broken his oath to this village, to you. I pledged to uphold his rule and follow his laws and he would offer aid in times of need. He tore this oath apart and stepped on our faces!" Blaze yelled.

People grew angry and started to mutter among one another.

"Rugrat and Erik were sent here. They only needed to survive the beast horde. They didn't need to protect us, to help us build up our strength, or improve our village. I decided that we should hold back the information right before the battle, not wanting to distract people and lead to greater losses." He let the quiet conversations go on for some time.

"Elise, Glosil, Jasper, Taran, and I have decided to follow them no matter what," Blaze said.

Erik stepped up and put his hand on Blaze's shoulder.

Glosil was reminded of the first time that Erik had addressed the people of Alva Village. The village couldn't be compared to what it was back then. Glosil, like the rest of the villagers, watched Erik's every movement, waiting for him to speak.

"According to our quest, the beast horde will not come back again. We have also been given a teleportation scroll and been made dungeon masters. I don't know what that means, nor where it will lead, but if any of you want to, you're welcome to join us in heading to the Beast Mountains Dungeon."

"You command—I will follow." Storbon pulled out his spear and stepped forward. He slammed it into the ground, steely determination in his eyes.

Others stepped forward.

Glosil looked to his fellow villagers. They'd been abandoned; everyone else had left them but Erik and Rugrat had stayed with them through it all. Glosil looked at them—their spears, swords, crossbows, and armor.

A crooked grin appeared on his face as they all looked at Rugrat and Erik.

Rugrat's stoic expression broke as he let out a laugh.

Erik's face also broke into a touched smile.

"All right, well, I guess we better start paying your wages!" Erik clapped his hands. This got a few grins and laughs. "Eighty percent of the materials and loot that we got from the beasts in the beast horde will be broken down and passed out to everyone. You can exchange with one another and the quartermasters once we've moved to the dungeon. We will be moving everything useful to the storage district tonight and tomorrow. Tomorrow night, we will activate the teleportation scroll. For tonight, we're not on rations. Eat, drink! Quick reaction force, you're on watch!"

People cheered, excited to leave Alva Village behind.

"There ain't no rest for the wicked." Erik stepped off the stage and addressed the department heads.

"Can't I just hit metal?" Taran complained.

"We've got to plan out how to move everything that's important. Break down the smithy, bring the components we need. We've only got a teleportation area one hundred meters by one hundred meters. We can't waste any space!"

So they set to work, planning out what they could take. Rugrat and Erik went with Jasper, marking out the one-hundred-meter radius teleportation circle.

That night, people celebrated. But knowing that they would be put to work the next day, they didn't go overboard.

Everyone was given tasks. Alva Village was torn apart and broken down. In the afternoon, they all went to the Village Hall. Blaze called up the village cornerstone. This was the core of the village and the basis of the village.

Blaze had planted this cornerstone when he had built the initial camp nearly twenty years ago.

A screen appeared in front of him. He hit a few commands and the cornerstone transformed into a token, landing in his hand.

He put it away as a notification ran out.

> The cornerstone of Alva Village has been removed. The village will cease to exist.

Blaze lost his title as the village became "abandoned," meaning that anyone could now take it over with their own base token or they could move into it and build on top of it without Blaze's agreement.

They spent the rest of the day piling all of their supplies up and distributing items to the different people and families. This made them responsible for their new goods. Many of them traded in their monster cores and other items at the store earlier to take more with them.

"It's time." Rugrat looked out at everyone who was all bundled up. The heavy infantry units were around the edges of where they had marked out the teleportation scroll's limits. Archers were behind them, with the old and young in the center, protected by the quick reaction force.

They simply didn't know what was waiting for them on the other side.

"Ready yourselves!" Erik barked.

Everyone gripped their weapons tighter, ready to fight.

Rugrat opened the scroll.

Teleportation Scroll (location locked)
Using this scroll, one will be teleported to the locked location. The teleportation circle will have a radius of one hundred meters.
Location: **Beast Mountains Dungeon**
Do you wish to activate?
YES/NO

"Yes." With Rugrat's word, Mana rushed in toward the scroll as a massive magical circle appeared underneath the feet of the villagers.

Lines, circles, triangles, and other shapes formed; complicated runes seemed to be written in the ground by an unseen pen. The children made surprised noises as they looked at the ground in shock.

The scroll floated away from Rugrat, rising up above him. The paper burned, condensing; runes on the paper burned in concert with the paper, forming on the ground.

The last rune was completed as the paper turned into a crystal.

There was a flash of light as the group disappeared.

A circle one hundred meters wide, which had been filled with people and supplies, was turned into barren dirt, no sign of the nearly two hundred people who had been there just moments before.

Silence fell over Alva Village. Wind whistled through the abandoned homes, the broken defenses and craters.

68
EGBERT

The village vanished in a flash of light. They were in a dimly lit cavern. The dim runes above them were the cavern's source of light, some thirty meters above them.

The floor near them was also glowing, its light dying down. It looked as if it were the fixed location for the teleport scroll.

The ground was smooth; one section showed a dimly lit line that led into the center of the cavern. Erik traced them back to three different buildings that were around a twenty-meter tall cylindrical device that was covered in bands of magical runes that slowly moved around.

The entire place gave off an old feeling, as if a once great power had once controlled this area but they had disappeared.

This sense made Erik eager to explore and discover more.

"Have the archers hold here. Section One, Two, and Three of the heavy infantry and quick reaction force will move with us to explore those buildings," Erik ordered Blaze and Glosil.

Quickly they got themselves organized and moved along the dim path toward the cylinder building and the three that surrounded it on one side.

As they moved closer, the buildings came into focus. The largest looked to be a sort of manor. Rugrat said that the other looked like a smithy.

Rugrat went to the cylinder. Erik went to the unknown building, with Blaze heading to the manor. Each of them commanded a heavy infantry section while the quick reaction force were tasked with looking over the smithy.

Erik had his shotgun out as he nodded at the heavy infantry soldier. They pulled open the door and Erik moved in, his shotgun up and looking around. The rest of the heavy infantry section followed in, their swords at the ready.

Erik was hit with the smells of old plants. Erik and the heavy infantry continued to push through the building, trying to discover its secrets.

"All clear," Erik said as they went through the last room.

Erik lowered his shotgun and looked at the cauldron on top of a cold hearth.

"What do you think this place is? Some kind of kitchen?" Sergeant Choi asked.

"No, I think this is an Alchemy workshop," Erik said.

The rest of the heavy infantry looked at one another.

"Let's see what the others have found," Erik said.

The people in the manor were still looking through the large building. The smithy was mostly open, with only the storage area and furnace being enclosed.

Storbon walked up to Erik to give his report. "Sir, we found some tools and ores in the smithy. We also found a large and complicated item that has magical circles on it. We don't know if it's a tool or not." Storbon sounded confused.

"Good work." Erik was about to say more when someone jogged over from the large cylinder building with the rotating bands of runes.

"Rugrat said to tell you that the building is the dungeon's core." The man looked to be disturbed about something, taking a moment before continuing. "He, uhh, well, he found something and, I'm not sure what it is, really."

Erik's brows knit together before he walked toward the dungeon core. "Sergeant Choi, go and help out Blaze. Storbon, patrol the area."

They moved to carry out his orders as he walked to the door leading into the dungeon core. He went up a set of stairs that spiralled upward. He could see into the center.

On the ground floor, there was a complex magical formation. It seemed to be drawing power inward to its center. The power collected together, forming a thin beam of blue light that shot up and into a series of floating inscribed metal bands. The bands went from small to big; the largest was fixed in position as the others slowly rotated in different directions.

From the main floating metal band, brighter blue Mana was channeled out, hitting magical circles, the power disappearing.

If I was to guess, then it looks like some kind of reactor. As he rose to the second part of the building, there was a crystal tube that extended from the magical reactor to the ceiling. Around it there were six shimmering and flickering images.

Rugrat was studying these different circles.

"This the dungeon core?" Erik looked around the room.

"Yeah. Look at this." Rugrat reached for the circle at the top and drew it out. The other circles became smaller as Erik was looking at a representation of the floor they were on, including the villagers who were moving around. It was like the village interface but this gave real-time updates on what was happening on the floor.

Erik could see Blaze exiting the manor and talking to the sergeants, sending them to patrol the area and sending a group to pass word to the villagers.

"So, only we can make building decisions in the dungeon and we can only make them in this room," Rugrat said.

"How did you find that out?" Erik asked. He hadn't received a notification.

"I told him!" a somewhat familiar voice yelled out with indignation.

A bony head appeared out of Rugrat's storage.

"Not now, Egbert!" Rugrat yelled, smacking the skeleton on the top of the head as it disappeared back into his storage ring. "You were saying?" Rugrat coughed, as if nothing happened.

Erik pinched the bridge of his nose. "Is there a skeleton in your storage ring?"

"*Maybe.*"

"Is there a *talking* skeleton in your storage ring?"

"*Maybe.*"

"*Why* is there a TALKING SKELETON IN YOUR STORAGE RING?"

"I wanted a souvenir?"

"I'm not a souvenir!" An angry voice came from Rugrat's ring.

"Don't make me come down there, Egbert!"

"You named it Egbert?" Erik asked.

"Not an it! I'm a *he*." Egbert's head appeared, all skull and glowing blue flames in his eyes.

"Egbert, not the time!" Rugrat stuffed Egbert back into his storage ring.

Erik looked at the ceiling, as if seeking strength from it. "Let the damn talking skeleton out of the storage bag."

"Come on, I thought he'd be a cool party guest—you know, let people think he's a mannequin and then he moves." Rugrat started laughing as he imagined it. "We'd get so many people!" Rugrat had to clear a tear out of his eye from the laughter.

"I am not a mannequin!" An indignant voice came from the storage ring.

Erik looked at Rugrat before the latter gave in.

He let out a sigh as "Egbert" was revealed.

"You're pretty skinny, huh?" Erik asked.

"I'm a damn skeleton—what do you expect me to be, overweight?" the skeleton yelled back.

Rugrat made eye contact and tapped his finger on his storage ring, sharing a look with Erik.

"No, you're not going to stuff him back in your storage ring," Erik reprimanded.

"But—" Rugrat started.

"Go and play with your rifle in the corner," Erik said.

"*You* go and play with your rifle in the corner," Rugrat muttered, kicking a rock that went flying into Egbert's ribcage, knocking out a rib and rattling around.

"I just fixed that one!" Egbert complained as Rugrat put his hands behind his back, whistled, and walked away as he looked up at the ceiling.

"You're the voice that gave us tasks!" Erik snapped his fingers, remembering the grandiose voice that kept on messing up and even got exasperated when Erik and Rugrat had rested for a few days instead of directly challenging the Beast Mountains trial.

"Yes, that was me. Oh, I guess you both became Dungeon Masters of Beast Mountains Dungeon."

A screen appeared in front of Erik.

> Egbert, the skeleton and caretaker of the Beast Mountains Dungeon, swears his undying loyalty to you and to carry out your orders with the best of his abilities.

Just reading this, Erik could tell that this oath wasn't like those that the other department heads had made. This basically made Egbert do everything that they said, without consequences.

If they ordered the department heads to do something they didn't like, then it might go against their conscience and they would break their contract based on their unwillingness to carry out these tasks.

"All right, Egbert, why are you here? What is the Beast Mountains trial really and what happened to this place?"

Rugrat stopped trying to look away and focused on Egbert as well.

"These things are directly connected. First, this Beast Mountains Dungeon was created in large part by a group of gnomes. They were a very advanced group of gnomes and looked to creating their own world away from the burning sunlight. They created the different levels of the dungeon. My master led them, wanting to create a utopia. That was, until a human entered the dungeon. He was but a child and my master took mercy on him.

"He raised the boy as his own, taught him what he knew. The gnomes accepted him as well, but their trust was misplaced.

"The boy grew up and created his own plans. He broke the power formations in the dungeon, opening it up to the Beast Mountains and letting in the powerful beasts around us. He even looked to steal the Mana seed that rested in the heart of the dungeon core.

"When my master, who considered himself the boy's father, confronted him, the boy, drunk with power, used the Mana seed on his body and attacked my master.

"My master was close to death, but not willing to let his mistake hurt others, he killed the boy he considered his son.

"The gnomes had taken too many losses. Many were killed; others had escaped.

"My master sealed off this level from the others and ordered me to start the Beast Mountains trials. He stored a piece of his soul before he passed away to assess those who might become the master of this dungeon.

"The Beast Mountains trial was not made for people to just kill beasts; it was made to find the new dungeon master, or masters. The ability to react to threats without thought was the trial with the snakes in the grass, to take one's time and plan was sneaking around the second beast. To know not only how to fight but also have other skills and desires. To look out for others and have a good character." Egbert didn't need to say anything more. These directly related to the trials and parts of the quest that they had gone through.

"The current state of the Beast Mountains is due in large part to that boy's actions. Most of the dungeon was in chaos. Multiple buildings were destroyed here. I cleared them away and even destroyed others to use their resources to fuel the dungeon core and keep it active. I kept my master's home in honor of him, the smithy to fix the few Vzztpsshts that were left, and the Alchemy workshop to create powders to assist my own body and allow me to keep living. There are six levels in total." Egbert pushed the expanded floor they were on back into place. "We are on the Neutral floor at the top. Below us there is the metal floor. This floor was made with massive metal attribute gathering formations and arrays. Rare metal seeds were added to this area, as well as different metal Affinity beasts, creating an entire ecosystem.

"In the same style, the next floor is the Earth floor. This is covered in growing pastures, with a natural light that gives one the warmth of the sun, without the damaging effects that affect gnomes. Then there is the Fire floor. This is a world of magma and volcanoes. Below that is the Wood floor, a vast forest with all kinds of natural druids, nymphs, will 'o wisp and other woodland creatures.

"The sixth floor is the Water domain and one of the deepest. This floor has a radius of one kilometer and is thirty meters tall. The lower domains or levels have the diameter of ten kilometers and are three hundred meters tall, except for the Water domain that is three kilometers from surface to its depths.

"When the boy opened the teleportation arrays and allowed other creatures into the different domains, they turned from a peaceful ecosystem into a war zone. There are many unbonded creatures that roam around wildly that are no longer connected to this dungeon.

"Their actions have inflicted massive damage on the different formations and arrays. I have been unable to repair or care for them as I neither have the knowledge nor the ability. My combat functions were locked by my previous master as he wanted me to focus on finding a new dungeon master. There are massive Mana gathering relays that connect the different floors. These were meant to draw power in, to grow the Mana seed that is downstairs. The power flow is just not enough to do so. The relays have been broken off and disconnected and there isn't much ambient Mana in this domain. I have needed to supply it with Mana stones. I have enough to run the dungeon for another five centuries—well, I *did* until some people decided to bring nearly two hundred people and their crap with them," Egbert grumbled.

"How much power do we have left?" Erik asked.

"Enough for five months on standby," Egbert said.

"If we wanted to teleport everyone out of here, with our power usage, how much power would it take?"

"About thirty Mana stones. After four months, there would not be enough power left to teleport everyone out."

"Is there a way to repair the relays and increase the amount of power we gain?" Rugrat asked.

"Look at the brains on this one, right? Like, I'm only made of bones and I can figure that one out." Egbert's blue flame orbs rolled in his eyes.

"No need to be a dick about it," Rugrat complained.

Egbert looked at his femurs, while raising his hands. "Low blow, dude," Egbert said.

Just what I needed, another friggin' comedian. Erik somehow felt that the old dungeon master was laughing at his pitiful expression.

69

A NEW PLACE, A NEW PROBLEM

Quest: Restoring Beast Mountains Dungeon Part 1
Congratulations! You have taken control of the Beast Mountains Dungeon. Its condition isn't the best and it will require work to repair. I hope you brought a hammer! Or crafters.
Requirements:
Repair the main Mana Gathering formation
Repair the secondary Mana Gathering formations (0/10)
Repair the Metal Beast controlling formations (0/3)
Repair the containment formation
Repair containment formation sub-arrays (0/12)
Activate KnghTNG mining machines (0/4)
Rewards:
Up to 200 ore per day
+100 Mana per day
+1,200,000 EXP

The screen appeared in front of Erik and Rugrat.

"What's a KnghTNG?" Erik asked.

"A KnghTNG breaks down rocks and pulls them out of the ground. The gnomes' naming conventions were a bit *different.*"

Rugrat and Erik looked to him with clear questions.

"Okay, so they named things based on the sounds that they made most of the time."

"So what's a Vzztpssht?" Rugrat followed up.

"There are a couple different types, but they're basically Mana-powered items that can do the work of people. They were used for jobs that no one else wanted to do, primarily," Egbert said awkwardly.

"A genius race that named a robot Vzztpssht," Rugrat muttered.

Egbert looked as if he were trying to find some thread of hope to grab onto. "Yes," he finally said, deflating as much as a skeleton could.

"What is the power used for?" Erik asked.

"A part is used to keep the different formations running, as well as the Vzztpsshts that maintain them. I have needed to activate more formations upon the arrival of more people, so that the city's air isn't toxic. More power is needed to use the smithy and Alchemy workshop."

"Okay, so what are our options for getting more energy?" Erik asked.

"The first is to repair the formations in the metal domain. First, we need to reconnect the formation there to the one we control here. With that active and if the formation in the metal domain isn't too broken, we'll be able to gather some more Mana. Then go system by system, repairing them. I would not suggest this method. I would instead suggest we go with the second and third option. We fuel the dungeon with Mana stones and gather Mana cornerstones, or you take the core of another dungeon."

"How do we take the core of another dungeon and what is a Mana stone or cornerstone?" Erik asked.

"Now you are dungeon masters, if you are to beat a dungeon and make it to the end of the dungeon, you can control it—take it over for your own, or you can destroy it. You take the resources of the dungeon and its core. Mana stones are stones formed from Mana. They have different grades but they are useful for people looking to increase their Mana Gathering system, or any Mana-based system. They're the primary currency in the higher realms. A Mana cornerstone is the seed of a Mana mine. If given enough time, they will increase the ambient Mana in an area and produce Mana stones. These are more long-term power solutions. Given enough time, then the entire dungeon can run off these, but they're incredibly expensive and rare."

Erik was filled with even more questions.

"Okay, first, do you have any information on the formations, like pictures or documents?" Rugrat asked.

"Certainly. I have all information resources contained in here as well as other valuable supplies." Egbert pulled one of his finger bones out; the rest of his finger didn't collapse as he held it out.

Rugrat pulled his head back into his neck trying to get away without moving, revealing a few unflattering chins. "That ain't natural."

Erik took the finger bone; even he shivered a bit as he looked inside the ring.

It was filled with books and scrolls. It wasn't a simple storage device, either: it had sixteen square meters of room, putting it in as a Lesser Earth grade storage item, worth three hundred gold.

There were some potions and other organic goods kept inside as well.

"The main Mana Gathering formation looks like this." Egbert moved his hands through the light in the center of the room. A massive formation appeared. Multiple shapes were linked together. The hologram became layered; not only were there shapes within shapes, but they were up to twelve layers deep within that.

"Do you know what needs to be repaired?" Erik asked, seeing Rugrat's lost look as he tried to find something familiar in the image.

"This section needs to be fixed to link our floor to the Mana Gathering relay there." Egbert circled a section and expanded it.

To Erik, it looked like a pile of coding. He had no idea what it was trying to tell him.

"Will the robots be able to fix it?" Erik asked, seeing that Rugrat was still clearly in over his head.

"They can perform maintenance but they don't have the ability to repair the formation," Egbert said.

"Looks like we're going to need to get a dungeon core." Erik sighed.

"Yeah, that shit is way too complicated." Rugrat shook his head. "Leave me with my weapon formations—those massive area arrays are a nightmare."

"There are a lot of different dungeons," Egbert said.

"A skeleton!" Blaze's voice came from the stairs as he looked at Rugrat and Erik talking to Egbert.

Erik realized that Blaze was pale as he shivered slightly, holding up his sword.

"Blaze, this is Egbert. You can lower your sword; he's controlled by Erik and me," Rugrat said, reassuring Blaze.

"It's a skeleton, a creation of dark magic and necromancy!"

"Hey! You tell your mom and dad that!" Egbert said indignantly.

A weird expression appeared on Erik's face.

"You insulting my parents, demon-born!" Blaze yelled, his color coming back.

"You insulting mine, you pipsqueak ting user!"

"Ting?" Erik had to ask.

"That thing." Egbert pointed at the sword.

"Gnome naming conventions?" Rugrat and Erik looked at each other.

Blaze looked thoroughly confused at Erik and Rugrat's relaxed manner.

"What's going on, Blaze?" Erik asked.

"We've found another building on the level. It looks to be some kind of stables. We haven't sent people to investigate. There are also piles of materials stacked with some weird machines around them. They look like the one that is in the smithy. The villagers are moving to the central area." Blaze lowered his sword even as he looked sideways at Egbert, who bit his teeth together loudly.

"Egbert, stop growling at the guests," Rugrat said.

"Wasn't growling," Egbert complained under his breath.

Does he even breathe? Erik disregarded this and cleared his throat.

"Good work, Blaze. We'll be down in a minute," Erik said.

"Sir." Blaze cast another look at Egbert, who was making a fist, rotating his hand around the other.

His pinky finger flipped up. "Oh sorry, I didn't know that would happen!" Egbert said, sounding pure as virgin snow.

Blaze looked to Erik and Rugrat, clearly confused as well.

"I think he meant the middle finger," Rugrat said.

Erik nodded while Blaze's confusion increased.

"So, dungeons and their cores?" Erik asked.

Blaze walked away, opening his mouth and closing it as the others talked. He simply shook his head and walked downstairs, talking about the devil's creatures and their curses.

"There are three kinds of dungeons. Free or random dungeons that aren't controlled by anyone and have been randomly created or formed. Then there are controlled dungeons; these have been created by something or someone, meaning that they usually have their own dungeon master. Then there are special dungeons; these dungeons can be controlled, but they cannot be destroyed. Only a dungeon master can destroy or take over a dungeon."

"So we need to destroy a dungeon, take its core, and then that should increase the amount of power that we get?" Erik asked.

"Doesn't sound too hard," Rugrat said.

"There are only a few dungeons in the First Realm. Most are in the higher realms. With them having more ambient Mana, it is easier to support their Mana needs. I can give you a skill through the Ten Realms that will allow you to sense dungeons." Egbert waved his hand; a golden spell formation appeared above his hand and he passed over two parchments.

Skill: Dungeon Sense
You can sense dungeons within a 5km radius. As you increase the level of your dungeon, your dungeon sense's power will increase.
Can be cast once per day.
Cooldown: 1 day

"Is there anything else we can use to increase the Mana we have?" Rugrat asked.

"Anything that contains power, really. If you cast spells, not all of the Mana is used—most spells are pretty wasteful—the Mana Gathering formation will naturally collect this Mana and bring it back to the Mana seed. If one just pours their Mana out while in the Mana Gathering formation, again, this will increase the flow of Mana. Monster cores, people or creatures dying." Egbert shrugged.

"Monster cores?" Erik tossed Egbert a Lesser Mortal monster core.

"Really? Monster core and you give me this bauble? I'd need about fifty of these to have enough power for one more day," Egbert said.

"Should give us a few more weeks," Rugrat said.

"How much power does it take to teleport five people back to the Beast Mountains Range?" Erik asked.

"One Mana stone, though you can just take the emergency exits," Egbert said.

"If we had the people killing in the Beast Mountains Range, they could increase their strength, get more resources, go to the border villages, and sell off the goods we have, then feed the monster cores to the dungeon?" Erik thought aloud, looking to Rugrat.

"Doesn't sound like a horrible plan to me. Though, if we really want to solve this problem, we're going to need to head to the Second Realm as soon as possible to get another dungeon core to stabilize this one," Rugrat said.

"I'm interested in what might be waiting for us in the Second Realm." Erik couldn't deny the allure.

70

RETURNING TO THE BEAST MOUNTAINS

Quest: Restore Power
The Beast Mountains Dungeon is under threat. To a dungeon, Mana is its lifeblood. You must find a way to increase the Mana produced in the Dungeon or a new way to produce Mana.
Requirements:
[Use adventurers to increase your power]
OR
[Repair the main Mana Gathering formation]
[Repair the secondary Mana Gathering formations (0/10)]
OR
[Capture a common Mortal Dungeon core, or equivalent dungeon cores, to fuse with main dungeon core]
OR
[Use 50 Mana stones to recover the dungeon core]
OR
[Use Greater Earth grade Monster Core]
Rewards:
Dungeon core recovers partially [1/12]
Mana per day generated increases based on repairs (can use more than one method)
Experience (based on results and time)

Erik closed the screen and looked at Rugrat, who was scanning through the different manuals Egbert had given them. "Anything?" Erik asked.

Rugrat rubbed his eyes and let out a sigh. "From what I can tell, the gnomes who made this place were at least masters of formations. They might have been bordering on Expert. I simply don't know that much about formations. I've been looking into weapon enhancements with arrays, not massive ground-based formations like these. It'll take time before I'm able to get to that stage, or we'll need to find someone who's capable of repairing them."

"Looks like it's about time to head to the Second Realm," Erik said.

The room seemed to chill a bit as Rugrat's face turned cold.

"I haven't forgotten about Chonglu City," Erik said. His voice was calm but his blood boiled thinking about the attack. It was the closest city to them with a Ten Realms totem.

There was a noise on the stairs. Rugrat put away the reading materials he had been looking over as Erik rose to greet them.

Elise, Jasper, Taran, Glosil, and Blaze all walked into the dungeon Village Hall.

Blaze had warned them about Egbert, but they were still all stunned by his appearance.

"Oh, hey there, boys and girl," Egbert said, daintily waving his fingers on one hand as he crossed his knees and held a hand in front of his face as if he were blushing.

They all shivered and paused their steps.

"Little bit of flattery and they're all, 'It's a skeleton,'" Egbert said to Erik.

"Stop scaring them," Erik said.

Egbert seemed dejected but moved off to the side.

"Please, sit down. We've got a lot to talk about," Erik said.

Everyone moved to the seats and the table that Egbert had pulled out from one of his storage fingers. He had removed it from the room to be more efficient. Now it sat in the middle of the room with the six levels of the dungeon floating above it.

"This is Egbert, our resident guide to the Beast Mountains Dungeon. He's oath-sworn to obey all of Rugrat and my commands. He's a bit…*quirky* but we'll get used to him."

Egbert seemed pretty happy to be called quirky as he perked up at the side of the room.

"First of all, we have a power issue. We've got four months of power left in the dungeon. Rugrat has been looking at the plans and it won't be a simple thing to fix the dungeon and increase our power."

"Also, the creatures on the lower levels can be up to level twenty, at least what I've seen," Egbert added.

"So, we don't want to be going down there and we need to get more power somehow," Erik continued. "We've got a lot of options but ultimately, we need to have groups head to the Second Realm to try to get what we need. At the same time, we want to build up the dungeon here so that we have a base and a place to rest. First, we need to care for our own needs: food, water, housing, and infirmary."

"Umm, I might have forgotten something," Egbert said.

You have taken over the Beast Mountains Dungeon
Construction ability unlocked
Blueprint store unlocked
Resource interface unlocked

Resources
Food: 6,350 Units
Stone: 54,000 Units
Wood: 215 Units
Mana: 235
Gold: 91

Upkeep costs:
161 Units of Food per week
4 Gold per week
1 Mana per day

You have gained control of:
Dungeon Core
Manor
Beast Stables
Smithy
Citizens: 184 (Trained, Morale increases by 20%; working together, they are 10% more productive)

Erik felt as if he were directly connected to the dungeon now. As he thought of it, a large map appeared in his vision. It showed him everything happening on the living floor of the dungeon. He waved to the side and saw the metal Affinity floor; it was hazier than the living floor. When he waved his hand again, the next floor—Earth—was even hazier, and it was hard to make out any distinctive shapes.

Erik returned to the first floor and saw that there was a glowing blue outline around the dungeon core. The outline changed as the interior of the building was altered. It turned red as the building was unable to support itself. It took shape in a few moments.

"Okay, that's useful as hell," Rugrat said, calling Erik back to reality. He dismissed the screen as the others in the room looked at them with concern.

"Was that you messing with the building?" Erik asked, looking at the pieces of paper in front of Rugrat.

"Yeah, so the construction ability allows us to put down blueprints of buildings. So we can plan out buildings and place them down, just like you could in strategy games," Rugrat said. "The difference is that we can modify the blueprints or make them as we want. I'm guessing that we will be able to buy them from the store as we could in Alva Village."

"I've just got a message from one of my guards. It looks like a blueprint has appeared around the dungeon core," Glosil said.

"Will it be easier to build than if they were to make it themselves?" Erik asked. If he could groom a few architects, then they could design all of the buildings they needed instead of wasting their gold. The construction ability would allow them to use people who weren't trained in construction much more efficiently. As the fine arrow blueprint improved the quality and the speed that the people of Alva Village could produce arrows, this construction system would allow them to do the same.

"Egbert, can you put the living floor on the table?" Erik asked.

With a few gestures, the floor appeared in the middle of the table.

Now Erik could see information ringing his vision as he looked at the table. If he stared at the information, it would pop out at him, giving him a more detailed insight.

He selected the house that Rugrat had designed and put it in the middle of the table. It was a two-story structure with a living room, kitchen, and bathroom on the first floor; upstairs, there were two bedrooms and two bathrooms.

"Do you think it would be okay to do one house per family for now?" Erik asked.

"Wait, you want to give a family this house?" Elise asked.

"Yes," Erik said, finding her reaction strange.

"This kind of house is something that only nobles would find," Elise said.

Rugrat and Erik could see that this was a common idea between the others in the room.

"This will be the current standard for homes within the dungeon. In the future, we will make improvements and upgrades," Rugrat said.

"Other than houses, we will need to build a school, a hospital, an area that we can grow crops, and a warehouse district to hold the goods that we brought and the ones we will get in the future. Also, we will need to build a market square to allow people to trade among one another and sell to the trading houses that will venture out to the other villages and cities around the Beast Mountains." Erik looked into everyone's eyes.

"This is just the start of the Beast Mountains Dungeon. Going forward, we will develop the dungeon together. People will work—growing crops, building up the village, hunting and patrolling the area around the dungeon, or going on trade convoys to other villages and increasing their knowledge in the academy. To progress, we need to increase our strength first. I want to build up sources of food and the infrastructure of the dungeon, or at least have everything in place before we leave. We will leave you with a plan and as of right now, you are all part of the dungeon's council. A replacement can only be picked by us, but you can vote to build more things and change items in the living floor," Erik said.

A light appeared around the others as a screen appeared in front of their eyes.

Elise agreed to the screen and pushed it away. She was the first to do so. "Then we're going to need to build a marketplace if we want to buy new blueprints. Also, how can we upload new building blueprints into the system?" she asked.

"As long as the blueprints are brought here, then one can test them out. The construction ability makes it so that people don't need to design an entirely new blueprint. They can use building blocks from different buildings that are in the dungeon's storage. Think of it as a prototype and testing tool—you can check the building out here, then you put it down in the dungeon and people can see the parts they have to make to complete it. This way, with each building, you can accurately estimate the resource cost," Egbert said.

"It wasn't possible to do this in Alva Village," Blaze said.

"Did you have an architectural school of study in Alva Village?" Egbert asked.

"No," Blaze said.

"Then you wouldn't have been able to unlock this. The Beast Mountains Dungeon had one in the past. Certain things have been unlocked ahead of their time because of what the gnomes did and the fact that my master has given this to you freely instead of you taking over the dungeon. If you took it over, then you would have to start from the beginning. Now there are buildings you will need to create or things you need to do to unlock other abilities. You will not be able to just get Alchemy recipes because we have an Alchemy workshop and had alchemists in the past. I only have a few manuals from the gnomes that used to live here, but I still remember a lot of what I have read or the gnomes said around me. I don't know what all of it means so while I can give you the information you need to find people that are capable of using that knowledge."

As long as we can advance a little, then with the knowledge that Egbert kept from the gnomes, we'll be able to advance a lot further. Erik looked to Rugrat. He had some Novice knowledge of formations, but looking at the formations in the dungeon, he was lost. If he learned more, he might be able to understand them and advance his skill faster.

71
RAPID EXPANSION

Erik's idea was alarming, not because of his words but the scope of it.

"What about people who might want to leave?" Blaze asked. They had come to Beast Mountains Dungeon but some might want to leave to venture through the Ten Realms.

"They are free to leave and return as they desire but for our safety, they will need to make an oath to not reveal anything about Beast Mountains Dungeon. If they come into trouble and they need help, then we will do what we can to help," Rugrat said.

"On the military side of things, what do you want to happen?" Glosil asked.

"Sections of the military will be dispatched to protect our trading convoys, others to gain Experience in the Beast Mountains and secure a safe place around the entrance to the dungeon. They will protect and defend the dungeon and also look to go on scouting forays to see what is on the other levels." Erik roughly explained what was happening in the other levels that had been cut off, where the creatures had turned wild, being placed into essentially holy lands of different Affinities.

He didn't miss the glow that appeared in everyone's eyes. If they could get access to these areas, then their strength would only increase.

"Our first priority is to build up the dungeon, to make it habitable. Then clear the area around the dungeon and establish contact with villages to trade with. From there, we will focus internally in growing our own strength. This might be sending people on missions to other cities to establish ties, or to higher realms. I won't lie to you. I want to keep Beast Mountains Dungeon a secret as it will give us a base to increase our strength dramatically. Still, we must not become insular; we need to keep our eyes open, to create the role of recruiter. These people will look for those who might not have a high ability, but they are driven and loyal. If they are driven and loyal, then, with lessons and resources, we can turn them into powerhouses. Also, Blaze, I want you to set up a mercenary outfit, the Alva Mercenaries. This way, our people will be able to increase their fighting abilities and gain resources."

"I will see to it," Blaze said.

Erik picked him as Blaze had interacted the most with the outside world, being a knight captain and someone who lived in a massive city.

"Jasper, it will be your job to establish trade with other villages. This will be to sell our products and take on further building jobs. These jobs can be passed to the crafters who we will look to develop in the Beast Mountains. Both of you will be the eyes and ears of Beast Mountains Dungeon. It will fall on you to recruit talents and increase the dungeon's reach."

Jasper and Blaze stood a bit taller, hearing the importance of their new roles.

"Elise, you will be in charge of the city. At the beginning, this will be a multitude of building projects, then it will turn to managing the people as well as the workshops and the academy. The library will be free to access for everyone. If someone wants to attend the academy, they must pay a fee to show their commitment. They will be supplied with housing, food, and studying supplies to push them forward. Taran, I hope that you will assist Elise in this endeavor?" Erik looked to the burly smithy.

"You have my word." Taran wasn't one to bow, but his word was good.

"I plan on building not only an academy where teachers will be paid to nurture students and their abilities, but also a formation workshop, woodworking shop, tailors, and a cookhouse to raise formation masters, tailors, carpenters, and chefs. We have a great number of works from the gnomes on these different crafts. People may use these facilities, but they will need to pay a fee and supply their own materials. We have seen how just having a spear or a crossbow can greatly increase our fighting strength and a good meal can increase our recovery speed. With this support, I expect great things for Beast Mountains Dungeon. I also propose that we rename the dungeon to Alva Dungeon," Erik said.

His words were calm and slow, but they were nonetheless shocking.

"With this, we…I can't even begin to imagine what would happen. If we told people that we even had these kinds of workshops and an academy, people would come from miles around," Blaze said.

"I think that changing it to Alva Dungeon makes sense. I also agree with Blaze and it makes me understand why you want us to make oaths to not release this information. Other cities don't have this ability. Cities need to have a certain population or groups enter their cities before they can build these different places. With the gnomes' knowledge, we can pass this gap in one jump. If cities and people were to learn of this, they would come and wipe us out for these treasures. Forget the First Realm—even people from higher realms would be tempted," Elise said.

"We will move forward together to increase our strength." Erik knew that although he might be interested in a lot of different things, there was no way that he could complete it all by himself.

Rugrat was interested in smithing and formations; Erik in healing and Alchemy. Those were just four different paths. Backing was everything in the Ten Realms. If one was able to get good gear and to have the best training aids, then their path would be smoother and easier to travel.

Erik and Rugrat didn't have this kind of backing, nor did the people of Alva. If they could rely on themselves to create it, they wouldn't need to worry about these issues anymore.

They took another couple of hours to iron out the details before the meeting came to an end. All of the department heads gave oaths to not reveal anything about Alva Dungeon to any outsiders.

The dungeon was still dark when everyone left. There was a lot to be done still.

Erik and Rugrat stretched; their night was still young.

"Okay, so, blueprint time?" Rugrat asked.

"Blueprint time." Erik called up the construction interface.

Blueprints
Alchemy Lab
Smithy
Formation Workshop
Tailors
Cookhouse
Mana Mine
Stone Mine
Growing House
House
Beast Stables
Barracks
Market Square

Clicking on each of the blueprints, they could see the blueprint of each building with different modifications. Next to them was the resource cost. Most of them were blocked off as their Mana requirements were too high.

"First of all, we need to remove the need for these to rely on Mana. We can hook them up later when we have more power to spare," Erik said.

"Always with the hard stuff." Rugrat pulled out some diagrams and put them on the table. "Egbert, can these be added to the blueprints?"

Erik looked over. They were the plans for the logging camp, wall, watchtowers, as well as public bathrooms and showers. They had made all of these things in Alva Village. Rugrat, working closely with the construction crews, got a set of detailed plans that he was now using.

Egbert looked at the plans. He waved his hands and they disappeared. "You know, you could just use the input function," Egbert complained.

New Blueprints added:
Logging Camp
Wall
Watchtowers
Showers—public
Bathrooms—public

"Now we just need to build a hospital and an academy," Erik said.

"You want to do the hospital—I'll do the academy?" Rugrat asked.

"Works for me," Erik said.

With the blueprint tool, Erik was able to use components from the other blueprints and combine them in new ways, like blueprint copy and paste.

The hospital was extremely rudimentary. There was a seating area up front, a reception and then behind it, there was a large medical bay. Its layout was simple: a bunch of beds with dividing curtains. There were showers and bathrooms as well as supply rooms.

"Different from the healing houses I've seen," Egbert commented.

"Oh?" Erik said, as he entered the "hospital" into the system. Right now, he wanted to have the basic buildings. It would be up to later architects and crafters to update and modify them as needed.

"Most healing houses look like an upscale manor as they treat only the rich and nobles. This is much simpler, focused on treating as many people as possible, instead of making them feel important," Egbert said.

Erik looked over to Rugrat's designs. The academy had four entrances. It was shaped like a square, with L-shaped buildings at each of the corners; each corner building had six classrooms that could hold thirty people. Rugrat had only made the basic structure; again, modifying them would be up to the users.

Other than the classrooms, there was a main building in the middle of the academy's grounds. It was the largest by far and it had three stories, with each floor getting bigger.

It looked incredibly solid.

"What's the main building?" Erik asked.

"The library. On the first floor, there will be Novice-grade books; on the second level, Apprentice; the third, Journeyman. Other books will be held onto by the staff until we can build more floors."

Erik nodded. He liked the people of Alva, but he didn't know whether they could ignore the allure of Master and Expert books. The collection Egbert had given them was vast and mainly consisted of Expert-level information.

Erik looked at the map of the floor. "Shall we start?" Erik asked.

"All right, but we should group things together." Rugrat added a few modifiers as a circular grid line appeared around the dungeon core.

"To our nine o'clock, we have the beast stables. I think we both agree that the barracks should be there. Not only are they right next to the beast stables where they can get mounts, they'll be right on top of the emergency exit, allowing them to react if anyone tries to force their way in. We've also got a road already to that area, so we don't need to do anything else."

Erik nodded. Rugrat didn't waste any time and put down the barracks. It was based on gnome design but all of the formations wouldn't be added in. It was a simple courtyard for training, with places for soldiers to sleep, take care of their gear and learn new fighting skills.

"Tracing back to the dungeon. We have this free area from half five to one o'clock. We can turn that into housing, keep them away from all of the workshops," Rugrat said.

"Let's put a hospital as a midway between the dungeon core and the barracks. That way, if people are hurt in the living areas they can easily get aid—also, if we're in a fight, then the people at the barracks aren't too far," Erik said.

He put down his rudimentary hospital. Then they laid down where roads were going to be through the housing area. It was very linear as they didn't want to waste space. At the twelve o'clock position, they put down a large market that would meet up with the dungeon core and extend halfway down the housing district. Behind it would be a warehousing district; continuing clockwise, one would enter the academics and workshop area.

The cookhouse bordered the market area, and then the academy. It was the largest building, with the woodworking and formation workshop behind it, the smithy and Alchemy lab in front. Continuing down, there was the manor with the tailors behind it and several large growing areas. These were basically greenhouses that would supply the people with constant food.

"All right, so how are we going to sort out pay?" Rugrat asked.

"We will give everyone a house, but then they will sign a contract to build everything we've planned out. We will pay people who prove themselves to be capable teachers, as well as the military. Librarians and the merchants will get a commission based off what they sell and how much. People will pay a fee to use the market; warehouse space will be rented. We will pay farmers for the growing houses and we will own everything that comes out of them. Those who go to the schools will have to pay a fee, but they can sell whatever they make. We will take a ten percent tax on anything that is sold inside the city." Erik outlined his ideas in broad strokes.

"Priorities for building?" Rugrat fired off.

"Barracks, hospital, growing houses, homes, academy, workshops, warehouse district, and market square," Erik said after a moment's thought, looking to Rugrat.

"Makes sense to me. First, we need to have some defenses, then the military can kill beasts and we can start trying to grow crops, bringing resources in. Right now, we have places that people can sleep. They're not comfortable, but they're survivable. I would also say that we build temporary showers and bathrooms and a water treatment center. Roska would only need to use a separation and purification spell and our water would be clean. With formations, we could automate the process but that would take more power," Rugrat added.

"It always comes down to the amount of power we have. At least we've got tons of resources left over from the gnome buildings," Erik said.

"While your people work in shifts, the robots can also help to build the structures all the time. It will cost energy, so they're best used for laborious and time-intensive but simple jobs, freeing up your people to focus on studies and increasing their strength." Egbert, seeing he had their attention, continued. "They can also be powered by monster cores instead of straight Mana stones."

"Have them start taking supplies needed over to the barracks location and the growing areas. Egbert, I want you to talk to Elise and tell her about their abilities. Using a mix of our own people and the machines will save us time and effort.

"You think there's anything else that we might be forgetting?" Erik asked Rugrat.

"Probably, but I don't know what it would be. The sooner we go dungeon hunting, the better. I trust our people," Rugrat said.

"Yeah." Erik wanted to experience the building, but he needed to find that dungeon core.

"Looks like it's time for another adventure." He checked his quests. "I still need to get those damn Alchemy ingredients."

72
PARTIES

Elise woke up on the hard floor. It wasn't that comfortable but she had slept on worse before. She cracked her back and headed for the open area around the dungeon core. She stopped walking as she saw four-legged robots moving materials with their manipulators. They looked like some kind of beetle as they worked without pause.

Elise's eyes adjusted as she looked at the blueprints that appeared all around the main area. She was left in stunned silence by it all.

The houses were simple but they were much better than anything they had in Alva Village. There was an entire district made for teaching and learning, even a marketplace with stalls. Seeing it all, a sense of anticipation and excitement filled her. It was the first and most basic step, but it showed where they would go.

She thought on what had been said at the meeting. "We've got a long way to go, but nothing is impossible," she said to herself with a smile on her face.

Erik and Rugrat were sitting with the sergeants of Alva's fighting forces as well as Blaze and Glosil.

Everyone's attention was on Erik and Rugrat.

"So far, your training, weapons, armor, and skills were passed to you out of necessity and lack of time. You have built a foundation and now it's time to build upon it. We don't have massive numbers and we don't need them to fight effectively. We will fight in parties, when outside of the dungeon. You will be classed as Warrior, Ranger, Medic, Mage, and Support. This leaves each role sufficiently broad for future development and individual development. Not every fight requires a warrior with a shield and some people will probably excel at wielding a spear or two-handed sword, but they would still be stuck into 'tank with shield.' Your focus should be in finding what your talent is and pursuing it fully. Go to the academy, talk to Egbert, talk to your fellow fighters—gain knowledge here, test it out when you're outside of the dungeon in the Beast Mountains. Although the main focus of the military is to fight, parties need to be adaptive, to deal with all kinds of situations.

"Support will be a broad category. I envision this as anything from specialists gathering personnel who excel at getting difficult to procure metals and herbs to specialist beast tamers caring for mounts and long-range / stealth / secure communications 'pets' and smiths, repair troops, hunters. In the future, we will go to the other levels. We will encounter different beasts, different situations, need to repair formations or fight different creatures. We cannot be rigid in our thinking or our fighting." Erik looked around the room, making sure that his words struck home. People were excited but they were also focused on his words.

"Also, there will be combat fanatics among you. I wish to make a new kind of school, a fighting school that will focus on fighting techniques. It will be based in the barracks with people trading fighting techniques and information. Based upon people's performances, they might also join the specialized groups, like the quick reaction force, gaining permission to head to the higher realms in order to train and broaden their horizons. These spec teams will carry out the highest priority missions, encountering the greatest dangers."

A wave of muttering and excited chatter went through the room. On one side, there was increasing their power; on the other, there was rewards for doing well, the enticement of the Second Realm and beyond.

Erik smiled slightly, seeing the drive and excitement in their eyes.

"Sergeants will be in charge of groups no more than five. There will be mandatory missions. These might be to investigate an area, or if Alva Dungeon is under attack, all of you will return to your original positions and fight. When there aren't mandatory things for you to do, it is the duty of each party to increase your overall fighting strength. To this end, enrollment in the academy will be cut in half. You will get a bi-monthly wage, cheaper weapons, armor, and other items as they become available at the market. You may also get bonuses at the end of the year based on performances. If you die in the line of duty, then your family will receive a monetary benefit, equal to half of your yearly wage, paid out for ten years. You will become the scouts for Alva Dungeon in the other realms and in the surrounding area. You will also be their shield and sword, ready to defend and ensure the safety of the village," Erik finished.

Chris, one of the sergeants, had suggested the roles. It was based off the mercenary guilds and groups he had talked with before. With the party system, it meant that increasing their strength was their responsibility.

They were strong but they simply didn't have the numbers to create a true military. Instead, he went along the path of making a number of groups. He was looking to emulate Special Forces groups back on Earth. He would give them a mission and direction, letting them plan and execute their plan; through working together and relying on one another, they would become incredibly close. Erik knew that a well-coordinated section's strength couldn't be compared to a weak and uncoordinated platoon.

In their downtime, their training would be left to them. The better they did, the greater the rewards. It would create competition between the different parties, but as they all came from the same root, when called back they would work together to defeat the enemy.

"Over the next month, you will form these parties. Your orders will come directly from Captains Glosil and Blaze. Teams will be located in defensive and offensive roles, changing every six months," Erik said.

He could see the interest in the sergeants' eyes. They had grown quickly, but now it was their chance to prove themselves, to go and truly experience the world.

Adding in the fact that they would be working to make their home stronger and safer, it filled them with a sense of pride and anticipation.

"Captain Blaze, your missions are to scout and then secure the surrounding area. After that, there are retrieval missions." Erik pulled out prepared pieces of paper with information jotted on them. These were all of the locations for the different ingredients that Alchemist Tommins was looking for.

This would allow Erik to collect the ingredients he needed, test out the new party system and give him time to look over the day-to-day running of Alva Dungeon.

"Understood," Blaze said, accepting the missions and bowing slightly.

"We will leave you to it," Erik said.

The entire group rose to their feet and saluted as they passed.

The quick reaction force was waiting for them behind the sergeants, a lost look on their faces.

"Why do you look so down? Do you think we would forget about you troublemakers?" Rugrat laughed.

They all looked up, with interest.

"Storbon! Roska!" Erik barked out.

"Sir!" The two people stepped forward looking off into the distance.

"Storbon you will be leader of the first special team, Roska you will be in charge of the second special team. Storbon you and your people will have some time off before you head to Chonglu and the second realm. Once there, you will have four months to learn as much as possible before returning to the First Realm and Alva Dungeon. You will report to Glosil and Blaze for your next task," Erik said.

"Yes sir!" Storbon saluted.

"Roska! You will be under the direct command of Glosil and Blaze. The aim of your team will be to increase your combat strength and prepare for the return of the first special team to begin your own operations in the second realm."

"Yes sir!" Roska said, both Roska and Storbon's eyes were shining but their faces remained steady albeit twitching a bit.

There were shocked looks. A few people looked a bit lost. Being away from home for a long period of time and relying only on a few people around them—it wouldn't be simple.

"Don't worry, you can do this. I hope that in four months you'll have been able to greatly advance your own strength. Anything that you make on these trips is yours to keep," Rugrat said, reading their emotions easily.

Erik watched on. He could see that Blaze and Glosil were discussing what the new changes meant to the sergeants and the look in the quick reaction force's eyes.

I don't know where all of this will lead, but with a strong base and the ability to venture freely, even if they're only military in name, I hope that when called they'll be ready to assist. In the future, if we get more missions, we can offer these to the different groups, allowing them to increase their strength and gain more resources. Who knows, we might be something close to an adventurer's guild by the end of this all. I wonder if there is an adventurer's guild here? Erik thought.

On the night of the second day, construction started. Once they learned what the blueprints were all about and having them explained by Egbert—who they were wary of but were getting used to—they got to work.

Elise was running a tight ship, and Jasper was putting together a trade convoy that would travel with Erik and Rugrat up to the Wild Reaches Trading Outpost.

She caught snippets of conversation as she worked on the growing houses block.

"What do you think about this four month nonsense?" one man asked his friend as they worked.

"What about this place losing power in four months and us having to leave?" the other asked.

"Yeah, do you think that Erik and Rugrat will be able to keep this place running?"

"Well, we thought that we were all doomed with the beast horde coming. What's so hard about finding a dungeon core or whatever? They only had a week and a half and they saved us from the beast horde. Now they've got four months. I can't even imagine what Alva Dungeon will look like by then." The other laughed.

The first man let out a short laugh. "Too right! I was scared over nothing. I heard that there are also groups heading up to the surface, but one has to take oaths to not reveal our location. Smart move, I think!"

"It might be annoying, but if no one knows we're here then no one can threaten us. I want to start learning formation arrays. There are a lot of them in the dungeon, but no one knows how to repair them. If I can learn that, then I'll be able to take some of the weight from the department head's shoulders," the second younger man said.

"Formations, huh? I think I want to try my hand at cooking. I never realized the flavor one could put into a meal. And the buffs! I heard from Lucile's brother in-law that he was reading some of the Apprentice cooking books and they stated that one could recover their wounds just by eating higher level meals! Some could increase their strength!"

"You just want to eat all day!" his partner accused him. "And 'higher' level, do you mean journeyman level meals?"

Elise smiled and continued on with her work, finding Rugrat working on the growing area.

"Rugrat, I didn't know you were here." She was flustered that the dungeon master was helping to build up the simple structure.

"Thought I'd help out a bit. How is it going?" Rugrat asked.

Elise wanted to complain about him being out here and helping but she also knew he would just wave it off with that goofy grin of his. "Much faster than I thought. With everyone's high levels, people are stronger, faster, and better coordinated. While the robots continuously bring us supplies, the barracks is nearly complete and the hospital's foundation has been laid. And the first ring of roads has been started. It should take three weeks before we're able to complete the first stage of building, with the hospital, homes, barracks, water treatment plant and growing area; another two weeks to complete the second stage, with the workhouses and academy, marketplace, and warehouse district."

Rugrat's eyebrows rose slightly. "Damn. I still have a hard time trying to wrap my head around the fact that even a level three in the Ten Realms would be like a comic book hero back home." Rugrat shook his head.

Are they really from the Ten Realms? Every so often, they slip up and say something out of the ordinary. And they have different ways of doing things compared to people I have met in the Ten Realms.

"Well, I'll help finish this section off, then I said that I would go and do some smithing with Taran. He's going to beat me in climbing the skill ranks at this rate!" Rugrat joked.

Elise gave a half smile. She knew that Taran spent all of his time in the new smithy.

To him, the smithy was like a newborn: nothing was allowed to touch it without his say-so. He had got the fires in the furnace going and he worked until he fell asleep in the smithy, or was dragged away.

He looked disheveled, but Elise couldn't deny the increase in strength his techniques and creations had gained.

It wasn't this that plagued her thoughts, though. Finally she built up the strength to ask a question she had avoided.

"Rugrat, are you and Erik really from the Ten Realms? I've heard that every few thousand years, people from other places will be teleported into the Ten Realms, to change things up. Though I thought that this was a lie, but the way you train, your equipment, those *rifles* you used against the beast horde—they're unlike anything I've seen before." Once she started talking, she couldn't stop.

Rugrat's smile dimmed as he looked over Elise. She felt as though he were assessing and judging her.

"That's right, Erik and I aren't from the Ten Realms. We're from a place called Earth that doesn't have a lot of the things one might find here in the Ten Realms."

"Are there others?" Elise asked.

"Yes, there are others, but the fact is that we haven't run into any of them. There were some ten thousand people who disappeared, or must have been teleported here. There are a few billion people in the First Realm. Trying to find them will be incredibly hard and there is no knowing if they will help us or try to hinder us," Rugrat said.

"Do you want to find them?" Elise asked.

"It's not our job to try to find everyone who came from our planet. Even if we did, there's no knowing what might happen. We might meet them in the future." Rugrat shrugged.

Elise had suspected for a long time but it was only now that it had been confirmed, she felt embarrassed. "Unless you or Erik allow me to, I will not share this information with anyone till the day I die, I swear on the Ten Realms." The power of the Ten Realms descended as she made her oath.

Rugrat had a bitter smile as a screen appeared in front of him. "Seems like I have been seeing these oaths more often than not." He laughed and accepted it. He continued in a softer voice, "Thank you."

Elise only smiled. "Well, once we have the market up and running, I'll be able to put in the market interface. With that, we can start buying and selling to other dungeon masters and city masters."

"I'm interested to see what they're like," Rugrat said truthfully.

Elise didn't know how to answer him as she thought of the Alva Dungeon's scale. Looking around, she could just barely see the edges of the first floor and it was only half the size of the other four floors, with the last floor being at least twenty times the size.

73

RETURN TO THE BEAST MOUNTAINS

Erik and Rugrat left the dungeon core. On the ground, one could see markers that lined out the different buildings that they had input.

The Vzztpssht, beetle-looking machines, started to move around, carrying resources with their front forks and placing the building materials at the side of these marked-out areas.

One of the patrols was watching them warily, their weapons in hand.

"Sergeant Choi," Erik said.

"Mister Erik, Rugrat, what are the markings and those metal machines?" Sergeant Choi asked, his expression tense.

"Those are robotic helpers. It's their job to move materials to the new work sites. The markings are where we'll build houses, academies, workshops, and other areas for the dungeon," Rugrat said.

"Houses, an academy?" one of the soldiers asked, looking stunned.

"Well, we can't very well keep sleeping on the ground." Erik smiled.

The soldier looked away awkwardly as he caught Sergeant Choi's glare. "No, sir!" the soldier responded, embarrassed by his outburst.

Where the robots dropped off the materials, the marked-off area would show where the materials were to be placed.

"You might need this," Egbert said from behind Erik and Rugrat, tossing them two scrolls.

The soldiers all gripped their weapons tighter, seeing the skeleton.

"Don't worry about him. That's Egbert." Erik looked at the scroll.

It was a spell scroll.

"Binding scroll—it allows one to bind materials together," Rugrat said.

Technique Book: Materials Binding
Do you wish to activate this Technique book? Doing so will destroy this Technique book.
YES/NO

Erik called up Egbert. "How many of these scrolls do you have?" Erik didn't want to waste them.

"About fifty or so," Egbert replied.

"Do you have any other technique books?" Erik asked.

"I've got spells from Novice to Expert. Most are simple spells for building," Egbert said.

"Go to Elise when she wakes up and give her a full accounting of all the materials and items that you have," Erik said. *If I can get my hands on some healing spells, or on spell formations so that I can make my own spells…*

Erik was pleased with the spells he had, but it felt as if he were using a multi-tool for everything; he didn't have the tools for more complicated procedures or problems.

"Understood," Egbert said.

Erik closed the channel and pressed YES on the scroll.

The scroll started to burn up, shooting out a ray of light into his brow.

You have learned the spell: Materials Binding. Your spell book has been updated.

Rugrat did the same. The soldiers could only look on in anticipation.

Erik moved toward where the hospital was to be built. He easily picked up the stone bricks. His strength was great enough that the heavy slab barely weighed anything. He carried a handful of them and looked at where there was a glowing blue light. He placed a brick down where it appeared and another light appeared next to it.

Erik bound the stone with the floor. He pulled on it, but there wasn't the slightest bit of give. Satisfied, he repeated the process, putting the next brick into its place. The building blueprint showed him exactly where to place the next piece.

Erik quickly ran out of stones. As he stood up, he could see a percentage bar in the middle of the hospital.

Hospital: 1% Complete
8 Hours til completion

"Catch!" Rugrat yelled out.

Erik, catching the rock, looked over to Rugrat. "Really?"

"Speed things up a bit!" Rugrat yelled back.

Erik felt a new energy filling him. He put down the stone brick and bound it to the floor; he stood up, catching the next brick that Rugrat had thrown over and bound it. He moved forward, catching another, and continued the process.

"Much too dirty in here. Hopefully the new masters will be able to build the new homes quickly," Egbert tuttered as Elise's eyes trembled before she opened her eyes.

She frowned as she looked up at Egbert, who was inspecting the smithy she was sleeping in.

"Egbert?" She pulled up her blanket.

"It's not like you're naked. Look at me—I've got my bones out all the time. Much more freeing, I tell you. Erik ordered me to give you this. It's a full accounting of all the resources and items that I contain." Egbert pulled out a scroll and passed it to Elise. "I'll go and see if I can help out the masters now." Egbert turned and left the smithy.

Elise looked at the scroll in her possession. Egbert was a strange one but she didn't feel any malice from him.

Why do I feel that he's begrudgingly happy under it all? Maybe he's been missing contact with other people? Elise didn't know the workings of an undead skeleton's mind and let it go as she opened the scroll.

It was itemized into different categories with separate stats for different items. She opened it up and her shock only increased. There didn't seem to be many simple things. Spell technique books were something that were originally from the Second Realm. Only someone from a powerful nation or sect in the First Realm would be able to acquire them. Just looking at this list, there were dozens of different basic spell scrolls and technique books.

"Expert-level information books?" Her eyes went wide as she shook.

Finding these in higher realms is hard unless you have a powerful backer. Is this the information that Erik and Rugrat want to place in their library? Getting just the chance to read a Journeyman book might be some people's aspirations in the Mortal realms!

Elise quickly put the scroll away. She needed to find Erik and Rugrat. She headed out of the smithy to the main area around the dungeon core. Already Jasper had his people preparing breakfast. Elise looked around before seeing a patrol. She quickly moved over to meet them.

"Miss Elise," Sergeant Niemm said in greeting.

"Where is everyone? Shouldn't there be more people?" Elise asked.

"Ah, well, most of them are helping with the hospital and the barracks," Niemm said with a smile. "Mister Erik and Rugrat started working on it early this morning. Others who weren't able to sleep went over and started helping out. I've never seen a building built so fast!"

"Where is the hospital?" Elise remembered the two talking about it, but they had been planning everything out after she left.

"Down Nine O'clock Street that meets up with the beast stables." Niemm pointed to one of the rune roads.

"Thank you." Elise moved down the road and could see the one-story building. It hadn't existed last night but now it was in the last stages of building. There wasn't a slate or tiled roof; instead, the roof was made from furs to protect from the draft.

All around here, there were markings that broke up the space. Piles of bricks lay in the middle of these locations. Around the hospital, crews were hurling bricks from these piles to their fellows who laid them down, following the blueprint. Their hands glowed with magical runes as they cast spells on the bricks and the floor.

Elise was in shock as she looked around. *There are fifteen people who are using spells? There were only five spellcasters when the beast horde arrived! What's going on?*

She walked up to one of the blueprints where people were chatting with one another, quickly assembling the building at an incredible speed.

House: 15% Complete
4 Hours til completion

"Miss Elise, is there something I can help you with?" Gu Tao, a burly-looking fellow, stood at the pile of bricks. He was throwing the bricks as if they were nothing. Everyone's levels had shot up, greatly increasing their attributes.

"Umm…" Elise's mind was still reeling. "Will this house really be finished in four hours?"

"If we had more people, we could do it faster." Gu Tao frowned. "Also, these don't have any runes in them and they won't be finished with lights or a roof until the second crew comes through. We're just making the walls and then the structure for the first and second floor."

"Do you know where Erik and Rugrat are?"

"They're probably up at the barracks. I heard that they might be racing each other at who can lay bricks faster." Gu Tao laughed, looking toward the beast stables.

"Thank you." Elise followed where he was looking. She could see that there was a building in the distance now next to the beast stables.

"No problem, miss!" Gu Tao said.

As they were talking, he never stopped throwing, supplying three different bricklayers as they simply caught, cast their spells, and caught the next, moving along the wall at a walking pace.

Elise moved toward the barracks and looked around. It looked as though everyone who was awake was working in the outlined areas that were meant for houses. Egbert was talking with a group. Elise walked nearby, listening in.

"Now these are mining picks. Make sure that the edges are smooth. If they're not, it will be hard to fit all of the piping and the cover stones," Egbert said.

Elise watched as she was walking. The crews turned to face different ways; glowing squares appeared in front of them as they swung their picks. The front group was meant to break up the rock while the second cleaned up the excess.

With their strength, each blow with the pick sent rocks flying. Their picks started to get into a rhythm as they walked forward. Behind them, they left a two-feet deep path. Panels were brought over and laid next to this path. They were rune panels, complete with sewer lines. The runes had been left unpowered; otherwise it was completely fine.

She could see the entire dungeon being built up at a speed visible to the eye. The sense of progress had her excited about what was to come and pushed her fears away.

"And you were scared that this was the wrong decision," she chided herself. But making any kind of big leap like this would make one hesitant.

She made it to the barracks. The walls here were much thicker and different sections were in various stages of progress. She walked through what looked to be the main gate. The towers on either side were being built.

People were talking and the sounds of work could be heard all around.

The soldiers, in their shirts and pants, helped out. There was a cafeteria, housing, training areas, an armory, and then the massive thick walls that enclosed the entire place. There was enough room for two hundred people, not just the sixty or so who had stayed as part of the army.

They were only focusing on the walls and some of the housing; the rest would be completed later if more people joined the military.

She saw Erik and Rugrat were building the outer wall facing away from the city. The stone was as big as a man's torso, cut into blocks.

Erik and Rugrat handled them as if they were just large boxes, easily catching them, placing them down and using the spell she had seen the other builders using to fuse it to the other materials around.

To keep up with them, two soldiers were throwing to them each.

In the space of a few minutes, they had done the base layer and they were moving higher.

"Done!" Rugrat jumped off the wall just a few minutes later and dropped to the ground.

Erik put the last stone in place and jumped down to the ground as well.

"What's going on?" Elise asked.

"Just a bit of friendly competition," Rugrat said.

"No, like last night I went to bed and there wasn't anything—now there are houses popping up, you made a hospital, and there are roads going in!"

"Oh, that," Rugrat said. "We did some planning and then we wanted to test out how these blueprints really work."

Seeing the playful grins on their faces, she could tell that they were indeed telling the truth. The previous images were once again shattered as she couldn't help but show an amused smile.

"Oh, Egbert gave me this this morning." She held out a scroll to Erik and Rugrat.

Rugrat opened it, with Erik looking over his shoulder. He perused through the scroll, his eyes getting bigger as he looked through it all. Rugrat's hands paused as they got to the smithing materials section. "Where's that skeleton!" he yelled out.

Erik grabbed the scroll from Rugrat and moved through to the section on Alchemy materials. "You go toward the six—I'll go to the twelve! Get his finger bones!" Erik yelled. The two of them ran out of the barracks.

"He's down the road, near the hospital!" Elise yelled out.

The two idiots who had been sprinting to the right and left curved back around in a comical display of speed as they left trails of dust running into the city.

"What was that all about?" Blaze asked.

"Well…" Elise thought about the things she had seen on the scroll. "I think that we're in for some big changes."

"Big changes? You ever seen a house built in an *hour*?" Blaze asked.

"Not really," Elise said.

"Even though these are blueprints, making so many buildings, someone would be able to learn something about construction. I swear that half of the people here will reach at least Apprentice skill level in construction!" Blaze said, loud enough that the soldiers heard.

They had been paying attention to their conversation and slowed their actions down; now they sped up.

Elise saw the sly smile on Blaze's face. It was true that crafters could increase their skill level by working with a blueprint related to their skill. It guided them to build higher quality items than what they could make themselves. If they could learn from the blueprint, then they could increase the quality and level of their own creations.

One might need to grind out plenty of blueprints, but the allure of learning a skill was high: they could get a random item, more Experience, and the modifiers could make their lives easier.

Elise thought on the markings she had seen around Alva. There were plenty of buildings to grind out.

74
ACADEMY STAFF

Rugrat and Erik had found Egbert with Elise's instructions and looted his spatial bones. He cut a sorry figure, missing so many bones, as Erik and Rugrat rushed off again like bandits.

Rugrat ran right to the smithy while Erik went to the Alchemy lab.

Most people were awake and having breakfast, leaving only a few people in the smithy.

Taran was already heating up the forge. Thankfully, with taking down his old furnace, he could use his fuel to start this furnace instead of relying on the Mana-powered flames.

"Taran!" Rugrat stormed into the room.

"What is it?" Taran's brows knit together at Rugrat's wide smile and excited expression.

Rugrat didn't say anything but threw out several blueprints onto the work surface.

"More blue…" Taran's heart thudded in his chest as he unconsciously adjusted his hands, holding the blueprint like a cherished child. "Oh, look at you—just…perfect." There were tears in Taran's eyes as he stroked the top of the forging blueprint lovingly.

A few people nearby glanced at one another in question.

"Is Taran crying?"

"What did Rugrat give him?" another asked, looking in at the blueprints.

"I just have some coal in my eye, you bunch of eavesdroppers!" Taran yelled, rubbing at his eyes and slamming the door shut.

The two eavesdroppers looked at each other.

"Definitely crying."

The other nodded in agreement.

Taran moved to the workshop's surface and looked over the forging blueprints. There was three in total. Two apprentice and one Journeyman level forging blueprint lay in front of him.

Rugrat laughed and waved Egbert's fibula. Materials appeared across the furnace room—all kinds of metal ingots, and even five smithing manuals.

Taran stumbled backward, his face white as he looked at Rugrat's smiling face. He nearly sat down, but seeing it was a pile of materials, he hurriedly stood up, still cradling that first forging blueprint in his arms. Seeing this all, he had moved straight past crying to shock.

"Right!" Rugrat said, his eyes shining as he saw it all. "These are all from the gnomes who were here before as well as the previous master. He was a smith and formation master. Everything he had he gave over to Egbert, who gave it over to us now. Manuals, blueprints, materials."

This was the wealth of the gnome civilization that had lived in Alva Dungeon. Their inheritance wasn't light.

Rugrat looked at Taran. The look in his eyes made Taran hold the blueprint in his arms tighter.

"Though only people who attend the academy will have access to the blueprints, the manuals and other information will be for everyone." Rugrat had dropped the hook and Taran had gone for it completely. Now he was reeling it in.

Taran had a depressed look on his face. He had to admit that Rugrat had him good.

Manuals were good, but they were theoretical. Taran had reached this skill level in smithing making hundreds of items, working with all kinds of materials. Practical experience was the basis of his skill. To him, the manuals were only surface material compared to what he might learn using these blueprints.

"I'll be your damn smithing teacher," Taran muttered.

"Good to hear, Principal Taran!" Rugrat announced.

"Principal! Wait a damn minute!" Taran waved a finger as Rugrat started to stoke the furnace fire.

"You going to stand there or you going to forge something, man!" Rugrat yelled as he waved the leg bones again, collected the treasures back inside and tossed it to Taran.

"Why is it stored in a bone?"

"Egbert might have a new set of trust issues," Rugrat said seriously.

Taran opened and closed his mouth and looked at the leg, fighting between disgust and knowing what was inside. "Argh!" He let out an angry growl but put the forging blueprint down on the workstation and pulled out iron ingots from his own storage ring as he started to heat it up.

Jia Feng looked to the others who had been gathered with her by Jasper.

He had been given an order by Erik to round them up. Jia Feng was the most advanced cook in Alva Dungeon. Shi Wanshu was the architect of the logging camp and the watchtowers. Both of them had benefited from the different technique scrolls that they had been awarded.

The last member of their group was Zhou Heng. He was a quiet man with a strange appearance. He didn't look physically odd, but his clothes were immaculate. Even though he had repaired them multiple times, he took his time to make sure that the quality of his repairs couldn't be seen. He was a farmer by day but he had repaired most people's clothes. He even made the guards' old leather armor.

"Did Jasper tell you what this was all about?" Shi Wanshu asked Jia Feng.

"He didn't know. He just said that Erik wanted to see us all," Jia Feng said.

Zhou Heng looked over to the smithy that was going at full blast. One could hear hammers repeatedly banging metal into shape. There was little emotion on his face as he looked back to the Alchemy lab. "We will find out soon enough." Zhou Heng stepped forward.

The others were startled into action, following him.

They entered the lab. Even now there was an old medicinal smell to the place.

"You stole my femur!" Egbert's voice could be heard, with a noncommittal reply.

"I had to walk back using my knees as my hip joints! I lost a foot and a half!" Egbert's voice reached new heights.

Everyone paused when hearing this.

"Could you be quieter? It's hard to concentrate," Erik replied, seemingly unaffected.

"Y-you!" Egbert yelled.

"I thought that this was filled with nothing but information manuals! More than three quarters are these romance books, like the Lewd Knights, Wilderness Borne and the Lusty Argo..."

"Hey! Who said that they were all the gnomes books! A man has to read you know! You only needed to ask and I could lend them to you! Those are *classics*!" Egbert said.

"But," *You don't even have the mechanics, do skeletons get freaky... how would that! No mind! No why did you do that!*

"No stop that, get out of my head, ughh, oh god I think I'm going to be sick, how could a skeleton, *ughk!*

Erik dry heaved for some time as Egbert talked at him, extolling the virtues of each of the books. It seemed his interests were heavily in the romance category.

"You're not even paying attention! Fine, what are the four stages of Alchemy?" Egbert asked, his fury reaching new heights.

Erik, happy to have something to distract him about the thoughts of skeleton mating held his head as he replied.

"Growing, harvesting, preparing, and formation."

The three in the hall looked at one another, not knowing whether to advance or stay where they were.

"What do the stages mean?" Egbert demanded, pressing Erik.

"Growing deals with the growth of the plant. Many alchemists create their own gardens of items in different regions or specific formations that will improve the growth and quality of the different ingredients. Also, alchemists might splice together different plants and strains to create more powerful ingredients. Sometimes extremely rare ingredients won't be grown, but are found in hard to find and secretive locations, such as dungeons, ancient realms, and other special locations. Whether the ingredient is located in one's own garden, or within a hidden cave, harvesting is vitally important, as is storage.

"If the ingredient is not harvested properly, then it might become useless. Many heroes travel with at least one person who is well versed in harvesting so that they might claim these ingredients to sell or use them later. One must also store these plants in containers that complement the ingredient or else the efficacy might decline.

"Then there is the preparation. This is made when you confirm you want to make a specific alchemic product, such as a powder, potion, or pill. For different alchemic formulas, ingredients might need to be prepared in a variety of ways—sometimes boiled, other times burned, chopped up, ground down, frozen, or grilled. Methods of preparation of the ingredients will have a vastly different outcome when you move to the last stage, which is formation. Forming a powder is the easiest; a potion is much harder and creating a pill is in another level of difficulty.

"The more suitable and tailored growing conditions for the plant, the greater the efficacy. If it is harvested properly and stored in the right container, it will retain the highest level of efficacy, with the preparation drawing out this potential for it to be combined with other ingredients in the formation stage according to an alchemic formula to create a substance that will have a great effect on whoever consumes it."

Erik's words were calm and relaxed, as if this was all natural.

"Hmmpf. Well, it looks like you've learned something. You still need to practice growing, then harvesting and preparation. Forming a powder is too advanced right now. Build a firm foundation and you'll advance faster. Take this scroll. It's one of the five compendiums on ingredients. It should help you out greatly. You have guests." The door opened to the corridor as Egbert appeared. His upper legs were missing and he held one femur in his left hand. He was missing multiple finger bones and his left fibula.

The three in the hall looked at him in his disheveled state.

"Come on in," Erik said from the Alchemy room.

The three shuffled in. Egbert was about to leave when Erik stopped him.

"Egbert, I have a plan for you too." He tossed Egbert his other femur.

Egbert caught it. He seemed to think for a minute before he closed the door and moved to the side. He pulled his legs off and started to put himself back together.

"Jia Feng, our most skilled cook, Zhou Heng, the leading tailor in Alva, and Shi Wanshu, architect and woodworker." Erik looked at them each in turn. "I want to hire you all."

His words sat in the air, heavy and ambiguous.

"What job might we need to do that involves us all?" Shi Wanshu asked. He was the most familiar with Erik.

"I want to raise you to be grandmasters in your field. As you know, Alva Dungeon was once a city of gnomes. They had reached a high standard in all manner of crafting disciplines. I need people who are motivated to learn and are willing to teach others. You will be paid to teach others and you will have full use of the academy as well as the workshops. Resources can be subsidized at the beginning and will be sold to you at cheaper prices than they would be at the market. You might be called from time to time to assist Alva Dungeon in one manner or another for compensation. Anything that you create will be yours to do with as you see fit. Taran has already been given the position as principal of the academy. Jia Feng, you would teach cooking." Erik pulled out a thick book and put it on the preparation table in front of him.

Jia Feng's eyes went wide as she read the book's cover. *Apprentice's cookbook, simple but delicious dishes.*

"Zhou Heng, a teacher to tailors." Erik put out a tailor blueprint for a simple pair of pants that were elegant in nature, with simple designs running through them. *Discreet animal hide light armor pants.*

Zhou Heng's breathing turned faster.

"Shi Wanshu, a teacher of woodworking and hopefully architect." A model appeared on the table. It was a wood house but the detailing was exquisite, as if someone had just shrunk a house down.

"Egbert, I'd like for you to be in charge of materials and the library. You know much more than we do about these subjects and it will be your goal to assist people increasing their knowledge and skills by supplying them with the information that they require," Erik said.

Egbert slowed down what he was doing. "It would be my honor," Egbert said, sounding strangely serious.

Erik had a small smile as he looked to the other three.

"I would be honored," Zhou Heng said, losing his quiet and calm composure.

Erik's smile widened.

"Me too!" Jia Feng couldn't hold back. Seeing that book in front of her, she just wanted to snatch it up and read.

"I as well!" Shi Wanshu didn't want to be left out.

"I thank you all for your time. Egbert is well versed in a great number of these disciplines. There are plenty more information sources under his protection."

Erik tossed over a few bones at Egbert. A weird attraction force pulled them back into their original places.

"These are still materials of the academy, so do not lose or damage them. Otherwise you will have to pay or replace them," Erik warned.

Jia Feng slowed her hands and gingerly took the book instead of just snatching it. Just smelling the book made her mouth water.

"What will the academy be called?" Egbert asked.

"Kanesh Academy," Erik said.

Egbert looked deeply touched as he bowed. Erik lowered his head to Egbert as well before Egbert led them out of the room.

Erik pulled out a number of books, covering the table once again. In his hands, a large and heavy book appeared.

A bright white light came from under the door. Jia Feng looked back at the door in alarm.

"Mother fuc—" There was a thud of a head hitting a table before silence.

"Looks like he used the entire compendium in one shot," Egbert said simply, sounding a little impressed as he continued walking.

"Should we help him?" Shi Wanshu asked.

"If one uses technique books, there is a lot of information contained within. It can overload people's minds unless they are of a higher level. For lower-level people, it might be too much and they fall unconscious. Don't worry. With his recovery abilities, he'll be fine in a few hours," Egbert said.

They continued out of the building as Jia Feng finally asked a question that had been confusing her. "What does Kanesh mean?"

"Kanesh? It was the name of this floor." Egbert's voice turned sober.

Jia Feng understood now. It was paying homage to the gnomes who had organized and created this knowledge.

75

SCOUTS AND SECOND PHASE

Four days had passed since the academy teachers were appointed.

In those four days, Alva Dungeon had been a hive of activity. All of the department heads had posted recruitment posters for farmers, soldiers, traders, and more. People were rushing to apply for different jobs. By the third day, all the positions had been filled.

The first phase had been completed. Now all that was left was to build the academy, workshops, warehouse, and the market.

The different teachers were looking forward to having new facilities. They had unlimited access to the information left behind by the gnomes. Jia Feng had taken over the manor's kitchen. Zhou Heng had taken over an open plot of land, sitting there for hours, studying different fabrics, testing out new ideas with the materials he had.

Shi Wanshu altered between building plans on the construction interface in the dungeon core and whittling down wood, using different techniques to carve out incredibly detailed statues and other items.

All of them shut out the rest of the world, spending their time increasing their abilities. Erik spent his time in the growing areas, using his Plant Cultivation spell.

They had already gone through one harvest. Erik submersed himself in plants, focusing on the first and second stages, growing and harvesting.

If he focused on just one plant, then it was possible for him to bring them to harvest in a few hours. Like this, he grew multiple kinds of plants, growing his Alchemy skill.

Rugrat and Taran did nothing but use the smithy. Thankfully, with the houses completed, people could get away from them.

People also learned about what the academy offered and went looking for Egbert for reading materials. He had taken up residence in the academy grounds. He exerted his true strength, focusing on building the academy's library. He made some adjustments, turning the three-story structure into a proud hexagonal tower with six stories.

People could only watch in awe as he used spells, carrying hundreds of stones at once, stacking them on top of one another. The tower shot up in the space of a day.

He also commissioned bookshelves from Shi Wanshu.

Egbert was in charge of testing, the library, and counseling. He was blunt with his assessment but it was usually right on the mark. Armed with a magic testing crystal, he could tell the Affinity of one's magic. Based on his knowledge, with a few questions, he was able to figure out what discipline would best suit those who appeared in front of him.

Taran might be the missing head of the academy but Egbert was its heart. Taran had already handed over the running to Egbert. The skeleton complained but one could tell that he was excited to be around people again. His character didn't change much but his demeanor became softer dealing with people, making a genuine effort to advance their strength.

Other than the sounds of construction and work, the academy grounds were silent, with people reading all manner of books in the courtyards. If they were stuck on something, they would go talk to Egbert. Only when they passed a test he put forth would he offer his assistance and guide them forward, looking to correct the holes in their knowledge.

Erik opened his skill sheet. Although his gains hadn't been massive, with his growing and harvesting, he had been able to improve upon his Alchemy skill.

Skill: Alchemy
Level: 17 (Novice)
No bonuses at this time. You must prove your skills first.

He'd even gained some Experience. Although becoming a higher level would diminish the rewards that one would get from killing creatures of the same or lower level, when increasing one's skills, the Experience gain was constant according to levels. But when one reached a higher skill level or if they repeatedly made the same item or concoction again and again, then the skill level wouldn't increase. After all, their skill level was adjusted based on their ability, not on the number of times that they replicated the result.

Basically, if you wanted to get a higher level, you simply couldn't grind out the same dagger; if you improved the dagger or made it with higher stats and abilities, then you would get more Experience and your skill level could also increase.

61,234/195,000 EXP till you reach Level 16

Erik dismissed the screen and bent down to inspect the blood fruit at his feet. This was a juicy, bulbous-looking plant that shone in the light. It slowly moved the reflected light, which made the fruit look like a beating heart.

Erik felt someone approaching. He dismissed his Simple Organic Scan as he looked up. Around him, there was a small garden, just a ten-meter-by-two-meter space, full of all kinds of plants. Breathing in the air, one would feel refreshed by the aromas. Erik had gained these seedlings from Egbert and put his full effort into understanding them.

Erik felt it was ridiculous at first, but with time he came to understand the different ways the plants interacted with one another and even moved their positions so that they benefited one another.

Plants could have different Affinities. Putting them in the right positions would allow them to increase one another's strength, creating a type of planting array.

Erik had been totally focused on improving the speed that the plants grew at, but also the efficacy of the final product.

He had read about all of these different ingredients and absorbed their information through the compendium that had knocked him out. Reading about them and then handling them personally was two different things. He had learned the basics but applying that knowledge was no simple matter.

Erik felt as if he were learning to be a medic again. When in training, it was so simple, but when one had to carry out their job in the field, training could only get you so far; the rest was on you.

Rugrat looked around the garden, surprised by the rapid growth. "I can faintly feel that my Mana Regeneration has increased."

"Most of these plants are geared toward increasing one's Mana flow. They can be used in Mana recovery concoctions. Each of them complement the other, so that the products they excrete benefit the others. Come here." Erik moved to the middle of the plants.

Here one could feel Mana moving through their Mana channels. It was soothing and relaxing. If someone stayed here for months, they might see their Mana channels cleared out and the purity of their Mana increase.

Rugrat moved forward and let out a satisfied sigh. After a few seconds, he frowned and looked at Erik. "You—did you recover your lost Mana drop?"

"I recovered it and condensed another drop." Erik smiled. His total Mana drops had now reached three. If he could reach four, he would just need to condense them together into a core and he would open his final Mana gate.

Being at the focal point in the garden, the Mana he pulled in was refined by the different plants, making it easier to condense into a single drop.

In this garden, Erik's senses were heightened.

"You opened a new Mana gate!" Erik said.

Rugrat laughed and shrugged. He didn't hide anything as he activated all twelve of his Mana gates.

Mana in the surrounding area settled down as if their master had arrived, bowing in deference.

Erik felt that his own Mana system was slightly suppressed. "When using all of your Mana gates, there's a faint suppression on others in the same area?"

"Yeah, that makes sense with the new title," Rugrat said.

"New title?" Erik asked.

Rugrat stopped purposefully using his Mana gates. "Well, as one increases the Mana gates that they open, every one past your tenth, you get a new title," Rugrat said, coming clean.

"Little fucker. I should have known that you were keeping something from me."

"Well, you ready to check out the Beast Mountains?" Rugrat asked, quickly changing the subject.

"Fine, but tell me how you opened your twelfth Mana gate." Erik moved away from his garden and headed through the now defined Alva Dungeon. Around the dungeon Village Hall, the different buildings were all done except for the market; that would come with the second phase.

"As I've been training with smithing, I've been improving my control over Mana. I took some time not just forming my Mana into shapes, but trying to create different items—not just the form of a spear but a true spear, condensed down and with runes.

"I studied up on Mana Manipulation formations that could be used with weapons and added those to the Mana-formed weapons. It took me a number of days and I needed to do it multiple times with real metal and formation before I could do it with Mana-formed ones. Then I drove them into my Mana gate; the runes on the weapons focused and directed my Mana, increasing their strength and blasting through my Mana gate. Honestly, it was kind of like the Mana-created weapon was an electric motor plugged right into my Mana. I just had to focus on drawing in more Mana from around me and it fed into the Mana weapon, cracking open my gate," Rugrat said.

As they had walked, they passed through the center of the dungeon and were passing through the houses, almost reaching the hospital.

"If you can do that internally, I wonder if there is a way to do it externally," Erik said.

"A weapon to channel Mana into your body?"

"Right. If you hit something from just one direction, it's effective, but if you hit it from opposite sides at staggered intervals, you might cause more damage. Maybe it would be possible to break through faster. I'll have to ask Egbert," Erik resolved. "So how is your smithing skill coming along?"

"Pretty well. I'm in the late Journeyman stages, though I'm running into the problem that without a teacher, I have a bunch of ideas and I can try them out, but it's hard to find what works," Rugrat said.

It made sense. With his general knowledge from Earth, combined with the amount he had spent researching different topics, he had surged ahead in his skill. Still, he had questions. He searched for answers in different books and asked Egbert, but Egbert didn't know everything and books might have the information but it could be obtuse or hidden away. Smithing was primarily a practical skill. Most smiths spent weeks in their smithies trying out new methods and improving on their skills. Rugrat could do the same, grinding away with higher level blueprints, but his growth would be slower than if he had someone to guide him.

"I don't know if we'll be able to find anyone like that in the Second Realm," Erik said apologetically.

"I've already found an answer," Rugrat said, surprising Erik.

"Oh?" Erik slowed his pace as they reached the barracks.

"The Blue Lotus—you remember that auction house? Well, it's not a simple place. They have many experts working for them and their background isn't small. They're supposedly in every realm and there is no one who would be willing to challenge them. Those who have have been destroyed either by the Blue Lotus, or those looking to curry favor with the Blue Lotus. It is possible to not only get items from them, but to also get information. The hardest thing will be getting their attention, but I have a plan," Rugrat said.

Seeing that Rugrat wasn't going to say freely, Erik forced out his next question. "How will you get their attention?"

"I will take my Journeyman-level items there to be appraised. They aren't too interested in strength in these lower levels, but if someone is capable of making high-leveled products—they are a powerful entity; to keep their strength, they need to bring in new blood."

"I wouldn't mind checking it out," Erik said. The two of them walked into the barracks. They were stunned to see that not only were the soldiers from Alva there, the people of Alva had gathered as well.

All of them had solemn looks on their faces as they looked at Erik and Rugrat.

The two hadn't noticed how empty the streets seemed as they walked to the barracks, lost in their own discussion.

"Of our own volition, we swear upon the Ten Realms that we will not pass on information about the Alva Dungeon to any outsiders. We swear to protect Alva Dungeon, no matter how far we might venture from the dungeon. We swear to uphold the rule of law within Alva Dungeon and to follow the orders of the Dungeon Masters Erik and Rugrat as long as their orders are reasonable." Their voices rose as one: children, grandparents, and residents of Alva all talking as one.

A large golden halo settled over them all before shooting toward Erik and Rugrat. They had thought to organize an oath ceremony but hearing their oath, Erik and Rugrat were touched by their sincerity.

They accepted them as the power disappeared.

"All right, you lazy bums, get back to work!" Blaze said, but there was no anger in his voice.

The crowd dispersed, smiles on their faces as Erik and Rugrat awkwardly stood there, not sure what to say or do.

"Shall we move forward with the scouting parties?" Blaze asked, rescuing them.

"Yes, let's do that," Erik said.

"Why do I feel like we just got pranked? Haven't felt that awkward in a long time," Rugrat said.

The quick reaction force and three of the newly formed parties followed Blaze, Erik, and Rugrat.

They went past the beast stables where the panther cubs were playing with soldiers, eating and lazing about. With the right food, the panthers were growing quickly. Beasts only needed to consume more powerful meats and could continuously eat other monster cores to increase their strength. Already they were reaching teenage creatures. Egbert had plenty of taming contracts that had been placed upon the panthers. This allowed them to be bound to whoever rode them. People needed to purchase them from the beast stables if they wanted to have one. The price was high, but they would gain a loyal follower and increase their own combat strength.

Past the beast stables, there was a hole in the wall that circled the village. There was a guard post and alarm formation here so that Egbert would be able to fight back anything that tried to enter.

Now it was manned by Alva's military.

They passed through the defenses and to the steps beyond. The stairs were only wide enough for two people side-by-side to walk up. They had to travel for twenty minutes before they reached a large entranceway that ended in smooth stone.

Everyone formed up behind Erik and Rugrat, who were searching over the smooth stone. Finally, Rugrat found a button and pressed it.

A grinding noise could be heard as the massive stone door rolled to the side. Light streamed in with fresh air and they could hear the sounds of beasts and wildlife.

"Looks like we're back," Rugrat said as they looked out over Beast Mountains Range.

76
HEALING MOON HOUSE'S DOMINATION

The scouts under Blaze's orders went out to search the area. The quick reaction force were also dispersed, heading in the direction of the Wild Reaches. They followed along with Erik and Rugrat to the different locations that Tommins had given them.

It could barely be called a fight. The parties would lock down any beasts in the area, killing or driving them off as Erik would harvest the ingredients.

"Remember when we had to distract the beasts so we could steal the ingredients?" Rugrat asked as Erik simply shook his head and harvested the last ingredient.

The parties got used to the area and to know the lay of the land. Erik and Rugrat quickly gathered all the required materials and then headed for Wild Reaches Trading Outpost.

Erik and Rugrat hid their appearance under doupengs, a conical hat with cloth around it.

The guard didn't seem to mind, taking their fee to enter the outpost. "No killing inside the outpost," he said before allowing them inside.

Erik and Rugrat entered the outpost. Rugrat headed off to go find the quick reaction party that was supposed to meet them.

Erik headed off to go and see Alchemist Tommins. He didn't miss the eyes that fell on him as he entered the store.

"Is there anything that I can interest you in?" Alchemist Tommins asked.

"I'm here to hand in the different ingredients." Erik walked up to the counter, filled with different bottles that held an assortment of ingredients.

Tommins's face turned from bored to excited in a moment. He seemed to pause a second, looking at Erik, trying to peer through his doupeng. "You remind me of someone. Oh, there was a guy trying to learn Alchemy. Seems that he was lost to the Beast Mountains Range. I thought that he might be able to learn something." Tommins shrugged. At the edge of the Beast Mountains Range, some people gained great fame and wealth; others would lose their lives in the pursuit.

If it was the Erik of the past, he would try to get some more knowledge from Tommins. Now he could ascend to the second realm he might find more alchemists and gain access to more resources than in the first realm. Still, one needed gold wherever they went and Erik didn't want to get nothing for all of his effort.

"Here is one gold and seventeen silver." Tommins held out the money. Erik accepted it and Tommins made the ingredients disappear into his storage ring.

His notification bar flashed after the transaction. Erik turned and left the store without a word. He went some distance before he turned down an alleyway and opened the notification.

Quest Completed: Gathering Ingredients
Rewards:
1 Gold, 17 Silver
7,850 EXP

I guess because I finished all of the orders I got some more Experience. This little bit of Experience isn't much but all of it adds up.

Thinking of his Alchemy skill, Erik looked it up as well.

Grandmaster Eri looked over the two small figures that lay next to one another. His face was aloof and imperious, as if the children's maladies were just a simple cold.

Lord Chonglu's fist tightened. He wanted to beat the man until he healed his children. If he did that, then the Healing Moon House would send their enforcers and none of the healing houses would help Chonglu City.

He could feel their hands around his neck, suffocating him. He would do anything for his children and he saw how they were undermining his authority, poisoning a man in the market in broad daylight. The people had called for blood for weeks but he didn't give in to their demands, knowing that the Healing Moon House would stop healing his children.

Based on their actions, he felt that the Healing Moon House could heal them with ease but they were instead playing him along to try to gain more benefits.

So Lord Chonglu sat there, biting back his words as he watched the grandmaster moving around.

"What is your diagnosis?" Chonglu asked, his voice deep as he held his killing intent at bay. He was hidden in the corner of the room, the darkness hiding him from sight.

"This is indeed a powerful malady. Their odor is foul and their skin has been turned pale and lifeless. They are holding on but by a thread. If I was able to, I would assist them, but my hands are being tied by the Rosa House." Grandmaster Eri sighed and opened his hands pitifully.

"Might there be a way to remove this issue and gain this assistance?" Chonglu was tired of word games but he played along. He'd suffer a hundred times worse for his children.

"Lord Chonglu is indeed benevolent!" Grandmaster Eri's acting skills were superb as he made it seem as if the idea had sprung from Chonglu's lips.

"It's like this. Our healing services are of a much higher quality and we put a lot more effort into healing people, but still we are taxed at the same rate as the Rosa House. How is this fair? We are only taking a loss accepting these taxes," Grandmaster said, as if he were some pious saint.

Chonglu wanted to rip the sniveling little cockroach's neck out. Chonglu knew that the healing houses gouged their patients and the people for even the most basic of services. Who wouldn't be willing to pay everything for their health?

"Grandmaster Eri's words make a certain sense. Two percent tax will be removed from the Healing Moon House," Chonglu said.

"It would speed up the rate that I can get that assistance from the capital if there was *more…*" Grandmaster said, as if trying to find the right word.

"Two percent tax will be added to the Rosa House," Chonglu ground out.

Eri could sense that this was all he was going to get and beamed as he bowed deeply to Lord Chonglu. Both of them knew who was the winner in this game. Still, Chonglu could sense that Eri liked to play around, trying to look like some holy and pious saint.

Once his children were healed, Chonglu wanted to rid his city of these scammers who called themselves healers.

"How long until that assistance is ready?" Chonglu asked.

"It shouldn't be longer than two weeks," Grandmaster Eri said. "I will make the necessary arrangements." With that, he dismissed himself.

As soon as he left the room, Chonglu's fist slammed into the wall beside him. The solid stone was cracked and there was a fist print in it now.

The hidden experts in the room who protected his children didn't say anything or move from their positions, chilled by the killing intent that washed out of Chonglu's body.

"Snakes and fake promises! These healers will be removed from my city and if they let my children die, I will hunt them down to the root."

The wind in the room stopped moving, fully under Lord Chonglu's control.

Grandmaster Eri laughed in his room as he drank red-white wine, a rare delicacy that was not only delicious and could get one drunk, but it also increased the rate that they absorbed Mana. This relaxing feeling of having Mana circulate through one's body was wonderful.

"That little fool! Does he think that I would ever heal his children?" Eri laughed to himself, a cruel smile on his lips. Lord Chonglu's children were at death's door—anyone could see that. Eri didn't know what was affecting them, but he knew how to keep them from dying. As long as he kept them on that line between death and life, then Lord Chonglu was like a dog willing to do anything he asked.

A sound transmission request appeared in front of Grandmaster Eri from his secretary.

"Grandmaster Eri, nobleman Zhan Su wishes to talk to you," his secretary said.

"Oh?" Eri said.

Zhan Su came from one of the larger families in Chonglu City. It seemed that the nobles sensed that there was a change in the policies and the true leaders of the city.

Eri's smile widened as he chuckled to himself, enjoying this sense of power. He never thought when coming to this little Chonglu City that he would be able to take control of the city! He thought that he would just be a grandmaster of the Healing Moon House. Having the same power as the city lord—this was more than most grandmasters in the larger tiered cities and capitals!

Lord Chonglu wasn't accepting guests but Grandmaster Eri was, allowing him to further increase his backing with the nobles and consolidate his control.

"Send him in in ten minutes." Eri downed the wine in his hands, his expression turning red with excitement.

Erik let out a sigh as he put down the book he was reading and rubbed his tired eyes. "I guess this is how Rugrat felt after reading all of those smithing manuals." Erik let out a dry laugh.

"You losing your mind too?" Egbert asked as he walked through the manor, holding a duster and a frock he had found somewhere. The eccentric skeleton was well known to the people of Alva by now.

It had been a week since they arrived in the dungeon. Construction was still going on but the barracks had been completed and the growing area would be done soon.

If anything, the original Egbert seemed to be tamer than the current "maid" version.

"Is there any way I can return a defective skeleton?" Erik muttered to himself.

"I heard that!" Egbert said, dusting some molding on the manor's wall.

Erik felt a new headache coming on as he pinched the bridge of his nose. *Reading Alchemy books all day is better than trying to have a real conversation with him.* Erik put the manual back into his storage ring.

"Ready for some fresh air?" Rugrat asked Blaze as he and the two parties under his command for this mission checked their gear.

"Damn right." Blaze had spent his time working with the villagers to build more structures and carve up new runed roads.

"You having fun with your new teacher?" Blaze asked Erik, who was to Rugrat's side, a tired expression on his face.

"I hate plants," Erik said, his eyes dull.

The others grinned and laughed. It was good to see that their leaders were normal people just like them and had their own faults.

Rugrat snorted and shook his head.

77

FALL OF THE HEALING MOON HOUSE

Erik and Rugrat's speed couldn't be compared to what they'd shown when entering the Beast Mountains Range.

They were faster than one-hundred-meter sprinters on Earth but they were barely breathing hard as they dodged through the forest. As they approached the area that they had hidden their gear, their speed slowed.

A bear roared out as Erik and Rugrat ran through its territory. It was too slow to even catch them, but it alerted a pack of hyenas that rushed over, hoping to get some kinds of scraps.

Rugrat's arrows cut through the air with a sound of rushing air, taking out three. As Erik landed among them, he threw out two punches, killing the remaining two. These level eight beasts were nothing but obstructions in their eyes.

Still, they collected the materials, not wanting to waste anything.

"This seems about right." Erik looked around the area.

Rugrat checked his map quickly. "Should be some ammunition underneath this rock." Rugrat pulled out a shovel and started to dig.

After a few moments, there was a sound of metal hitting metal.

"Pay dirt." Rugrat smiled at Erik as he quickly uncovered one of the caches.

Using the first one as a reference point, Erik found a rotted-out tree, rolled it to the side and started to dig. It wasn't long until he found a rifle bag.

He opened it up, revealing the rifle that he had left behind.

GM6 Lynx (Big Momma)
Damage: Unknown
Weight: 11.5 kg
Health: 100/100
Base Value: Unknown
Range: Long range
Requires: .50 BMG Ammunition

He had a bittersweet expression on his face. He loved the rifle but with its bigger rounds, it would mean that more formations could be placed on them. He knew that his rifle was destined to be used by Rugrat. It saddened him but he knew that as he was fighting with his fists, it only made sense. Erik put it away in his storage ring.

They went to each of the hidden locations and pulled out the different buried caches. Once they collected the goods, they headed toward Chonglu.

Erik stood on a roof. Rugrat was beside him, crouched down as he used Big Momma to look over the Healing Moon House building.

Their silhouettes were hard to see in the night's darkness, only illuminated by the lights in the square below them.

In the center of the square lay their target.

"I count twelve guards around the perimeter. All of them are at least level eight, armored, decent weapons, high Novice grade, one with an Apprentice-level sword—must be the commander," Rugrat said, not looking up from his scope as he scanned the building.

Everything was quiet as most people were asleep in the noble sector.

"Got four hidden archers on each corner—saw them go on shift," Rugrat said.

Erik put away the rifle sight he had been using to scout the healing house, memorizing the different guard positions. He shifted his shoulders around, feeling the new armor that lay underneath. Rugrat had made it himself. The Golden Fox gear was up for sale and its strengths lay with swordsmen type fighters, not melee.

Though he didn't really agree with the new gear's names.

Nipple Chafer 2000 Cuirass
Defense: 87
Weight: 32.3 kg
Durability: 107/107
Base Value: 1 Gold, 12 Silver
Slot: Takes up chest slot
Innate Ability: Reduce magical attacks effect by 5%
Requirement:
13 Agility
15 Strength

Erik's Face Puncher's Gloves
Defense: 27
Attack: 13
Weight: 1.7 kg
Durability: 98/98
Base Value: 87 Silver
Slot: Takes up hand slot
Innate Ability: 3% chance to stun
Requirement:
17 Agility
4 Strength

Party Pants Greaves
Defense:
Weight: 5.3 kg
Durability: 90/90
Base Value: 2 Gold, 73 Silver
Slot: Takes up leg slot
Innate Ability: Increase Agility 4%
Requirement:
22 Agility
10 Strength

All of it had been darkened so it wouldn't shine in the dark. Other than his chest, his gloves and his greaves were lightweight to reduce noise and not get in the way when he was fighting.

"Plan?" Erik asked.

"I hit the archers, work the perimeter, thin them down. You move in close. I'll give you support, call out the enemy," Rugrat said.

"Works for me."

"I'll take out the archers, then put a silence spell on your armor so that you don't sound out so much."

"Works. Once we clear the perimeter, we'll go in loud—they'll find out sooner or later," Erik said. "Ready when you are."

Rugrat didn't say anything as Erik pulled off his cloak, revealing the dark armor underneath. The cloak and the doupeng disappeared into his storage ring.

Rugrat fired his gun, riding the recoil as he altered his aim. He fired again; the round traveled through an arrow slit to hit the archer beyond.

There was no more movement as Rugrat continued to change his aim: one shot, one archer fell until there were no more left.

Rugrat turned to Erik; a spell formed on his hand. It was black, nearly impossible to see in the dark as it shot out and landed on Erik's body, assimilating into his armor. "Good," Rugrat said.

Erik ran and jumped off the roof of the building. He came down over the fence that separated the Healing Moon House from the open square around it.

Erik pulled out a blade as he dropped onto one guard, his blade stabbing into their neck.

Another in front of him started to yell out; the blue flash of a Mana bullet from Erik's finger silenced them.

"Twenty yards around the corner, hold position, turning to face you," Rugrat said.

"Roderick, Chiao—you okay?" a voice asked.

Erik stayed crouched as a guard turned the corner. A flash of Mana was the last thing he saw as it ripped through his open visor, piercing his eye and brain.

Erik jumped forward, grabbing the man and lowering him gently.

"Turn right, five yards, get into the alcove." Rugrat was holding his rounds. The noise from hitting the armor would alert everyone in the healing house.

Erik moved forward into the alcove.

"Hold," Rugrat said.

Erik ducked into the alcove as two guards passed. Erik jumped up, placing his fingers against each of their necks and firing Mana bullets. They didn't have time to call out as Erik grabbed them and slowly lowered them to the ground.

He moved through the grounds; Rugrat called out targets as he cleared around the healing house, until it was just the gate guards at the front of the healing house.

The gates were shut. Erik moved up close to the wall. The bottom three feet was made of stone, the upper part made of iron rods that looked like crude spears.

"Ready?" Rugrat asked in Erik's ear.

Erik tapped the device on his wrist twice as he edged closer. He could hear the breathing of the two men at the gate now. He tapped on the device once.

"Ready?" Rugrat asked.

Erik tapped once again.

"Understood. Ready to fire. Five seconds, four, three."

Erik readied himself, thinking about his next action.

"Two, one!"

Erik jumped up as the guard captain to the right side of the gate crumpled, his helmet deformed by the heavy fifty-caliber round. Erik reached through the iron bars, grabbing the other guard's jaw and pulled his head up, making him unable to yell out as his right hand snaked out, pressing against his neck and firing a Mana bullet up into his skull.

The man's weight fell into Erik's left hand as he released him.

Rugrat moved out of the shadows, carrying a bow and arrow with him. He wore black leather with banded steel on it, made from the leopard pelts they'd collected and armor he'd made himself.

Erik opened the gate from the inside.

"Wha—!" The word ended in a gurgle as Rugrat moved through the gate.

Erik turned to see a healer on the ground, holding his neck in shock. He was so stunned by getting actually hurt he didn't even use any healing spells.

Rugrat jumped up the stairs. The noise of the armored guard being hit by Big Momma's heavy round made lights turn on in the Healing Moon House as some guards came to see what the commotion was.

Erik pulled the keys off the dead guard captain. He locked the gate again and broke the key off in the lock. He ran to follow Rugrat.

The entrance was a large opulent hall. One could see all the way to the ceiling where large windows allowed sunlight in. Now there were just a few magical lights on.

There were three stories. On the first was a reception, with private rooms behind it that the injured were attended in. There was a set of stairs at the back of the hall that went halfway up to the second floor before they branched off; this led to the healer's quarters. There were stairs in front of the healer's quarters that led to the administration offices and the quarters of the Healing Moon House's leaders' rooms.

Guards came down from the second floor.

"Who are you and what are you doing in the Healing Moon House?" a guard demanded. All of them had just woken up and they were mostly wearing just padded jackets and pants.

Who would be foolish enough to attack a healing house when it was inside a city? Most of these guards lived a charmed and easy life, simply looking good instead of training their combat skills.

"We've come to discuss some policies of the Healing Moon House—primarily, poisoning," Erik said.

The light caught his face as the guard looked at him. His eyes thinned, as if remembering the face. Then they widened abruptly. "Y-you're—you were the peddler in the market!"

A spell circle appeared at the end of Erik's finger. The guard didn't have time to react as the Mana bullet hit him in the face. His fellows were hit with his remains as he dropped to the ground.

Rugrat's arrow glowed with a spell as he released it. The arrow struck a guard near the back. The explosive spell on the arrow turned it into a small grenade as it went off, throwing the guards.

"Bingo," Erik said. Multiple Mana bullets shot out of his finger, almost in a stream, leaving behind destruction.

The Healing Moon House turned into chaos as healers started to come out of their rooms to see the guards being torn apart by explosive arrows and Mana bullets. The two men in dark clothes seemed untouchable, the guards not even getting close as the two ascended the stairs.

78
DISTURBING THE PEACE

Lord Chonglu's features were gaunt, his eyes not leaving his children's beds as they laid there, barely breathing.

He had personally administered the different concoctions he had been given and he was waiting on Grandmaster Eri's support. He could only curse inside as he gripped his fists together, hoping that the aid would come soon and he could stop their suffering.

Mira, what did we do wrong to bring this suffering down upon them? We thought that your father would be happy to know that you settled down and you were finally able to awaken your bloodline. Who knew that he would send members of the clan to take you away and poison our children?

Hot tears filled his eyes as he blamed himself for pushing his wife to pass word to her father. He knew how it hurt her so not being in contact with her family. He had hoped to repair things, but it had only made them worse.

There was a knock at the door.

Chonglu's pent-up anger and frustrations were released. His eyes turned cold as he beckoned at the door. It opened to reveal Quinn. Seeing and feeling the killing intent that rolled off Lord Chonglu, Quinn dropped to his knees.

"Lord, there is a commotion going on at the Healing Moon House!" Quinn forced out the words as his face was pale to the extreme.

"What!" Chonglu stood, his veins bulging out. He took half a step forward before he looked to his children. "Send out the guards to assist. You will lead them. Ronhou!"

The last word carried through the palace as it was answered by a howl.

There were noises in the palace before a large black beast dropped down into the corridor. It moved toward its master. The beast was smarter than average. A powerful aura surrounded it, making others feel oppressed. But when its eyes fell on Chonglu's children, its expression altered between sad and angry. Ronhou had seen them grow up and was highly protective of them both.

He was no young beast anymore; scars showed through his sleek black fur. To someone from Earth, he might look as if he was a mix between a tiger and a bear—a tiger's body with the mass of a bear and the face of one.

"You will obey Quinn and listen to his commands as if they are my own," Chonglu ordered.

Ronhou dropped his head in understanding. The mutual contract between them passed their feelings and thoughts back and forth.

It raised its head and looked at Quinn, assessing him before he turned to the side.

Quinn bowed to Ronhou and to Lord Chonglu. "Thank you for your trust." Quinn didn't wait any longer as he jumped up onto Ronhou's back.

The creature took off as Quinn started to send messages through his sound transmission device.

"Seal the palace." Chonglu's voice rang with power. He was the lord of this city, a level fourteen existence that had traveled across the Second Realm. His strength wasn't simple.

Hidden experts in the room passed the word as the lord's guard were awakened, moving to their positions.

The doors closed to the children's room as Chonglu pulled out a seal of office. This was directly connected to the city itself and allowed him to command the city interface.

Through it, he could see roughly what was going on.

Grandmaster Eri turned over in his sleep at the loud bang down below. He turned and grabbed at the woman to his right, waking her up.

She let out a stunned and then excited noise.

Eri couldn't help but smile as he played with her nipple. His eyes slowly opened and he frowned as he heard another noise from downstairs. He was about to continue what he was doing when the noise only increased.

With an angry snort, he got out of bed, pulling on his robe and checking his appearance before he strode for the door.

He lived on the highest part of the third floor. He went to the balcony that looked over the healing house. He looked down to see streams of Mana blue lighting up the scene below as fiery red explosions went off or arrows cut through multiple people.

His face turned white at the destruction below. *What Experts did we offend to have them come here?*

"Please, can we not resolve this matter!" Grandmaster Eri yelled out below.

The fighting stopped as the men looked upward. "Are you the leader?" one asked.

Grandmaster Eri gulped. Looking into those eyes, even three floors away, he felt his knees were weak and his back cold. There wasn't any explicit killing intent; instead, it felt as if he were the one being looked down on, some insignificant ant beneath this other person's shoe.

Eri could only nod.

"Good!" The man jumped up, reaching the banister of the first floor and jumping to the other side.

"Put down your weapons and I will not attack you," the other man with a bow yelled.

The aura of the Ten Realms was descending as some of the guards who couldn't take it anymore unleashed what attacks they had prepared.

The man's arrows cut them down. Others threw their weapons away, not getting into the fight. His accuracy and the power of his arrows left one shocked.

The other man was climbing up the banisters. He was already up to the second floor and leaping for the third.

Eri backpedaled, nearly tripping over his robe as he ran for his door. He slammed it closed and locked it. He looked around his room. The two women in his bed looked at him in alarm as he ran for his desk.

The door to his room shook once. The iron lock bent. The second kick broke the lock and bent the hinges.

The women in Eri's bed screamed as the man who had been downstairs walked into the room.

Eri was filled with fear as he tried to look through his desk. Something shot out of the man's hand, shredding the desk. The desk exploded and peppered Eri with splinters, but it revealed a piece of wood with runes on it and a crystal at its top.

Eri grabbed the wand, a fierce look on his face as he fired it at the mysterious man. The man dove but Eri knew he had hit him.

He got up, unable to see over the remains of his desk.

The man was waiting; his Mana bullet hit Eri's wand, causing the crystal to shatter and then explode.

He hit the wall to the side of his desk.

The man stood up and moved forward.

Eri looked up at him, whimpering. He could see the hole in the other's right arm. He had hit him, but the man didn't seem to care. There was even bone showing.

The man's arm started to regenerate before his very eyes. A healing spell appeared over the wound as he started self-healing.

"W-what do you want?" Eri asked.

"Grandmaster Eri, I've been hearing a lot about you." The man crouched down. "Heard that you don't like any opposition, that you're a miracle healer." The disdain was clear in his eyes.

"This is the Healing Moon House. If you do anything to me, you will be hunted across the First Realm!" Eri said, some fire returning to his eyes.

"I also heard that your disciple wouldn't do anything without your orders," the man continued, ignoring his words.

"I-I…" Eri's words died in his throat. He hadn't just okayed it, he'd been the one to suggest it to his disciple. He didn't expect it to be so public. With Lord Chonglu cowed for fear of losing the person that could heal his children. He had bragged about it to some of his rivals to incite fear and show his new strength in Chonglu City. Trying to take it back when he had said it was his plan all along was impossible now.

Eri's mind was still sharp, though. "You're the peddling healer!"

"Got it in one." The man stood, grabbing Grandmaster Eri's robe and lifting him up with ease.

Eri tried to struggle but it was like a baby trying to fight an adult.

"This is the city guard. Put down your weapons and come out. You are under arrest for disturbing the peace."

A chill seemed to run through the man's eyes. He threw Eri backward, breaking the large window behind his desk. "Count the peace as disturbed!" the man yelled out.

Eri screamed before he slammed into the iron spear-like fence below. His blood splattered on the city guard outside of the Healing Moon House.

79
INVITED

Captain Quinn had a grim look on his face as he looked up from the impaled body of Grandmaster Eri up to the man who stood in his window. One of the moons was up, light striking his features. Quinn felt that he looked familiar as the man turned around and headed back into the healing hall.

His arm—is it healing? The slight light of a healing spell could be seen working on the man's arm, putting him back together.

A chill ran down Quinn's spine at that gaze; even Ronhou lowered his head slightly.

Still, Quinn had his orders. "Break down the gate!"

The guards who had been splattered with blood were slow to react. They started to hit on the gate, taking a few moments before they made some headway.

The yelling and cries from inside dimmed down before there was a heavy sound like a body dropping. Quinn and the others winced at the sound.

The gate finally broke and they threw it wide, pushing into the Healing Moon House.

They started up the steps when two men started walking out of the healing house: one with a bow, the other without any visible weapon. Both of their faces were revealed.

The man without a weapon was the one who threw Eri, the other—

"You're the man who fled Chonglu!" Captain Quinn's eyes snapped to the other man. He hadn't been able to see him as he'd been on the large man's back as he ran out of the city. "You cured the poison?" Quinn asked.

"And did your job for you. Seems that Chonglu City hold some people in high regard, but not others." The man shook his head as he looked at the guards with disdain.

"We couldn't do anything," Quinn said, the words sour even to him.

"Couldn't do anything? There is a rule of law in this city but you decided not to listen to it. Very convenient. Don't worry—I did your dirty work. Now you can stand off to the side and let this go, you know, like the bunch of spineless shits you are." The man's words weren't angry but straight up looking down on them.

Ronhou let out a roar and rushed forward to attack the man.

The man let out a roar of his own that seemed to be like a physical thing. It was as if they had walked into the depths of hell as the man unleashed his strength. That same dread Quinn had felt, the senses that he had trained continuously, all warned him that this was an Expert who had crawled through a sea of bodies to get to the point he was. He hid it well, but when enraged or fighting, he would turn into a demon.

Ronhou couldn't stop his momentum. As the man's foot snapped up, Ronhou was sent flying back over the fence and crashed into the ground, whimpering.

"Stay down, pup." The man's voice was a command.

The pup tried to get up as Quinn dropped to his knee, his brain working quickly.

"We did it to save Lord Chonglu's children. The Healing Moon House was the only group that said that they could heal them," Quinn said. He couldn't win, but maybe there was another path.

The killing intent from the man's body was pulled back. He seemed to be judging Quinn.

Quinn kept his head bowed. His guards had pale faces and their hands were slick with sweat. This reaper in front of them had swept through the Healing Moon House in just a few minutes. Even going up against Ronhou in pure strength, he'd won.

Ronhou was a powerful Mana beast that Lord Chonglu had raised himself. His strength wasn't any less than a level fourteen and he had great strength coming from a powerful beast bloodline.

"Swear that this is the truth," the other man with a bow said.

Quinn looked up at them both. "I swear on the Ten Realms I speak the truth!"

The power of the Ten Realms descended and then disappeared. This oath made Quinn feel weak as it stole ten percent of his Experience to call the energy of the Ten Realms when using it to ascertain whether one was speaking the truth.

The man's hand on his bow relaxed some.

"Take us to see Lord Chonglu." The man started walking down the steps slowly, the other man following.

Quinn was stunned for a moment before he recovered. "Yes, sir." Quinn stood and waved for the guards to clear a path. They moved back, edging away from the two and spreading out, still not feeling safe enough to put their weapons away.

Quinn sent a sound transmission to Lord Chonglu.

"He is waiting for us," Quinn said as he started walking toward Lord Chonglu's palace.

"Good. Someone will need to clean up the guards, Eri, and his apprentice Deng," the man with the bow said.

Hope flared in Quinn's chest. *If they're not all dead, then we might be able to mend some of our relationships with the Healing Moon House.*

Lord Chonglu was standing outside of his children's room when he saw Quinn approach. The two men were not what he was expecting. They both wore grim expressions, though there was only a faint aura around them.

One's aura is one's soul and emotions. For them to not have true killing intent and be calm and collected—just who are these two demons?

Even as he was shocked, he didn't show it. His features were tired. And he had learned that one had been infected while he was fleeing the city; for him to appear healthy and fine, even healing his arm that Quinn noticed—these two men weren't simple.

"You have my deepest apologies. I swear on the Ten Realms that if you are able to heal my children, I will let you go peacefully," Lord Chonglu said. The Ten Realms created an oath between them both.

"We swear on the Ten Realms that we will look in on your children; if it is in our power, we will heal them. We will also leave Chonglu City peacefully unless otherwise provoked," the shorter man said.

Chonglu was inwardly shocked as the oath was completed.

The other trusts him so much to agree with this kind of oath; they're not even brothers.

> Erik and Rugrat have sworn oaths to you. If they break their oath, then the Ten Realms will punish them.

Feeling much safer, Lord Chonglu opened the door behind him and walked into the room. The experts hidden in the room all watched Erik and Rugrat as they walked inside.

80
POISON IN THE MARROW

Erik moved to the two. There was one girl and one boy, their features similar and their ages the same. "Twins," Erik surmised. He placed his hand on the boy's head as he cast Simple Organic Scan. His hand moved from the boy's head to his shoulders, down his arms and then his chest.

Erik paused, his expression darkening as he continued his examination.

To use such a thing on children, it's despicable, but it might be the poison that I need to temper my bones. In Erik's mind, he knew he could heal the two children. Gaining the poison, he could use it to temper his bones and bring his body to the Body Like Stone realm.

He moved to the girl without pause. After some time, he pulled his hand away from the girl, shaking his head.

Lord Chonglu's expression fell. He seemed to age decades in a moment. "It's okay. It's just the wild ambition of this old man to help them recover."

"What—you don't want me to even tell you what is happening to them or possible treatment plans?" Erik growled.

Lord Chonglu's hand stopped in the air as his body shook. The light seemed to flicker within his eyes as he looked to Erik.

"I don't know what poison this is, but it's nasty as hell. It has assimilated itself into the marrow of both children in different spots. You have placed them into a comatose state through probably some kind of Alchemy solution to stop them feeling pain. The healing potions, healing attempts, and apothecary treatments deals with the effects but it is unable to resolve the main issue. Maybe this could be resolved with a higher healing potion. That I don't know. What I do know is that this poison has taken over the marrow and is infecting the marrow around it. It is excreting a poison into the bloodstream. As time goes on, you will need stronger and stronger healing potions to deal with this infected blood. But not dealing with the marrow, it will only come back." Erik's words were like thunderbolts ringing out in Quinn and Lord Chonglu's skulls. They looked at Erik as if looking at some kind of monster.

Rugrat moved to the children, using his own Simple Organic Scan to check them over.

Erik didn't stop talking. "Now, option one: we get a healing potion that is powerful enough to heal this kind of damage. Seeing as this hasn't happened already, it means that the healing potions here aren't powerful enough. Two: we cut out the infected marrow and then regrow their bones and marrow. Three, which might be needed to be used in combination with two: we go through intensive rounds of healing to clear out the marrow of this infection. It will take a hell of a lot of Mana and time, plus we will be fighting against time. Would need tens of healers working for months to resolve it at this point," Erik said.

Lord Chonglu looked to Quinn with a dazed look.

"Now this is what I know of, but I haven't been here long and there might be other solutions."

"You said that you wish to cut out their infected marrow?" Lord Chonglu asked.

"I'll use knives and saws to break the bones and cut out the infected sections of marrow, pour in some healing potion or use healing spells to help them recover their lost bones and tissues," Erik said confidently. He had recovered his legs and arm with magic before; if it was just growing a bone, it shouldn't be too difficult. "They'll need time to recuperate, but it will be the fastest method."

"All of the other healers simply wished to use spells. I have never heard of one tearing out the infection," Quinn said.

"Well, that's 'cause they're healers. I'm a combat medic. Without Mana, I don't have to worry about infections and I can remove the root issue, bypassing instead of having to deal with it directly," Erik said.

Quinn and Chonglu shared a puzzled look once again.

Finally, Chonglu seemed to recover some. "What do you need?"

Erik looked to the children. "Healing potions, pills, powders, also Stamina ones. That should be all." Erik looked back to Lord Chonglu. He might be a big and powerful man but he reminded Erik of many other soldiers he'd seen—all mean on the outside but once they were around their kids, they turned into teddy bears. Seeing his kids laid up like this was tearing him apart.

Erik could charge him whatever he wanted, but he wasn't that heartless.

A screen appeared in front of Erik's vision.

Quest: Poison in the Marrow
Requirements:
Heal Young Master Feng
Heal Young Mistress Felicity
Rewards:
Lord Chonglu's blessing
3450 EXP

Erik waved the quest to the side. "I would've even without the rewards," Erik said before his tone suddenly dropped. The room turned cold. "My one question for you is how did they contract this poison?"

Lord Chonglu's face twisted with an array of emotions before landing on anger. "My wife is from a powerful clan that lives in the Earth realm. She was adventuring in the Second Realm when we met up. We adventured together for some time before coming back to the First Realm and establishing ourselves here, looking to settle in and have a family.

"Little did we know that her family had other plans. They sent people down from the Fourth Realm to deal with us. They took my wife and told me that they would never allow me, or the spawn that I had desecrated Her Holiness with, to survive.

"They left and I thought that their words were empty. I looked for her and started to make plans to ascend the realms once my children were old enough. I didn't know that they had infected my children, who were just toddlers, with this poison. It seeped into their bone marrow and took root. It was only two years ago that their condition turned to how it is today. In my mind, they wished for me to watch as my children died, knowing that I was nothing but a scourge to their family name for stealing one of their own and having children with her.

"With my impure bloodline, I was nothing more than trash in their eyes, my children a blight." As Lord Chonglu talked, his aura billowed to new heights, making it hard for Erik to stay upright under the pressure.

"I had meant to just take my wife back, but now—now I will not rest until I have my foot on their necks and wipe them out from the realms."

From what Erik knew, ascending the realms was no simple task. With the look in Chonglu's eyes, it seemed as if it was not a matter of how he would raise himself up to the higher realms, but rather when. This kind of willpower and the clear love for his children and wife garnered Erik's respect.

"All right, you gather the supplies and we'll see about getting them healed as soon as possible. Do you have a side room here?" Erik asked suddenly.

"Yes. Quinn, please take them to the room next door. I will get the supplies you need gathered," Chonglu said.

"Make sure to have a sharp blade and a strong saw—that would be for the best," Erik said.

Chonglu paused before he nodded.

Erik and Rugrat left the room, Quinn taking them to a nearby room.

"Well, shit," Rugrat said when they were alone. He and Erik shared a look. Seeing the state of the kids hurt both of their hearts.

"Well, we'd best do our part and get them back on their feet," Erik said.

"Taking out their bones—it's not going to be easy," Rugrat said.

"Nope. That's why we're going to have to try it out first." Erik moved to a chair with armrests. "I'm going to open up my arm, cut out a bit of bone, then heal it all up. See what the effects are and modify what I'm going to do so that we put as little stress on the kids as possible."

"Lovely." Rugrat moved over as Erik started to put things out on a nearby table. Rugrat grabbed a chair and sat beside him, arranging the different items on some boiled cloth.

Erik put more cloth on the armrest as Rugrat passed him Wraith's Touch salve.

Erik put a glove on his right hand and then started to put the salve on his arm.

"Do you want to do an IV of a Stamina or healing potion?" Rugrat asked.

"For this, I just want to do it with my own skills. That way we know that it can be done. Then we can try it out with the different potions and see how it goes."

Rugrat nodded. After all, he had spent hours in his smithy going through numerous trials to increase his smithing ability.

He waited until his arm was numb. "Scalpel." Erik held out his hand and Rugrat passed him the tool.

Erik pressed it against his arm; he didn't feel anything and continued. Using his Simple Organic Scan, he could see what was happening as he cut through the skin and muscle.

Blood welled up and came out of his arm. The blood loss wasn't too much, so he refrained from using a healing spell.

"Retractor." Erik held out the scalpel; Rugrat traded with him.

Erik used the retractor to open the wound up more, allowing him to see through the layers of his arm and look at the bone underneath. "Hey there, bone."

"When did this become normal?" Rugrat asked.

"Shut up and pass me the chisel." Erik gestured to the table. As if realizing his words, he looked up and over to Rugrat.

"Chisel." Rugrat held it out to him.

Erik put it against the bone.

Rugrat swung a hammer. With a crisp, cracking noise, the bone broke.

Erik changed the chisel position and Rugrat hit the chisel again. He took the chisel and hammer away, passing Erik forceps.

Erik slowly pulled the bone out of his arm.

Erik put the bone to the side, sorting his tools. He poured Mana into the Focused Heal spell. The marrow rapidly grew forward and out, meeting up with the marrow of the other side of the bone. The layers of the bone formed together before creating a complete bone once again. Erik swept it with his Simple Organic Scan before pulling out the retractor and applying spells to seal up his arm.

He sat back in his chair, applying a healing spell to himself to return blood.

"Okay, so there's red marrow that makes stuff in my hand and that grew back fine and is fully functional. When I cut bone that was inside my body and then healed it, it grew back nice and quickly. But what we're talking about, that poison, is in those kids' ribs, feet, and hips."

A sudden thought appeared in his mind.

"If I was able to remove most of the poison and halt its progression, maybe we could see the evolution of this place to increase their ability to fight back against the poison. Not only would it make it easier for me, it would mean that the poison would never again flare up as they would have built up an immunity to it. It worked with the other poisons I've used to temper my body." Erik tapped his chin in thought. "I can remove their feet easily and the ribs aren't too difficult. Regrowing both of those, then resist poisons and cure poisons—I need to practice more."

Erik looked over to Rugrat.

"Why do I have the feeling that I won't like this?" Rugrat asked.

"What made you think that?" Erik stood.

"My balls being located in my stomach right now." Rugrat shrugged.

"I'm going to need to test out a few ideas. Healing my body is harder. As I've tempered everything but my bones, it takes more Mana to recover. You haven't undergone Body Cultivation so I can heal you easier. The more tests and trials, the greater surety I know we can heal those kids," Erik said seriously.

Rugrat sighed and switched places with Erik. "Don't forget the damn Wraith's Touch." Rugrat pulled out a smithing manual with his left hand to start reading.

Erik smiled. Rugrat was one of those men, all hardass and angry on the outside, but inside he would put his life on the line for any kid, any man or woman he considered a brother, sister, or innocent.

Erik started to work, repeating the procedure. His eyes were lit up with the glow of healing spells. He wasn't simply trying to heal Rugrat; he was trying to learn the components of the spell. He had been looking for ways to improve his healing abilities. Just using Focused Heal would waste his energy. But if he could fuse bones, heal them, have spells to knit muscle back together and have skin adhere perfectly, he wouldn't waste his energy on the Focused Heal trying to heal everything in an area.

81
TWO DIFFERENT SIDES

Wren Silaz was in his office, looking over the different reports. He made a notation in a workbook as there was a knock at the door.

He didn't look up until he finished the note. He activated an array that would make it impossible for someone to see the work on his desk as he sat up in his chair and arranged his clothes and rubbed his face a bit.

He looked outside. It was already dark. He let out a short snort, shaking his head before he recovered his regal disposition.

"Enter!" he yelled, his face serious as he looked at the man who entered.

"Young Master Wren, those two that Domonos talked about have returned." The man's words were simple, his tone calm and subservient as he took a knee and looked at the floor.

Wren's carefully prepared appearance changed as his head swung to the side. He looked over to a certain area within his family's home. The most perfect house and gardens lay there and was the home of his little sister Qin'er.

"Tell me everything," Wren demanded. He wanted to rush out and demand their help, but remembering his actions before, he could only wince and try to gain more information on these two men to know whether they might be able to help his sister.

Nothing else mattered if he was able to save his sister from her fate.

"They entered the city at some point, then ambushed the Healing Moon House. They entered the healing house, killing Grandmaster Eri and his direct apprentice, Xui Deng—the two people who planned out poisoning one of the men. Afterward, Lord Chonglu's mount Ronhou confronted them but it was sent flying with a kick. The two men were escorted to Lord Chonglu's palace."

The man fell silent as Wren's mind started to turn over. A chill fell over him as he thought of what he had asked his older brother. *Thankfully he wasn't as rash as I was and gathered more information.*

Wren was a proud son of the Silaz family, but he had not been interested in fighting. Instead, his strengths lay in the business; he wasn't the strongest nor did he have the strongest will, but he was a great administrator.

Domonos would lead the family to greater heights and Wren would support him from behind. Yui was focused on training and he, too, would have a bright future fighting and even as he did call out, his brother Wren would still support him. The display outside the walls of their family home made them look fractious but it was a ploy.

That way they could draw out the sly ones, thinking that they could back a person in the family, only to find themselves being played.

"Were any others killed?"

"Those on guard and those who didn't surrender. The two men didn't care for their lives, only those who had attacked them and removing any alarms so they wouldn't get away."

They only kill who they have to—their revenge isn't blind. For trying to kill one of my family, wouldn't I do the same? Would I be able to be as calm?

"Prepare my carriage and people. Get two Greater Mortal grade monster cores and come with me to Lord Chonglu's palace," Wren said. Once he had decided something, he wouldn't step back down.

"Yes, Young Master." The servant seemed shocked, not having seen this dominating side of the young master in a long time.

Wren did away with his mask. This matter was much more serious than keeping up appearances—this was about his sister's life.

Seeing the servant bowing and being respectful, Wren grew frustrated. "Move! We don't have time to waste and let them go!" Wren stood from his table. He might not have any fighting prowess, but that protective and determined light in his eyes, his presence was that of a lord.

The servant rushed out to attend to their duties.

Wren's face darkened in thought. "I hope that they are agreeable to helping me." A flash of worry appeared on Wren's face—not worry for himself, but letting this opportunity slip through his fingers and Qin'er continuing her suffering.

Wren flicked the sleeves on his robe and strode forward. Even at this time, he could hear the distant sounds of Yui training. He nodded to himself, proud at his brother's accomplishments and his drive.

Yui had hidden his abilities so that he wasn't accepted by the Willful Institute. The sect was filled with snakes and Yui was too straightforward. Domonos could deal with these problems but not Yui.

I will have to find him another sect or group that he can join and increase his strength.

Wren dismissed such thoughts and focused on the task at hand. Those under his command were moving, rushing to prepare a carriage and the goods he had requested.

"Enter." Lord Chonglu opened his eyes as he looked up at the door.

It opened to show a servant.

"Young Master Wren has appeared at the gate to the palace." The servant bowed deeply as they reported.

"I am not taking guests," Lord Chonglu said in a deep voice.

"Lord, he is not trying to gain entry but waiting there in the rain." The servant had a hint of anxiousness in their voice as they were scared of overreaching their limits.

Lord Chonglu frowned. "Why is he waiting?"

"He says that he wishes to apologize to the two guests staying here."

"Oh?" Lord Chonglu's eyes moved over to Quinn.

"There was a commotion with Young Master Wren in the Silaz trading house and two strangers a few weeks back. Maybe those two strangers are our guests?" Quinn said.

"He must have learned like we did that they are healers." Lord Chonglu's face softened. He knew Mister Silaz well and of his daughter's ailment. He didn't know the true details and had only seen her a few times. Although others might not be able to tell and think he was sheltering her from the outside world, Chonglu's senses were not simple and he could tell that she was suffering from some kind of health issue.

"Let him wait. I do not want to distract them. It will be up to them how they want to resolve their issues." Chonglu pushed it to the side.

"I'll go and see how things are progressing," Captain Quinn said.

Erik put his tools down. He had been working on Rugrat for some time, the latter having fallen asleep and snoring in his chair as Erik worked.

"When using healing spells, it looks like I'm just converting Mana into energy that makes the body regrow, a combination of their current state and when someone is born and their cells change into different systems and parts. I've been trying to focus on the physical differences between the parts of a body, but what if I was to alter the kind of energy? Like how dogs can hear higher frequencies, or a radio has different channels—I just need to tap into the right channel." Erik called up the spell formation of the Focused Heal in his mind. He had taken some time to study spells and the way that they functioned.

"There are three things primarily: one, the power; second, the function; and the direction. Right now, with the Focused Heal, I give it power, and it creates a healing energy that I direct with my thoughts, altering the direction. Changing the function can turn it from Focused Heal to a fireball. So I'm the human battery; the function is like plugging in a flashlight, or plugging in a railgun. If I, the battery, have enough power, I can do both. Right now I'm spending a lot of Mana on just directing the spell. If I was to fix the direction, so just bones, or just veins, then I could heal system by system, reduce the energy cost. Changing the function, that'll be harder. The function is the body of the system—the coding, the brains. The direction just says where it has to work."

Erik wanted to alter the function to improve the spell, but it would take time and effort. Time that he didn't want to waste. So he focused on changing the direction.

Erik focused on the spell formation. He altered the direction of the Focused Heal. He could do it easy now, but he focused on the alterations that he saw in the directional ring of the magic circle.

He let out a small trickle of power so he could focus on the changes. Meticulously he altered the parameters, changing them and testing them out.

He didn't know how long went past before a notification rang out in his ears.

You have learned the spell: **Heal Bone**. Your spell book has been updated.

Heal Bone
Novice
Fuse bone together as if it was never broken.
Consumption of Mana based on area and effect.

For teaching yourself a Novice ranked spell, you gain: 5,000 EXP

61,534/195,000 EXP till you reach Level 16

Skill: Healer
Level: 48 (Apprentice)
You have become familiar with the body and the arts of repairing it.
Healing spells now cost 5% less Mana.

"Learning a spell increases Experience and it increases the correlating skill—me likey," Erik said.

Excited by his new find, Erik focused on what he had learned, and once again started to alter the direction component of the spell.

As he'd done it once before, it was much easier for him to repeat the process. It wasn't long until he had two new screens in front of him.

Heal Scars
Novice
Remove scar tissue and replace with healthy tissue.
Consumption of Mana based on area and effect.

Heal Muscle
Novice
Repair muscle with ease.
Consumption of Mana based on area and effect.

For teaching yourself 2 Novice ranked spells, you gain: 10,000 EXP

71,534/195,000 EXP till you reach Level 16

There was a knock at the door. Not wanting to wake Rugrat, Erik moved to the door and opened it. "Come on in. I think we're almost ready." Erik moved into the room.

Quinn opened his mouth to talk and then looked at the bloody cloth, Rugrat's still open arm, and the tools that were beside him.

And the fact that he was snoring *loudly.*

Erik followed his gaze. "Rugrat!"

"I'm awake! What's happening!" Rugrat started to get up.

"Sit down, you idiot. Your arm's open still." Erik called up his Heal Bone spell. The bone formed tens of times faster than before as he altered the spells. Now that each of them were fully concentrated, they were much faster and cost less Mana.

Rugrat blinked as his arm sealed up. "Damn, I was dreaming about *Baywatch*," Rugrat complained.

"Mhmm." Erik doused the different tools in alcohol and started to clean them.

"I need to find a woman, you know, like one who'll be there in the good times and bad," Rugrat started.

"Not this again. And we've got work to do," Erik said.

"Huh?" Rugrat looked over and saw Quinn. He turned to Erik again. "We good?"

"Yeah. I even got a few spells, gained some Experience for learning them," Erik said.

"Oh come on, how did you do that?" Rugrat asked in a low voice.

"Practice," Erik said. "We good to head over now? Has everything been collected?" Erik asked.

"Yeah," Quinn said, recovering slightly.

"Good." Erik moved for the door. He glanced out of the window. The morning was starting to be revealed.

82
FOUR COPPERS

The room had been changed, with two tables being set out.

Rugrat pulled out tools and the IV stand. As he checked over the different potions and solutions on the side, a man came forward, discussing what they were.

Lord Chonglu brought his son Feng first. The boy was pale and weak-looking, not much left but the bones on his body. Lord Chonglu placed the boy down on the table.

"I'm going to have to remove the infected bone. It won't be pretty, so it might be best if you leave the room." Erik held Lord Chonglu's gaze.

"Do what needs to be done." Chonglu bit out his words.

Erik nodded and pulled out a marker. Using his Simple Organic Scan, he was able to find the infected marrow. He circled these areas, checking them a few more times before he turned to Rugrat.

"We've got a mix of powders, healing and Stamina recovery. I've found two that can be mixed together in water to create a solution—run an IV bag filled with it?" Rugrat asked.

"Sounds good to me," Erik said. With the assistance of the solution, it should help to reduce the strain on the two twin's bodies, allowing him to violently cut away the infection.

Rugrat moved to Feng's arm. He put gloves on and cleaned himself up, even pulling on a frock before he put the IV into the boy's arm.

Erik finished marking the boy's body and looked over the tools. Finally, he moved to the boy's feet. He quickly checked the marked location before applying tourniquets above the marks, tightening them to cut off circulation.

With quick and precise movements, Rugrat inserted the IV needle into the boy's upper arm. It was hard to find a good vein on the boy's withered skin.

With gloves on, Erik put Wraith's Touch around the line on the boy's leg.

Rugrat helped him put on a clean frock and his sanitized ballistic eyewear.

Erik and Rugrat held their hands up, ready. They looked at the boy on the table. He was skinny and emancipated; even unconscious, his features seemed to be in pain.

"Let's begin. Saw." Erik held out his hand to Rugrat.

"Saw." Rugrat gave him the saw Lord Chonglu had acquired and had been disinfected.

The infection was so bad in the foot it would be hard to just remove the infected sections of bones. Erik started sawing through the boy's lower leg, just above the ankle.

It didn't take long for him to remove the foot. He passed the saw back and Rugrat started to clean it as Erik was already using Focused Heal on the boy's foot while releasing the tourniquet.

The boy's foot grew back, small and disproportionate, as if a babe's as it was rebuilding it all at the same time. Erik used Focused Heal instead of the smaller spells; healing with the smaller spells, he would have to build layer by layer. Without the other layers then the bones would grow, but then fall apart as they didn't have tendons, muscle, or skin holding them in place.

The foot grew bigger, until it was the same size as the foot that had been removed.

"Stable. All good." Rugrat monitored everything with his Simple Organic Scan.

"Good." Erik took a few breaths and moved to the other foot that was also badly infected and repeated the procedure.

Then he moved to Feng's ribs. Applying Wraith's Touch, he opened up the boy's side and cut out the infected ribs. He repaired them with Heal Bone and the subsequent layers with different spells. The skin didn't show any signs of being cut open at all.

Chonglu watched everything, ready to destroy Erik and Rugrat in a moment. After Erik removed Feng's first foot, he relaxed, his anxiousness replaced with shock.

This healing ability—it's not something that I have seen in the first two realms. Mira didn't talk about anything like this either! Just how powerful are they to do all of this? Normal healers would fight the poisons and cleanse the body, but they're simply removing the infection by lopping it off and then replacing the damaged areas.

Even though his fingers were digging into his palms and drawing blood as he saw Feng being cut up, he wasn't rash or stupid enough to stop them.

Everyone in the room held their breath as the two men bent to their work, wholly absorbed in helping Feng.

They worked together without any flaws or disruptions.

Hope bloomed in Chonglu's chest.

"Switch to the Stamina-only drip," Erik said.

"Understood. Looks stable. Take a look." Rugrat switched over the feed for the IV needle, allowing the pure, stronger Stamina solution flow into Feng's veins instead of the mixed IV.

Erik placed his hands on the boy's body. He used a healing spell on him again. Erik had been holding back, only pouring in a small amount of Mana, but now the Mana in the room seemed to charge toward him and into Feng.

Chonglu could even faintly feel that his control over Mana was reduced.

"You save up your energy. I can do that," Rugrat said.

"Yeah—king." Erik shook his head.

Rugrat grinned and shrugged before he used the same healing spell.

A chill passed through Chonglu as he felt the Mana in his body being pulled toward Rugrat slightly.

"All right, let's have a look at Felicity, shall we?" Erik looked to Chonglu as he washed his gloves with a bottle of powerful alcohol.

Chonglu's fears and anxiousness had been pushed away. He didn't dare to waste time and quickly moved to bring Felicity over.

He looked at her pained expression, feeling relieved. "It'll be over soon." His words were soft and caring, breaking the image of the iron-fisted lord of Chonglu City.

He looked up to Erik. He didn't see the cold killer in there anymore, but a man who truly cared about saving lives instead of taking them. It left him a bit stunned, but it somehow made sense.

Didn't I fight ferociously alongside my raiding party but then we joked and laughed when away from the battle?

Rugrat completed checking Feng. Chonglu looked over to his son. His features were relaxed and calm, his body showing a healthy color instead of the mottled skin that gave off a faint rotting smell.

He watched Rugrat and Erik work. Their actions were like watching a crafter, going through different processes, moving section by section.

It was early afternoon by the time Erik and Rugrat switched Felicity's IV from Stamina and Mana to just Stamina.

Erik and Rugrat started to clean up and put their gear away.

Erik and Rugrat chewed on some forest fennel leaves, moving to the side for Chonglu to check on his children. He waved one of his friends forward and they checked over the two twins.

"They've been nearly completely healed. The infection has been removed from most of their bodies, but it seems that they're fighting back against it?" the man said after casting a few spells.

"We removed most of the marrow that was infected. It was still in their blood so we healed different systems related to blood. Their bodies are now actively fighting the poison. In fact, they might take a few steps along the path of Body Cultivation," Erik said, as if it were a simple thing.

"Body Cultivation?" Chonglu asked. "That is a road that only people in the higher realms with pills and massive resources can walk down."

"Well, this was a nasty poison. Their bodies were weak. By overcoming it, their bodies will be tempered. Also, they won't be infected with the same poison again." Erik pulled off his frock and glasses.

"I'll take the IVs out of them, but just Stamina recovering powders, food, water—that should be fine, slowly, and with soft foods and water at first, then more substantial meals," Rugrat said.

Chonglu nodded, burning the information into his mind.

Erik and Rugrat checked the children again before clearing away the last of their gear. The two children looked much healthier now.

"Have a good day," Erik said to Lord Chonglu as he and Rugrat left the room. No one stopped them and they were already out of the door when they heard a yell from behind them.

Rugrat and Erik looked to see Lord Chonglu running after them.

"Will you not stay for longer?" he asked desperately.

"We have other things that we need to do," Erik said.

Chonglu nodded, a sour look on his face.

Erik felt some goodwill toward this man, this father. "In my mind, it will take no more than a week, two at the most, for them to completely recover." Erik smiled.

Lord Chonglu let out a heavy sigh before he put his arm on Erik's shoulder. "I know that they are not healed yet but I have come to trust you and you've yet to fail me." Lord Chonglu pulled out a card from his ring and passed it to Erik.

A screen appeared in Erik's vision.

Quest Completed: Poison in the Marrow
Requirements:
Heal Young Master Feng
Heal Young Mistress Felicity
Rewards:
1,000 gold
Title of Noble
3,450 EXP

"We do not need the title or the gold." Erik was tempted but he shook his head, pushing the ring back toward Lord Chonglu.

Lord Chonglu smiled awkwardly. The Noble title was a way to connect them together and the gold to create some goodwill.

"I will see you out then," Lord Chonglu said.

He looked back to his children. Seeing them resting there and Lord Quinn and Ronhou, who had recovered from his wounds, standing there, he was reassured.

He led them out of the palace. When they got to the gate, there was a young man standing with all of his knights. The man looked tired but stubborn as he looked up at the gate.

Chonglu ignored them for the two men in front of him. "Is there nothing I can give you?" Chonglu asked, feeling that he was taking advantage.

Erik held up four fingers.

Four thousand gold? Mana cores? Swords, houses?

"Four coppers," Erik said simply.

Behind him, Rugrat laughed. "Too cool." Rugrat clapped Erik on the shoulder.

"Four coppers?" Chonglu said, stunned. Then he remembered a piece of information, something he had thought irrelevant: Erik and Rugrat had accepted two coppers per person who visited their stall.

With this, it was as if they were declaring that everyone was equal, from the lord's children to the farmers.

Knowing their strength and their ways, Chonglu wasn't offended; instead, he was humbled by the experience. He took out four coppers and passed them over. He bowed deeply to them both. "Thank you for saving my children," he said, no hint of nobility in his voice or actions.

"Look after them well. We'll be around in the future," Rugrat said approvingly as he pulled Chonglu back up.

Chonglu found the two men smiling. When he had seen them for the first time, he would never think that their entering and leaving of his home would be so different.

"Man, I wish we had shades and suits," Rugrat said.

"What for?"

"Be badass as fuck! Hey, doesn't that kid look familiar?"

"Do you think we're the Blues Brothers? Yeah, he does. Why is he kneeling?"

"Maybe he got hit by a horse in the head?" Rugrat muttered.

Still, Chonglu's ears twitched as the glowing image of the duo faded. A smile appeared on his face as he remembered his own raid party and old friendships.

Good luck and hope you make it through the realms safely.

83

CHANGE OF FATE

Wren had been standing out front of Lord Chonglu's palace all night and morning. He was faint, hungry, and tired from standing for so long. Still, he remained there, not moving from his spot.

Finally, it was reaching mid-afternoon when two men, escorted by Lord Chonglu personally, were led out of the palace.

Others might not know the truth but Wren did: Lord Chonglu never left the side of his children since they had fallen ill. Seeing him out in the sunlight, sending these people away, Wren's mind could only shake.

They must've healed them. If they were able to heal the twins whose issue couldn't be resolved through the healing houses or medicines, they could help Qin'er.

This thought was at the front of his mind. But there was also a smaller voice that chided him for his previous actions.

Because you were lacking, you turned arrogant, falling into your role heavily and attacking others without care. What would Mother have thought? What was Father trying to tell you when you hid your emotions and wanted to lash out at them?

Wren's stomach turned. His own actions turned over in his mind again and again to the point that he had imagined himself in their shoes. It didn't feel good.

He was angry for not doing what he set out to do, for not becoming strong enough. He shouldn't have put this on others.

The guards and servants all moved around awkwardly as the Lord Chonglu bowed to these two men. One of them lifted him back up with a smile.

Then the two men were chatting to each other as they walked down the hill, looking over Wren and his entourage.

Wren dropped to his knees and kowtowed in the dirt. "Great masters, this lowly one is Wren Silaz. I slandered you and talked out of spite when we first met. If you wish to punish me, I will accept it all. I only ask for you to help someone who is innocent!"

"Silaz?" one man asked.

"Trading shop, monster core," the other replied.

"Ah, okay, yeah, that makes sense," the first said.

Erik and Rugrat looked at the young man in the dirt. His guards all took a knee behind him and kowtowed, too, with grimaces on their faces.

Erik and Rugrat had been angered by the boy's actions but they took them as actions of an arrogant youth who needed to learn some lessons.

Since then, they had been through a lot.

Erik squat down and looked at the boy. Rugrat was behind him; he looked relaxed but he was watching Erik's back even now. His finger traced one of his storage rings, ready to pull out a weapon if he needed it.

"Raise your head," Erik said. Kowtowing in the ground was good and all, but he wanted to see whether the boy had changed, whether he was different.

The boy did so, not meeting Erik's eyes.

"Give me your hand," Erik said.

The boy held it out freely, gritting his teeth as if he expected to lose it the next second.

Erik held the boy's wrist and used Simple Organic Scan. With it, he could pick up the speed of the boy's heart and figure out whether he was lying or not.

"Your name is Wren, correct?" Erik asked, working to establish a baseline.

"Correct," Wren said.

"Your last name is Silaz?" Erik asked.

"Correct," Wren said, confused by the questions.

"Do you believe your actions were wrong that day? Yes or no."

"Yes," Wren hissed. His face turned red.

"In the future, will you treat others as you wish to be treated, no matter their position? Yes or no?"

"Yes," Wren said, recovering some strength as he looked up at Erik slightly.

"Who do you want to help?" Erik asked.

"My sister."

"Is she hurt?" Erik asked.

The boy flinched as if he had been stabbed. "Yes."

Erik could hear the helplessness and feel the truth in his words. Erik released his hand and stood. "Well, let's go and check up on her then. And don't be such an arrogant prick in the future, or we'll come and kick your ass." Erik's voice dipped slightly into a growl as his aura leaked out a bit, focused on Wren, who shivered under it.

"Y-yes," Wren said, goose bumps covering his body.

As soon as it arrived, it left.

Erik pulled Wren up from the ground with ease. "Lead on, Wren."

Elan Silaz smiled as he looked out over the garden. It was one of Qin's good days. She sat across from him, looking at the pieces on the board. Her brows were pulled together in serious concentration, giving off a childish charm.

She moved one of her pieces on the board as her father looked at her move. She held her finger on the piece, checking her move and analyzing it.

Looks like she saw through my sneak attack.

Elan pushed his lips together as she let go of her piece.

"Your turn, Dad!" she said, excited to see what he would do.

A woman at the side of the room cleared her throat.

Silaz looked over, his hand in the air.

Qin also looked over. Elan couldn't help but frown as their private time was interrupted.

"Young Master Wren seeks an audience with Head Silaz and Young Mistress. He left last night to stand in front of Lord Chonglu's residence all night and morning, kowtowing before two men who departed. They are the ones who acted upon the Moon Healing House and the ones young lord Domonos talked of," the woman said in a rush.

Elan felt a mix of emotions: hope, fear of that hope, pride at his son having learned from his losses.

"Wren apologized?" Qin couldn't help but ask.

"That is correct." The servant looked awkward before nodding.

Elan lowered his hand and seemed to be deep in thought.

What if they can't help her? Will this just be another wasted visit and test? Raising her hopes only to break them—it would be too cruel.

Just as he was about to speak, another voice interrupted him.

"Dad, we should see them at least," Qin said.

Elan looked over at her. He could only sigh. She had seen through him easily.

"Very well." Elan smiled at Qin and then turned to the servant. "Bring them here."

It wasn't long until Wren entered the room with two men right behind him.

The men wore blackened clothing. At a glance, Silaz could tell that they were fighters, but they didn't seem to be interested in fighting, instead looking around the gardens and his home in interest.

"Father." Wren stopped and bowed to his dad.

The two men didn't bow and instead looked at Qin.

Elan felt his anger building, but he didn't see any lust in their eyes. Instead, they seemed to be appraising her, checking her condition as he had seen many of his people look over monster cores. They looked at her the same way.

"These two healing *grand*masters have agreed to visit and lend their aid to Qin," Wren said.

The stress and respect in Wren's tone made Elan look over the two men again.

"What would you need to do?" Elan asked.

"Just need to use a spell to see what the issue is. From there, we can figure out what might make it better," one man said.

Elan looked to Wren and then the man and finally Qin.

As if understanding what he was going to say, Qin smiled softly. "Please do your spells." She offered her hand.

The man nodded and stepped forward. He didn't take her hand but instead held her wrist and closed his eyes. "I never thought this was possible!"

"What is it?" the other man asked.

The first man used a sound transmission to the other so they couldn't hear him.

"No way! If I had that!"

Another sound transmission followed.

After a flurry of them, the first man released her wrist and they started to talk freely through their sound transmission devices.

Their expressions were animated and then they slowly darkened before they frowned. Then they seemed to reach an accord.

"We have a plan that might work, but it relates to some skills that we don't want others to learn, so we would have to ask that Qin would have to swear an oath that she wouldn't tell others what happened and that no one else would record or try to gain any information while this is going on." The man's eyes landed on Elan.

"You can help Qin?" he demanded.

The men looked at each other.

"We believe so."

"I will need an oath that you will do nothing to harm Qin and only look out for her best interests," Elan said.

"These oaths are getting tiring," the taller one complained.

"We swear on the Ten Realms that we will do nothing to harm Qin and only look out for her best interests unless otherwise provoked," the other man said.

With the oath established, Elan nodded. "I swear that I will make sure that there is no one who tries to learn of your techniques while you are assisting Qin Silaz," he said, establishing overlapping oaths.

Erik, Rugrat, and Qin were guided to a secure room that was used for conversations that the Silaz family didn't want getting out.

Once inside, Erik started stretching. "Dude, I swear the right shoulder is all kinked to fuck."

"Come on, I just made it like last week." Rugrat inspected the shoulder.

"It's pinching me in the back!" Erik said as Rugrat checked on the shoulder.

'"You've just got fucked-up shoulders."

"You made fucked-up shoulders," Erik complained.

Qin wrung her hands as she looked at the two "grandmasters" arguing about armor.

"Look, you check it out." Erik pulled off the straps and gave it to Rugrat.

Rugrat sighed and looked the shoulders over and put his head inside. "Fuck, you need deodorant," Rugrat complained.

"Yeah, you need a shower and all," Erik shot back as he stopped in front of Qin.

She looked up at him timidly. He had a handsome albeit rugged face, and the black shirt under his armor showed his muscles. She looked up into his crystal-blue eyes and she somehow felt a bit safer.

"You've got crystals in your Mana channels, kid." The man grabbed a chair and sat down. He didn't have any of the air of a grandmaster as he lounged there, looking more like a mercenary.

Qin jumped as there was a banging noise behind him.

"Will you shut it!" Erik yelled to Rugrat.

"You want a fixed shoulder or not?" Rugrat shot back as he continued to work on the shoulders, putting them back into place.

"You admitting they're fucked up?"

"No!" Rugrat said, but even to Erik's ear, it sounded like a kid not getting their own way.

Erik revealed a grin to Qin and winked.

She moved her hands faster. She hadn't really seen that many people outside of the family in her life; seeing these two lively fellows seemed to be a lot for her.

"Umm, these crystals, w-what does that mean?"

Erik let out a sigh and leaned forward slightly, trying to relax her a bit. "It looks like there was a mutation in your body. You see, you have Mana channels that run through your body. They pull Mana in from the outside world, store it in your belly, or your dantian; you can draw this out and through spells, create phenomena in the world," Erik said.

Qin nodded her head, her hands slowing their speed as she looked at him, interested.

"Now, these channels, usually they're clear, but yours got filled up with crystals. In fact, it made a gem in your dantian. First, I want to test something out." Erik held out his hand and indicated for her to come forward.

She did so. Erik held her wrist again and then allowed a thin strand of Mana out of his Mana gate and allowed it to touch the Mana gate in her wrist.

Not only were her veins filled with Mana crystals, her gates were crystalized as well!

He watched the thread of Mana with his Simple Organic Scan as it touched the Mana crystal. He felt a tugging sensation as the Mana gate pulled on his Mana. He continued to let out a small amount. The Mana gate seemed to become more refined. As her Mana channels swelled, Qin'er let out a low hiss of pain.

Erik pulled his Mana back as he looked at her. Her legs were shaking and there was sweat on her face.

Her Mana channels swelled as if they were trying to draw the Mana in. The crystal seemed to crave it. It almost looks like when someone has a punctured lung and it separates inside—you need to bleed out the air or else they can't breathe.

He had seen the same when someone was wounded and he healed them: their body wanted that healing energy.

The same thing went for the crystals.

Having an idea, Erik turned to Rugrat. "I need you to make a needle that can pierce skin and bone as well as Mana gates. I want it to be able to hold Mana. Like how we attack them from the inside, this'll be from the outside," Erik said.

Rugrat nodded slowly. "Okay, I can make basically a shard of metal that will be Mana conductive. I don't have the skill or the smithy to work on anything in-depth here."

"That should be enough," Erik said.

Rugrat put the armor to the side and then he sorted through his storage rings. "Where are you?"

While Rugrat searched around, Erik looked to Qin.

"It looks like you have a special constitution, one that has changed your Mana channels and gates. What I want to do is open a small hole in one of your Mana gates. This should allow Mana to pass into your body, equalizing the pressure inside and out," Erik said.

"O-okay," Qin said with a pale face. She had a weak body, with the constant pain being in places that had high Mana. By remaining at home most of the time, her body was incredibly weak.

Still, she was stubborn and she had endured through the pain, covering it over so that her father and brothers wouldn't worry.

She sat down on a chair offered by Erik as Rugrat finished up with the needle.

He cleaned it up with some fire and gave it to Erik.

Erik took out Wraith's Touch and put it on Qin's wrist.

He focused on the needle. He poured Mana into it, finding that it circulated easily. It was a rough-looking needle, more of a metal shard that Rugrat had knocked off a piece of ore.

He would have never used this back on Earth; now he wasn't so worried.

He built up more and more Mana in the needle until it glowed blue faintly. "Rugrat, I need more!"

Rugrat moved over, holding the needle as well, and poured in more Mana so that it was showing blue lines. The light of the needle was brighter than that of the lights in the room.

Erik jabbed the needle into her Mana gate. The sudden blast of direct Mana didn't break open the gate but it drilled a small hole through it.

It was as though a vacuum had been opened. Mana in the room rushed toward Qin; it slammed into that opening and rushed into her Mana channels. The crystals in her channels started to change. They seemed to almost liquefy; her Mana channels grew bigger and turned into crystal. As Mana passed through her Mana channels, it was refined repeatedly. Her Mana system seemed to come alive as it reached down into her dantian, being sucked in by the crystal there.

"Look at the Mana gate," Rugrat said.

Erik moved his scan back to see that under the influx of Mana, Qin's Mana-deprived body was drawing in a massive amount of Mana. The Mana was like water rushing through a mud wall; chunks of the Mana gate were being torn apart as it was forced open. The Mana in the room only picked up speed as her entire body underwent a massive transformation.

The crystal in her body started to dissolve and integrated into her Mana channels.

The crystal in the middle of her body was condensed multiple times over, pulling in the neon-blue Mana.

That pure white crystal started to take on a blue hue, becoming more vibrant as it condensed further and further.

"Core Compression stage," As Rugrat focused on the Mana Gathering system, he could identify what was going on inside of her body.

The now pinky nail-sized sphere started to rotate slowly within her dantian.

Qin'er let out a gasp as the Mana running through her body stopped moving. The rush of air settled back down. The disturbed dust and letters that had been on a nearby desk floated back to the ground.

Qin opened her eyes. They looked like aqua-blue pearls.

Erik, who had been using Simple Organic Scan, noticed the blue channels that had been glowing brightly now dimmed down slightly. He broke out of his daze and looked inside her body.

"It looks like the crystals are actually refining the Mana as it passes through her body. When it reaches her dantian, it is naturally accumulating. With such purity, the Mana gathers naturally instead of needing to be forced together," Rugrat said, explaining what they were seeing.

"This must be like the modifications that Mana Gathering cultivators use to improve their abilities," Erik said.

"Right, to break through into the compressed core stage in one shot, leaves one jealous," Rugrat said.

"Umm, what happened?" Qin asked in a daze.

Erik and Rugrat let go of her wrists and looked at her. She was just a girl, a little lost with everything that had happened.

"You opened your first Mana gate. You had a lot of pressure inside your Mana channels. We opened one of your Mana gates so that the pressure would balance out. You've got a high talent for Mana," Erik said.

"I only have one Mana gate, though? I thought one needed more Mana gates to be stronger?"

"They do and they don't. There's a lot of theory and information about it all," Rugrat said. Even he hadn't been able to understand it all and he had access to the gnomes' records.

"Qin, what do you want to do in the future?" Erik asked.

Qin was kind of struck with his question. "I…umm." She looked kind of lost for a few moments but gathered herself.

"Well, I guess I can do a lot now, but I'm not really good with fighting. I don't want to hurt people and I wouldn't want to run the business—too many meetings and stuffy old men." Qin scrunched up her face, making the other two smile at her expression.

"Talking about this with anyone else will break your oath." Erik pulled out an emblem. This emblem was something that Rugrat and Taran had made together. It was an invitation. It was nearly impossible to fake. The idea was that the person with this would go to the Wild Reaches Trading Outpost, hand this to a contact there, and then be taken to Alva Dungeon.

Qin wasn't well suited for fighting and she didn't want to run a business, but she was smart and she could think quickly, as Erik had seen already. The sects and other schools would ask for her to fight. Kanesh Academy would be a place that she could grow her talents.

She could learn to make different things, or build on current theories. Erik was also being selfish. Right now, she had just awakened her magical abilities. If he could open her other Mana gates that were still sealed with crystal, just what would the result be?

Qin's attention was focused on Erik and the simple-looking piece of metal.

"This is an invitation to a place that you won't have to fight, to a place that you can learn more about your abilities, about crafting, growing your skills and other pursuits, where you can find a path. If you are looking for an option, try this one out." Erik passed it to her.

"How does it work?" She turned it around in her hands.

"Go to the Bloody Ram in the Wild Reaches Trading Outpost at dusk and look for a person wearing this on their clothing," Erik said.

She nodded and looked at the piece of metal. "Thank you," she said, honestly.

"Get some rest, little one, and take your time getting used to your changes. Only tell your father what has happened." Erik saw the way that Elan Silaz looked after his daughter; he would know the correct thing to do.

"Could I be a healer like you with this?" Qin held up the invitation.

"You can be whatever you want." Rugrat grinned.

Erik nodded and looked to Rugrat.

"Your shoulder should be fixed now," Rugrat said.

Erik pulled his armor back on as Rugrat checked everything in his storage rings.

They left the room. Elan, Wren, and the elusive Yui were all there. As the door opened, they looked behind Rugrat and Erik into the room. Seeing Qin there, they couldn't help themselves and rushed forward.

Elan slowed his steps and looked to Rugrat and Erik. "What can I do to repay you?"

"Two coppers, please." Rugrat smiled.

Elan froze, before he pulled out two coppers, a confused look on his face.

"Have a nice day," Rugrat said as the copper disappeared into his storage ring.

Erik and Rugrat walked away.

Elan had been willing to give up his trading house, everything he had built, but they let it go just like that?

"Father." Qin's voice reached him.

He turned to see her smiling there. She had hidden the signs of pain before, but now he could see her truly relaxed expression. He couldn't help but feel burning hot tears fall down his face, seeing his daughter healthy and not suffering anymore.

Erik and Rugrat walked through the streets of Chonglu. It was late afternoon and people were moving through the low light, heading home, getting drinks with friends. It seemed almost peaceful.

They both wore cloaks, hiding their appearances and their armor.

People moved out of their way as they headed through the city.

"Did you hear about the Healing Moon House?"

"Grandmaster Eri—tossed from the highest window. I didn't like him, but isn't that kind of overboard?"

"Haven't you heard the announcement by Lord Chonglu denouncing Grandmaster Eri and laying his crimes bare? Healer? More like crook in flashy robes!"

Erik turned a deaf ear to it all as they entered the largest square in Chonglu City. In front of them lay Chonglu City's Ten Realms totem.

They walked up the steps toward the totem. No one moved to stop them but people watched them in interest.

"Are they going to try ascending?"

"I want to ascend too!" a young boy said.

"It's dangerous going through the realms! You'll scare your mother, talking like that!" his mother berated him.

"But I'll bring back a princess and make you a queen!" the boy said, living in his heroic fantasies.

Somehow I doubt it's going to be that easy. Erik looked up at the totem as they paused in front of the massive pillar.

Erik and Rugrat looked at each other.

"Teleported into the unknown—sounds familiar," Erik said.

Rugrat laughed. The two of them had gone through life and death, but from it, they still wanted to venture more, to see what these Ten Realms had to offer. They had people in Alva Dungeon relying on them. Their path might not be easy, but they could take it one step at a time.

A screen appeared in front of them.

You have reached Level 10, meeting the requirements to ascend to the Second Realm.
Do you wish to ascend?
YES/NO

"Second Realm, here we come!" Rugrat yelled, selecting the YES. A flash of light enveloped them.

"Another two off to try the Second Realm." A man drank from his mug.

"I wonder if they'll make it back?" one of his friends asked as the sun started to dim and the moons rose over Chonglu.

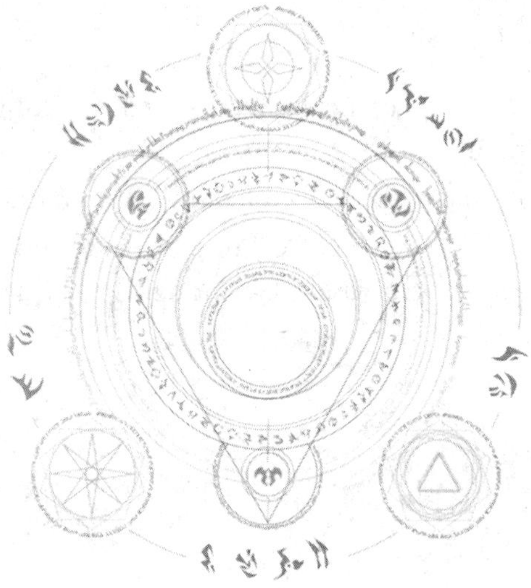

AUTHOR'S NOTE

Thank you for your support and taking the time to read The Two Week Curse.

The Ten Realms will continue in the **Second Realm**. If you've enjoyed The Two Week Curse, please leave a **review**!

Do you want to join a community of fans that love talking about Michael's books?

We've created this Facebook group for you to discuss the books, hear from Michael, participate in contests and enjoy the worlds that Michael has created. You can join using the QR code below.

Thank you for your continued support. You can check out my other books, what I'm working on, and upcoming releases with the QR code below.

Don't forget to leave a review if you enjoyed the book.

Thanks again for reading!